Brenda Clarke w... Ministry of Labour and National Service until her marriage in 1955. With her two children at school she found the time to indulge her long-held ambition to write, and her first novel was accepted for publication in 1968. Since then she has published, under various pseudonyms, another thirty books. Brenda Clarke lives in Bristol.

Sweet Auburn

BRENDA CLARKE

WARNER BOOKS

A *Warner* Book

First published in Great Britain
by Little, Brown and Company in 1995
This edition published by Warner Books in 1995
Reprinted 2000

A CIP catalogue record for this book is available
from the British Library.

ISBN 0 7515 1237 0

Printed and bound in Great Britain by Clays Ltd, St Ives plc

Warner Books
A Division of
Little, Brown and Company (UK)
Brettenham House
Lancaster Place
London WC2E 7EN

'Sweet Auburn, loveliest village of the plain'

Oliver Goldsmith, 1728–1774

Prologue
1900

The long-case clock in one corner of the room chimed midnight, its sweet, clear notes sounding loud in the silence. Almost at once, despite the tightly shut windows and heavy plush velvet curtains drawn closely across them, a faint noise of cheering could be heard outside. Some revellers were banging on saucepan lids; voices were raised in laughter and greeting as people emerged from their cottages, or the Ring O'Bells further along the village street. At the same moment, St Peter's bells rang out to celebrate not just the first day of a new year, but also the first few moments of a new century.

And what a century the twentieth promised to be, thought Arthur Burfoot, warming his coat-tails in front of his brother-in-law's fire. With England – the other nations of the British Isles counted for little or nothing in Arthur's book – riding high in all quarters of the world, with the tentacles of her mighty empire stretching around the globe, there was nothing that could not be achieved in the years ahead. What a truly glorious future lay before his two boys, three-year-old Donald and Ernest, a twelvemonth younger. There might be a little trouble in South Africa just at the moment, but the English were bound to win in the end. They always did; and it stood to reason that a parcel of Dutch settlers weren't going to get the better of the victors of Trafalgar and Waterloo, Sebastopol and Balaclava. He raised a glass of the best vintage champagne, which he had brought with him from Abbey Court, then noticed with irritation that no one else in the room was drinking. They were sitting, tense and strained, waiting for the first cry of the newborn child from upstairs.

Arthur slapped his brother-in-law on the shoulder. 'Come

3

on! Drink up! Your son's going to be the first inhabitant of
Staple Abbots born in the twentieth century. Helena will be
fine this time! If you're that worried, perhaps you should
have attended her yourself, instead of bringing old Richardson out from Westbury.'

Marcus Gilchrist compressed his lips. 'It wouldn't be
ethical, you know that. And Jack has always been her doctor.
If I'm worried, it's because she's had three miscarriages in the
past nine years, and she's not a young woman any longer.
She's twenty-eight, for God's sake!'

The woman seated at the round table, a scattering of
fashion periodicals on the red chenille tablecloth before her,
gave a little cry of disapproval. 'Marcus! You know how
blasphemy upsets me – and dear Helena. You shouldn't take
advantage of her absence, particularly at such a moment.'

Arthur Burfoot nodded approvingly. 'Quite right, Mrs
Jardine, ma'am. Quite right. Your brother tends to be lax
from time to time in the company of ladies.'

Henrietta Jardine coloured prettily and fluttered her
eyelashes. Her patrician features beneath the widow's lace
cap were very like those of her brother, allowing for the fact
that Marcus was ten years her senior and tanned from being
out and about amongst the sick of the village in all winds
and weathers. Her eyes were the identical shade of blue, her
hair a similar fairish brown. At the ages of forty and thirty
respectively, brother and sister were a handsome couple, like
their late parents before them.

The same, however, could not be said of their elder sister,
who had arrived at Rosemary Villa two days earlier from her
Bristol home. At the age of forty-two, Josephine Gilchrist
was used to hearing herself described as a 'fine figure of a
woman'; which, as she herself was the first to admit, meant
that she had a tendency to stoutness, offset by her commanding height. Indeed, her mother had always maintained that
it was this Amazonian appearance which had frightened
possible suitors away; while others, most notably her
younger sister, held by the view that what scared the men

was Josephine's habit of always speaking her mind, plus her extremely radical opinions on almost every subject under the sun, but particularly on the role of women.

'We aren't meant to know about such things, Jo!' Hetty had often wailed in the past, as yet another young man had angrily quit the family home in Clifton after being told that his views on the Irish question were positively medieval, or that his notions on parliamentary reform would disgrace a child.

Their late parents had always backed Hetty. It was Marcus who had been Josie's ally; Marcus who, having become a doctor like his father, and nurturing a passionate admiration for reformers such as Lord Shaftesbury, had intended to devote his life to working among the poor. But Marcus, Hetty reflected with satisfaction as she glanced round the comfortable, almost opulent parlour furnishings, had slipped and fallen by the wayside; and in her opinion, very sensibly too. For what man in his right mind would not prefer a wholesome country practice, together with a pleasant house provided rent-free by his wealthy brother-in-law, to struggling among the disease-ridden Bristol slums? And what a blessing it had proved to be for her when, two years ago, darling Herbie had died and instead of finding herself a well-to-do young widow, she had discovered she was liable for heaven knew how many debts! For Captain the Honourable Herbert Jardine, late of the Coldstream Guards, had been an inveterate gambler, whistling down the wind not only most of his pay but also a modest fortune inherited from an aunt. And when, after his untimely death from liver failure, his aristocratic parents had made it plain that they wanted nothing more to do with a daughter-in-law socially their inferior, things might have been very difficult indeed. But Marcus and Helena had insisted that she come to live with them, an arrangement which suited both ladies admirably – one being in need of a comfortable home, the other looking for a companionship impossible to find in a husband with whom she had nothing whatsoever in common. Yes, it had all worked out very satisfactorily, Hetty decided, turning the pages of her fashion periodical and noting that dresses for the coming spring would have even smaller waists, with lavish trimmings of lace or silk braid.

'Well, Hetty, how are you going to enjoy having a baby in the house?'

Hetty started nervously at the sound of her sister's voice. There was something very intimidating about Josie; there always had been. For one thing, she was twelve years older than Hetty, but it wasn't just that. Josephine Gilchrist was the author of a series of children's books which not only sold, but sold well enough to make their creator a financially independent female, still something of a phenomenon even though women in general were beginning to make their ideas and presence felt in a way unthinkable a decade or so ago.

'Oh, I shall be delighted,' Hetty answered. 'And I can be such a help to dear Helena, you know.'

'No, I don't know,' her sister retorted bluntly. 'You're years younger than Marcus and me, you've no children of your own, so how you can have any idea what to do with a small child is beyond my comprehension. On the other hand, you did live with Herbert for seven years, and I suppose he couldn't have had a mental age of much more than three.'

Hetty coloured indignantly. 'Really! That's a horrid thing to say.'

'But true, nonetheless.' Josephine regarded her sister with a smile of derisive affection. 'Are you happy here, Hetty? If you ever get tired of living in the country, especially in a spot as remote as this, you know you can always come back to Holly Lodge. It's your home as much as mine; it's the house we grew up in.'

Hetty barely repressed a shudder. The mere idea of going to live with her sister in the rambling house overlooking the Downs filled her with dismay. It had been enjoyable enough when dear Mama and Papa were alive and Marcus had been at home, but just her and Josephine? The very suggestion of it was sufficient to make her turn pale.

Her sister's smile deepened. 'My dear Hetty, you need not look so alarmed. I'm not pressing you to come. I'm more than happy with my own company, as you well know. But you've always been one for city pleasures, and I was afraid you might be missing them. The back of beyond on Salisbury Plain is not, I should have thought, your ideal milieu.'

Hetty felt somewhat surprised at this observation because, until that moment, she had not seriously considered how remote the village was. Staple Abbots and its attendant hamlets of Lower and Upper Abbots were isolated, it was true, surrounded as they were on all sides by the vast, empty tracts of Salisbury Plain, much of which belonged to the War Office and was used in the training of soldiers. But so much went on in the villages during the course of a year, so many events which centred upon either the church or Abbey Court or the changing seasons, that there was little time to feel cut off from the mainstream of civilization. And the towns of Westbury and Warminster, at a distance of some six or seven miles, were only an hour or so's ride away by pony and trap, while Salisbury itself could be reached from either by that miracle of the nineteenth century, the railway.

'There is as much going on here as there is in Clifton,' Hetty replied with spirit, raising her voice just enough to attract Arthur Burfoot's attention.

'That's right, my dear Mrs Jardine! You set the record straight. City dwellers always think nothing happens in the country. You should take a long holiday here sometime, Miss Gilchrist. Do you good, put the roses back in those pasty cheeks. Just say the word, and I'll put a cottage at your disposal – rent-free of course – for the whole of next summer.' He chuckled richly. 'Might even find yourself a husband. There are a couple of widowers hereabouts looking to remarry.'

Josephine swivelled round in her chair until she was directly facing Arthur Burfoot, her blue eyes – a deeper and

8 Brenda Clarke

richer blue than either of her siblings' – expressionless. Then
she reached into a pocket of her navy-blue serge skirt and
pulled out a silver cigar case. From this she extracted a
cheroot which she proceeded to light by rising from her chair
and kindling a taper at the fire. Drawing herself up to her
full five feet, ten-and-a-half inches, she inhaled deeply before
blowing out a cloud of smoke which made Arthur cough and
splutter.

There was a moment's complete silence, even the noise
from the street having ceased temporarily. Then, in spite of
his worries about his wife, Marcus began to laugh.

Arthur rounded on him. 'You think it's funny, do you, to
encourage your sister in such outrageous behaviour? Smoking is ... is unwomanly! Not to be tolerated. She needs a
man to school her. If ever I caught my Mabel smoking, I'd
tame her, I can tell you!'

'For heaven's sake!' his brother-in-law snapped impatiently. 'Josie's forty-two. No one can treat her like a child.'

'It's all right, Marcus, you don't have to spring to my
defence.' Josephine threw the remains of her cheroot on the
fire and smiled grimly at Arthur Burfoot. 'These two
widowers of yours,' she said consideringly, 'do they have this
propensity for "taming" women? I suppose that could be
rather fun.'

The silence this time was more profound, more outraged,
and even Marcus slanted a swift, shocked look at his elder
sister. Before anything further could be said, however, there
was the sudden, unmistakable cry of a newborn baby from
above their heads and, after what seemed an eternity, the
patter of feet on the thickly carpeted stairs. A moment later
Ellen Lightfoot, the kitchen-parlourmaid, who had been
fetching and carrying for the doctor and midwife, burst into
the room, her round, homely face wreathed in smiles.

'Oh, sir, please sir,' she gasped, addressing Marcus, 'the
Doctor and Mrs Pollitt say will you come up, sir? The baby's
born, sir. A lovely little girl.'

But Marcus had already gone, bounding anxiously up the

stairs. Arthur Burfoot frowned, a look of disappointment momentarily shadowing his face.

Josephine regarded him with amusement, no whit abashed by the animosity she had recently provoked. 'Dear, dear,' she mocked, 'another recruit to John Knox's monstrous regiment of women.'

Arthur pulled himself together. 'You're talking your usual nonsense, Miss Gilchrist. Another Burfoot, that's what matters. And I've two splendid boys of my own to carry on the family name. Besides,' he added with growing enthusiasm, as he detected a hitherto unrecognized advantage in the situation, 'she'll be just the right age for marrying either Donald or Ernest in twenty or so years' time.'

For a few seconds Josephine was bereft of speech, but having recovered her voice, she remarked ironically, 'How very stupid of me not to have thought of such a thing for myself! But of course she'll have to marry Donald, so that she can be mistress of the Staple Abbots estate. I'm sure dear Helena wouldn't want her daughter to wed a younger son.'

Impervious to sarcasm, Arthur Burfoot shrugged. 'Wouldn't matter if she did. The estate's not entailed ... never has been. I can leave it to whomsoever I like.' He grinned complacently. 'Good arrangement, as successive generations of elder Burfoots have discovered. Keeps the younger ones on their toes; none of them can take anything for granted.'

'A place for everyone and everyone in his place,' Josephine murmured, as she sat down again on one of the old-fashioned, balloon-backed dining chairs drawn up to the table. 'What an extremely well ordered existence you seem to lead.'

Arthur was saved from having to reply by the re-entry of Ellen Lightfoot, who bobbed a curtsey and said, 'Master asked would you like to come up one at a time, please, and see the baby? He also said to tell you the mistress is doing well.' And overcome by the sense of her own importance, she retreated hastily upstairs again to see if either Doctor

Richardson or Mrs Pollitt had anything further for her to do.

*

The heat in the front bedroom of Rosemary Villa was almost unbearable. A huge fire burned in the grate, on which kettles of water needed for the confinement had been boiled. The four-poster bed, like the rest of the furniture, was made of mahogany, dark and heavy, while every available surface was crowded with ornaments and knick-knacks. The marble mantelpiece was draped with loops of blue silk plush. The wilder extravagances of home decor might be growing more restrained in towns, but the more affluent housewives of Staple Abbots preferred what they had grown up with, and change was slow to gain a hold. The cradle which stood beside the bed, looped and frilled with Honiton lace, had served the last four generations of Burfoot babies, and had been brought from Abbey Court several months ago in preparation for the new arrival. It was in vain that Marcus had protested that he would prefer something more modern; Helena had been close to tears at the mere suggestion, and her husband made to feel like a criminal for upsetting her in so delicate a condition. And like most women, she had made the most of her pregnancy, for it was the only time when men were of less importance than their wives. The feeling of power was exhilarating, and of all too short a duration.

Marcus's first thought on entering the room was for his wife, and as he bent over her the midwife drew back, but not too far. Her hovering presence was a reminder that her ministrations were more necessary than his caresses just at present, and a further proof, if one were needed, of female ascendancy in these matters.

'How are you?' he whispered, smoothing back a tendril of sweat-darkened hair from Helena's forehead. All the Burfoots had red hair of one shade or another, ranging from Arthur's fiery thatch, streaked as yet with only a thread of grey, through young Ernest's carroty mop and his brother's sandy curls, to Helena's rich, copper-coloured mane. And a glance at his baby daughter, lying in the crook of her mother's left arm, showed Marcus that she too was a Burfoot in this if nothing else, for the soft fuzz covering the tiny head could be described by no other word than auburn.

'Tired. Very tired,' came the faint response to his question, at which Mrs Pollitt immediately took charge, elbowing Marcus unceremoniously out of her way, lifting the freshly washed and clothed little bundle from her mother's side and placing her in the cradle.

Marcus turned to Jack Richardson, who was still in his shirt-sleeves and looking exhausted from his labours. 'Is it all right if the others come up? Arthur will want to see the latest addition to his family.'

If the older man detected an underlying note of bitterness, he did not let on.

'Yes, but tell them only one at a time, and their visits must be brief. Helena's had a hard time.'

Marcus gave Ellen her instructions, then turned back to his colleague. 'Was it bad?'

'Bad enough for me to advise you, Marcus, that this must be her last attempt at childbearing. You will have to be satisfied with the one. I know how much you both hoped for a large family, but I'm afraid it's not to be. After those three previous miscarriages, it was touch and go whether or not she carried this child for the full nine months.'

'And thanks to you that she did so.' Marcus pressed the other man's hand. 'I can't tell you how grateful I am for all your care of her.'

The bedroom door opened to readmit Ellen, with Arthur hard on her heels.

'Come on, then!' he exclaimed jovially. 'Where is she? Where's this niece of mine?' Ignoring the midwife's frowns provoked by his hearty tones, he stooped over the cradle, parting the lace curtains adorned with white satin bows. 'Well, she's a beauty and no mistake.' He chuckled with pleasure. 'And a proper Burfoot by the look of her hair. Now what colour d'you call that?'

'Auburn,' his brother-in-law admitted grudgingly, 'but it could very well change. Babies don't always keep the colour of hair they're born with.'

'She will,' Arthur predicted confidently. He turned his attention to his sister – that sister seventeen years his junior whom he had always regarded with an affection more paternal than brotherly, and who was the apple of his eye. 'Well done, my dear!'

The delicate, flower-like face crumpled and thin arms were raised to entwine themselves around his neck. 'Oh, Arthur, thank you. I was so afraid you'd be upset because the baby isn't a boy.'

Jack Richardson, packing away his instruments in his doctor's bag, glanced up at Marcus, noted his wooden expression and smiled to himself. The child he had just delivered might have the Burfoot colouring, but in the matter of upbringing she was likely to prove a Gilchrist if Marcus had his way. And if it came to a battle of wills, he would bet – if he were a betting man, that was – on Marcus outfacing both Helena and her brother; for whatever Arthur Burfoot liked to think, his brother-in-law was a very determined man, the more so because Marcus had betrayed his principles by coming to Staple Abbots in the first place. He would resist allowing himself to be compromised again. The doctor looked at his watch; it was gone one o'clock. He touched Marcus on the shoulder.

'I must be off. I'll drive over in the morning, but in the meantime Helena will be in Mrs Pollitt's capable hands.' The midwife smiled complacently. 'Let Helena sleep as much as she can.' Dr Richardson broke off, chuckling. 'Listen to me! Teaching my grandmother to suck eggs. Are you coming downstairs now, Arthur? The quicker Mrs Jardine and Miss Gilchrist see their niece and your sister, the sooner Mrs Pollitt can get them settled for the night, or what's left of it. By the way, a Happy New Year to you all!'

He left the bedroom accompanied by Arthur, who promised his sister that he would also be returning in the morning; and by the time Josephine had trailed upstairs after *her* sister, and added her congratulations to those of Hetty, Marcus heard the wheels of the doctor's pony-trap rattling away from the house on its homeward journey across the Plain. He stooped and kissed his wife a second time, but Helena was already drowsy, soothed by the flickering firelit patterns playing over the carpet and walls.

'Excuse me, Doctor,' Mrs Pollitt whispered as he wished her good night, 'what name have you and Mrs Gilchrist decided on for the child?'

Marcus hesitated, recalling that their discussions on this subject had been perfunctory, all Helena's concentration being centred on male names, so certain had she been that the child she was carrying was a boy. There was no urgency in the matter; it could perfectly well wait until tomorrow when Helena could make her wishes known. But the memory of his wife clinging to her brother, together with Arthur's confident assertion that the child was a Burfoot, made him say, 'Eve. We shall be calling her Eve, Mrs Pollitt. It was my mother's name.'

The midwife nodded approvingly. 'That's nice. And fitting somehow, for someone born on the first day of a new century.' She peeped into the cradle with a proprietorial air. 'Bless her! You can't imagine them growing up and growing old when they're as young as this, can you? Just think! If she lives to be a hundred, she'll be celebrating her birthday on the first day of another century. Fancy that!'

Marcus smiled. 'But not just the first day of another century, Mrs Pollitt, the first day of a new millennium! The year two thousand. Now that really is a thought. She'll have seen out a thousand years that started with Ethelred the Unready on the throne of England and the Norman Conquest still sixty-six years away.' He saw by the midwife's blank expression that she found it difficult to assimilate such a length of time, and added kindly, 'Don't worry about it.

It's all a long time ago. And if Eve should live to be a hundred, one thing's sure; you and I won't be here to see it.'

'That's true enough,' Mrs Pollitt answered briskly. 'Good night then, Doctor. I hope you have a peaceful night without any calls of your own.' And she turned to build up the fire before making herself comfortable in the armchair until such time as either Helena or the baby should need her. Ellen Lightfoot had long since been despatched to her bed in the small attic room next to that of Mrs Kellaway, Rosemary Villa's housekeeper-cum-cook.

Marcus thanked her and went downstairs, where he found his elder sister in sole possession of the parlour, smoking a cheroot.

'Your brother-in-law asked me to say his farewells for him, as he had to get back to give Mrs Burfoot the glad news; she apparently insisted on waiting up until his return. Hetty has gone to bed with one of her nervous headaches, but whether this was brought on by the excitement, the lateness of the hour or my reprehensible conduct I should be afraid to hazard a guess. I just hope I don't wake her when I go up.'

Marcus poured himself a brandy, then sat down opposite her on the other side of the fire, which was almost out.

'I'm sorry you're having to share with Hetty, but now the baby's born I'm afraid I'll be using the guest room for a while.'

Josephine finished her cheroot and threw the stub on the coals. 'No more than I expected. And I'm the one who should be offering apologies for my conduct tonight.'

Her brother smiled. 'Don't be sorry. I rather enjoyed your passage-at-arms with Arthur, even though you did perhaps go a little too far.'

'Pompous creature!' Her eyes kindled. 'How dare he imagine that every woman's goal in life is marriage with a man!'

Marcus threw back his head and laughed. 'Honestly, Josie, the things you say! If we're talking about marriage, what other alternatives are there?'

She tilted her head to one side, regarding him straitly. 'It's good to hear you laugh like that. You don't do it very often nowadays.'

He coloured self-consciously. 'Nonsense! What are you implying?'

'That you've lost that *joie de vivre* you had as a young man. You're far too serious.'

'But I'm not a young man any more. I'll be forty this year. I'm married, with responsibilities.'

'You had a lot more responsibilities before you met Helena – that practice you ran from Milk Street – but it never curtailed your sense of humour that I recall.' Josephine sighed. 'Whatever happened to all those dreams you cherished of helping the poor?'

Marcus's colour deepened. 'How priggish you make me sound . . . and as to what happened, I fell in love, that's all. Not an uncommon or unusual story. I couldn't have expected Nell to share the risks and dangers of Milk Street. She's delicate, it was out of the question.'

'But did you have to bury yourself in the depths of the country, and your talent with you? You were a good doctor, Marcus. You had ideals.'

'There are plenty of poor people in the country, you know,' he said stiffly. 'Here in the village, and in Lower and Upper Abbots. A farm labourer only earns fifteen shillings a week, and if he should be sick he loses even that.' The long-case clock chimed the three-quarter hour. 'Anyway, I think it's time we were both in bed. It's almost two o'clock and tomorrow will be a busy day.'

*

Yet late as it was, Marcus found, once he had undressed and got into bed, that he could not sleep. For one thing, the unfamiliarity of the spare bedroom, the unexplored contours of the mattress, the looming shapes of furniture in unexpected places, was not conducive to repose. For another he slept, as did many doctors, with half an ear cocked for the knock on the front door, the urgent nocturnal summons which would disturb his rest. And tonight he listened also for the cry of his newborn child; the child he had thought he would never see; the child who had been so long in coming. Three sons all born prematurely – and now, at last, a girl. Perhaps that was why she had made the nine months' journey safely. In his experience, girls were hardier than boys in many ways.

He tossed restlessly from side to side, tried lying on his back, then his stomach, but without success. Sleep still refused to weight his eyelids. His nightshirt wriggled up around his knees and the bedclothes, like the room, were icy cold. In all the confusion, no one had remembered to pass a warming-pan between the sheets or fill one of the stone hot-water bottles. So in the end he gave up, staring into the darkness and thinking over his conversation with his elder sister. Josephine was right, of course; he *had* betrayed his ideals by allowing Arthur to persuade him to give up the Milk Street practice and settle in the comfort of Staple Abbots. What would have happened, he wondered, if he had never met Helena? If he had never gone with friends to that dance at the Grand Pump Room Hotel at Bath and finally, at the age of thirty, been smitten by a pair of blue eyes and a profusion of curls the colour of beaten copper?

It had been useless for people to warn him that he would be tired of her company in a couple of years at the most; that there was nothing in that lovely head except what gown to wear for which occasion and how to furnish the pretty house which her doting brother would provide for them, rent-free, in the village where she had grown up. In any case, Marcus knew it for himself, but was so bowled over – he who had resisted so many women until he was the despair of his mother and younger sister – by Helena Burfoot that he was a lost soul, giving up everything to do as she asked. At the time it had seemed like fate that Jack Richardson should have decided, two months before the wedding, to quit Staple

Abbots and move to Westbury, thus leaving the village practice open for Marcus. It was five years before he stumbled on the truth: that Arthur Burfoot, owner of every cottage and farm in the district, lord and master of all he surveyed, had brought pressure to bear on his old friend to go and so clear the way for his prospective brother-in-law. And by then, it was too late.

But it had always been too late, from the moment he had succumbed to a pair of dove-like eyes and a complexion as white and translucent as alabaster. 'Dora,' Josephine had called Helena behind her back, comparing her with Dora Copperfield in Dickens's novel; and although Marcus had at first been angry at the reference, finally he was compelled to recognize its justice. In the beginning, God forgive his presumption, he had tried to educate his Helena, but had been forced to give up for lack of response. And so they had continued over the years, growing further and further apart, but only he understood why. Helena was like a bewildered child, aware of the distance between them but unable to comprehend the reason for it, turning more and more to her brother and his wife for comfort and companionship . . . and to Henrietta. Yes, Marcus had to admit that having his younger sister to live with them, after she was widowed, had been a blessing in disguise. He had made the offer grudgingly and prompted only by a sense of duty, but it had worked out far better than he could ever have imagined. Helena had found in Hetty a friend and a sympathetic ear. Hetty had found a safe haven.

A baby's thin, high wail, loud enough to penetrate two stout oaken doors, pierced the silence, only to break off abruptly as the child's needs were attended to. A new life, a new beginning; Marcus felt a sudden thrill of optimism. This was his daughter, as well as Helena's; a Gilchrist as well as a Burfoot. Eve was the future. He recalled Mrs Pollitt's words. His little girl might live to see in the twenty-first century, the new millenium. Science and medicine were advancing at a rate never conceived of before; the human race

was becoming more enlightened. With luck and common
sense there might be no more wars. Tolerance, brotherly
love, Nature harnessed for the good of mankind – this would
be his child's inheritance, and it would be up to him to guide
her first tottering foosteps along the path leading to these
realms of gold. Ultima Thule.

Marcus turned on his side and fell sound asleep, a little
smile curving his long, thin mouth.

Part One
1908-1918

Chapter One

She always loved the early morning, particularly when the days grew longer and lighter, and the sun filtered through the rose-patterned curtains of her bedroom to lie warm and gentle across her face. She could hear the birds singing in the lilac tree outside the window, and Ellen calling softly to them as she scattered crumbs. For Ellen was up and busy, polishing fenders and blackleading grates long before the rest of the household was astir. Presently there would be the appetizing smell of frying bacon as Mrs Kellaway began cooking breakfast, but first Ellen would come upstairs with the trays of tea and biscuits for Mama and Papa, hot chocolate for Aunt Hetty and herself.

Eve wriggled into a sitting position, propped against the pillows, wondering why it was she woke so promptly and so easily during the holidays but found it so difficult to get up in term-time. It wasn't that she didn't like school or Miss Jillard, the village schoolmistress, nor did she find the work particularly hard; she was invariably top of the class. It was simply that she hadn't made many friends during the past three years and tended to be lonely. The other children resented her; the way she was dressed, the 'proper' way she spoke, the facility with which she absorbed and understood the lessons, the fact that she was the doctor's daughter and Squire Burfoot's niece. If they had been able to give voice in any comprehensive fashion, they would have agreed with Helena, who had argued passionately and tearfully that Eve should be educated by a governess at home.

'You can't mean for our daughter to mix with all those common village children!' she had sobbed when Marcus first announced his intention of sending Eve to school.

And Hetty had added her mite. 'Really, Marcus! I never heard anything so absurd! How can you possibly expect Eve to grow into a lady when she's exposed all day to rough speech and manners? She'll turn into a hoyden!'

But it was Arthur, after a long tirade about free-thinking, liberal nonsense, who had put his finger unerringly on the one real weakness of the plan.

'The villagers won't thank you for it. They won't want Eve mixing with their children any more than Helena wants Eve mixing with *them*. Eve'll make them feel uncomfortable, not only because she's brighter and smarter than they are but also because they'll regard her as a spy. I'm her uncle, and they'll feel they've to watch their tongues every minute of the day in case she reports back to me what they say. You're a city man, Marcus. You don't understand the country and its ways. Village folk are conservative; they know their place as I know mine and as you should know yours. We prefer it like that. So take my advice and don't go upsetting the *status quo*.'

But Marcus had stuck stubbornly to his guns, and in spite of all Helena's hysterical pleading, Hetty's tears and his brother-in-law's admonitions, Eve had attended the village school since she was five years old.

'I don't want my daughter growing up in an ivory tower, knowing nothing at all of the rest of the world,' she had heard her father say more than once. And when Uncle Arthur protested, as he often did, that in any case education for girls was a waste of time, Papa just folded his lips until they almost disappeared, as though he were controlling his tongue with an effort. Not that he always managed to exert such self-control. Eve had only a very vague idea what the word 'politics' meant, but she knew that there were some loud family arguments about them.

But today the school was closed for the Easter holiday, the sun was shining and there was nothing to do except decide how to spend the empty hours stretching ahead of her in a long, indolent procession. She wiggled her toes beneath the white cotton counterpane in an ecstasy of anticipation.

There was a knock on the door, and in answer to her 'Come in!' Ellen appeared, her rosy cheeks flushed with exertion, carrying a cup of steaming chocolate on a tray.

'Morning, Miss Evie. Did you sleep well?'

'Very well, thank you, Ellen. It's a lovely day.'

'It is, Miss. I'll just draw back the curtains for you, then you can see it proper like. There, that's better. I'll bring up your hot water in about fifteen minutes. Breakfast's a bit earlier this morning; it's the doctor's day for Lower Abbots and he likes to get off before ten.' Ellen paused in the doorway to glance admiringly round the room. She said, not for the first time: 'Mrs Gilchrist *has* turned this into a lovely room. I remember when it was just the guest room, dark red wallpaper and heavy brocade curtains and a counterpane the colour of stewed tea. And now it's all rose and white.' She added, without a trace of envy, 'You are a lucky girl, Miss Evie and no mistake.'

Eve nodded her agreement although later, when she was pouring hot water from the brass can into the white china bowl with red and white roses painted round its rim, she made the mental reservation that her luck might be considered greater if this wasn't the day for visiting Abbey Court with Mama and Aunt Hetty. She supposed she quite liked Aunt Mabel, a pretty, quietly spoken little woman, but she found her cousins Ernest and Donald, three and four years her senior, noisy and self-opinionated, inclined to be rough and patronizing. As for Uncle Arthur, his loud voice and the way he invariably insisted that she sat on his knee made her uncomfortable. He smelt of tobacco-smoke and leather, while the rough tweed of his jacket rubbed against her arms and the moustache – as fiery as his hair – which he had grown in recent months tickled her face whenever he kissed her. However, they wouldn't be driving over until teatime, and the day was her own until then.

She slid into the dining-room just as Mama was pouring the coffee and Aunt Hetty was hesitating between bacon, fried bread and devilled kidneys, or haddock topped with poached eggs.

'I do wish you'd try to get downstairs on time, Evie,' Helena said, mildly reproachful. 'I don't know what you do upstairs.'

'I'm sorry, Mama,' was the meek reply. Eve was old enough to know that she was extremely fortunate in the way her parents treated her. At Abbey Court, and also in many of the village households, children had to be at table, and remain standing, until their father appeared and sat down. And they were expected to be seen and not heard, whereas Eve was positively encouraged by Marcus to contribute to mealtime conversation. She didn't think Aunt Hetty altogether approved, but after all this time she must be used to Papa's unconventional ways. She did occasionally say discouragingly, 'In my young days, we had meals in the nursery until we were nearly ten.' To which Papa would answer a little shortly, 'Eve is a part of the family, not someone to be hidden away as though we're ashamed of her.'

He looked up now from his laden plate to smile at Eve. 'No school today then, my darling. It's my morning for surgery at Lower Abbots and I wondered if you'd like to come with me? It's a beautiful day and you can play outside. The Mailer boy will look after you until I've finished.'

There was an immediate outcry from his wife and sister.

'Really, Marcus! The boy's uncouth. You can't let him look after Evie!' This was Hetty, who had no knowledge of the Mailer family except that the father was a farm labourer at Abbey Court Farm, where in all probability he would soon be joined by the son.

Helena said, with that tearful quaver in her voice which her husband had learned to know and dread, 'Oh, Marcus! How can you even suggest such a thing? It's bad enough Eve having to play with children like that at school, without mixing with them socially as well. There are plenty of things she can do at home here to help me and Hetty.'

'Eve.' Her father's tone was carefully controlled. 'What

would *you* like to do, my dear?'

Avoiding her mother's eyes, Eve said gratefully, 'I'd like to come with you, Papa, please, if I may.'

'That's settled then.' Marcus returned to his breakfast. 'Be ready to leave by half-past nine. Ellen, will you please run round to the stables and tell Naysmith I'll be needing the pony and trap after breakfast?'

Eve picked up her spoon and began eating her porridge, trying to ignore her mother's hurt silence. Aunt Hetty remonstrated, 'I never heard the like, allowing a child that age to make her own decisions!' But it was a half-hearted protest because she knew from previous experience exactly what to expect.

So, promptly at half-past-nine, Eve took her place beside her father on the front seat of the trap, her new chip-straw hat tied securely over her auburn curls with a broad navy-blue ribbon, her navy serge dress with its wide sailor collar banded in white carefully brushed, her black leather boots polished until they gleamed, her woollen stockings smoothed free of wrinkles. 'For if you have to go visiting that kind of person,' Aunt Hetty had told her, 'you can at least set an example.'

Helena had kissed her sadly. 'Aunt Hetty's right, darling. Show the Mailers how a really well-brought-up little girl behaves.'

But now, bowling along the road to Lower Abbots with the warm breeze fanning her cheeks, the needle-sharp sunlight laying shadowy strips like tiger-skins across the rough, unmade track, Eve forgot her promises in the sheer enjoyment of being alone with her father, and free of the restrictions of petticoat government. The trees were budding in a haze of soft spring green, fleecy clouds scudded across a pale blue sky, and the hedgerows were spangled with wild primrose and wood anemone. Eve hummed 'Sweet Lass of Richmond Hill' under her breath.

'You sound happy,' her father said, smiling. 'Do you know the Mailer boy? Frank? I thought you might have spoken to

him in school, but of course he's four years older than you.
Nearly twelve. He'll be leaving in the summer, George
Mailer tells me. Joining him at the farm. A pity. Frank's a
bright lad and he deserves something better.'

'I have spoken to him once,' Eve acknowledged, 'on my
first day at school. Some of the other children were bul ...
well, not being very nice, and he came across and told them
to stop it.'

She recalled the occasion vividly, the ugly, menacing faces
of her fellow pupils clustered around her, herself terrified and
alone. And Frank Mailer had wandered up, a thin, dark,
undernourished-looking boy with fierce brown eyes, wearing
shabby knickerbockers and jacket a size too small for him,
obviously someone else's cast-offs (her cousin Donald's, Eve
had hazarded shrewdly). He had said, 'Stop that! You lot
leave her alone!' and knocked a couple of heads together. To
Eve's surprise, no one had resented his tone; in fact, they had
all looked rather sheepish and slunk away, and she had
discovered later that he was one of the most popular boys in
the school. The other children liked and respected Frank
Mailer, and not just because he was pugnacious and able to
use his fists. He was the bane of the teachers' lives, standing
up to Miss Jillard and her assistant if he thought anyone was
being unjustly discriminated against, but equally, in his
careless fashion, keeping an eye open for the bullies who
found their sport in making the smaller ones' lives a misery.
That first day at school, she had tried to thank him for his
intervention, but he had been off before she could stammer
out more than two or three words, and back to kicking a ball
around the playground.

Marcus gave her a sidelong glance, feeling uncomfortable
at the revelation of an incident he had previously known
nothing about. Had she often been bullied, he wondered,
during the past three years? It was on the tip of his tongue
to ask, and he knew that he should. But he did not really
want to know: the truth might be disturbing and force him
to the conclusion that Eve would be happier being educated

at home, and where would that leave his much-vaunted theories of equality?

So all he said was, 'That's good, then. You and he won't be complete strangers, and there aren't any other Mailer children for you to play with. The other three all died young.'

Eve found this information neither shocking nor particularly sad. Lots of children, both rich and poor, died in infancy; it was a fundamental fact of existence. But she was interested in so far as it pertained to Frank Mailer. The hero-worship she had felt for him since that day he had come to her rescue made any knowledge of him welcome, and she realized how little she knew about him.

They were by now approaching the hamlet of Lower Abbots, which comprised a scattering of farmworkers' cottages and a long, low, single-storey building designated as the local inn and dignified with the name the Cat and Fiddle, but in reality closely resembling the Spartan simplicity of an ale-house in the Middle Ages. There was no village store or green, and the Methodist Chapel which most of the inhabitants attended was in Staple Abbots, a few hundred yards along the road to Upper Abbots and entailing a walk, every Sunday morning, of three to four miles.

'Here we are,' Marcus said, pulling up in front of the first of the cottages. 'This is the Mailers', where I hold my surgery. Hop down and come along in.'

Frank emerged from the cottage door. 'Hello, Doctor. I'll see to the pony. Ma's got the other room all cleaned up for you, so you can start as soon as you like. Here, let me carry your bag indoors first.' His eyes fell on Eve and a faint blush coloured his cheeks. 'Oh! Didn't know you was coming.'

'I thought she would enjoy the trip,' Marcus said cheerfully. 'I'm relying on you to look after Eve for me while I'm busy.'

Mrs Mailer had joined them, wiping her floury hands on her apron. 'Of course he will, Doctor. Be pleased to, won't you, Frank?' And she clipped her unresponsive son around the ear.

'Yeah. Of course.' Heaving the heavy leather Gladstone bag from the back of the trap, he began to walk up the path, then glanced over his shoulder at Eve. 'You'd better come with me, then.'

She followed him round to the side of the building and in through the door of a lean-to scullery, where a strong odour of paraffin was all-pervasive. This emanated from a drum containing fuel for the oil-lamps which, with candles, provided the cottage's illumination. At the far end of the scullery was a large bundle of kindling, made up mainly of hedge cuttings, a pile of logs, and a small heap of precious coal used only with the strictest economy. There was a bread oven built into the thickness of the cottage wall, two wooden tubs piled one on top of the other, a broken-legged stool, various garden implements, a chipped and much stained sink and a pump. There was also a huge wooden pail of water which she later learned was for drinking, the supply from the pump being unsuitable for this purpose. The drinking water had to be fetched from the well in a neighbouring garden, some twenty yards further up the lane.

The main room of the cottage was about twelve feet square and served the function of kitchen and living-room rolled into one. The floor was stone-flagged with a scattering of faded, home-made rag rugs; and a high-backed settle, standing just inside the scullery door, formed a kind of passage into the room and prevented the worst of the draughts reaching those gathered around the fire on a winter's evening. A large table occupied the centre of the floor, while a stout wooden armchair and half a dozen ordinary wheel-backed ones provided, together with the settle, the necessary seating. A fire was kept going all year round, and over it hung a big iron kettle suspended from a chain in the chimney. The fireplace was flanked by two more wall ovens, and a narrow, twisting stair in one corner of the room led to the bedrooms above. A door in the opposite corner opened into a second lean-to room, equipped with the basic furnishings of a doctor's surgery.

'It's all ready for you, Doctor,' Mrs Mailer assured Marcus as she led him through. 'I scrubbed the table and floor and washed down the walls first thing this morning. Frank! Get them chairs in a line there. Sorry, Doctor. I thought 'e'd already done it. Lazy young so-and-so! If I don't keep my eye on 'im every minute of the day, 'e's off larking about.'

Frank grimaced at Eve, but immediately began arranging the wheel-back chairs along the wall between the front door of the cottage and the surgery door, a job which took him no more than a couple of minutes. Marcus refused the offer of a cup of tea, having already noted two of his patients coming up the garden path, and whisked himself out of sight in order to unpack his bag. Mrs Mailer welcomed her neighbours in, settling down to a detailed discussion of their ailments until such time as the doctor should be ready to offer more professional advice.

Frank looked at Eve consideringly. 'What d'you want to do then?'

'I . . . I don't know,' she stammered, blushing furiously.

He sniffed. 'Well, you can't do much in them clothes. You can't go birds-nesting or kicking a ball around. Looks like I'd better just take you for a walk.'

'Thank you,' she said humbly, uncomfortably aware that she was spoiling his morning, and was stopping him from being out and about with his friends. 'It's very kind of you,' she added.

He grinned at that. 'No, it ain't. Ma would belt me good and proper if I didn't do as I was told. Do you like apples?' Eve nodded, and Frank disappeared momentarily into the scullery, returning with two of last year's 'fallers' from Arthur Burfoot's orchard, one of which he handed to her. 'Here you are, then. Now, I'd best go and see to that pony or Ma'll have me guts for garters. After that, we'll walk down as far as the barrows.'

'The barrows?' Eve queried, following him out of doors and watching while he unhitched the pony from between the shafts of the trap and turned it loose in the nearby field.

'Oh, they'm not real barrows,' he explained as he rejoined her, picking up his half-eaten apple from the stone where he had left it and taking a large bite. With his mouth full, he continued, 'Not burial mounds like what Miss Jillard told us about in school. Your dad says they're probably what's left of the original village.'

They set off down the lane, past the other cottages from which several people were emerging, obviously intent on making for the doctor's surgery, to the open spaces of the plain beyond. The distances shimmered blue and pink in the morning sun, and the grass was green and lush after a recent spell of rain. Frank left the verge and led the way to a spot some hundred yards or so from the road where the ground was very uneven because of a cluster of humps and tussocks.

'Is this it?' Eve asked, disappointed. 'These aren't barrows.'

'I told you they wasn't, didn't I?' Frank was justifiably irritated. 'The doctor says it's where Staple Abbots stood in olden times.'

'The medieval village?'

'Yeah. Told me all the villagers died during the Black Death, and when the village was rebuilt later it was sited three miles north of here. Said we was lucky. Lots of places just disappeared completely.'

Eve took off her hat and sat down on one of the grassy hummocks. 'Papa knows about a lot of things like that. Does he talk to you often?'

'When I see him, yes. In the holidays.' Frank finished his apple and tossed away the core. 'I don't suppose I'll see so much of him in future, though, unless I'm sick. I'm starting work at Home Farm when I leave school this summer.'

'For Uncle Arthur?'

'Yeah.' Frank scratched his head. 'Of course, Squire's your uncle, ain't he? I was forgetting. So why'd your dad send you to the village school? Your cousins was taught at home before they got sent off to that what-d'you-call-it school in Salisbury.'

'Prep school – short for preparatory.' Eve, too, finished her apple and threw the core into some bushes, although she had an uneasy feeling that Mama would not approve. A lady never made litter. She tried, unsuccessfully, to explain. 'Papa feels that, well ... that people oughtn't to be, well, different ... so different from one another. They should be more sort of ... equal.'

Frank was nonplussed. 'You mean he belongs to this new Labour Party thing?'

But Eve had no knowledge of any 'Labour Party thing' and shook her head vehemently. 'Oh no, I don't think so. Papa's a Liberal like Sir Henry Campbell-Bannerman and Mr Asquith.'

'Oh well!' Frank shrugged and abandoned the subject. 'What d'you want to do now? There ain't all that much *to* do around here.' He seemed suddenly to have lost interest in her. He added hopefully, 'I could take you back to the cottage. It's Ma's baking morning; you could watch her make bread.'

Eve felt a pang of disappointment. She didn't want to lose his company. She liked Frank Mailer, liked him a lot. She had to admit that he wasn't much to look at; small, wiry and dark, not at all like her big, redheaded cousins or some of the other village boys who showed the characteristics of their Saxon forebears: blond hair, blue eyes and sturdy, solid frames. But she couldn't detain him against his will. 'All right,' she agreed dejectedly.

They started back the way they had come. 'You don't get trouble any more from those kids at school, do you?' he demanded all at once. 'Jim Tucker and Hester Zeal and that lot?'

'No.' Eve swung her hat by its ribbons. 'They don't like me,' she added candidly, 'but then, I don't really blame them. They don't bully me, though, thanks to you.'

Frank turned his head and looked at her, as if seeing her properly for the first time. 'Hasn't been easy for you, has it, being at that school? Haven't you made any friends?'

'No, not proper ones. Papa thinks I'm to blame, and I expect he's right. I don't find making friends easy.'

Frank whistled tunelessly for a moment between his teeth. Then he said, 'Nah! It's not your fault.' There was a pause in the conversation while he resumed his whistling, but after a moment he asked abruptly, 'How'd you fancy me as your friend?'

She thought she must have misheard and waited for him to repeat the question. When he did, she whispered breathlessly, 'Oh yes. Yes, please. Oh, please!'

He grinned. 'Steady on, I haven't offered you the crown jewels! Funny little thing, aren't you? All right, I'll be your friend, but there's no need to go telling everyone. It'll be our secret. Understood?'

Eve nodded ecstatically, and her joy was compounded when she discovered, on reaching the Mailers' cottage, that he had no intention of leaving her at the gate but went in with her. As they entered the scullery, Mrs Mailer came through the opposite door carrying the first batch of loaves, made from dough which had been proving in front of the living-room fire since early morning.

'You back already? Well, now you're 'ere, Frank, you c'n rake out the ashes in the bakin' oven. 'Urry up, for God's sake! I 'aven't got all day.'

Frank did as he was bid, grabbing a shovel, opening the oven door and scraping out the charred remains of the brushwood-and-twig fire which had heated the fireclay bricks inside. Eve stared fascinated as Mrs Mailer scattered a handful of flour over the oven floor to see if it had reached the correct temperature. Apparently it had, because she elbowed Frank out of the way and, with the help of a long-handled wooden shovel, put in the loaves, slamming the door shut behind them. It occurred to Eve that this sort of thing must go on at home, but she rarely went in the kitchen at Rosemary Villa, preferring to spend her spare time reading rather than watching Mrs Kellaway at work. Now, all at once, baking bread seemed the most fascinating of occupations. She smiled shyly at Frank as he sucked one of his knuckles where the hot ashes had burned him. He winked, and she felt as though her cup of happiness was running over.

'People still waiting to see the doctor?' he asked, and his mother grunted. He thought a moment, then rummaged in a cupboard crammed to overflowing with all sorts of objects, eventually finding what he wanted, a wooden box. He jerked his head at Eve. 'Come on outside, and I'll teach you how to play marbles.'

Chapter Two

'Eve!' She could hear her mother calling from the hall. 'Hurry up, dear. The carriage is at the door. Don't keep your uncle's coachman waiting.'

Eve sighed, dragged a hairbrush through the tangle of auburn ringlets and picked up her hat from the bed. Mama had reluctantly agreed that she need not change, so she was wearing the same dress she had worn that morning. She had managed to conceal the fact that the hem of her skirt was dusty from kneeling in the dirt, playing marbles. She wished Papa were going with them, but during luncheon Marcus had been sent for by old Mrs Yelling who lived some way along the Westbury road. Eve had detected a look of relief in his eyes, and she suspected that her father no more relished a visit to Abbey Court than she did.

'Eve! Hurry!' The summons was growing more urgent. She sighed, put on her hat and descended the stairs to find her mother and Aunt Hetty standing by the open front door.

'At last!' Helena's glance took in her daughter's appearance and she noticed for the first time a smear of dirt near the hem of Eve's dress. 'Oh, for heaven's sake, you've mud on your skirt. I knew I should have insisted on you changing.' She seized a clothes-brush from the hallstand and, kneeling down, scrubbed at the offending mark. 'There, that's better. What were you doing this morning to get your frock in that state?'

It never for a moment occurred to Eve to prevaricate. Her candour, even when it worked to her own disadvantage, sometimes verged on the foolhardy.

'Frank Mailer was showing me how to play marbles.'

Aunt Hetty gave a shriek of dismay. 'It's all Marcus's fault,' she moaned. 'No good will come of these egalitarian notions of his. They're not natural.'

They walked down the garden path between borders of nodding daffodils and white narcissi, interspersed here and there with small, flame-like spears of purple crocuses, to where the Burfoot carriage was waiting for them beyond the gate. Across the lawn, the forsythia bush stood like a golden shower, and an early-flowering rhododendron was already in bud, deep crimson petals bursting through the green.

The Abbey Court coachman – a thin, cadaverous man whose naturally severe expression had become even sourer of late as his position was threatened by the ever-increasing popularity of the motor car – had just finished walking the horses for a second time.

'If looks could kill,' Hetty murmured as they climbed into the open carriage, 'we'd be dead.' In a louder voice, she apologized prettily for their tardiness and was rewarded by what might have been the beginnings of a smile.

Helena squeezed her sister-in-law's hand gratefully. She had never been able to overcome her childhood nervousness of superior servants. The coachman flicked his whip and they were off, bowling along the village street, past the post office and general store, past the Ring O' Bells with its painted sign showing a circle of bellringers in a belfry, pulling on red-and-white striped ropes, past rows of thatched cottages which visitors to the village described sentimentally as picturesque, but which Marcus called flea-infested and insanitary. Behind them lay the cross-roads to Upper and Lower Abbots, the butcher's shop, the bakery, the chandler's and the forge. Here and there, swinging on a garden gate, Eve recognized one of her schoolfellows and waved, but her tentative salutations generally went unreturned. A couple of hands were raised, but mostly there was resentment at seeing her perched on high in the Burfoot carriage when only days ago she had been sitting beside them in the classroom, sharing lessons.

Abbey Court was about half a mile clear of the village and was approached by a winding drive which had once been the cart-track leading, in the seventeenth century, to a simple, well proportioned farmhouse with chamfered windows and tall chimneys. To this original building, succeeding generations of Burfoots had added a wing here, a terrace there, until the place was a hodge-podge of various styles and shapes. Inside, short flights of stairs of perhaps three or four treads led from one part of the house to another, from one room to the next. Architectural purists might throw up their hands in horror, but the casual visitor found it intriguing and the villagers regarded it with pride. They referred to it always as 'the Big House', and there was a great deal of rivalry among village girls for vacancies as members of the domestic staff. Arthur Burfoot was popular as both Squire and landlord, and it was generally agreed that he kept his place. You knew where you were with him, was the consensus of opinion; there was none of this nonsense about mixing on equal terms. The men and boys touched their forelocks, the women and girls bobbed a curtsey and Mr Burfoot raised his hat. He and his family had their own pew at the front of the church, he presided over the Harvest Supper every autumn, the carol singing at Christmas, and threw open his gardens each July for the Summer Fête. Most petty crime was referred to him for judgement, especially by the village constable, so there was rarely any need for recourse to the Warminster police. Arthur was the great man of the district, the main employer, approachable but not over familiar. Which was as it had been for centuries and, as far as anyone could see, would be for centuries more.

As Eve descended from the carriage, the front door opened and Aunt Mabel came out on to the top of the steps to welcome them. She was a small woman with the kind of faded prettiness that had never been startling, but which had diminished further during the years of her marriage. The piled hair was a mousy brown, her eyes a watery blue. It was, thought Eve, as though everything about Aunt Mabel was designed to blend into the background, leaving her healthy, vital, red-haired husband and sons to occupy centre stage. Even her voice was depressed and quiet. She spoke now barely above a whisper.

'Helena. Henrietta. How lovely to see you. Marcus isn't here. Oh dear! Does that mean he's been called out? Eve, give me a kiss.'

She led the way into the hall, where a parlourmaid was waiting to take their hats and coats, and then into the drawing-room. Here, Arthur was standing with his back to a fire which, in spite of the warmth of the spring day, had been lit on the big, open hearth which had served the original farmhouse. But an ornate marble overmantel had been added since those days; and with the walls papered in a dark red flocked wallpaper, a matching rich red Turkey carpet covering the floor, a welter of furniture, ornaments and knick-knacks crowding every available space, there was little else to indicate that this had once been the very heart of the house, an airy, stone-flagged kitchen.

Arthur kissed his sister affectionately on the mouth, placed an equally resounding earnest of his affection on Hetty's cheek and swooped to gather Eve up into his arms.

'How's my little princess?' His enquiry was always the same.

Eve, seeing Mama's anxious eyes upon her, restrained her natural impulse to wriggle down. 'Very well, thank you, Uncle Arthur,' she answered primly.

'That's a good little puss.' He set her on her feet again. 'Glad to see you haven't lost your manners, mixing with those village children. Where's Marcus? Oh, sit you down! Sit you down! Mabel, have your wits gone woolgathering, leaving guests standing like this?'

His wife immediately looked flustered and patted a large, velvet-covered sofa with a trembling hand, urging Helena and Hetty to a seat. Eve felt sorry for her aunt, as she always did when Arthur bullied her.

'Marcus was called out to old Mrs Yelling,' Helena

explained as she arranged the skirt of her new pale green, silk brocaded suit which she had collected from Miss Ellice, the village dressmaker, only last Friday. A lace jabot cascaded from the neck of the white blouse underneath, disguising what she felt was the cross she had to bear, the lack of an ample bosom, a definite drawback in this year of the much admired 'Gibson Girl'.

Arthur had been looking forward to goading his brother-in-law into an argument and was disappointed by Marcus's absence, but he managed to disguise his feelings.

'Perhaps it's just as well, or we should have ended up having words about this Liberal Government. Now then! Where are those two young rascals of ours, Mabel? Haven't you sent for them to play with their cousin?'

'They'll be here as soon as they get in from riding, Arthur.' Mabel Burfoot twisted her hands together nervously in her lap. 'You know you said it was all right for them to go out with Thomas this afternoon.' She forced an affected little laugh. 'They do so miss the horses when they're away at school.'

Hetty smiled reassuringly at her. 'I'm sure they do. Such nice boys, the pair of them. I must congratulate you both.' But her coquettish glance was for Arthur. 'Such little gentlemen. Only what one would expect, of course. But it's so much more fitting for Eve to be in Donald's and Ernest's company than that of the Mailer boy.' She deliberately ignored Helena's warning glance, feeling that Arthur Burfoot had a right to be kept informed of her brother's wilder fits and starts.

'Mailer boy?' Arthur's sandy brows snapped together and his moustache, Eve noticed, fairly quivered with indignation. 'You can't mean George Mailer's lad, surely!'

Helena pressed a hand to her chest to still the sudden acceleration of her heart-beats. She hated unpleasantness of any sort.

'It was only that Marcus took Eve with him to Lower Abbots this morning, and while he was in surgery it was natural that Frank should look after her. Marcus rents a room from the Mailers,' she added by way of further explanation.

'Yes, yes, I know that!' Arthur was testy. 'But why did Marcus want the child to accompany him in the first place? Let alone allow her to associate with young Frank!' He turned to face his sister, wagging a spatulate forefinger. 'It's high time you put your foot down, Nell! No good'll come of all these damn queer notions of his. Reading people like this Shaw fellow and H.G. Wells!' He drew a scathing breath. 'I've even known him stick up for a scoundrel like Oscar Wilde! I wouldn't have believed it if I hadn't heard him with my own ears!'

Helena was about to protest that she had no influence over Marcus's radical ideas when the door opened and Donald and Ernest Burfoot entered the drawing-room, washed and changed after their exercise, red hair neatly brushed, freshly laundered Eton collars turned down over the necks of their navy-blue serge jackets, socks pulled up smoothly beneath their knickerbockers. Donald was nearly twelve, Ernest almost exactly twelve months younger, their birthdays being within three days of one another in May. Of the two, Eve liked Ernest best, finding him less pompous than Donald who was very conscious, young as he was, that he would one day be Squire Burfoot of Abbey Court.

'Don't count your chickens!' Ernest would tease when he wanted to annoy his brother. 'Papa could leave it all to me, you know. The estate's not entailed.' But they both knew that would never happen. Arthur Burfoot was a stickler for tradition.

Hetty was now chatting animatedly to her hostess on her favourite subject, royalty, both British and European. There was no newspaper article about King Edward and Queen Alexandra or any member of their family that she did not avidly read, and she knew the exact relationship of every crowned head to every other crowned head on the Continent. When Queen Victoria died, seven years previously, Hetty had gone into deep mourning for months. It was the one subject on which no one would dare challenge the accuracy of her knowledge; and her scrapbooks with their elegant marbled covers, which every lady of taste and refinement kept for her pleasure, were filled with royal portraits and lovingly hand-scripted family trees.

Arthur took the opportunity to sit beside his sister and possess himself of one of her hands, prepared to offer the sympathetic ear which she had always needed for her little grumbles and grievances. Marcus had no time for them, telling her abruptly that she had everything to be thankful for and nothing to complain about: she was a very lucky woman.

'I know I am very fortunate. I know I am,' she moaned tearfully to her brother, 'but Marcus just doesn't realize the responsibilities involved in running a home successfully. Thank goodness I have Hetty to back me up, or I don't know how I'd survive.'

The children, left to their own devices until such time as tea should arrive, stared balefully at one another. It was Ernest who eventually suggested that they go outside.

'We can walk down to the stables and you can see our horses,' he said to Eve, who remained infuriatingly unexcited by the prospect.

'I'd rather walk over to the farm,' she said, wondering if there was any possibility that Frank Mailer might be around, helping his father during the holiday.

But her cousins had no interest in sheep and pigs and cows. They had no inclination to get their shoes muddied unless it was in the stables, which according to them was a different kind of muck.

'We're wearing new shoes,' Donald pointed out. 'Mother would be furious if we ruined them.'

Eve could not imagine Aunt Mabel getting furious, but you never knew. 'Would she have your guts for garters?' she enquired with interest.

Her high-pitched young voice was clearly audible in every part of the room, and there was a sudden deathly silence.

'Eve!' a scandalized Helena was at last able to exclaim. 'Wherever did you hear such a common expression?'

'Well, it's obvious where she heard it.' Arthur turned his wrathful gaze on Ernest, who was showing a marked tendency to giggle, unlike his brother who maintained a stuffily scandalized expression. 'It comes from letting her loose, unchaperoned, in Frank Mailer's company. It's no good relying on you to do anything, Nell. There, there! Don't start to cry, sweetheart. I'll have to have a word with Marcus myself.'

*

Arthur was as good as his word, making a special visit to Rosemary Villa the following morning, but the only result – as Helena had already predicted to Hetty – was to make his brother-in-law more stubborn than ever.

'If Arthur thinks he can come here and tell me how to bring up my daughter, he's a more pompous, self-opinionated fool than I already took him for!'

The tirade was delivered over lunch, with the result that Helena retired to her room for the rest of the afternoon, nursing one of her sick headaches. Hetty, for once in her life, was wise enough to keep her thoughts to herself, relying on her brother's conscience to do her work for her; and instead of quarrelling with Marcus, she spent her own afternoon writing to her sister. When minded, Hetty had a subtle intelligence for which few people gave her credit, and without mentioning the actual cause of the present rift between Marcus and the Burfoots she managed to convey a family riven by tensions which, as ever, centred upon Eve.

'If you could possibly see your way, my dear Josie, to inviting the child to stay with you for a couple of days – without, of course, mentioning that I have asked you to do so – I would myself be only too willing to travel to Bristol with her, and fetch her again at the end of the holidays.' Self-sacrifice, Hetty felt, could hardly go further.

She walked down to the post office herself and posted her letter, and a reply was received within a very few days. If dear Helena and Marcus could spare her one and only niece for the remainder of the holiday, Josephine would be delighted to have Eve to stay.

'And you need not fear that the child will be bored,' Josephine continued, 'for my friends have at last persuaded me that the internal combustion engine is the only way to travel, and I have bought myself a Singer 4-cylinder tourer, so we shall be able to go on expeditions much further afield than before. If you reply by return of post and name a day, I will travel to Warminster by train to meet Eve, so no one at your end need be troubled. I have just finished my latest book and sent it to the publishers, so there will be no question of my work being interrupted.'

'Well?' Marcus asked, having read the letter aloud over the breakfast table. 'What do you say, Evie? Do you want to go?'

He had anticipated an unequivocal 'Yes' and was puzzled by his daughter's hesitation. But Eve found herself unexpectedly torn between a holiday with her beloved Aunt Josephine – with the added inducement, if one were needed, of trips in a motor car – and seeing Frank Mailer again when Marcus next had a surgery in Lower Abbots. She remembered his offer to be her friend and was afraid of losing him if she went to Bristol. She had never wanted anyone as her friend so badly as she wanted Frank.

'It would make a change for you,' Hetty said firmly.

Marcus ignored his sister. 'It's for you to make up your own mind, Eve. But I must admit, I thought you would jump at the chance.'

'Yes, but . . .' Eve hesitated. She knew, however, that Papa would prefer her to be honest. 'I should like to visit Aunt Josie very much. It's just that I shan't see Frank again if I do, and he was going to teach me how to go birds-nesting.'

Both ladies let out a simultaneous groan, Helena clutched her forehead and Hetty turned reproachful eyes on her brother. But the admission had taken even Marcus aback. He said gently, 'Girls don't climb trees, and taking their eggs is unfair to the birds.'

'And you have all those lovely toys to play with,' Hetty scolded. 'I'm sure you've hardly touched that dolls' house I gave you last Christmas.'

Eve sighed. 'It gets lonely, playing on my own.' She was seized by a sudden inspiration. 'You don't think Frank could go with me to Bristol? I'm sure Aunt Josie wouldn't mind!'

Marcus had his mouth open to say that this was not a good idea — even he was beginning to be a little troubled by the success of his experiment — when he was interrupted by a furious cry from Hetty.

'No! I've never heard such nonsense! Marcus, you can't condone such a proposition. It's monstrous! You can't foist a common farm lad on to Josie. He wouldn't know how to behave! I'm sorry I ever wrote and . . .' Her voice tailed off and she bit her lip, realizing that she had given herself away.

'And asked Josephine to invite Evie to stay with her. Is that what you were going to say?' Her brother's voice was glacial. 'That explains the suddenness of the invitation. You wanted to remove Eve from my sphere of influence, and also that of young Mailer, for the remainder of the holiday.' His eyes glinted angrily. 'You may be my sister, Hetty, but you are nevertheless a guest in this house. Please try to remember that. I will have neither you nor Arthur nor anyone else meddling in my affairs.'

Helena rose shakily to her feet, her handkerchief pressed to her lips. 'I must go and lie down,' she said. 'My headache has returned. Hetty, would you send Ellen to me, please? I need my smelling salts.'

'Now look what you've done!' Hetty cried, also rising. 'I'll have to go after her. She's in no fit state to be on her own.'

The dining-room door closed with a defiant click, and they heard the patter of her feet on the stairs. Ladies, according to Hetty, never ran, but she came as near to hurrying as she dared without ignoring her own dictum.

Marcus looked at his daughter. Her face was white and her
hands were clasped tightly together in front of her on the
table.

'Are you all right?'

Eve tried to smile but her stomach, as it so often did, felt
as though it were doing somersaults. Why were people
always arguing over her? Why was she the subject of so many
rows? Was it her fault? The prospect of going to stay with
Aunt Josie seemed very desirable all of a sudden.

Before she could speak, however, Papa astonished her by
saying, 'I have to go to Westbury this morning. While I'm
there, I'll go to the post office and put through a call to Holly
Lodge.' Staple Abbots at this time had neither telephone
cables nor electricity nor running water. 'I'll ask your Aunt
Josie if she would be willing to have Frank Mailer as well as
yourself, if his parents will let him go. It would do the boy
good. He's like all his kind; too thin and undernourished for
his age.'

'But Mama and Aunty Hetty...' Eve faltered. 'They
won't like it.'

'Maybe not,' her father answered grimly, 'but I am master
in my own house, and I shall do as I think fit, a sentiment
which even your Uncle Arthur would approve of. Speaking
of whom, if the Mailers do agree to let Frank accompany you,
it may be as well that your uncle should be kept in the dark.
Therefore, we had better say nothing of our plans to your
mother and aunt. We shall not lie to them, we shall just not
tell them all the truth. Regretably, that sort of deceit is
sometimes necessary. It is called expediency – remember
that, Eve.'

'Yes, Papa.' She was so happy, she would have agreed with
anything as long as Frank could go with her as Aunt Josie's
guest. And such was her faith in Marcus's ability to arrange
matters that it never occurred to her that things would not
work out.

Nor was her faith misplaced, for he found time that day
not only to telephone Josephine and obtain her blessing, but

also, between visiting patients and consulting with the local nurse, to drive to Lower Abbots and talk the Mailers into giving their consent. This was not easy, and to begin with Frank himself did not want to go; he was appalled at the thought of having to be on his best behaviour for several days, to mind his manners and try not to drop his aitches. But the prospect of going for drives in a motor car, in addition to travelling by train, won him over and made him argue as hotly for the proposed treat as he had originally been against it. Neither of his parents wished him to go, fearing the visit would imbue him with ideas above his station, and shrewdly seeing it as just another of the doctor's weird schemes to disturb the regulated order of their lives.

But in the end they gave in, partly because they were in awe of anyone with superior education, and partly because Lizzie Mailer was unable to deny her one remaining child anything he had truly set his heart on. And George knew from experience that to upset his wife was to make his own existence miserable. Their one stipulation was that the Squire should not be told, for they feared his anger and being turned off the farm. It was therefore arranged that Frank should set off with his few belongings at daybreak the following morning and walk the six and a half miles to Warminster station, where he would be met by Eve and her father who would make the journey by pony and trap. Josephine would travel down from Bristol by train and take the children back with her.

Eve considered it all the most exciting adventure, and any qualms she might have had about deceiving her mother and Aunt Hetty were speedily laid to rest when Papa told her it was necessary for the sake of Frank and his family. She had the most awful fear that something would happen to prevent Frank from coming, but when she and Papa arrived he was already waiting for them on the station forecourt, dressed in his Sunday suit, a clean spare shirt and an extra pair of socks packed in a cardboard box which he carried under one arm. She grinned shyly at him as she descended from the trap.

At first the conversation between them was somewhat strained, but by the time Josephine arrived on the south-bound train, they were chattering away without reservation. Marcus handed over his charges and returned to where he had left the pony and trap, grimly elated that he had foiled his sister and brother-in-law, but also prey to some uncharacteristic misgivings.

Chapter Three

In later years, Eve remembered those few days as one of the happiest times of her life; a time never to be repeated; days of endless spring sunshine and pale, primrose-tinted skies; the beginning of everything, the end of nothing. The whole world lay open to her to do as she pleased in the company of the two people she was fondest of, Frank and Aunt Josephine.

It was strange how soon she knew that Frank was important to her. She had expected to feel tongue-tied, diffident, for her acquaintance with him was formerly so slight, and he was four years older than herself – growing into manhood, soon to go out to work. But she found him easy to talk to, and because of his small stature was able to forget his age. It was Aunt Josie, however, who was really at the heart of the relationship, who made things smooth. Eve was too young at the time to understand what it was about her father's elder sister that made everything right; but when she was older, she realized that to her aunt Frank was a person, a real person, not a farmhand's son, not an inferior; nor was he a social experiment, nor the means of a defiant gesture at Arthur Burfoot and his kind. He was just a boy.

As for Frank himself, he soon forgot his shyness. To begin with he was overwhelmed by the idea of living at Holly Lodge, even for a few days. The high-ceilinged rooms with their solid, old-fashioned, Victorian furniture, the four-poster bed in which he was put to sleep, the lace-edged, linen sheets which enveloped him, the napery, the silver, the china were all as alien and as intimidating to him as if he had suddenly been transported to the court of Siam and expected to know how to behave. The city, too, seemed immense and

the amount of traffic frightening. Josephine had left her
Singer on the forecourt of Temple Meads station and the
drive to Clifton was both exhilarating and worrying,
especially when the car stopped three times on the steep
incline of Park Street and passers-by had to give them a
push. Frank counted at least half a dozen other motor cars on
their way to Holly Lodge, and there were lots of horse-drawn
vehicles as well; brewery drays, removal vans, and innumerable carts of all shapes and sizes carrying milk and coal, bread
and vegetables.

And the shops! He had never seen so many shops in his
whole life, nor such a variety of goods. And hotels and houses
and churches. Long before they reached the open spaces of
the Downs, his head ached with so much staring. The first
night he found it difficult to sleep because of the distant
rumble of traffic, but he was amazed how rapidly he got used
to it and how comforting the sound became. The next
morning Josephine, having assessed the meagre contents of
Frank's cardboard box, took both children into town on the
pretext of getting Eve a new dress. But, she said, it would
be impolite to buy anything for her niece without also
buying something for Frank, so she purchased a blue merino
shirt, two pairs of socks, a cap and a silk tie for the reasonable
outlay of two shillings and tenpence-halfpenny. Afterwards,
they went to Melhuish's at the top of Castle Street for the
café's shilling lunch.

'And what would you like to do when we've finished
eating?' Josephine asked, smiling with pleasure at the way
Frank scraped every last morsel of meat and potato pie from
his plate.

'Trains,' Frank said, his mouth full and his eyes following
a waiter who carried two large, shallow, flat-rimmed bowls
filled with apple tart swimming in bright yellow custard.
'I'd like to see trains.'

Josephine signalled to their own waiter, hovering close by,
and ordered two helpings of pudding. 'None for me,' she
sighed regretfully. 'I'm heavy enough as it is. Eve, what

would you like to do? Ladies should always be allowed first choice.'

'Oh, I'd like to see trains, too,' Eve fibbed, and was rewarded by a glowing look from Frank.

So they went to the station and stood on the platform to watch the great expresses thundering through to London or South Wales. The engines all had names. One was called 'The Lord of the Isles', which Eve thought was particularly splendid and conjured up visions of kilted Scotsmen running through the heather. Some engines were squatter and smaller than others, with water tanks on top of their boilers; and a friendly young man who was standing nearby, writing down locomotive numbers in a halfpenny notebook, told Frank that they were saddle-tank engines, known familiarly as 'Billy Busters'. Frank, prompted by Josephine, thanked him politely, and Eve gave him a smile. The young man was, she judged, about sixteen or seventeen, very tall and extremely pale and thin, as though recovering from a recent illness. He was beautifully dressed in a grey cashmere overcoat over a darker grey suit, and wore a black bowler hat perched at a rakish angle on his fair wavy hair. He was a great train enthusiast, and told them about the biggest locomotive of the lot, the 'Great Bear', so huge that on her maiden trip her outside cylinders had fouled the platforms. And no doubt he would have regaled them with even more information, his pale blue eyes shining with excitement, if a uniformed chauffeur had not at that moment approached and touched him on the arm.

'Your mother is waiting, Master Lawrence.'

The young man gave a sweet, sad smile. 'Very well, Robinson. Say I'll be with her directly.' Then he shook hands with the three of them, very solemnly, before turning and walking towards the platform entrance.

Altogether, it was a very happy and pleasant afternoon, and Eve enjoyed herself far more than she would have imagined possible. They caught the omnibus back to Clifton and had tea sitting in front of the fire in the drawing-room at Holly Lodge. Afterwards, when the parlourmaid had cleared away the tea-things and the two fat cats, Powder and Puff, had curled up contentedly on the hearthrug, Eve and Frank sat one on either side of Josephine on the sofa, while she read to them from one of her own novels, all about a family of children called the Mortons who had the most amazing adventures.

'And tomorrow,' she promised, finally closing the book and packing them off to bed in spite of their protests, 'we'll take a trip across the Suspension Bridge to Leigh Woods.'

The holiday was over all too soon; a magical progression of days, travelling by train to Weston-super-Mare, where they made sand castles on the beach, exploring the shadowy reaches of Nightingale Valley, taking trips in the Singer to the opposite side of the Avon Gorge. And in the evening, when the curtains were drawn and the lamps lit, Josephine either continued reading to them from *The Mortons Abroad*, or introducd them to what she called 'worthier works': fairy stories from the Brothers Grimm and Hans Andersen, or Lamb's *Tales from Shakespeare*. And one evening she read from *She Stoops to Conquer*, playing all the parts in different voices and making her charges double up with laughter. And when she finally closed the weighty, leather-bound volume, she handed it to Eve.

'The combined works of Oliver Goldsmith,' she said. 'Keep it. It's yours for when you're older. You'll enjoy *The Vicar of Wakefield* and the poem, *The Deserted Village*.' She quoted: '"Sweet Auburn, loveliest village of the plain,"' adding, 'That could almost apply to Staple Abbots, couldn't it?'

Frank pulled one of the shining strands of hair tumbled about Eve's shoulders. 'More like you,' he suggested. 'You could be called Sweet Auburn; it could be your nickname.'

'I'm not going to be called after a village!' Eve exclaimed indignantly, but she laughed, spoiling the effect of outrage. She pushed her hair back from her face. Normally, it hung in tight ringlets, but since being at Holly Lodge she had not bothered to curl it up in rags every night before she went to sleep. She supposed sadly that she would have to do so this evening, for tomorrow they were going home and she dared not risk Mama's disapproval, which would rebound on Aunt Josie.

The following morning, they piled for the last time into the Singer, Eve's case and Frank's cardboard box stowed on the back seat, and drove to Temple Meads station. Josephine accompanied them as far as Warminster, where Marcus was waiting to meet them with the pony and trap for Eve, but Frank would have to walk to Lower Abbots. Josephine shook his hand.

'Goodbye, Frank. I have enjoyed your visit. You must come to Holly Lodge again sometime.'

He shot her an upward glance from his shrewd brown eyes. 'P'raps,' he said gruffly. 'Thank you for having me.'

They left Josephine waiting for her return train to Bristol, and Eve clambered into the trap beside her father.

'You won't say anything to anyone, Eve, about Frank having been with you,' Marcus instructed, as they set out on the journey home. 'There is no need to lie. Just be very careful what you say. Don't mention Frank, that's all, he won't be going with you again.'

'But Papa, Aunt Josie didn't mind. She liked having him, she told me. And he's my friend.'

'I'm not saying you can't mix with the village children, my darling. I want you to, but there are degrees of familiarity, and in this instance I have to confess that I made a grave mistake. Now, we'll say no more about it. Just try to remember what I said. No word to your mother or Aunt Hetty.'

Eve watched the familiar fields flash by on either side of her until at last they gave way to the more open spaces of the Plain. She felt confused and suddenly unhappy. Home and its conflicts seemed to be closing in on her again. But there was one thought she clung on to; she liked Frank and he liked her, and there was nothing anyone, not even Papa, could do about that.

*

When Eve was eleven years old, there was a big celebration
at Staple Abbots; bigger even than the Harvest Supper or
Summer Fête. In the bright June sunshine, trestle tables
were set up in the main street outside the Ring O' Bells and
the general store. Red, white and blue bunting was criss-
crossed from roof to roof and the Union Jack flew proudly
from the flag-pole on the church tower. Every woman in the
place had been baking for days, making sausage-rolls and
tarts, jellies and blancmanges, seed cakes and fruit cakes of
gigantic proportions; and on the day itself enough sandwiches were cut to feed, as Mrs Jenks from the bakery shop
put it, the entire British Army. Two enormous tea-urns had
been provided courtesy of St Peter's Church and the Methodist Chapel, and a brass band had been hired from Salisbury
for the afternoon at Arthur Burfoot's expense. Everyone who
was neither ill nor infirm was expected to attend, and indeed,
there was hardly anyone who had not been looking forward
for weeks to the Coronation tea.

King Edward VII had died in the May of the preceding
year and now, thirteen months later, King George V and
Queen Mary were to be crowned. Celebrations were being
held in every part of the United Kingdom, and Staple
Abbots was no exception.

'I want this to be the biggest do we've ever had,' Arthur
told the other members of the Coronation Committee.
'Bigger than we had for King Edward, bigger even than for
the old Queen's Diamond Jubilee. And no shirking with
either money or time. After all, now this Government's
actually paying people just for being old, there's no excuse
for anyone to plead poverty.'

The Old Age Pensions Act, passed by Parliament in 1908,
was a very sore point with Arthur and was a continuing bone
of contention between himself and his brother-in-law whenever they met. The idea of giving people over seventy years
of age five shillings a week – seven and sixpence in the case

of a married couple – 'as of right' was anathema to Arthur.

'If they haven't the gumption to save for their old age, they deserve to go into the Workhouse.'

'How on earth can they save on the pittance you and other employers pay them?' Marcus would retort furiously, and off they would go hammer and tongs, as Helena tearfully complained.

But today all differences were to be set aside; all was to be harmony and light as the village gave itself up to the celebration not just of Their Majesties' Coronation, but also of everything British.

'The greatest nation in the world,' Arthur said in his opening speech. 'An empire on which the sun never sets, that is this country's stupendous achievement! And I think I can safely say that every man and woman of this village can take a little credit for it. The British spirit! That's what's made England the power that she is today. We don't have revolutions like they do on the Continent. We don't envy people who are better off than ourselves. So, before you all fall to and enjoy this delicious spread, I ask you to give three rousing cheers for Their Majesties, King George and Queen Mary, God bless 'em! Hip-hip . . .'

Everyone stood and cheered like mad, but with half an eye on the food to make sure that no one took unfair advantage by starting betimes. Then with much scraping of chairs and light-hearted banter they sat down, reaching out eager hands towards the nearest plate, children being scolded by parents to 'mind your manners, now do!' and amidst reminders of 'sandwiches first, cakes after!' From her place at the top table, wedged between Uncle Arthur and her mother, Eve could just make out Frank a long way down on the right-hand side, seated outside the saloon-bar entrance of the Ring O' Bells.

He had left school three years ago, at the end of the summer term and three months past his twelfth birthday, to work in Arthur Burfoot's fields alongside his father. Without the daily contact of the playground, and with an age gap which seemed to widen between them, he and Eve had seen less of one another, but when they did meet the bond of that shared holiday was still strong. No one had ever found out about it: Josephine and the Mailers had kept discreet tongues in their heads and when Eve, on two occasions, had almost let something slip, she had managed to cover up successfully. But there was no doubt that the real barrier to their friendship was that Frank, at fifteen, was now a man, with a man's appetites and instincts, while Eve was still a child whose main preoccupation each Saturday was whether to spend her penny-a-week pocket money on two farthing strips of liquorice and two farthing gob-stoppers or owls' eyes, or to blue the lot on one reckless purchase such as four ounces of mixed boiled sweets.

At last the gargantuan meal was over and an army of willing helpers began to clear away, the women carrying off the piles of stacked crockery to the pub kitchens, while the men let down the trestle tables and returned them to the church hall whence they came. The brass band, which had played stirring patriotic tunes throughout the tea, packed up their instruments, received their fee from Arthur's bailiff, climbed into their hired waggon and set off down the road to Lower Abbots and thence across country, back to Salisbury. And then it was the turn of old Tom Ormes, once the village carpenter and handyman, now seventy-five if he were a day, but who still played the fiddle – as he had done for as long as anyone could recall – at every local function where dancing was required. After some tuning up, which set everyone's teeth on edge and provoked cries of "'E's throttlin' that there cat again!' he broke into a lively reel and everyone lined up for the first country dance.

Eve had been promised that she should stay up until at least nine o'clock, which she thought might well be stretched to ten if she stayed discreetly in the background and didn't force herself on people's notice. Her parents were leading the first set for Sir Roger de Coverley, and Arthur had asked Aunt Hetty to lead the second with him, leaving poor Aunt Mabel to stand at the side of the road and chat with the other matrons. Eve withdrew into the shadows of the narrow gap between the Ring O' Bells and its neighbouring cottage, to be quiet and observe. She could smell the delicious scents of the cottage garden, the heady perfume of scarlet-headed roses, honeysuckle and late-flowering lilac. A drift of pinks lay near the open gate and wisteria climbed in purple profusion round the door. In the cloudless evening light it looked like the setting for some Hans Andersen fairy tale, but only last week she had heard her father inveighing against the village's lack of running water and an adequate drainage system.

'You have no soul, Marcus!' Aunt Hetty had cried impatiently. 'Staple Abbots is beautiful, everyone who comes here says so.'

'It's a breeding ground for germs and disease,' Papa had snapped back at her. 'Art for art's sake is all very well, but let's have proper drains for God's sake. Don't you agree, Michael?' And he had rounded on the hapless Reverend Michael Ellice, vicar of St Peter's, who had been paying one of his parochial visits.

'Oh . . . ah . . . quite so,' the vicar had answered, with one eye on Helena, who was Arthur Burfoot's sister. He didn't want any complaints going to the Bishop. 'But Mrs Jardine is also right. We mustn't discount the aesthetic side of life altogether. Practicality has its uses, but so does beauty.'

Marcus had lost his temper. 'Sitting on the church fence, as usual, Michael? Trying to serve God and Mammon?'

Eve hadn't stayed to hear the rest of the discussion but had taken herself off to her room – as she always did whenever she felt trouble was brewing – to read the Goldsmith given to her by darling Aunt Josie. *She Stoops to Conquer* still made her laugh even though some of the antiquated language was difficult to understand on her own, and she loved *The Deserted Village* because it reminded her of Frank . . .

'Well, well,' said a soft voice behind her, and a hand covered her eyes, 'if it isn't Auburn herself! Sweet, sweet Auburn.'

Eve jumped and spun round. 'Frank! Oh, you did startle me! Where have you come from? I thought you were in the street, dancing.'

'I was.' He grinned. 'But I needed to use the pub's earth closet. I've been down at the bottom of the yard.'

Eve blushed faintly. Bodily functions were rarely mentioned at home, in spite of her father being a doctor.

Frank gave her a brief hug, having first made sure that no one could see them. 'I've embarrassed you. Sorry.'

'No, you haven't.' She gave him a shy kiss on one cheek.

In the past three years, he had filled out and grown taller. He was still small and wiry for his age, but he had lost the fragile, undernourished look which had captured Josephine's heart.

'Why aren't you dancing?' he demanded.

'No one's asked me. The boys from the village won't, and my cousins are away at school. I'll have to wait until Papa or Uncle Arthur are free.'

'I see.' And he did. Nothing had changed. She was still on her own, not accepted as a village child despite her schooling, but with no contemporaries of her own social class close at hand. Frank made up his mind. 'Come on!' he said, grabbing her wrist and dragging her forward. 'You can dance with me if you'd like.'

Of course she would like, that went without saying. They joined the end of a set which had just formed and, within minutes, Eve was smiling at the top couple as they sped, hands linked, down the middle of the two rows. Her eyes sparkled with happiness, the auburn ringlets bounced to the rhythm of her clapping and her toes, in the blue kid boots which exactly matched her frilled lace dress with its broad satin sash, tapped impatiently. At last it was her and Frank's turn to dance, and the music from Old Tom's fiddle grew faster and louder until her feet scarcely seemed to touch the ground. Up and down between the two lines of watchers they bounded; hands across and whirl around. It was over all too soon, and it was only when she finally stopped, laughing

and breathless, that Eve noticed her mother and father
standing on the grass verge at the side of the road.

'Hello, Frank.'

'Hello, Doctor. Mrs Gilchrist.' He tugged his forelock
respectfully. 'Be seeing you, Eve.'

He was gone, to join his friends and receive their good-
natured chaff about cradle-snatching, leaving Eve to stare
wistfully after his departing figure.

Helena glanced at her husband. 'Papa was looking for you,
to ask you to dance.'

Marcus nodded and held out his hand. 'Would you do me
the honour, Miss Gilchrist?' he enquired with mock solem-
nity, but his eyes failed to meet hers and the fact made Eve
curious. Papa was uncomfortable about something and she
wondered what it could possibly be.

*

'So you see, darling, you won't be very far away. You'll be
able to get home at weekends if you want to, and there will
be holidays as well.'

A bird was singing in the elder tree outside the window
of Marcus's study, which also doubled as his surgery. Eve
knew the room like the palm of her hand: the big, leather-
topped desk, the rows of glass-fronted cabinets containing
medicines, the straight-backed chair for patients to sit on,
the red, much worn Wilton carpet with its pattern of beige
and brown, the deep armchair near the marble fireplace, the
copy of Frans Post's *A Village in Brazil* blending into its
background of tobacco-brown wallpaper. Yet suddenly
everything appeared strange and unfamiliar, as though she
were looking through a distorting mirror. The door was
slightly ajar, and she could hear Ellen clattering the plates
and cutlery as she washed up the breakfast things.

'But why do I have to go away?' she asked.

Marcus took one of her hands in his. 'Because you'll soon
be too old for the village school. There's only one class above

the one you're in, and that's for thirteen and fourteen-year-olds. But your education isn't going to finish then. So, Mama and I have been looking around for somewhere not too far distant, but which has a good reputation for scholastic achievement, and Mayfields Academy seems to fit both of those requirements. It's a lovely old country house between Lower Woodford and Salisbury, and the Miss Milwards who run it are two very nice ladies with splendid academic qualifications. They are both Cambridge graduates, so you can see that you will be in good hands.'

'But ...' Eve began again, then stopped, biting back her objections. For it had suddenly occurred to her that she was not averse to the idea of continuing her education: she enjoyed learning and had never found schoolwork difficult. She had a good memory for facts and figures, and a natural curiosity which made her want to enquire into the origins and mechanics of things. She spent hours reading, and the thought of being encouraged to do this, rather than having Mama and Aunt Hetty constantly chiding her for hurting her eyes – 'You'll end up having to wear spectacles and that will ruin your looks!' – was really quite agreeable. On the other hand, it would mean leaving her friends.

What friends? mocked the voice inside her head. You haven't any friends except Frank Mailer, and after last night ... For he had not asked Eve to dance with him again. He had spent the rest of the evening either with his pals or in the company of Jenny Slade. And Eve hated Jenny Slade. Jenny was in the class above her and would leave school at the end of this summer term; a big girl for her fourteen years, with hair the colour of ripe wheat, a full red mouth and bold blue eyes that stared impudently from beneath thick, fair lashes. 'Brazen', Aunt Hetty called her, and prophesied that she would 'come to a sticky end'. Whatever that meant. Certainly, most of the village lads clustered round her like bees round a honeypot, including Frank, and yesterday he seemed to have been picked out for special favours. Jenny Slade had danced with him nearly every dance, laughing and tossing her head at the rest of her frustrated admirers. It had worried neither of them that they were so unequally matched in height, and Frank had kept Jenny in a perpetual state of giggles with the things he whispered in her ear whenever they were close together.

'But what?' Marcus queried gently, watching his daughter's face and wondering what was going through Eve's mind. A secretive, solitary child in many ways, boarding school would do her good, bring her out, force her to mix with girls of her own age and intelligence.

Eve raised her eyes, her lips arranging themselves in a bright, acquiescent smile.

'Oh, nothing. When would I go to Mayfields?'

'In January, after your twelfth birthday. And there would be Christmas to look forward to first.'

Eve nodded. 'That's all right, then.'

Chapter Four

This was her last Christmas at home.

Well, not exactly, Eve thought, as she peered into the brightly-lit windows of the village shops, with their paper streamers and sprigs of evergreen which gave a festive air to the more mundane, everyday objects such as loaves of bread and joints of meat. She would, of course, be home for the holidays, but it would not be quite the same. She would not be here to participate in the early preparations, to catch that first whiff of barely definable excitement when the realization that it would soon be Christmas enveloped the village as a whole. She would no longer go out with the other children to gather mistletoe and holly to decorate the classrooms and the school hall, or watch for the arrival of the carter with his barrow-load of fir trees, soon to be transformed, even in the poorest homes, with ribbons and candles and tinsel bows.

Eve turned into the shop run by Mrs Crocker and her husband, Bert. On this December evening Bert Crocker was ensconced behind the wire grille of the post office, while his wife's ample figure was to be found in its customary place at the counter of the general store. A row of large sacks, containing sugar, dried peas, oats and bran, was ranged in front of the counter, and Mrs Crocker was at that moment employed in twisting a sheet of stiff blue paper into the shape of a cone and then scooping sugar into it. She placed this carefully on the scales and balanced it against one of the big brass weights.

'That's one pound exactly, Miss Ellice. That'll be a penny ha'penny. Is there anything else I can get you?'

The vicar's sister nodded. 'Two pounds of currants, please.

I'm making my Christmas puddings.'

Mrs Crocker made an even bigger cone, this time from a sheet of brown paper, and dug another scoop into one of the wooden boxes which stood on top of the counter. Eve amused herself by looking at the rows of brightly coloured metal canisters, containing different sorts of tea, from which Mrs Crocker skilfully made up the blends to suit the varying tastes of her customers. Miss Ellice was still busy with her purchases: half a pound of streaky, cut from one of the sides of smoked bacon hanging from hooks in the ceiling, a pennyworth of treacle drawn from the tap of a big metal drum in a corner of the shop, four ounces of mixed biscuits from the tins of different assortments on the shelves.

'And four eggs. I think that's everything.'

She stowed her shopping in her basket, and waited for Mrs Crocker to add up her bill.

'That's one shilling and threepence, if you please.'

Miss Ellice sighed as she produced a green chamois leather purse from her coat pocket.

'Oh, dear! I don't know where the money goes these days. Milk's gone up to a penny a pint, and I had to give one and eleven-three for a pair of slippers in Salisbury last week. It's so difficult to make ends meet.'

'I don't know what the world's coming to,' Mrs Crocker agreed comfortably. 'What with the Post Office asking everyone to post their cards no later than Christmas Eve and these nasty, smelly motor cars everywhere ...' She turned to Eve. 'I hear the doctor's bought one?'

'It's not a brand-new one,' Eve said defensively, feeling that she was being criticized on behalf of Marcus. 'He bought it from Doctor Richardson when he retired last month. It's an Argyll, and specially designed for the medical profession.' She had heard Papa use exactly those words and was proud of herself for remembering them.

'Well, I wouldn't know about that,' Mrs Crocker responded. 'But I do know horseback or a pony and trap has always been good enough in the past. However, times change, I suppose. Now, what can I do for you?'

Eve produced some of her carefully hoarded pocket money and bought two bars of Fry's Chocolate Cream to give to Aunt Hetty for Christmas. If she could persuade Cook to keep them on the marble meat slab in the pantry, they shouldn't melt in the next three days.

By the time she finally left the shop, sucking an owl's eye – a gift from the soft-hearted Mrs Crocker – darkness had descended. After the drizzle of the past few days, the weather had suddenly taken a turn for the better. It was a clear, dry evening with a touch of frost in the air, and a sky that fairly crackled with stars. Lighted windows were strung like golden beads along either side of the village street, and the shapes of Christmas trees were silhouetted against drawn blinds. Eve was reminded of a scene from her currently favourite book, *The Wind in the Willows*, when Mole and Ratty were returning across country to the River Bank from a foraging expedition. Holding tightly to the brown paper bag containing her chocolate bars, she started in the direction of Rosemary Villa.

'Auburn! I thought it was you. I haven't seen you for ages.'

It was Frank, barring her path, a grin splitting his face almost from ear to ear.

'You look like the Cheshire Cat,' she said crossly. 'What are you doing here?'

The grin became, if possible, even wider. 'I've come to buy my Dad an ounce of Old Shag for Christmas. What's happened to put you in such a bad mood?'

'Nothing!' Eve tossed her head so violently that she nearly dislodged her woollen tam o'shanter. 'I suppose you're still seeing a lot of that Jenny Slade.'

'Oho,' he said. 'So that's it.' He tapped her on the tip of her nose with a grimy finger. 'You should know there's only one girl for me, Sweet Auburn. Besides,' he added, completely ruining his effect, 'what with me working all hours at Home Farm, and Jenny under-parlourmaid up at the

Court, there's not a lot of chance for us to see one another.
Your uncle doesn't believe in too much spare time for his
employees.'

Eve felt hot tears sting the backs of her eyes, but she
answered with spirit, 'I'm going away to school after
Christmas, so *we* shan't be seeing a lot of each other, either.'

'I heard about that. Doctor told Ma last time he was at the
surgery.' Frank's tone was not noticeably less cheerful than it
had been, and Eve could have screamed with vexation. 'You'll
soon be a proper lady, Auburn, instead of one of us scruffy
village children.' He leaned forward and brushed her cheek
with his lips, in a brotherly fashion. 'Try not to get too grand,
though, will you?' He moved on towards the general store,
then paused and looked over his shoulder. 'I often think of that
holiday, you know. She's a nice lady, your Aunt Josephine.'

He disappeared inside the shop and Eve was left, rubbing
her cheek where he had kissed her. The door of a nearby
cottage stood open, and a stream of golden light poured out
into the road, which glittered with the first skimming of
frost. She took the owl's eye out of her mouth to see how
many layers of colour she had sucked away, and if she had yet
reached the liquorice centre. The familiar ritual was somehow reassuring, and prevented the tears from spilling down
her face. Yellow . . . she was only at the yellow layer. From
long experience, she knew she still had white and brown to
go. She put the sweet back in her mouth and crossed the road
to Rosemary Villa.

*

'This is what I like.' Arthur's voice boomed out genially
from his place at the head of the dining-table. 'This is as it
should be. All the family together at Christmas!'

He directed a particularly beaming smile in Josephine's
direction, eliciting only the sketchiest response. Apart from
a natural resentment at being included in the ranks of the
Burfoot family, Josephine was wondering why she had
agreed to come to Staple Abbots for Christmas. She would

have been much happier at Holly Lodge, among her own friends or being quiet by herself. She did not like the festive season – being, if not an atheist then certainly an agnostic, and consequently finding it lacking in meaning. She considered, moreover, that there was a great deal of hypocrisy attached to the giving of expensive presents to people as well-off as oneself, while millions of others were starving. Surely, if there were any meaning to the Christian message at all, it was to bring aid and succour to the poor.

She glanced around her at the white damask napery, the sparkling crystal glasses and silver cutlery, at the Wedgwood dinner service and its load of food. A huge turkey on an enormous carving dish, sauce-boats of cranberry and bread sauce, vegetable dishes full of boiled and baked potatoes, winter greens, Brussels sprouts, turnips, carrots and parsnips, two tureens of gravy and four bottles of wine ensured that there was hardly an empty space on the sideboard. Josephine found herself wondering about the Mailers and what they were having for Christmas dinner. She always enquired after Frank whenever she managed to get Eve on her own, but this year had found her niece singularly uncommunicative on the subject. Eve seemed more concerned with going away to school, which Josephine supposed was unsurprising, for she sensed a natural anxiety in the child facing her first real break with home.

Marcus, too, was reticent concerning Frank Mailer.

'But I thought you wanted Eve to mix with the village children,' Josephine had protested, 'not to feel herself superior to them.'

'There's a difference between not feeling superior and being over-friendly,' her brother had retorted. 'That holiday I arranged for him to spend with you was a mistake, and I'm extremely grateful to you for never having mentioned it to Helena these past three years.'

Josephine remained dissatisfied, and could not help reflecting that her brother's attitudes were beginning to alter. She noticed a certain complacency in the way he looked across the table at Eve, who was chatting companionably to Donald Burfoot. Josephine knew from Hetty that one of the long-term plans laid by both Helena and Arthur was that a match might one day be possible between the cousins.

Had her aunt but known it, Eve was extremely bored by Donald's anecdotes of life at Marlborough and his own prowess on the sports-field. But he seemed to think that she should be flattered by his attentions. At fifteen, he regarded himself as a bit of a 'blood' who would not normally waste his time talking to a girl not yet twelve years of age, even though they were related. But he had always considered Eve, with her auburn ringlets and creamy complexion, to be extremely attractive, if a little young. And Donald had an eye for a pretty girl. He was fully aware of Jenny Slade's presence in the room, as she assisted at table.

Shortly before the start of dinner he had encountered her, not quite by accident, in the long, dark passage which led from the kitchens to the front hall. He had slipped an arm about her waist and tried to kiss her, and his lack of success had been due more to the appearance of the head parlour-maid than to Jenny's unwillingness. Throughout the meal, his eyes rested thoughtfully on her every now and then as she moved quietly and efficiently between sideboard and table.

It was nearly four o'clock before the final spoonful of plum pudding and brandy butter, the last morsel of Stilton cheese had been consumed, the dregs of wine drained from glasses. And in an hour or two it would be time for the tea-trolleys to be wheeled into the drawing-room, with their burden of sandwiches and muffins, cake and mince pies. Eve, escaping from the dinner-table and her cousins' company, headed for the bathroom upstairs. As she crossed the hall, Jenny Slade emerged from the kitchen passage. They were alone, and Jenny permitted herself a whispered jibe.

'If it isn't Miss Evie,' and she dropped a mocking curtsey. 'Uncle's little pet! We always knew we had to be extra careful what we said in front of you at school, pretending to be one of us and then running home to tell tales.'

Eve felt the colour burn in her cheeks; her heart began to pound, and she was about to scuttle upstairs when she suddenly discovered a reserve of courage, swung on her heel and went back to face her tormentor.

'And if you don't watch your tongue, I'll be running to my uncle with another complaint.' She made no effort to lower her voice. 'I fancy you won't retain your place here very long if he discovers you've been cheeky to his niece.'

The words were no sooner spoken than she felt bitterly ashamed. She wondered what Papa and Aunt Josephine would say if they could hear her. Yet she also felt a surge of elation. It was nice to know that she could stand up for herself if necessary. A little of her fear about going to Mayfields Academy evaporated. And without waiting for Jenny Slade's reaction, Eve turned and marched up the thickly carpeted stairs. By the time she came down again, Jenny had vanished and the rest of the family were opening their presents. Uncle Arthur was making another speech. Even Mama, on a recent occasion when she had thought Eve safely out of earshot, had remarked to Papa that, really, she did so wish dear Arthur would stop addressing her as though she were a public meeting.

'He won't. He likes the sound of his own voice too much,' Papa had answered shortly.

Eve made her way to the fire and stooped to fondle the two spaniels lying on the hearth-rug. One of the great regrets of her life was that Mama would never allow her a pet. Although brought up in a home where animals abounded, Helena had never liked them.

'They grow old and smelly,' she objected, 'and their fur gets everywhere.'

'Well, young lady,' her uncle began, as Eve sat beside her mother on one of the big settees, 'and where have you been? We thought we'd lost you.' Fortunately for Eve's modesty, he did not wait for an answer and continued, 'You nearly missed your presents. I was just going to open them for you. But before you do, I'll repeat for your benefit what I've been saying to the others.' Everyone except Mabel gave a small, resigned sigh. 'It's been a marvellous year, and I'm not simply referring to that wonderful summer weather. We've a new King and Queen safely on the throne, and that's very important. You've only to look at what's been happening in other countries to realize the dangers of republicanism, and that's a fact. Mexico, for example. And France and Germany at each other's throats over Agadir!' He gave a rumble of laughter. 'I'll tell you this, my girl, if we'd sent in a gunboat like the Germans, *we* wouldn't have tamely withdrawn and waived our claims! Not the greatest nation on earth! But nothing changes in this country except for the better. Stability, continuity, they're what matter.' A shade of dissatisfaction passed across his heavily jowled face. 'Pity, though, that Scott has allowed that fellow Amundsen to steal a march and get to the South Pole ahead of him. A Norwegian, too! However, I suppose one can't be too grudging. Got to let the underdogs have a bone now and then, to keep them happy. And Norway hasn't achieved anything like the launch of the *Titanic*.'

Later, as they were being driven home to Rosemary Villa in the Burfoot Daimler, Eve wedged uncomfortably on Hetty's lap, Josephine demanded of her brother, 'Why on earth didn't you say something, Marcus, when Arthur started holding forth like that? Pompous man! I'm sorry, Helena, I know I shouldn't belittle him in front of you, but he makes me so angry. However, as an outsider, and in his own house too, I didn't feel it my place to speak.'

Marcus hesitated before replying. 'There is something in what Arthur says, you know, Josie.' His tone was measured, almost placatory, as though he accepted that this view would not be shared by his elder sister. 'Things do go on the same in this country from century to century. I thought only yesterday morning, when I was passing the saw-pit on the edge of the village, that men have been cutting timber like that in rural areas since the Middle Ages, and Arthur's right: it does give an enormous sense of stability and continuity.

They'll probably still be doing it the same way in another three or four hundred years.'

Josephine snorted. 'What about the motor car? What about the transatlantic telegraph? I don't suppose Doctor Crippen felt nothing had changed when he was arrested miles out to sea, on board the *Montrose*. Once upon a time, you could count yourself pretty safe from the arm of the law if you left the country.'

'I'm talking about the basic fabric of life. Of course there must be some progress.'

But the mention of wife-poisoner Harvey Hawley Crippen had sparked off a rival conversation between Helena and Hetty, who proceeded to review the scandalous doings in Hilldrop Crescent for the remainder of the homeward journey. Eve's head drooped against Hetty's shoulder and her eyes closed. She was tired of the sound of grown-ups' voices. It was all so boring. Soon she would be away at school, surrounded by girls her own age. She wasn't sure whether to be glad or sorry; she wouldn't see much of Frank in future, but what did it really matter? Nowadays, when they met, he treated her like an indulgent elder brother. He was probably walking out with Jenny Slade on her days off. She hated Jenny!

The Daimler drew up in front of Rosemary Villa. Everyone got out while Compton – Arthur's chauffeur, who had replaced the old coachman – reversed the car and started back to the Court. Josephine and Marcus continued to argue as they went indoors, while Hetty and Helena were still discussing the more ghoulish elements of the Crippen case with relish. Eve wondered sleepily why it was that murders seemed to hold such a fascination for her mother and aunt, who both turned faint at the sight of blood.

The house was quiet, Cook and Ellen having been given the day off to visit their families, with permission to remain at home for the night. This was a great sacrifice on Helena's part, for it meant that she had to get up next morning and lay the table for breakfast. It was understood, of course, that to eat there would only be toast and boiled eggs, which would in any case be prepared by Hetty. Nevertheless, she felt herself generous to a fault for having made such a concession, even though it was at Marcus's instigation. Eve said her good-nights and climbed the stairs to bed, carrying her Christmas presents with her: a new dress from Mama and Papa, some hand-embroidered linen handkerchiefs from Aunt Hetty; a recently published book, *The Secret Garden*, from Aunt Josephine; a leather pencil box with her name on it, tooled in gold letters, from Uncle Arthur and Aunt Mabel; a thin silver bangle from her cousins. She put everything away, then went to sit on the window-seat, pushing up the lower sash and letting in the scents of the garden – a blend of damp earth, cold air and an acrid whiff of bonfires. A drift of stars twinkled between the branches of leafless trees, and she could see the ghostly outline of the winter-flowering jasmine on the other side of the lawn. The grass itself was rimed with frost and sparkled in the faint light thrown by the gas-lamps in the drawing-room, where the curtains had not yet been drawn against the night.

In two weeks' time, she would be leaving all this. Eve withdrew her head, closed the window and stared around the familiar, safe room. There was the dolls' house Aunt Hetty had given her, the old rocking-chair covered in a patchwork blanket, the rose-patterned curtains and counterpane. She knew that Mama did not want her to go away, and Aunt Hetty had declared openly that it was barbaric to send girls to boarding-school, an institution intended only for boys. As for Uncle Arthur, he had poured scorn on the very idea of women's education.

'A sheer waste of time and money, Marcus! What's she going to do with it? Earn her living?' And he had roared with laughter at the very idea. No woman in the Burfoot family had ever soiled her hands with labour. 'No, she's going to get married, of course. Become a wife and mother. That's what Nature intends for women.'

'Oh?' This exchange had taken place some time ago, before Eve had noticed, as had Josephine, a slight sea-change in Marcus's attitudes. 'What about all those who are employed at Abbey Court? What about all those poor unfortunates who slave in London's East End sweatshops? What about schoolmistresses and shopkeepers' wives like Mrs Crocker? Are you telling me they're not really women?'

'Now you're being stupid!' Arthur was smug. 'You know very well that I'm referring to *ladies*!'

Eve undressed and washed, cleaned her teeth, brushed her hair and tied it up in rags so that it would be curly again in the morning. Then she climbed into bed and blew out the candle. Perhaps, she thought, snuggling down beneath the blankets and pulling up the chintz-covered eiderdown around her ears, it was just as well that she was going away to school, for it demonstrated that Papa did not regard her as a lady. And that was fortunate, for she fully intended marrying Frank Mailer when she grew up, and no lady could marry a farmhand. This sudden decision took her by surprise: she had no idea how she had reached it. A few days, even hours, ago, she had regarded Frank as lost to her. Now, however, her confidence had returned. Perhaps it was because she had stood up to Jenny. That encounter had shown her what she was capable of and made her feel that anything was possible.

She would marry Frank, she didn't care what anyone said. She had made up her mind.

*

Mayfields Academy was a mellow old Georgian house, standing in its own grounds and set well back from the road which ran between Lower Woodford and Salisbury. The two sisters who owned it, Flora and Emily Milward, were waiting at the top of the steps to greet the new arrivals. Eve's first impression of Miss Flora Milward, the headmistress, was of a tall, imposing woman with a stern but kindly expression who would stand no nonsense. Although still in her late forties, her hair was already grey, parted in the middle and looped over her ears in the style known as 'earphones'. The hazel eyes were directly appraising, but there was a lurking spark of humour in their green-flecked depths. She wore a tailored grey suit and mannish grey-and-white striped blouse, with a fob-watch pinned to her ample bosom.

But if Miss Flora was the iron fist, Miss Emily was the velvet glove. No less imposing a figure than her sister, with the same iron-grey hair and steadfast gaze, she nevertheless managed to convey a gentleness, a willingness to overlook small misdemeanours, apparently lacking in the older woman. It was she who came forward to fuss over the new girls, directing the porters to carry in their cases and telling them exactly where to go. The headmistress herself was content simply to have a brief word with the parents, advising them not to hang about too long.

'The children will be better once you have gone. Just leave them to us. I assure you that none of them will be unhappy.'

In the long dormitory overlooking the gardens at the back of the house, Eve sat on the edge of the bed allotted to her and stared miserably at the case she was supposed to be unpacking. Mama and Aunt Hetty had refused to make the journey, so she had only had to say goodbye to Papa. She had clung fiercely to him until he gently loosened her arms.

'You'll be all right,' he had said. 'You'll soon make friends.'

She became aware that the girl who had the next bed was watching her, a small, plump child with round brown eyes the colour of toffee, and two short mousey pigtails.

'I'm Rose Druitt,' the unknown finally volunteered, adding enviously, 'You arrived in a motor car.'

Eve nodded and gave her name. 'My father's a doctor,' she explained apologetically. 'He needs one to travel around.'

'You are lucky! My father hasn't got one because Mama says they're noisy and smelly and pollute the atmosphere. But I expect Papa will buy one in the end.' Rose came and sat beside Eve on her bed. 'You're new, too, aren't you? So, as we're next to one another in the dormitory, shall we be friends?'

'If you like.' After a moment, Eve held out her hand and the two girls linked fingers. The human contact was reassuring. Perhaps boarding-school wasn't going to be too bad, after all.

Chapter Five

Mayfields Academy closed its doors for the summer vacation of 1914 on Friday, the 17th of July. Marcus arrived promptly after lunch in the 4-cylinder Ford Model T, which had replaced the old Argyll, to collect not only Eve but also Rose Druitt, who was to spend the first two weeks of the holiday at Staple Abbots. Watching them both descend the front steps, trim in their white poplin summer dresses, the wide-lapelled collars banded in navy-blue, their broad-brimmed chip-straw hats, also bound with navy ribbon, set at the prescribed angle on their burnished and neatly pigtailed heads, he was suddenly aware that Eve was no longer a child, his little girl, but almost a woman. Since Whitsun, when she had last been at home, she had mysteriously blossomed. Marcus wasn't quite sure where the difference lay, for she was as thin as ever and her face, no longer framed by plump ringlets – the Miss Milwards forbade all artificial curling aids for girls under the age of sixteen – was as delicate and small-boned as it had always been. Perhaps it was the air of quiet confidence which made her appear so mature.

She and Rose, laughing and chatting together, waved goodbye to friends, paused to 'read the riot act' to some errant first-former who had no business to be using the front-entrance steps, shook hands with Miss Emily, who had come out to wish her girls a happy holiday or to take a tearful farewell of those who were leaving for good, then turned to find Marcus.

'Papa.' Eve kissed his cheek, pleased to see him but knowing that he did not like overt demonstrations of affection. 'Now, where's our luggage?' She scanned the array of cases, brought out earlier by the porters and lined up on the gravel sweep.

'Already strapped to the back of the car. I thought I might as well do it while I waited. It's clearly labelled.' Marcus held out his hand to Rose, which she shook with her customary vigour.

'Jolly nice of you and Mrs Gilchrist to invite me again,' she beamed. 'I've very much enjoyed my previous visits.' She ran an admiring hand along the side of the Ford. 'Splendid machines, aren't they? My father has one. Twenty horse-power. Flywheel magneto.'

'Oh, get in, do,' Eve expostulated, laughing, 'and stop waffling on about matters neither Papa nor I understand. Papa just drives the thing. If it goes wrong, he gets a man out from Warminster to put it right.' And she climbed in beside her friend on the back seat.

Marcus cranked the starting handle a couple of times, got in as well and they sped off down the school drive.

'As a matter of fact,' he said, 'that might soon prove unnecessary. Albert Naysmith's lad is talking about opening a motor car work-shop next door to his father's stables.'

'In Staple Abbots?' Eve was incredulous. 'Surely there aren't enough cars in the village to keep him busy?'

'Not in the village itself, no.' They passed through the school gates and turned right towards Lower Woodford. 'But there's more traffic about than there used to be. We're not quite so isolated any more. Nowadays we get people travelling across the Plain, on business *and* pleasure. And sometimes cars break down, not to mention Army vehicles. There have been a lot of troop movements lately, and only last week we had a couple of soldiers come into the village, asking if anyone could help, because their lorry had stalled half a mile along the road and they couldn't restart it. In the end, your Uncle Arthur had to send one of the grooms into Warminster for them. Besides, Jim Naysmith would still assist his father with the stable. The workshop would be a sideline.'

'It all sounds jolly exciting,' Rose enthused. 'I wonder what sort of Army lorry it was. Could it have been a Napier?'

It was Marcus's turn to laugh. 'I've no idea!'

Eve looked at the countryside, bathed in warm golden sunlight, at the road winding ahead of them through stands of ancient beeches and oaks, at the tall spears of red and yellow hollyhocks, beds of sweet-scented lavender, red-hot pokers, pinks and carnations in cottage gardens. She drew a breath of pure pleasure. The summer holidays were here again. Soon she would see Frank.

Rose was speaking. 'A lot of girls at school are saying there's going to be a war. What do you think, Doctor Gilchrist?'

Marcus half-turned his head as the Ford began the long haul across the open Plain towards Staple Abbots. 'I shouldn't think so, for a moment. It's all bluff and counter-bluff, and double bluff piled on top of that. If the British Government is worried about anything, it's that there's going to be civil war in Ireland. That's much nearer home than some little flare-up in the Balkans.'

Helena and Hetty were waiting at the door of Rosemary Villa to greet them. Ellen Lightfoot was no longer in evidence, having suddenly decided, at the almost old-maidish age of twenty-nine, to marry Jeb Marston, who had been courting her for the past ten years. The wedding had taken place two weeks earlier at the Methodist Chapel in Upper Lane and Ellen, together with her new husband, had retired to a farm cottage at Lower Abbots, not far from that of the Mailers. It was the fact that the cottage had fallen vacant and been offered to Jeb by Arthur Burfoot which had precipitated the event.

'Though I do feel badly about the way we got it,' Ellen had confided to Helena on the morning she handed in her notice. 'If Old Pete Ottewell hadn't been kicked by that horse, he'd still be working, and he and his missus wouldn't have been carted off to the Workhouse.'

Her mistress, however, had not shared her sentiments. 'My dear Ellen, they're very well looked after in those places, you know, and there's nothing to pay. All the cost falls on the

Parish. You're being foolishly sentimental.'

So Ellen, reassured, had enjoyed her wedding, and Helena
was left with the arduous task of training a new girl how to
wait at table, how to dust properly, not forgetting skirting-
boards and the tops of cupboards, and how to assist Mrs
Kellaway in the kitchen. Although in fact it was Hetty and
Cook herself who did most of the instruction, this did not
prevent Helena from complaining.

Eve's first encounter with the new maid, Doris Hosier,
was fraught with embarrassment, as they had been classmates at the village school. Doris, however, unlike some of
the other children, had never resented Eve's superior social
status and therefore had no difficulty in coming to terms
with the situation. But she did forget, from time to time, to
add the prefix 'Miss' when addressing her former fellow-
pupil, thus incurring Helena's wrath.

'It's all your fault,' Helena scolded Marcus one lunch-
time, after Doris had offered Eve a dish of cabbage with the
words: 'Here y'are then, Evie girl. That'll make yer hair curl.'
'You should have had Eve taught at home, as I wanted.'

Before Marcus could defend himself for the thousandth
time, Rose said warmly, 'Oh, no! I think it was a splendid
gesture on the doctor's part, Mrs Gilchrist. Governesses are
absolute hell, believe me.' Oblivious to the startled faces
around the table, the gasp of horror from Hetty and Marcus's
attempt to stop himself from smiling, she continued, 'Eve's
one of the brightest girls at Mayfields, and Miss Milward
reckons it's because she's had such a sound grounding in the
three Rs. Governesses are more concerned with useless
things like embroidery, playing the piano and deportment.
That's why my parents decided I must go away to school
before it was too late, if I wasn't going to grow up an even
bigger chump than I am already.'

Marcus said as gravely as he could, 'Thank you, Rose, for
your support. And what are you two up to this afternoon?'

'It's such a lovely day, we thought we'd walk up to Long
Meadow and watch the haymaking.' Eve tried to sound

casual, trusting that no one would attribute any ulterior motive to such an innocent-sounding excursion.

Her mother and aunt were more concerned that she and Rose would get tired and dusty from a long walk in the heat, but Marcus gave her a quick sidelong glance, bright with suspicion. He made no comment, however, for which Eve was grateful. After luncheon, she and Rose set off to walk the two miles to Long Meadow without anyone making any attempt to prevent them. Rose was buoyed up by the possibility of seeing farm machinery in motion, Eve by the almost certain knowledge that Frank would be one of the haymakers.

Neither girl was disappointed. As they approached, Eve could see both Frank and George Mailer among the team of workers handling the crop. Frank was loader, and was seated on top of the great pile of hay being forked up to him by his father and two other farmhands.

'That'll do,' Eve heard him shout. 'I'll have to start roping down now.'

Eve nudged Rose. 'Let's sit in the shade a moment. No one'll notice us until they've finished. Roping down's a tricky business.'

So they sat in the lee of the hedge which bordered the field and watched while everyone stopped what they were doing and helped Frank tie down the cartload of hay for safe transportation to the rickyard. By the time they had finished, sweating and straining, Jeb Marston had returned with an empty wagon pulled by two more of Home Farm's great Shire horses. It was then the turn of one of the other men to see the full wagon to the rickyard, a welcome diversion from all the stooping and heaving.

Frank made his precarious descent from the huge pile of hay and stood rubbing his hands down the sides of his corduroy breeches.

'I reckon we deserve a break,' he grunted. 'The Gaffer'll never know if we take five minutes.'

George Mailer gave a crack of laughter. ''E'll bloody know

all right if we ain't cleared this field by sundown. Get on with it, Frank. You ain't long 'ad yer dinner.'

'Two hours or more . . . All right, I'm coming.'

Frank was about to jump up on the empty cart when Eve got to her feet and waved at him.

'Hello, Frank! We've come to watch you working.'

A delighted grin nearly cracked his face in half. 'Auburn!' He came across the field towards her, holding out a hand in greeting.

Eve, however, caught him by the shoulders and kissed him, French fashion, on both cheeks, as was the custom amongst pupils and staff at Mayfields Academy. There was a ragged cheer from the rest of the men, and Frank's face burned with embarrassment.

'Well,' he said, when he had recovered his balance, 'you've grown up since I last saw you.'

Eve smiled coolly and turned to Rose. 'Rose, let me introduce you to an old childhood friend of mine: Frank Mailer. Frank, this is Rose Druitt, and nothing would please her more than a trip to the rickyard to watch them using the boom and cable.'

Frank scratched his head. 'Funny thing for a girl to want to see, I'm buggered if it isn't.' He recollected his manners and apologized hastily for swearing. 'But I can't get away now, Auburn. Dad's right, there's still a lot to do and Squire won't be pleased if we haven't finished here by evening.'

Eve shrugged. 'Oh well, I'll just have to show her myself. Come on, Rose, follow me.'

'I say,' Rose breathed, as they picked their way across the field and out through the gate, 'your parents must be awfully broad-minded, letting you mix with boys like that. Fancy being able to kiss one in public and nobody minding.'

'Papa's always been extremely liberal in his attitudes,' Eve replied airily, 'which is why he sent me to the village school instead of having me tutored at home by a governess. And it isn't as though I kissed Frank on the lips.' But deep down, she doubted Marcus's approval of the little scene just

enacted, and hoped that news of it would not reach his ears.
Young ladies with pretensions to gentility did not go around
kissing farmhands, and even Papa might well be scandalized,
let alone Mama and Aunt Hetty who were quite liable to
faint from the shock. She did not really know why she had
done it. Bravado, perhaps, or a desire to wipe that comradely
grin from Frank's face. She doubted if he greeted Jenny Slade
in such a fraternal fashion.

'Why does he call you Auburn?' Rose panted, her short
legs working hard to keep up with Eve's long ones.

'Because of the colour of my hair, of course.' Any more
involved explanation, Eve felt, was unnecessary.

'But I mean . . . Well . . . He's quite familiar.'

'For a farm boy is what you're saying. But there again, you
see, we were at school together, and he once saved me from
some bullies in the playground.'

'Gosh!' Rose's round, toffee-coloured eyes grew even
rounder. 'It's all terribly . . . I don't know . . . romantic, isn't
it?'

Eve burst out laughing and paused to hug her friend.
'Rosie! Rosie! You're absolutely right. It *is* romantic. If I tell
you a secret, you must promise faithfully not to tell anyone
else.'

Rose licked her forefinger and made the sign of the cross
over her heart. 'I promise. May I be nibbled to death by
ducks if I breathe a word to a living soul!'

'All right, then.' Eve took a deep breath. 'I love Frank
Mailer. He doesn't know it yet, but I intend to marry him.'

'Golly!' Rose was thrilled, but also practical. 'Your parents
would never let you.'

Eve lifted her chin. 'When I'm twenty-one, they won't be
able to stop me. And I'm certain Frank will wait for me, once
he understands what's in my mind.' She spoke with all the
confidence of youth.

Rose would have liked more details, but they were just
turning into the rickyard and all her attention was immediately claimed by the horse-powered boom and cable hoist,

which came into operation as soon as each rick grew too high
to manhandle the hay to the top. The building of ricks was
a tricky business, particularly in the early stages when any
misjudgement could eventually result in either a lop-sided
or a collapsed one. And to ensure the proper concentration
of his labourers, Arthur had sent along Donald and Ernest to
oversee the farmhands.

Ernest, in his shirt-sleeves, was mucking in with the
others, taking his turn at either managing the horse, whose
manipulation was vital to the entire operation, or climbing
up on top of the rick, ready to receive and spread the hay
when it was released from the grip of the forks. Donald, on
the other hand, was issuing a spate of instructions and
criticism from the sidelines. Eve touched him on the
shoulder.

'Hello, Don.' She made no attempt to kiss him, but went
straight into introductions. When these were finished, she
enquired, 'How does it feel to have left school? When will
you be going up to Oxford?'

Donald, at once conscious of strange – if not very
attractive – female company, drew himself up to his full six
feet and struck a stance which showed off a body honed to
perfection on the rugby and cricket pitches. His hair glinted
redly in the afternoon sun.

'Shan't be going, shall I, if there's a war? Still, it'll only
be a postponement. Everybody says we'll have licked the
Boche by Christmas. One Englishman's worth a whole
regiment of Krauts.'

Rose regarded him briefly with her bright, round eyes,
like a biologist inspecting an interesting specimen. 'I
shouldn't think that's at all likely,' she said. 'The Prussians
are a very military-minded people.'

Donald, unused to being contradicted by a girl, stared at
her in astonishment, but was relieved from the necessity of
replying by the arrival of three of the maids from Abbey
Court, bearing big wicker baskets. These contained great
mugs of sweet tea and jars of cider, 'doorstep' meat and

cheese sandwiches, and thick slabs of fruit cake. Ernest climbed down the ladder at the side of the rick and came over, wisps of hay sticking out of his carroty hair. Eve made further introductions.

Donald glanced round at the maids in their black afternoon dresses and crisp, frilly aprons. 'Where's Jenny Slade?' he asked of the nearest.

The girl bobbed a curtsey. 'She's gone down to Long Meadow, Master Donald, with Iris and Susan.'

Donald looked annoyed, but said nothing. As the girl moved away Eve saw her wink at one of the others, who quickly stifled a giggle. Eve wondered fleetingly what her cousin's interest could be in Jenny, but she had no time to spare to ponder the answer. Her overriding desire was to return to Long Meadow. She abandoned her mug of strong tea and looked about her for her friend, but Rose had vanished. After a moment or two Eve located her standing beside Ernest, listening intently to his explanation of how the boom and cable fork-lift operated.

'Rose!' Eve interrupted without compunction. 'I'm going back to Long Meadow.'

'Oh!' Rose was disappointed. 'I suppose, in that case . . .'

'I'll see her safely home to Rosemary Villa,' Ernest volunteered. 'I'll get her back in time for dinner, I promise.'

Eve glanced from one eager face to the other. 'Well . . . Yes, all right. If you don't mind, Rose?'

But her friend had already turned away to inspect the cable and pulley. Satisfied that she was in good hands and enjoying herself, Eve gathered up the skirts of her green poplin dress and sped out of the rickyard, back to Long Meadow. Her white leather boots were tight and had been pinching her toes all afternoon, but she hardly noticed the discomfort as she ran along the road. All she could think of was Frank and Jenny Slade together.

The men were finishing the remains of the picnic meal and the maids had gone. Frank, too, had disappeared. Eve buttonholed George Mailer.

'Mr Mailer, I want to speak to Frank. Where is he?'

The man's face was secretive and sly, but he had his answer ready.

'Well now, Miss, 'tis a delicate matter t' speak of to young ladies.' His voice became confidential and Eve could smell the cider on his breath. 'A call o' nature.'

Eve didn't believe him for a moment, but she thanked George politely and retraced her steps. Once outside the gate, however, she took the left-hand lane which led to Abbey Court instead of going back to the rickyard. Here it was cooler, the rutted track shaded from the sun by the overhead interlacing branches of the trees. A cluster of buttercups and an attendant clump of delicately nodding, purple-headed crane's bill would at any other time have tempted Eve to stop and pick them, but now she hurried on, unaware of their presence. A bee hummed past her ear, a lark soared skyward, but she had eyes for neither. Once she twisted her ankle, but she was not even conscious of the pain.

She was getting close to the house now. Maybe, after all, she was wrong and Frank had not walked Jenny back to the Court, risking being seen and incurring the subsequent wrath of his employer. Maybe, even at this moment, he was haymaking in Long Meadow with the others. The lane curved sharply to the right, widening for a yard or two to accommodate a grass verge and a circle of elms. Jenny Slade, her empty wicker basket on the ground beside her, was leaning against the trunk of one of the trees, pressed hard up against it, and Frank was kissing her. He had not noticed Eve because his back was towards her, but Jenny saw and, after the first momentary shock of being discovered, her eyes gleamed triumphantly. She raised her arms, which until that second had hung slackly at her sides, and locked them around Frank's waist. His thin body pressed even closer, taut and wire-drawn with urgency, and one hand began to fumble at Jenny's skirts, pulling them higher to reveal black lace-up boots and coarse black woollen stockings.

Eve felt sick. She wanted to turn and run, but her feet seemed rooted to the ground. She watched, fascinated, as the black poplin skirt and flurry of white cotton petticoats rose above Jenny's knees, and as Frank thrust his questing hand between the ample thighs. Jenny gave a moan of pleasure before raising one hand to tap Frank's shoulder.

'We've got company,' she whispered.

He cursed and pulled away from her, letting her skirts fall once more to her ankles. His face, as he turned, was white with apprehension, expecting to see Arthur Burfoot or Donald or Ernest. Therefore, his anger was commensurate with his relief when he recognized Eve.

'What the bloody hell are you doing here? Following me around? Spying on me? So what are you going to do now? Run and tell Uncle?'

Eve could have ignored the violence of his language, the recriminations, but the old false accusation that she was a tale-bearer, and from Frank of all people, broke her spirit. She was unable to control the sudden flood of tears which poured down her face, the noisy sobs which racked her.

'I hate you!' she screamed, all her carefully acquired poise shot to flinders. No longer one of Miss Milward's 'Young Ladies,' she stumbled back along the track in the direction of the village.

'Eve!' She could hear Frank shouting her name, the sound of his hobnailed boots ringing against the stones. 'Eve, stop a minute. I'm sorry!'

But she only ran the faster. Perversely, now that he was ready to apologize she did not want him to. She wanted to wallow in her misery, let her sense of ill-usage fester. She forced her legs to take bigger strides, but suddenly tripped and fell, sprawling in an undignified heap on the ground. Moments later Frank flopped down beside her, trying to take her in his arms.

She resisted with all her strength, transformed by anger and injured pride into a wild-cat, spitting and clawing. After a minute or so Frank's own control snapped and, seizing her

by the shoulders, he shook her unmercifully. When she
continued fighting him, he suddenly slapped her hard across
the face. Astounded that anyone should dare to treat her in
such a fashion, Eve stopped lashing out with her fists and
stared in astonishment. Then she collapsed, half crying, half
laughing, into his arms.

'That's better,' he said. 'Look, I really am sorry for what
I said back there. I didn't mean it. But . . .' and he shifted
uncomfortably '. . . there are times when a chap don't want
to be spied on.'

'I wasn't spying,' she denied furiously. 'At least, not inten-
tionally. And it's 'doesn't'. A chap *doesn't* want to be spied on.'

'That's just what I'm saying.' He gave malicious grin,
then began kissing her cheek gently. 'Auburn, you're my
friend. I don't want us to quarrel.'

Eve pulled away from him, sniffing and straightening her
clothes, which were dusty and rumpled. Tendrils of hair had
escaped from the two thick braids which hung over her
shoulders.

'Is that all I am to you?' she asked. 'Just a friend?'

He regarded her, suddenly serious. 'You're only fourteen
years old. I'm eighteen, I'm a man. It makes a difference.'

She clambered slowly to her feet and brushed down the
pale green cotton of her dress. 'I shan't be a child for ever.'

'No, that's true enough.' His voice was sombre. 'But you
won't be for the likes of me, even when you're a woman. It
would be more than your family, or mine come to that,
would tolerate.'

Eve looked at him, her pale face resolute. 'We'll have to
see about that, won't we, when the time comes?' She leaned
forward, and kissed him full on the lips. 'Meanwhile, don't
do anything silly like marrying someone else.'

She swung on her heel and, resisting the temptation to
look over her shoulder, walked on down the lane.

Chapter Six

The second Easter of the war was late, the last complete weekend of April, and in consequence the church was bright with blossoms on Sunday morning. Miss Ellice and her helpers had decorated the pulpit, the font, window embrasures and tops of pews with a variety of flowers: daffodils and tulips, anemones and double daisies, huge rhododendron heads from the vicarage garden, wallflowers and narcissi. A copper vase to the right of the altar was filled with armfuls of bluebells gathered by the village children, and smaller pots of lily-of-the-valley perfumed the air like incense. The sun came through the stained-glass windows, painting jewel-coloured lozenges on the worn stone flags and tinting the faces of the congregation with their brilliant hues.

The final words of 'Christ the Lord is Risen Today' faded into silence; the last notes of the organ rumbled and died. Everyone sat down except the Reverend Michael Ellice, who cleared his throat and gripped the edge of the pulpit as if for support. His unnatural hesitation fixed all eyes upon him and people stopped fidgeting with their gloves and prayer-books. Why was the service not proceeding as normal?

'You may,' he began, 'have remarked upon the absence this morning of Albert and Edith Naysmith.' There was some nodding of heads and also some looking over shoulders, by those who had so far failed to miss the couple. Backs and necks grew suddenly rigid with the anticipation of bad news. 'Late last night,' the vicar continued, 'I was called to their cottage to pray with them and give what comfort I could.' The church was now so quiet that a pin dropping would have sounded like the chiming of Big Ben. Michael Ellice raised his head. 'Their son, James, whom we all knew, who grew up amongst us here in Staple Abbots, has been killed in Flanders. He is the first young man from the village to be lost. Let us pray to God that there will be no more.'

It was a sombre crowd which half an hour later spilled out into the churchyard, where the carefully tended graves lay in neat rows beneath the dark green shelter of the yews. There were many graves belonging to the Naysmith family, going back generations; but now one of their number would be buried in foreign soil, never to return again. It was this fact, more than any other, which brought the war home to Staple Abbots.

It was almost twenty-one months since hostilities had been declared between Britain and Germany; since wave upon wave of eager and enthusiastic young would-be heroes had volunteered to fight for 'King and Country' and to save poor little Belgium from the ravages of the Hun. It was going to be the war to end wars, the Government said; a kind of Herculean cleansing of the Augean stables. And it would all be over by Christmas because the Germans had no stomach for a fight. A few people had been sceptical; Marcus was one of them.

'The Germans are as stubborn and aggressive as we are. They won't give in easily.'

He had been proved right. By August 1915 the Western Front had settled into a line which snaked from the Belgian coast to the Swiss border, and thus it seemed set to remain, with only the slightest variation, while men massacred each other in oceans of mud. Donald and Ernest were both in France and so far had survived the slaughter. But as the months passed, Eve noticed a subtle difference in their letters. At first they had been full of chauvinistic pride, bragging about what the British were doing, and would do, to the enemy. Nowadays, however, they were far more restrained, and she increasingly detected a *leitmotiv* of despair.

Last Christmas, Ernest had written: 'Are you still friends with that roly-poly girl – I forget her name – who was with you at the haymaking the summer before last? How very,

very long ago that seems! If so, would you please ask her to write to me?' Eve passed on the message, omitting Ernest's description and the fact that he had forgotten Rose's name, but she had an idea that the information would not have troubled her friend. Rose had immediately begun a correspondence with Ernest and his letters to Eve had dwindled.

Not that Eve cared. Her main concern with the war was that Frank should not enlist. As a farm worker, he was needed on the land, and Arthur had persuaded him that his place was in Staple Abbots. But in February this year the British Military Service Act had come into force, giving the Government the previously unheard-of power of conscription. Once again Frank had considered volunteering before he was forcibly recruited, and once more Arthur had pulled a few strings.

'It's not what you know, it's *who* you know,' was one of his favourite maxims. And Frank had remained at Home Farm.

Eve was delighted at the news, which she gleaned second-hand from an overheard conversation between her mother and uncle. Neither of them thought to lower their voices, for as far as her family was concerned Eve's friendship with Frank Mailer was a thing of the past. She had had very little to do with him since that afternoon at the haymaking, and did not even mention his name nowadays to Rose, who came to the same conclusion as everyone else: it was a passing infatuation which had burned itself out.

But Eve was simply biding her time.

*

Eve struggled up through layers of sleep to the sound of someone knocking urgently on the door of Rosemary Villa. A moment later, she heard her parents' bedroom door open and her father's footsteps as he descended the stairs. Bolts were drawn back and the front-door key scraped in the lock, then came the murmur of voices. She got out of bed and crept out on to the landing, leaning over the banister. She recognized Frank's voice, although she could not catch all the words.

'... come at once, Doctor ... very bad ... difficulty breathing.'

'You'd better come in and wait while I get dressed.' Marcus held the door wide and Frank entered, a brown woollen muffler wrapped about his neck against the chill of the night. 'Go into the parlour. It's warmer there.'

Eve waylaid her father at the top of the stairs. 'What's wrong?'

'George Mailer's suffering from a bad bout of bronchitis and it seems to have worsened since I saw him yesterday. Go back to bed, my dear. There's nothing you can do.'

'I'm coming with you. You may be glad of another pair of hands.'

Marcus was peremptory. 'What nonsense! You'll be more of a hindrance than a help.'

'No, I shan't.' Not for the first time, Marcus reflected that his daughter was growing into a very determined young woman. 'I helped Mama nurse Aunt Hetty through bronchitis, the Christmas before last. I know all about steam tents and kettles. Anyway, I'm wide awake now. I shan't get to sleep again for ages, so I might just as well go with you. It'll be good experience.' She did not say what for, but as all women needed, at some time in their lives, to nurse husbands or parents or children through various illnesses, Marcus accepted her statement without too much argument.

'Oh, very well. I'll tell Mama. Go and get dressed then, quickly.'

Twenty minutes later, her coat thrown on anyhow over a mismatched blouse and skirt, her boots only half-laced, her hair bundled on top of her head and escaping untidily from its pins, Eve found herself in the back of the Ford, acutely conscious of Frank's proximity. The smell of the leather upholstery mingled with the sweaty animal scent of his workaday clothes. Throughout the journey to Lower Abbots he neither looked at her nor spoke, confining himself to answering Marcus's questions; but Eve knew from the abstracted way in which he replied that he was as aware of her presence as she was of his.

A lighted candle stood in the front window of the Mailers' cottage, and as the car drew to a halt the front door opened and Ellen Marston, formerly Lightfoot, emerged. She came down the path towards them.

'I just come in to lend a hand and keep Lizzie comp'ny till you arrived, Doctor. But I got to get back. Jeb needs his rest, getting up at four in the morning. And he don't sleep if I'm not with him. Hello, Miss Eve! What you doing here?'

'How's Dad?' Frank asked, getting out of the car and coming round to the near side.

Ellen shook her head. 'Not good; he's coughing something shocking. All that phlegm rattling round in his poor chest. Breaks my heart to hear him. Never mind. You're here now, Doctor and he'll soon be all right.'

Marcus took his bag and disappeared inside, while the other two lingered to say a whispered good night to Ellen. At the front door, Frank stood aside to let Eve go ahead of him.

'It's good of you to want to help Dad,' he said shyly.

She turned back to face him. His features were a blur in the darkness.

'I want to help you, Frank.' She added deliberately, 'I love you.' Then, appalled at her own temerity, she hurried indoors and mounted the narrow wooden staircase to the bedroom. She was shaking all over. Well-brought-up girls simply did not make such declarations; it was enough to put a man off her for life.

She could hear George Mailer's distressed breathing before she opened the bedroom door. The tiny room with its small, high window was very cold, and in winter must have been icy. There was no fireplace and therefore no means of heating, no rugs on the bare floorboards, and only the minimum of furniture. Most of the space was occupied by an iron bedstead, around the head of which had been placed an old screen – once the property of Abbey Court – and across this sheets had been draped to make the 'tent' necessary for the treatment of bronchitis. Beside the bed a kettle of water simmered gently over a spirit lamp, emitting a steady flow of steam scented with Friar's Balsam.

Lizzie Mailer was talking in a low voice to Marcus. 'He's a bit easier on his chest than he was, Doctor. I'm sorry to have called you out in the middle of the night like this, but Frank would fetch you. And his father did seem real poorly an hour ago, but as I say, he's coughing a bit less now.'

Marcus opened his bag and prepared to examine his patient. 'Don't apologize, Lizzie. Frank was right to come and fetch me if you were worried. Eve, if you want to be useful, go downstairs and see that there's plenty of hot water to keep this kettle going. And ask Frank to bring up a bucket of earth or sand or something, in case the spirit lamp should get knocked over. You should always have some fire precaution in the room, you know, Lizzie. If the spirit was spilt, it could easily get set alight.'

Eve sped downstairs again, to find Frank hovering at the bottom.

'How is he?'

'A little better, by the sound of it.' She passed on Marcus's instructions. 'The water from the pump will do for the kettle. No one's going to drink it.'

She preceded Frank into the scullery, where he lit a candle and pumped water into the biggest saucepan he could lay his hands on, then carried it back to the kitchen fire and set it over the embers to heat. He then found a bucket, filled it with earth from the garden and lugged it upstairs. By the time he came down again, Eve had made a pot of tea and discovered where Lizzie Mailer kept her crockery.

'The drinking water's getting low,' she pointed out, glad to have this mundane topic of conversation. 'You'd better fetch some up from the well first thing in the morning.' She busied herself pouring a stream of rich brown liquid into Lizzie's precious bone china cups, patterned with irises and part of a set costing half-a-crown from a travelling salesman. 'Is there a tray anywhere? I'll take some tea up to your mother and Papa.'

'I shouldn't, not for a moment. The Doctor's still examining Dad.' Frank came and stood close beside her: she could feel his breath against her cheek. 'Auburn ... Did you mean what you said just now?'

Eve felt the blood rush to her cheeks and she kept her head lowered, but she wasn't going to back down. 'Yes,' she said. Her heart seemed to have stopped beating altogether as she waited to find out what he would say or do next.

He said nothing, but pulled her into his arms and kissed her. She had never experienced a kiss remotely like it in her life before. It made her knees buckle and her senses swim; it stirred feelings within her that were new and strange; the blood coursed along her veins and her whole body seemed to be on fire; most peculiar and most frightening of all was the hollow sensation in the pit of her stomach. She pulled away, eager to repeat the experience yet also frightened by it.

Could Frank have made her pregnant with that kiss? Common sense told her it wasn't possible; people kissed each other all the time. But not quite like that, not with their tongues almost locking. She wished desperately that she knew more about such things, but no one had ever talked to her about them. Helena certainly never had, and would consider it extremely improper to do so. The same went for Aunt Hetty. Even the Miss Milwards, advanced in so many of their ideas – anxious for their girls to be interested in current events, to train for professions, not to be completely dependent upon the opposite sex – never made any allusions to what happened between a man and a woman after marriage.

And sometimes before marriage ... Eve knew that some girls managed to have babies without having a husband, but when she had asked Hetty once how that was possible, her aunt had replied with a shudder, 'Nicely-brought-up young women have no need to know such things,' and refused to say any more on the subject. Eve had never bothered to ask Aunt Josephine who, being a spinster, presumably knew no more than she did herself.

'What's the matter?' Frank asked. 'Why did you push me away like that?'

Eve hesitated, but she had to know. She couldn't lie awake all night, and all through the coming weeks, worrying.

'You haven't . . . you haven't made me pregnant, have you?'

He stared at her for a moment in complete bewilderment, his mouth half fallen open, before he suddenly realized that she was serious, that her question was not some tasteless joke. She really did not know and was scared for the consequences. Eve was not like the village girls who, brought up in thin-walled cottages where every sound could be heard from their parents' bedroom next door – and some of whom even slept in with their parents for lack of space elsewhere – were aware from an early age of the facts of life. And what they didn't know from first-hand experience, they soon gleaned from friends and relatives. But girls like Eve were ignorant of the world. Even though she had gone to the village school, she had remained isolated.

He put his arms around her again, but gently so as not to frighten her. 'No, of course I haven't done anything to hurt you. Did you really think I would? Don't you trust me?'

She trusted him with her life and said so. 'We will get married, Frank, won't we? Promise you'll wait for me.'

'Auburn, they won't let us. You must know that. Not your uncle, not your mother, not your father. I'd lose my job, and I daren't do that. With Dad ill each winter, Ma needs my money more than ever.'

Eve said confidently, 'They can't stop us once I'm twenty-one. That's only five years, Frank; it's not for ever.' The way he was feeling just then, five years *was* like for ever, but he said nothing and let her continue. 'I'll be leaving school in two years' time, and I've made up my mind. I shan't go on to university, as Papa and Miss Milward want me to. I shall come home to Staple Abbots and wait until we can marry. We can elope. You'd find a job somewhere . . . and we'll have lots of children. You and I are both only ones, so we must make up for it and have a big family. You'd like that, wouldn't you?'

He gave himself up to the fantasy and began kissing her again. 'Three boys for you and two girls for me. So, where shall we run to? What part of the world do you fancy? By that time, the war will be over and we can go anywhere we choose.'

Eve returned his kisses, savouring the feel of his lips on hers. 'I don't want to leave this country. Let's go to Cornwall. I always enjoyed holidays there when I was a child.'

'All right, Cornwall,' he agreed. It didn't matter: it wasn't going to happen. And yet ... he loved her, just how much and how deeply he had only just realized, and she loved him. Perhaps, after all, their dream was not impossible. It just needed sufficient determination to make it come true.

There was a clatter of feet on the wooden staircase and they sprang apart as Marcus appeared, his stethoscope still hanging round his neck.

'Papa! I was just going to bring you and Mrs Mailer some tea.' Eve noticed guiltily that what she had already poured was cold and skimming over. 'Er ... this isn't very nice. I'll get rid of it and make some fresh.'

*

The rest of the Easter holiday passed in a daze, with only one thought uppermost in Eve's mind: how to see Frank as often as possible without arousing suspicion. She listened with only half an ear to talk about the rising in Dublin and the arrest of Sir Roger Casement. All the arguments between her father and uncle about the rights and wrongs of Irish Home Rule had little to do with the world she inhabited with Frank; a world of secret meetings and stolen, passionate embraces, exploring the wilder, remoter corners of the village where they could be alone. The warmer weather made it possible for Eve to argue the need for exercise and the pleasure of walking, a pleasure shared by neither Helena nor Hetty and for which Marcus was too busy, owing to an outbreak of measles in the village. She also became a frequent visitor to the Abbey Court kitchens, and joined the maids in carrying the midday baskets of cider and sandwiches to the men in the fields, oblivious to the winks and giggles behind her back. Frank saw them, and those of the other farmhands, but was confident that no one would inform Arthur Burfoot because no one believed him to be serious where Eve was concerned. They thought her just a silly girl with an infatuation for one of her uncle's workers.

On the eve of her return to school she met him as he walked home to Lower Abbots, tired after a long day which had begun at five that morning and was ending only now, as the sun disappeared over the western horizon. George Mailer's illness had been a blessing in disguise, for it had meant that Frank was alone each evening.

'Frank!' Eve was sitting on the stile overlooking the bridle path leading to Upper Abbots, but she jumped down as she saw him approach. She descended from her perch in a flurry of lace-edged petticoats, revealing long and shapely legs as far as the knee. She was wearing a poplin dress with a tucked and feather-stitched bodice, in her favourite shade of pale leaf-green, and her hair, brushed until it shone like burnished copper, was tied at the nape of her neck with a big green velvet bow. At times she looked so cool, so sophisticated, in short so grown-up, that Frank had to keep reminding himself that in ways that mattered she was still extremely young. She might be able to recite poetry, talk knowledgeably about the plays of William Shakespeare, correct his arithmetic and grammar, but when it came to making ends meet on a very small wage and, above all, where sex was concerned, she was a child. He found her both enchanting and maddening, and his relationship with her deeply frustrating. Unlike the village girls, who knew exactly what passions they were arousing when they led boys on, Eve was both provocative and sensual without any idea of the restraint he was forced to exercise.

Yet tomorrow she would be gone and he would miss her dreadfully. In the past week or so, she had become necessary

to his peace of mind. Infuriating she might be, but he was
miserable when she was not around. He slid his arm about
her waist and kissed her cheek.

'Will you miss me when you're back at school?'

'You know I shall. The question is, will you miss me?
You'll probably be off with that Jenny Slade as soon as my
back is turned.'

At the mention of Jenny, Frank felt guilty. In the past year,
he had seen enough of her for people to begin linking their
names together; for his mother to regard them as 'walking out'
and to speak, once or twice, of 'when you are married'. Lizzie
had stopped short of naming Jenny as her future daughter-
in-law, but it was obvious that she regarded it as only a matter
of time. And it would make a lot of sense, both for himself and
his mother. Jenny would make him an excellent wife.

'Let's sit down a minute,' he suggested. 'I'm late enough for
supper already for another five minutes not to matter.' He
guided her to the grass verge at the side of the lane, and when
they were seated took both her hands in his. 'Eve –' it was so
rarely that he called her by her proper name that her head
reared suspiciously '– I know you say you mean to marry me
now, and God knows it would be the dearest wish of my heart,
but ... it isn't possible. You're the doctor's daughter, the
Squire's niece, and I'm just an ignorant farmhand.'

She interrupted him fiercely. 'We've been through all this,
Frank. We've said we'll go away where no one knows us,
away from our families, as soon as I'm twenty-one.'

'That's just the point.' He gripped her hands so tightly
that he almost crushed the bones. 'You won't be twenty-one
for another five years! How can you know how you'll feel by
then? You could have met someone else, someone much
more suitable. You might fall in love with your cousin,
Donald. That's what everyone wants you to do, isn't it?
Squire Burfoot and Mrs Gilchrist?'

Eve wrenched her hands free and jumped to her feet.
'You're trying to get rid of me, aren't you? You're trying to
tell me you don't love me. Why else would you be saying

these horrible things?' Frank scrambled up and attempted to repossess her hands, but she beat him off angrily. 'Why did you say you love me if it isn't true? I hate you!'

Frank removed his cap and ran a hand through his tousled dark hair. 'I do love you! I swear I do. I'm just trying to warn you that five years is a long time to wait.'

'So you keep saying, but it won't seem that long if we just remember that we'll be together for always at the end of it.' Her chin jutted belligerently. 'I can wait if you can.'

Suddenly, he felt too tired to argue any further. He was beset by a host of fears and anxieties, all of which he knew he should heed. She was so naïve! She thought she had only to say 'I want' and everything would fall into her lap; she had no real conception of the difficulties and problems that lay ahead. He, on the other hand, knew better; he ought to put a stop to their relationship here and now, but he didn't have the willpower. He wanted Eve, not in the way he wanted Jenny Slade, but as his wife, for ever. He supposed it was what people meant when they talked about love, and he was shrewd enough to guess that as an emotion, it was less common than was generally supposed. Love was a word used very loosely, a conclusion he had reached many years ago.

'You think too much,' his mother had often told him. 'People of our sort aren't meant to think; we do as we're told.' But he couldn't stop himself thinking. One of the reasons he loved Eve was because she talked to him; she taught him things that he would not otherwise have known. She appealed to his reason as well as his senses.

He drew her into his arms and this time she made no move to stop him. 'Auburn,' he murmured, nuzzling his cheek against her hair. 'Sweet Auburn, I'll wait. I promise . . . if you can wait for me.'

Miss Ellice, out for her evening constitutional, had walked as far as the bridle path, looking for periwinkles to add to her recently started dried flower collection. Finding a patch in the shadow of her hedge, she crouched down to pick them. Neither Frank nor Eve noticed her as they went past.

Chapter Seven

'So you see,' Miss Ellice finished, 'I felt I just had to come and tell you what I saw.' She was perched uncomfortably forward on the edge of her chair, back ramrod-straight, nervous hands fidgeting with her white crocheted gloves. 'I don't like telling tales, I really don't, but on this occasion I felt it to be my duty. Eve is only sixteen and still very much a minor. Frank Mailer, on the other hand, is over twenty and a man. Kissing and cuddling there, in the middle of the bridle path where anyone might have seen them – these things can only lead to trouble. And Frank! A nice enough lad, I'm sure, but only a farmhand. I do most fervently assure you both that not a word of this has passed my lips to anyone else, not even to my dear brother. You can rely on my discretion absolutely, but I did feel you might want to speak with Eve.'

'Eve returned to school this morning,' Marcus said, 'accompanied by my sister, Mrs Jardine, so for the time being she is safely removed from Frank Mailer's vicinity.' He glanced at his wife's tense white face and hoped that Helena would not be so foolish as to create a scene in Jane Ellice's presence. The only way to stop gossip was to treat it as lightly as possible. Hysterical reproaches would simply confirm the vicar's sister in her obvious belief that she had stumbled on a domestic rift of significant proportions. 'But the truth is that the friendship between Eve and Frank Mailer goes back to their schooldays, when Frank was kind enough to take Eve under his wing. I am sure that what you witnessed yesterday was nothing more than the affectionate farewell between two old friends. Eve would naturally wish to say goodbye before leaving home for the summer term.'

And Marcus glared warningly, daring Helena to contradict him.

Jane Ellice also glanced at her hostess, but to Marcus's relief his wife made no attempt to speak. The older woman sniffed and rose to her feet. 'Of course, if you're satisfied ...' She let the rest of the sentence go and pulled on her gloves, moving towards the drawing-room door where she paused to look over her shoulder. 'We are all aware of the doctor's liberal views, and perhaps as Christians we might feel obliged to sympathize with them. But I wouldn't want a daughter of mine to find herself forced to marry a farmhand. I should say that was carrying equality a mite too far, and I'm sure Squire Burfoot would agree with me. I can't see him welcoming Frank Mailer as his nephew-by-marriage. No, no! Don't bother to see me out. I can find my own way.'

'Insufferable woman!' Marcus exclaimed as he heard the front door of Rosemary Villa close behind her, but his tone was half-hearted. His real concern was with the news she had brought them.

Helena spoke through bloodless lips, her voice constricted. 'Well?' she demanded. 'What are you going to do about it?'

'What am I going to do about what?' Marcus was playing for time, warding off the moment when her recriminations could no longer be contained.

'About Eve and Frank Mailer!' The sluice-gates opened and he was engulfed as the tears poured down Helena's face. 'This is all your fault, Marcus! Your fault! Hetty and Arthur and I have warned you repeatedly over the years that these ideas of yours would lead to disaster! That you were filling Eve's head with stupid notions of equality – and where has it led her? Straight into the arms of Frank Mailer!' Her voice was momentarily stilled, choked by emotion, then rose again to an even more hysterical pitch. 'Suppose Eve's ... Suppose she's going to have a baby! You can't rely on a farmhand to act like a gentleman! He wouldn't be able to control his ... his ...'

'Animal lusts?' Marcus's tone was cold, but a worm of fear was gnawing away inside him. He was gripped by a strong sense of self-disgust as he realized that Helena was only giving voice to his own secret thoughts. He asked angrily, 'Why should you assume that because a man is from the working classes he has no moral sense? That his instincts are baser than those of his social superiors? A study of history hardly lends that hypothesis credence.'

Helena rose to her feet, her ravaged features suddenly revealing how much her prettiness relied on health and peace of mind.

'Stop lecturing me!' she hissed, the delicate bow of her mouth almost non-existent as her lips thinned to a narrow, savage gash in her colourless face. Marcus had never before seen her so furiously angry. Gone was all her customary dislike of creating a scene. 'What are you going to do? That's what I'm asking! I don't want any more of this high-faluting nonsense. I want a practical solution to a situation which is entirely of your making and has got thoroughly out of hand!'

All at once, Marcus could see a hitherto unremarked resemblance between Helena and her brother. The soft blue eyes held a hint of steel, and the high-piled, copper-coloured hair seemed a more fiery shade in spite of the grey threads which salted it. But it was the belligerent set of the jaw, the accusing stare, the harder timbre of the voice which really marked the emergence of this new, previously dormant Helena and was so reminiscent of Arthur. Guilt settled on Marcus's shoulders like Christian's burden, and he suddenly felt every one of his fifty-six years.

He said quietly, and with as much authority as he could muster, 'Pull yourself together, my dear. Becoming hysterical will serve no good purpose. If it's any comfort to you, I agree that something must be done, and with that end in view I intend going down to Mayfields Academy tomorrow. There are no emergencies on my list at present, and if I telephone Jack Richardson straight away' – telephone and

electricity cables, along with water-pipes, had been brought
into the village, for those who could afford to make use of
them, six months earlier – 'he'll take the morning surgery for
me. He likes to keep his hand in now he's retired.'

'What good will it do to see Eve?' Helena cried impatiently. 'You want to go to Lower Abbots and warn off
Frank Mailer! Warn him that he and his father will lose their
jobs and home unless he agrees never to see our daughter
again.'

'Because I want to hear Eve's side of the story first.'
Marcus sat down abruptly on the black leather horsehair sofa
and turned his head to look out of the window. The afternoon
shadows inched their way slowly across the lawn, and the soft
spring sunshine spun a web of bright gold. Hetty's carefully
tended borders of tulips and wallflowers turned their faces
towards the uncertain warmth, and the rhododendrons
cautiously unfurled their crimson petals. 'I refuse to take
what might turn out to be an unnecessary step on the
unconfirmed tittle-tattle of Jane Ellice.'

His wife's tense posture relaxed a trifle, although she
continued to dab at her eyes with a lace-bordered handkerchief, and when she spoke her voice had lost something of its
frightened clamour.

'Perhaps you're right. But if Eve confirms Miss Ellice's
suspicions, you swear you'll do something about it? Marcus?
Marcus, I want you to promise!'

The note of querulous insistence had returned, and he
answered hastily, 'I give you my word.' But he wished he
didn't despise himself so much for agreeing.

*

She seemed somehow younger than he remembered her from
the holidays. Perhaps it was the white summer uniform dress
with its navy-blue-banded collar. Or the fact that the long
auburn hair hung down her back in a thick pigtail, ending
in a navy-blue ribbon bow, rather than being piled on top of

her head in more sophisticated fashion. But maybe it was because he was seeing her for the first time in ages simply as a sixteen-year-old girl, in danger from a man four years her senior and well versed in the art of sexual practice. At least, Marcus suspected that Frank Mailer was well versed, having seen him about the village not only with Jenny Slade but with a number of other local girls, and probably not one of them as virtuous as she should be.

'Papa!' Eve carefully closed Miss Milward's study door and crossed the intervening stretch of no-nonsense, plain fawn carpet to stand in front of her father. 'Is anything the matter? Mama's not been taken ill, has she? I know it can't be Aunt Hetty. She was as right as rain when she left here yesterday.'

Marcus got up from the armchair by the window and kissed his daughter. 'No, no,' he assured her. 'It's nothing like that.'

Relieved of her most pressing anxiety, Eve was immediately beset by others. Summoned from her mid-afternoon geography class to the headmistress's study, she had been met in the ante-room by Miss Milward herself, who told her that her father was here and asking to speak to her urgently on a private matter. Illness of one sort or another had naturally been uppermost in Eve's mind, but now that this was denied other unpleasant possibilities surfaced. Had Papa run foul one final time of Uncle Arthur, and were they to be thrown out of Rosemary Villa? Unlikely. Uncle Arthur would never do anything to hurt Mama. Had she done something wrong at school and Miss Milward had sent for Marcus before she expelled her? Eve's heartbeat quickened for a moment before recollecting that she had been back at Mayfields for less than a day, and any misdemeanour from the previous term would have been dealt with earlier. With a guilty start, she remembered Donald and Ernest fighting in the trenches, and realized that she was inclined to forget the war because no one she really cared about was involved in it. Had one of her cousins been killed? She was just about to ask, in suitably muted accents, when Marcus forestalled her.

'Eve, dear, sit down. You know how I dislike prevarication, so I won't beat about the bush.' He took a deep breath and asked, 'Is there anything between you and Frank Mailer apart from friendship?'

It was the last question Eve had expected, and for a moment she was at a loss how to reply. She took her father's vacated seat in the brown leather armchair beside the long, sashed window which gave on to a view of the terrace and the gravel walk beyond. Panic set in. Her skin paled and her eyes grew wide and dark with fear as she half-rose from the chair.

'Why, what's happened to him? He's not ill, is he? He hasn't had an accident?'

If Marcus had been hoping to have his worries allayed, he knew in that instant that he was doomed to disappointment. He had never seen such naked emotion in any woman's face as he saw in his daughter's now. Her love for Frank Mailer was writ large in her terrified expression.

'No, nothing like that, I promise. And I think you've answered my question.' He told her briefly about Jane Ellice's visit, and went on, 'Mama and I want you to stop seeing him.'

Eve frowned, as though not quite certain that she had heard her father aright. 'Why?' she asked bluntly.

'Oh, really, Eve!' Marcus turned away so that he would not have to look directly at her, and began prowling around the room. 'You're an intelligent, sensible girl. You must know the answer.'

There was a silence before she said, 'You mean you and Mama don't think Frank's good enough for me. Well, I expected Mama to feel that way, but not you. You're the one who's always taught me that people's jobs don't matter; it's the people themselves who count. And Frank's a good man, Papa. We love each other. We're going to be married as soon as either you give your consent or I pass my twenty-first birthday. I'd rather hoped until now that it might be the former, but in any case it doesn't matter. Frank will wait for me. He's promised.'

Marcus had been staring at a fine reproduction of a Bellotti without seeing any of the picture, but now he turned sharply. 'You may feel very differently about him after you've been to university.'

'I'm not going to university,' Eve answered calmly. 'I'm returning to Staple Abbots once I leave school, to be near Frank until we can marry. And it's no use arguing with me, Papa. You know how obstinate I can be when I've made up my mind.'

He did know, and the knowledge did nothing to ease the turmoil inside his head. He stopped pacing and came to sit on the window-seat close to her, taking one of her hands in his.

'For heaven's sake, Eve, you're deluding yourself. Frank Mailer isn't going to wait the best part of five years without looking at another woman. My darling child, he's a man, and men have ... well ... appetites that nicely-brought-up single young women know nothing about.' Was that true? his conscience mocked him. If it were, how had Miss Ellice been able to make her insinuations?

Eve smiled patiently and laid her left hand on top of the one clasping her right.

'Papa, I'm not as innocent as you seem to think. You saw to that by sending me away to school. In a community of women, there are always those with knowledge who are willing to share it.' She saw the anxiety in his face, and it was her turn to do the reassuring. 'Frank would never do anything I didn't want him to do.' She couldn't bring herself to admit that she still did not really understand the mystery of what went on between men and women after they were married; she only knew the strange urges she experienced whenever she and Frank were alone together. Nevertheless, she was convinced that nothing improper had taken place, and she trusted Frank implicitly to see that it didn't. 'Frank loves me, and I love him.'

'I see.' Marcus noted the tender expression on her face and was seized by such a feeling of jealousy that it left him emotionally reeling. He stood up and Eve rose with him.

After a moment, he went on, 'If marrying Frank Mailer and being the wife of a farm labourer is what you truly want, I suppose there's nothing I can do about it. But I won't and can't pretend that I'm not bitterly disappointed. With all your advantages, I had hoped for something better.'

'Papa, I'm sorry. But it is truly what I want, and thank you for being so understanding. With you behind us, even if you don't exactly approve, Frank and I will find it easier to overcome the other opposition. And I know there will be a lot to contend with: Mama; Aunt Hetty; Uncle Arthur. Not Aunt Josie, of course. She'll feel the way that you do.' She flung her arms around her father's neck and hugged him. 'Dear Papa! Once again, thank you.'

Gently, he unclasped her hands. 'You may yet change your mind,' he suggested, but Eve shook her head.

'No, I won't, Papa. I love Frank. I'll always love him.'

*

'What do you mean, you didn't forbid her to marry Frank Mailer? I don't care about her not going to university – in fact I'd rather she didn't – but Eve certainly isn't going to marry a farmhand! Marcus, how can you possibly entertain the notion for a single instant?'

Hetty, equally dismayed, came to Helena's support in an outraged treble. 'Marcus! You must have taken leave of your senses!'

During a belated dinner, put back a couple of hours until his return from Salisbury, Marcus had refused to discuss the day's events with his wife and sister, knowing that the subsequent chorus of protest would upset his digestion. He had therefore delayed his disclosures until they had withdrawn to the comfort of the parlour after the meal. There, seated in his favourite armchair and drawing on his favourite pipe, he had given an account of his interview with Eve. The reaction was everything he had expected.

'I won't allow it!' Helena was shaking all over and beginning to cry.

'You can't possibly mean to aid and abet her,' Hetty stated with conviction. 'Something must be down about it.'

Marcus lay back in his chair and regarded the two women through a haze of smoke. After a moment, he said quietly, 'I agree. It can't be allowed to happen.'

Helena, puzzled, gulped back her tears. 'But ... But you told us ...'

Marcus stretched his slippered feet to the fire which was still necessary on these cold, early May evenings. Josephine had written from Bristol that coal, along with many other commodities such as sugar and butter, was in short supply and rationed, but there seemed no shortage of anything, not even fuel, here in the country. Nevertheless, the realities of war were daily drawing closer; there had been an unprecedented amount of military activity on the Plain as he drove home today.

'I told you what was said between Eve and me, that's all. My dear Helena, if you think that forbidding our daughter to marry Frank Mailer would have done any good, then you don't know Eve as well as I do. It would only have made her more determined. She is quite capable of eloping with him, and if you want her involved in that sort of scandal, it's more than I do. No, outright opposition would have been fatal.'

'What ... What do we do, then?'

Marcus pulled again on his pipe. 'I'm not quite sure yet. I thought,' he added reluctantly, 'that I'd call on Arthur tomorrow morning.'

His wife and sister heaved a concerted sigh of relief and approval.

'That's the first really sensible suggestion you've made,' Hetty said with sisterly frankness. 'If anyone will know what to do, it's Mr Burfoot.'

Helena nodded her agreement. 'Oh, yes, he will. Oh, Marcus, thank you. Arthur can get rid of the Mailers. They can be gone from the district before Eve comes home for the summer holidays.'

'No!' Marcus's tone was bitter. 'I won't hear of them being

sacked or losing their cottage. George Mailer is still far from well, and in any case I'll not be a party to depriving anyone of his livelihood and dwelling. Besides,' he went on, wearily rubbing his forehead, conscious of a nagging little headache behind his eyes, 'such a move would be extremely imprudent. It would solve nothing where Eve is concerned, and even if she were unable to trace Frank, she would grow to hate us as the people responsible for separating them.' He took a deep breath. 'I'm afraid that this is a situation which calls for cunning, and far more than I possess.'

Helena, her spirits restored, said comfortably, 'Arthur will think of something.'

Her husband sighed. 'I'm sure he will.'

*

'It's your own bloody fault, you know that, don't you?' Arthur Burfoot regarded his brother-in-law with undisguised contempt. 'If you hadn't filled Eve's head with all these gimcrack notions about everyone being as good as everyone else – sending her to the village school and so forth – this would never have happened. Marry Frank Mailer, indeed! Does the silly child really believe I'd stand by and do nothing to prevent it?'

'I don't think she's given much weight to your reaction, Arthur,' Marcus replied with quiet venom.

'Then she bloody well should have done!' Arthur's chest swelled with righteous indignation. 'Doesn't Eve have a thought for anyone but herself? Hasn't she considered my position?'

'Apparently not. But then, the young are so selfish.'

The irony was lost on Arthur, who nodded. 'That's very true. Well, well! We'll just have to do something about it ourselves then, won't we?'

Marcus glanced up quickly. 'I don't want the Mailers turned out with the loss of their home.'

Arthur raised his bushy eyebrows. 'Who said anything

about turning them out?' He strolled across to the sideboard and poured two whiskies with soda, one of which he handed to his brother-in-law. 'I certainly don't intend losing a couple of my best workers, especially at a time when manpower's so scarce. I'm not so stupid.' He chuckled and downed his drink in almost one gulp. 'There's more than one way to skin a cat, you know, Marcus; ways that won't turn young Frank into a martyr, either. In fact, just the opposite.'

Marcus said hurriedly, 'I don't want to know what you're planning, Arthur. Just get on with it.'

His brother-in-law sneered. 'I always thought you were a hypocrite, but I didn't know the half of it. All your fine sentiments count for nothing, do they, when it comes to your own daughter? You don't have the courage of your convictions. But more than that, you don't even have the courage to do anything about it. You have to get someone else to do the dirty work for you, but you salve your conscience by keeping your hands clean. A regular Pontius Pilate!'

Marcus slammed down his untasted whisky on the dining-room table, slopping some of the liquid on to the polished surface. Two hectic spots of colour flamed in a face which was otherwise paper-white. There was nothing he could say in answer to the charges, however. Much as he despised Arthur, he despised himself far more.

'Never mind tearing my character to shreds,' he said thickly. 'If it's any satisfaction to you, I entirely agree with your diagnosis. Just do what you have to do, that's all.' He drew a shaky breath and retained a precarious hold on his temper. 'I trust the boys are all right? I imagine you'd have said if there was any news to the contrary. Give my love to Mabel and make my apologies for not stopping to see her. Don't bother summoning Simmonds. I can find my own way out.'

He felt that if he did not leave immediately, he would stifle. The dining-room at Abbey Court – with its heavy oak furniture, gravy-brown wallpaper and dark, shinily varnished reproductions of hunting dogs with dead animals in their mouths – depressed him at the best of times and today threatened his sanity. He muttered a brief goodbye and went.

Left alone, Arthur abandoned what remained of his drink and rang the bell, which was answered promptly by the butler. He indicated the spilled whisky.

'Get someone to mop up that mess and then polish the table. I'm going to my study. Tell Jenny Slade I want to see her there within ten minutes.'

The study was the pleasantest room in the house, at the end of a long corridor which was part of the original farmhouse, and built into the corner of a wing erected by Arthur's grandfather. With windows set into the south and west walls, it commanded the best of both morning and afternoon sun and was light on even the dullest day. Comfortably furnished with a big roll-topped desk, a black leather swivel armchair, a well-worn, brocaded sofa, a filing cabinet for the estate accounts and book-filled shelves lining the two windowless walls, it nevertheless struck terror into the heart of anyone summoned there by Arthur, including, in earlier years, his own two sons. It was therefore with a heart beating faster than normal that Jenny Slade knocked on the door and was told to 'Come in.'

'You sent for me, sir?' Her face was very pale and she twisted the edge of her white cotton morning apron between restless fingers.

Arthur was seated in his swivel chair and indicated another upright chair on the opposite side of the desk.

'Sit down, girl. Sit down. Don't be nervous. You haven't done anything wrong.' Jenny did as she was bidden, relief making her even paler, and her employer went on, 'Ever thought of getting married? Silly question. Of course you have; every woman has. Marriage and children, that's what you're here for, all part of the divine plan.'

'I . . . Yes, sir,' Jenny stammered. But her confidence was gradually returning. She stopped playing with her apron, folded her hands demurely in her lap and sent Arthur a provocative upward glance from beneath her lashes.

He grinned in appreciation. 'Yes. You're what my dear mother would have called a minx. Had a few kisses and cuddles with my two sons, I daresay, in the past. Oh, I'm not blaming you. Couple of hot-blooded lads and a pretty girl, only to be expected. But time now, I think, that you settled down. So what do you think of young Frank Mailer, eh? Seen you in his company on more than one occasion. A bit small and dark, a bit foreign-looking, but a presentable enough chap, wouldn't you agree?'

'Y-yes, sir.' Jenny was still unsure where this was leading.

Arthur leant across the desk towards her, sinking his voice to a confidential whisper. 'Well, there you are then. You could have a husband, a cottage to start your married life in and – and this is strictly between you and me – a hundred pounds in cash on your wedding day to do with as you please.'

A hundred pounds! A fortune! Jenny could scarcely hide her excitement. All the same, she managed to maintain a calm exterior as she raised her head and stared her employer straight in the eye.

'I think you'd better tell me what this is really all about, don't you, sir?'

Chapter Eight

The summer evenings were longer now that 'daylight saving' had been introduced. In general people objected to this tampering with the clock, and sermons had been preached against the idea in churches throughout the British Isles. But farmers found it a boon, as it meant they could work their labourers for an extra hour each afternoon without the necessity of offering extra pay, while at the same time expecting them to start as normal the following morning.

'Something to be said for Asquith, even if he is a Liberal,' Arthur declared during Sunday tea at Abbey Court, attended ritually once a month by the inmates of Rosemary Villa. But this attempt to provoke his brother-in-law proved to be as much a failure as all his others. Marcus was very quiet, even in public these days, and he avoided all private conversation with Arthur if he could possibly manage it, afraid of becoming the recipient of unwelcome confidences. And when Hetty impatiently enquired from time to time, 'But what *is* Arthur doing about Eve and Frank Mailer?' her brother would hunch his shoulders and change the subject.

Helena had no misgivings on that score. 'If Arthur has promised to fix matters, then he will. You have no need to worry, Hetty dear.'

Such blind faith only served to irritate Marcus even further, adding to his personal sense of guilt and self-disgust. In normal circumstances he looked forward to Eve's return home for the summer holiday, the longest of the school calendar, but this year he found himself dreading it, wondering how he was going to face her.

Conscious now of his brother-in-law's mocking gaze, he forced himself to join in the general conversation, which had inevitably reverted to the national tragedy of Lord Kitchener's death, drowned at the beginning of June when the cruiser HMS *Hampshire*, in which he was travelling to Russia, had struck a mine off the Orkneys. Most of the crew had also perished, a fact which caused Mabel to say tremulously, 'I can't help thinking of all the mothers. I just can't stop thinking about them.'

Helena squeezed her sister-in-law's hand, knowing that what Mabel was really thinking about was Donald and Ernest at the Front; and with rumours of a big Allied offensive about to take place, her anxiety had doubled in the past few days. Where these rumours came from, or how they originated, no one really knew, but they had proved uncannily accurate on previous occasions – which, with so many military personnel scattered across the Plain, was perhaps not surprising. Army activity had greatly increased, and for a few months earlier in the year the inhabitants of Staple Abbots, along with those of other villages, had been allowed out of the area on only three days a week. It was a state of affairs which had not lasted too long, but long enough for people to complain that it felt like being under siege.

'For God's sake, woman, don't get all maudlin!' Arthur admonished his wife, but the brusqueness masked his own anxiety for the safety of his sons.

The drawing-room door opened and Jenny Slade came in, wearing her afternoon uniform of black poplin dress with white frilled cap and apron. Although she addressed Mabel, Arthur was conscious that she was watching him from the corner of her eye.

'I wondered if I could clear away the tea-things a little early, m'am. I've been promised a couple of hours off this evening.'

'Oh ...' Mabel blinked unhappily. 'Oh, well, yes, I suppose so. If it's all right with Mrs Dowson ... if she says you can go ... yes. I think we've all finished. Arthur, did ... did you want another cup of tea?'

She cast a scared glance towards her husband, recalling past tirades on the subject of her inability to be firm with servants, but for once Arthur was complaisant.

'No, no! Let the child go. Just so long as she really has permission from Mrs Dowson.'

'Oh, I have, sir.' Jenny's demure smile concealed the truth, that Arthur himself had instructed the housekeeper to allow her any time off, within reason, that she requested. Mrs Dowson, thin-lipped and disapproving, had her own mistaken ideas as to why this was so.

'No better than she should be, that Jenny Slade,' she confided to the butler, but Simmonds refused to be drawn. Unlike the majority of domestic staff, he believed that his employers' business was their own.

Jenny gathered up the dirty crockery, the plates of leftover scones and sandwiches and cakes, until the tea-trolley was fully loaded and ready to be wheeled from the room. Returning to the kitchen, she barely paused to push it inside the door before saying, 'Well, that's it, then. Ta-ta, folks. I'm off.' She had discarded her cap and apron by the time she reached her attic room, and pulled her dress over her head without stopping to draw the blinds. In any case, who was there to see her, apart from the birds, up there under the eaves? She poured cold water from the jug into the basin and splashed it over her face and arms, then rummaged in the plain deal cupboard which served as a wardrobe for her best summer dress. Her only decent summer dress, if it came to that, but she would be able to afford many more clothes when she got her hands on that hundred pounds. She added her old chip-straw hat, freshly trimmed with blue ribbon and a bunch of artificial flowers, but having no mirror in her room was unable to assess the effect as a whole. She was confident however, that she could still turn male heads wherever she went, in spite of having reached the ripe old age of nineteen years. Then she ran quickly down the back stairs, let herself out through the kitchen door – ignoring an appreciative whistle from Compton, the chauffeur – and cut

across the fields in the direction of Lower Abbots. She kept
her fingers crossed that Frank would be there already,
waiting.

*

From his perch on the gate which opened into Three Acre
Field, Frank saw her before she saw him, and felt his pulse
begin to race. He cursed softly, angry as always at the way
his body betrayed his heart. For the truth was that Frank did
not care for Jenny Slade – he thought her selfish and grasping
– but she held a strong physical attraction for him which he
found it difficult, if not impossible, to overcome. And in the
past two months, she had shown a flattering desire for his
company, seeking him out, preferring his attentions to those
of her other numerous suitors, visiting his mother on her
days off with little gifts, such as a posy of wild flowers or a
pot of her own mother's home-made jam.

Frank tried to make himself think of Eve, but when she
was at school she seemed remote. She had written to him,
telling him of Marcus's visit and his promise of support,
speaking confidently of their future together and how easy
everything would prove to be. Frank wanted to believe her,
but his greater knowledge of life made him cynical: he could
not really imagine that Arthur Burfoot and the Gilchrists
would allow Eve to become his wife without lifting a finger
to prevent such an unequal marriage. And there were still
five years to go before she reached her twenty-first birthday.
His friends had lately started to rib him about his self-
imposed celibacy; and although he knew better than to
credit every tale of sexual success which circulated among
the younger men of the village, he nevertheless knew that he
was probably the only one living the life of a monk.

And why should he? It wasn't fair that Eve should expect
it of him. He was a man. Women didn't feel these bodily
urges; at least, not nice women, the sort men eventually
married. There were the other sort, of course, like Jenny

Slade, but they were fair game, so why should he be barred from the hunt? Girls such as Jenny knew how to take precautions, how to look after themselves. Well, didn't they? It stood to reason that when they made advances as openly as she did, they must surely know what they were about.

Frank stifled his qualms that this might not be the case, and slid down from the gate. Jenny saw him and her full red lips curved into a smile. Her breasts thrust against the blue cotton print bodice of a dress which was slightly too small for her, and she lifted her skirt in unnecessary precaution as she stepped across a muddy patch of ground, revealing the lower half of a shapely, black-stockinged leg.

'Hello, Frank.' Her arms were about his neck, her lips pressed against his before he could even return the greeting. 'I was afraid you might have changed your mind.' She brushed a stray dandelion seed from the lapel of his best Sunday suit.

'Why should I?' he asked, a trifle breathlessly. 'But I thought you might've done. Lot of soldiers about nowadays. Lot of 'em in the Ring O' Bells most nights, lonely and homesick.'

'Frank!' Jenny drew back from him a little, her deep blue eyes sparkling with indignation. 'I'm not that sort of girl, you know I'm not! Whatever could make you say such a thing?'

This fine display of outrage, however, failed to convince Frank. He laughed, put one arm about her waist and began to walk with her along the lane towards Three Acre Copse on the crest of the rise.

'What sort of girl are you, then?' he asked. 'You tell me.'

'One who wants a good man and a home and children of her own, of course.' Jenny felt his arm stiffen and wondered if she might have overplayed her hand. At the same time, it was necessary to establish this fact. The task Arthur Burfoot had set her was in one way relatively simple; she could have seduced Frank Mailer a dozen times over during these past eight weeks. What was not so easy was to convince him that when she eventually let him have his way, he was the one taking advantage of her, and that her surrender was because of her affection for him. Frank had proved less gullible than expected. 'Don't you believe me?' she asked him.

'Of course!' But he spoke lightly, with a laugh in his voice.

They had reached the edge of the copse by now, and as the green shade of the trees closed over their heads Jenny stopped and turned to face him.

'I love you, Frank.' She slid her arms about his neck. 'You must have guessed that by this time. Oh, I know you think I'm silly and feckless; and I'll admit that, in the past, I've been a bit fond of the lads, like. But that's all over now, and has been for ages.' She saw the startled, wary expression in his dark brown eyes, saw his mouth open to speak. It was this moment or not at all; if she allowed his protest then all was lost and she could say goodbye to that hundred pounds.

She kissed him, using both lips and tongue in a way which was instinctive with her. No one had ever taught Jenny the art of love-making, for it was a subject never mentioned at home, the Slades being strict Methodists. But just as some people had a gift for drawing or singing or playing the piano, so she somehow knew from childhood how to do all that was necessary to please men. She felt Frank's rigid body suddenly slacken; felt him tremble and his arms tighten around her waist; felt him, after an initial reluctance, return her kiss with a savagery which told more plainly than words how hungry he was for a woman. She pulled him, unresisting, down on to the grass, and there, in that sub-aqueous gloom between the trees, they made love with a quiet and loveless intensity.

When they had finished, Frank rolled on to his back with groan which seemed to come from the depths of his being. He stared for a moment or two at the patterns of leaves and flickering sunlight above him, then flung one arm across his eyes. Jenny sat up and straightened her clothes before reaching out a hand to touch him.

'Frank? Frank, speak to me. Didn't you enjoy it? You're not being very gallant, are you?'

'Go away,' he muttered. 'Go away and leave me alone.'

Jenny's eyes sparkled triumphantly. 'I love you, Frank. I've never done that before with anyone. Now we'll *have* to get married.'

'No,' he said thickly. He scrambled to his feet, buttoning up his trousers. It was the first time he had ever made love properly to a woman, contrary to the reputation he had so carefully fostered, and he had no previous knowledge of exactly how things should be. But he had listened to the older farmhands talking, and suspected that it had not been the first time for Jenny. Everything had been too easy and she had been too bold. Yet he could be misjudging her. He reflected uneasily that no village lad had ever boasted of laying Jenny Slade, and such a conquest would surely not have gone unsung. He added in a softened voice, 'I don't love you, Jenny.'

She had foreseen this and laid her plans accordingly. She held out a hand, and when he had helped her up she retained his clasp. Slowly, she let her wonderful eyes fill with tears, a trick she had mastered as a child in order to disarm her father. 'But I love you, Frank. I'll always love you.' She disengaged her hand and ran down the slope to the lane, her shoulders hunched and shaking.

Frank called her name, but she ran on until she rounded the bend and disappeared. He made no attempt to pursue her, but sat down again on the grass and buried his head in his hands. He felt, as Jenny intended he should feel, a callous seducer who had taken advantage of an innocent girl for his own carnal satisfaction. Yet, even as Frank reviled himself, intuition warned him that Jenny's declaration of undying affection lacked the ring of truth. It was too sudden. They had known each other all their lives and had 'walked out' together on several previous occasions, sharing their inexpert sexual fumblings, but never once had she expressed any preference for him over the rest of the village boys. On the other hand, there had to come a moment in any relationship when friendship and liking turned to love. He and Eve had both made the discovery, so why not Jenny? Why should he doubt her word?

It was time to go home. It must be almost mid-evening and his mother would be wondering where he had got to. His father was still not in the best of health, and she relied on Frank to perform more than his own share of the household chores.

'You ought to get married,' she kept insisting. 'You did ought to be settling down at your age. And the Brownleas' cottage has just fallen empty. Squire would let you have it if you so wanted it, I'm certain sure he would. And that Jenny seems a very nice girl.'

Lizzie Mailer so plainly envisaged a future with her son and his wife living conveniently only two doors away that Frank, thinking of his plans to marry Eve, felt racked by guilt. It was more than likely that even with Marcus Gilchrist's support, they would have to move right away from the area. Arthur Burfoot would never countenance the marriage.

Frank stood up and began retracing his steps towards Lower Abbots. His body felt pleasantly tired, as it did when he had done a good day's work in the fields, but his mind was like lead. He felt confused and unsure of himself, not knowing what he wanted. Jenny or Eve? The safety of an existence he had always known and where everyone knew him, or the insecurities of an uncertain life which might open up all kinds of exciting possibilities? He reached home without having come to any conclusion.

*

But he thought he knew as soon as he saw Eve again, three weeks later.

Within hours of her arrival, she walked up to Home Farm to find him. Her eyes glowed with love and tenderness as she approached, carefully skirting the edge of the field to avoid the swishing scythes. She had dropped all pretence of being there by accident. Now that her parents were aware of her feelings, she saw no need to hide them from the rest of the world.

'Six whole weeks,' she had gloated to Rose that morning, as they travelled to Warminster by train. 'Six whole weeks without a visit to Cornwall or Aunt Josie in Bristol. Thank goodness taking holidays is no longer the patriotic thing to do.'

'But I'm having a holiday with you,' Rose protested. 'Am I being unpatriotic?'

'Of course not!' Eve was swift to refute the suggestion. 'You're on essential war work, visiting the injured.'

For Ernest had been wounded in the left leg on the very first day of the present Somme offensive and, after a fortnight in a field hospital in France, had been sent on sick leave to recuperate at home. His request to see Rose had resulted in an invitation to her to spend the beginning of the summer holiday at Rosemary Villa; an invitation which had been eagerly accepted, in spite of her father's reservations.

'You're only sixteen, Rose,' Mr Druitt had warned anxiously. 'It doesn't do, at your age, to get too fond of one particular man.'

But his wife had other ideas. 'Don't discourage the girl, Wilfred! The son of a man as rich as Arthur Burfoot is a good catch, especially for a girl as plain as our Rose.'

So Rose arrived at the villa to her usual warm welcome from Marcus and Helena, and after lunch walked up to Abbey Court, Eve accompanying her part of the way, as far as the farm.

'Auburn!' Frank threw down his scythe and came towards her, a grin on his face so wide that it seemed he might never stop smiling. 'You're home!'

'Yes, I'm home.' She stretched out her hands and their fingers linked. They just stood there, struck dumb by their delight at being together again. Eve was vaguely aware of the nudges and mutterings among the other men, but only had eyes for Frank. He, in his turn, was not even conscious of the sensation they were causing until his father thrust suddenly between them. George Mailer's face, haggard and sallow in spite of its sunburn, registered horror.

'What the bloody hell d'you think you're doing, lad? For God's sake, behave yourself, or I'll be turned off as well as you if this gets to Squire Burfoot's ears.'

Eve smiled reassuringly. 'It's all right, Mr Mailer. My father knows all about my ... my friendship with Frank. He knows that when I leave school we intend to be married. I thought Frank would have told you.'

'You stupid bugger!' George rounded furiously on his son. 'D'you think Squire'll let you get away with this if he ever finds out? Do you? 'Cos if you do, you're a bigger bloody fool than I took you for. I tell you straight, it'll kill yer mother.'

'Mr Mailer!' Eve intervened before Frank could reply. 'Please don't be angry. Frank and I really love one another, and I'm sure when my uncle appreciates that he won't try to part us.'

George Mailer curled his lip. 'You don't really believe what you're saying, Miss Gilchrist.'

'Indeed I do.' She knew that Uncle Arthur of his own accord would never countenance her marriage to Frank, but they had her father's support; and although, since arriving home a few hours ago, she had had no chance to speak with Marcus in private, she had no fear that he would renege on his promise. But more than that, the friendliness of both Mama and Aunt Hetty had been a pleasant and welcome surprise, especially as she had steeled herself for hysteria and reproaches. If those two had accepted that she was going to marry Frank, then Uncle Arthur might be reconciled to the idea, also. Mama had always been able to twist him around her little finger.

'Then you're as big a fool as he is!' George Mailer spat, jerking his head in his son's direction. There was a murmur of agreement from the rest of the men who, abandoning their scythes, had gathered round to listen. 'And I'm not having Squire thinking I'm a party to this nonsense. I'm going up to the Big House right now and tell him so, before he thinks I've encouraged you in it.'

'You can't do that!' Eve grabbed George's arm. 'He knows nothing about it yet, and I'd rather he heard it from me or my parents.'

'Yes, leave it, Dad,' Frank pleaded. 'Leave it to Dr Gilchrist.'

George Mailer hesitated. He had great respect for the doctor, but common sense told him that even Marcus's powers of persuasion would not be sufficient to avert the full force of Arthur's wrath from falling on his and Lizzie's heads if he thought that they had been in any way a party to their son's folly. But if he could get to the Squire first with the news, disclaiming all knowledge of Frank's intentions, then there might be a chance of retaining his job and home. In his book, it was certainly worth trying.

He freed himself from Eve's clasp. 'I've made up my mind, and you can't stop me. If you didn't want trouble, you should've thought of that before you started this madness. How long's it been going on, eh, Frank? And her not yet seventeen! There'll be the devil to pay, and so I'm warning you. I'm dreading telling your mother.'

George Mailer stamped angrily towards the gate and out into the lane. Eve called desperately, 'Mr Mailer!' but Frank shook his head.

'It's no good, Auburn. Once the old man's got the bit between his teeth, there's no stopping him.' He squeezed her shoulders. 'Cheer up. We'll be all right, whatever happens.' But he spoke without conviction. Things had suddenly got out of hand, like a team of horses he had once seen bolting, and he wished that he were a hundred miles away.

When she had walked into the field a quarter of an hour ago, he had experienced such a surge of love for Eve that he had forgotten all else in his desire to reach out and hold her; a thoughtless impulse which had pitched him headlong into a situation which he had found impossible to control, and which was forcing him to come to a decision. Eve or Jenny? During the past three weeks he had avoided Jenny like the plague, refusing to speak to her when she came out to the fields to look for him, not meeting her eyes in Chapel on Sundays. But every now and then his body betrayed him, and he was filled with a fever of physical longing which he found difficult to ignore.

Eve kissed his cheek, to the embarrassed sniggers of the other men who were reluctantly picking up their scythes again and getting on with their work.

'Of course we'll be all right,' she said confidently. 'As long as we've got each other.'

*

George Mailer knocked on the scullery door and told the kitchenmaid who came to answer it that he needed to see Mr Burfoot urgently.

'Wait here,' she said. 'I'll speak to Mr Simmonds.'

She vanished into the house, returning after some little time with a demand to know what it was that he wanted.

'My business,' was the surly rejoinder.

She disappeared again, returning a second time, after an even more protracted period, with an invitation to him to step inside. 'But wipe yer feet,' she ordered. 'Mr Simmonds've spoken to Master, and 'e'll see you in the little study downstairs. Follow me.' As she led him along the stone-flagged corridor which bisected the kitchen regions, and through the baize-covered door which opened into the hall, she added, 'It must be one of those co-in-cidingces what Mrs Dowson's always on about, 'cos Master was seemingly on the point of sending for your Frank, so Mr Simmonds said.'

'Sending for our Frank?' George Mailer's heart thumped unpleasantly fast. 'What for?'

The girl shrugged her skinny shoulders. ''Ow do I know? Mr Simmonds wouldn't tell me even if 'e knew, which I doubt. It's that door over there. Not the double ones, that's the dining-room.'

George Mailer knocked on the door she indicated,

wishing he hadn't come. He was too late, after all. Arthur Burfoot knew about Frank and his niece already, and George would receive the full brunt of his wrath. A voice called 'Come in!' He turned the handle and entered . . .

Jenny Slade. What was she doing there with the Gaffer? And why did she look as though she were crying?

'Ah, George!' Arthur Burfoot rose from behind his desk, solemn but not angry. 'This is most fortuitous. I was just about to send for Frank, but it's perhaps just as well that you know first. Draw up a chair and sit down.'

Chapter Nine

It was a day of wind and driving rain when Frank Mailer married Jenny Slade in Staple Abbots Methodist Chapel.

Sudden squalls of bad weather had come roaring up out of the west, howling across the Plain and dispersing the hot August sunshine. Eve sat at her bedroom window, staring through the streaming panes at the storm-tossed garden. A scattering of white rose-petals lay on the sodden grass, and some of the flowers which bordered the path had been flattened by last night's gale. A branch had been torn from one of the apple trees at the back of the house, and had come to rest against the rhododendron bushes. All in all, a fitting day, she thought, for such a marriage.

Rosemary Villa was strangely quiet. Doris Hosier and Cook were both out, invited to the wedding, and Marcus was at Upper Abbots, sent for by the husband of a diphtheria patient whose condition had deteriorated during the morning, indicating severe toxaemia. And Helena and Hetty were downstairs, tip-toeing about and talking in whispers as though in the presence of mortal illness. There was no disguising their delight at what had happened, but their affection for Eve, and her obvious distress, made them feel a little guilty.

The news that Jenny Slade claimed to be pregnant by Frank Mailer had spread like wildfire throughout the village and both hamlets. At first, Eve had refused to believe it.

'She's lying,' she said confidently when Helena had told her. 'Jenny Slade would lie the hind leg off a donkey.'

'Well, you'd better ask Frank about that,' her mother answered, trying to keep the note of triumph out of her voice.

'I shall. I'll go up to the farm this morning.'

But Frank wasn't there. Jeb Marston said he'd been given time off by the Squire to 'get himself sorted', and offered to give her a lift on the back of the hay-wagon as far as Three Acre Field, adding, 'You can walk to the Mailers' cottage easy from there.'

The familiar smell of paraffin had greeted her as soon as she entered, bringing back poignant memories of her first visit all those years ago. Frank was in the kitchen with his mother, who was baking the weekly batch of bread. It had been a warm day, and the room was made even hotter by the fire in the oven. He was seated in the rocking-chair, staring moodily ahead of him, sunk deep in thought.

'Frank!' Both he and Mrs Mailer jumped at the sound of her voice. 'I've just heard, and I want you to know I don't believe a word of it – that Jenny Slade's baby is yours, I mean.'

Frank got up slowly, gripping the back of the chair to still its motion.

'Eve, I didn't hear you come in.'

Her breath caught in her throat. She couldn't recall the last time he had called her by her proper name.

'I . . . I'm sorry, I came in the back way. I hope you don't mind, Mrs Mailer?'

The older woman glanced up but made no comment, dropping her eyes again almost immediately to the dough she was shaping into a loaf. Frank moved closer, but ominously made no attempt to take her hand.

'We'd better go for a walk. The oven's nearly up to heat, Ma. Can you manage?'

'Of course I can manage!' Mrs Mailer was scathing. 'How do you think I go on when you're not here? And anyway, I'll soon have a daughter-in-law to call on, if I need her, won't I?' She spoke with enormous satisfaction.

Eve followed Frank outside without remembering how she got there. 'What did she mean, Frank? You're not going to marry Jenny! You can't be! Why should you?' Her voice shook with fear. 'You haven't done anything wrong with her, have you?'

He recognized the question as being a plea for reassurance rather than an accusation, and refused to look at her, scuffing up the dirt with the toes of his boots.

'It probably is my child,' he answered.

Eve took hold of his arm, forcing him to stop, oblivious of prying eyes in the neighbouring windows. 'What ... What are you saying?'

He tugged his arm free, a bad conscience making him cruel.

'I'm going to marry Jenny, that's what I'm saying. As soon as possible. Squire's letting us have the Brownleas' old cottage.' He threw out his hands. 'What else can I do, Auburn? She's going to have my baby.'

Eve put up her hands to her burning cheeks. She wished she were dead; she might as well be, because her life had just ended. 'I see,' she whispered.

'No, you don't see. You're too young, and that's always been part of the trouble.' It was his turn to seize her arm as he dragged her along the rutted track, out of sight of the other cottages. Suddenly he had gathered her into his arms, holding her so close that she could feel the trembling of his body. 'Auburn, Auburn! I do love you, but it would never have worked – you must see that. They wouldn't have let us marry, not when it came down to it. And even if we defied 'em, and ran away and got married, it still wouldn't work. You're a different class. You're educated ... refined. I'm just a rough labourer. You'd've got tired of me in no time and we'd've quarrelled. It's no good you shaking your head, you've never been poor. Money, lack of it, is a terrible thing for making rows between a man and a woman.'

'We'll make it work,' she told him fiercely.

'No. It's no good, Auburn. I can't wait five years until you're twenty-one. I thought I could, but I can't. And anyway, I couldn't leave Jenny in the lurch. The whole village'd be against me.'

'That doesn't matter. We shan't have to listen to them. We'll run away! Tomorrow!'

He released her, giving her a little push which almost sent her flying. She grabbed the top of a five-barred gate which opened into a field where sheep were grazing.

'You're talking nonsense. You're only sixteen! Before I knew it, I'd be behind bars. Is that what you want? To see me in prison?'

Eve hadn't meant to cry; she'd meant to be grown-up and dignified, but the tears welled up of their own accord and started to trickle down her cheeks.

'I love you,' she sobbed. 'I don't want to hurt you.'

'Then don't make a fuss.' He pulled her into his arms once more, smothering her upturned face with kisses. 'I love you, Auburn, but I've got to marry Jenny.'

'Why? You can have children with me. Lots of them. We always said we'd have a big family.'

'I know!' He rocked her to and fro, swaying on the balls of his feet. 'I *know*.' But had he ever truly believed it? To him, talking about their future together had always seemed slightly unreal. Deep down, he had known it would never happen.

She raised her head, cupping his face in her hands. 'I want children, Frank. Your children.'

He tried to smile. 'You'll have children, Auburn. A lovely girl like you, you're bound to get married.'

She answered fiercely, 'I don't want anyone else's children. Just yours.'

His lips found hers in a long passionate embrace, and she felt her senses swimming ... Then, suddenly, he tore her arms from around his neck, pushed her violently away and said hoarsely, 'Goodbye, Auburn.' A moment later he had gone, running as hard as he could along the track until he reached the hamlet. By the time she had recovered her balance and followed him, he had disappeared indoors, and somehow she knew that it was useless to try to see him again. There had been something in the quality of that last goodbye which left her in no doubt that he meant it. He was going to marry Jenny Slade. It was over.

She had walked home, hardly aware of the distance. Neither her mother nor Aunt Hetty had questioned her as to the outcome of her visit to Frank, displaying a tact and understanding over the past two weeks which, perversely, had only served to underline their secret satisfaction that the whole sorry business was finished and done with. Only her father had attempted to put his feelings into words.

'You're very young, Eve. Your life's barely begun. Come September, you'll be back at school among your friends. You'll soon forget Frank Mailer. It's all for the best, my darling. You'll see that for yourself one day. You'd never have made a farm labourer's wife. It would have been a disaster.'

Eve had made no response. No one really understood her feelings for Frank, not even Rose, who had extended her holiday by a week and moved to Abbey Court at Arthur's and Mabel's invitation, to be nearer Ernest.

'It wouldn't have worked, Evie,' she had said, trying to be sympathetic.

And now there was no more hope. Eve glanced at the clock on her bedroom mantelpiece. Half-past-two; the service was over, Frank and Jenny Slade were married. She couldn't even cry; all her tears had been shed and she felt empty inside. All that was left was school and work and her sudden determination that whatever happened, whatever Mama and Uncle Arthur said, she was going to become a teacher.

*

It was late in December, her first day of the Christmas school holiday at home, when Eve overheard Doris Hosier and Mrs Kellaway talking.

Hetty had asked her to find out from Cook how many pots of mincemeat were in the store cupboard before they started on the afternoon's marathon of making tarts. The door was ajar as Eve approached the kitchen, and she could hear what the women were saying, although both had lowered their voices.

'He was in the Ring O' Bells again last night, so I hear, getting drunk.' Mrs Kellaway was clattering the saucepans as she prepared to dish up luncheon. 'S'pose you can't blame him, the way she deceived him.'

Eve was about to enter when she heard her own name mentioned, and she paused in the act of opening the door.

'D'you think anyone's told Miss Evie?' Doris asked. 'This soup's about ready, Mrs Kellaway.'

'Take it off the range, then, there's a good girl. No, I shouldn't think so. Not that she won't find out, now she's home again.'

'What will I find out, Cook?' The two women looked up in startled dismay as Eve entered the kitchen.

'Oh, my goodness, Miss Evie, you did give me a fright.' Mrs Kellaway pressed a hand to her starched white bosom. 'I didn't know you was out there.'

'What will I find out?' Eve persisted.

The others exchanged glances. 'I don't know, Miss, as it's our place to tell you.' Doris Hosier expressed their reluctance.

'Nonsense.' Eve was brusque. 'It obviously concerns Frank Mailer, so I might as well hear it from you as from anyone else. Come on, Doris, we were at school together. Just pretend we're back in the classroom.'

But the housemaid continued to hesitate. There was something a bit forbidding about Eve which she had never noticed before. Still a few weeks short of her seventeenth birthday, she seemed very adult, as though childhood was gone and lost for ever.

'Oh, all right. Sooner or later, someone's going to have to say something.' Doris took the empty soup tureen from one of the ovens, where it had been warming. 'Jenny Slade wasn't having a baby, after all. It was a mistake on her part.'

'I see.' Eve was astonished at how little emotion she felt on hearing this news. Over the past few months, while she wrestled with history and English literature, geography and mathematics, she had trained herself to think of Frank and his wife with detachment, as though they were no more to her than the rest of the villagers. Success had numbed her. She went through the motions of daily life, but she was dead inside. 'Jenny always was a liar. Mrs Jardine wants to know how many pots of mincemeat are in the cupboard, Mrs Kellaway.'

'Well! She took that pretty coolly!' Doris Hosier exclaimed as soon as Eve was out of earshot. 'P'raps all those stories that she and Frank were planning to run away together weren't true, after all. Always seemed a bit far-fetched to me.'

Eve said nothing to either her parents or Aunt Hetty about what she had heard, and if they didn't wish to say anything to her, that was up to them: it wasn't their fault that Frank had allowed himself to be taken in. It was only when Aunt Josie arrived to spend the holiday at Rosemary Villa that she eventually mentioned the subject.

It was two days before her seventeenth birthday, that limbo time between Christmas and New Year. Eve and Josie had decided to take a walk after luncheon, leaving Helena and Hetty lying down on their beds for an afternoon nap, while Marcus had been called out to see a patient. It was a dull day, grey and overcast, and there was a pervasive air of gloom that had nothing to do with the weather. As the country embarked on its third successive year of war, there was little to make anyone cheerful. The casualty lists from the great Somme offensive, begun in July and not called off until the beginning of November, had been staggering in their numbers of dead and wounded. Two families in a place as small as Staple Abbots had each lost one of their menfolk. And it was small consolation to read that food was rationed in Germany, for at home shortages of almost everything were increasing daily. Young men like Donald and Ernest, the latter now fully recovered from his leg wound, came home on leave like ghosts of their former selves – taciturn and morose – or wildly boisterous, as though seized by madness.

There was a new British weapon, the tank, first used in September, harbinger of the kind of mechanized warfare which the world had never seen before. Gone were the days of the cavalry charge: the horse would soon be obsolete, everyone said so. There was a general belief that now Lloyd George had become Prime Minister in place of Asquith, the war would be prosecuted with greater resolution, but it was more of a hope than a certainty. These things apart, life went on much as normal, unless one lived in London where they suffered under Zeppelin air-raids.

'What will you do when you leave school?' Josie asked as they walked, well wrapped-up against the cold, along the lane at the back of the chandler's shop and cottage.

'I'm going to teach.' Eve rearranged her red woollen scarf more cosily about her neck and pulled her hat further down over her ears. 'I've talked it over with Miss Milward, and I shall apply to take a degree course in Modern History at Bristol University.' She hesitated. 'I wondered ... I wondered if I could come and live with you at Holly Lodge? I mean, I wondered if a lodger would interfere with your writing?'

'My dear child, I'd be delighted to have you. You must regard the Lodge as your home, and come and go as you please. Do your parents approve of this decision?'

'Papa's delighted, as you can imagine. Mama and Aunt Hetty, not to mention Uncle Arthur, think any education for women is a foolish waste of time. But they're all so thankful that I was prevented from marrying Frank Mailer that they've refrained from saying very much.' There was a brief pause before she added, 'I suppose Papa told you all about that?'

Josie carefully avoided a half-frozen puddle. 'He did write to me now and then, to let me know what was happening.'

'And you thought I was young and stupid, like the rest of them.'

'It wasn't my place to think any such thing. Let me take your arm, my dear. At fifty-eight, I'm not as young as I was; I occasionally feel in need of a little support. My weight makes me easily breathless.' Her aunt's tall figure belied how heavy she really was, as Eve soon discovered when Josie leaned on her. 'It's your life, the only one you have, and you should be allowed to decide what to do with it. Heresy, I know. Perhaps it's just as well I never had any children.'

'You'd have made a wonderful mother,' Eve assured her, squeezing her arm.

'No, I wouldn't,' Josie answered decisively. 'Children need discipline and guidance, and woe betide the society which ignores that fact. There, you see, I'm preaching against my own principles. Life is so difficult, and knowing what to do in the best interests of other people is the most difficult thing of all. Have you ... seen Frank since his marriage?'

The lane had petered out in a muddy track, fit only for animals, so they turned and began to retrace their steps.

'No ... Jenny Slade wasn't having a baby, after all – Doris Hosier told me. So Frank needn't have married her. If only he'd listened to me! I warned him she was a liar.' The numbness of the past months was suddenly melting. The sense of hurt and betrayal was reaching out towards Eve with long, coiling fingers; tears were very near the surface.

Josie patted her niece's hand in silent sympathy, trying desperately to stop herself from giving advice, and failing.

'Eve, my dear, whatever the circumstances, he's a married man now and there's nothing you or he can do about it. You have to accept it, put it behind you and try not to be bitter. You have your whole life ahead of you and you have to get on with it.' She sighed. 'Oh, dear! I expect you've heard that a dozen times before; said it to yourself over and over. But it isn't any less true for all that. Clichés only become clichés because of constant repetition.'

Eve wiped a stray tear from her face with the back of her red woollen mitten. 'I know. I'm so pathetic! I thought I'd trained myself not to care.'

'You must never stop caring ... not about anything. I don't believe in God, haven't for years, but I do believe in love if you have the gift for it. I haven't; I've always been too

self-centred. But you have, so make the most of it. Share it
out among others as much as possible. And now,' Josie
added, laughing, 'let's go in and sample one of Hetty's
delicious teas before we get too serious.'

*

The first half of 1917 was eventful. There was revolution in
Russia and Tsar Nicholas abdicated; the United States
entered the war; Vimy Ridge was taken by the Canadian
forces; and on June 19th the royal family renounced all
German titles and names, rechristening themselves the
House of Windsor. Various items of food remained in short
supply, and Arthur decided that part of the parkland should
be turned into a vegetable garden. Some of the farmhands,
including Frank and his father, were diverted from their
normal work to dig up the lower meadow.

It was a hard job on a hot day and Frank, for the first time
in his life, got a touch of sunstroke. He foolishly removed his
cap because his head was aching, and by midday his senses
were reeling. He ate his dinner, brought out by the maids
from the house, and drank one cup of cider before being
violently sick.

'Go home, Frank,' his father advised him. 'We'll square it
with the Gaffer.'

There was a general murmur of agreement from the other
men and Frank, feeling a lot worse than he would admit, was
at last persuaded to abandon his spade and begin the long,
hot walk to Lower Abbots. For the first mile he felt too ill
to do more than put one foot in front of the other, and on
more than one occasion was forced to sit by the side of the
track with his head between his knees. After a while,
however, the very act of walking, together with a slight
breeze which had sprung up, made him feel a little better.
His head stopped lurching, his legs recovered some of their
strength and he began to move at a swifter pace. But the
trouble with feeling better was that his thoughts returned,

as they always did nowadays, to Jenny and his marriage.

Had she tricked him? Or had she genuinely believed herself to be pregnant? When he protested that she had trapped him, she countered with the accusation that she had also trapped herself, for she had very quickly dropped all pretence of being in love. ('A temporary infatuation', she had called her erstwhile seeming affection for him.) So he had little choice but to believe that she had been telling the truth. There was otherwise no good reason that he could see for her to have chosen a loveless marriage.

Frank reached the cottage to find that Jenny was not at home, but this did not altogether surprise him. Lizzie Mailer, her hopes of cosy domestic intercourse between the two households soon dashed, complained that her daughter-in-law was always out, gallivanting off somewhere or other.

'Though where she finds the money for all these excursions of hers and the bits of finery she decks herself out with, is beyond me. You must be giving her too much house-keeping money, Frank.'

Frank took no notice of his mother, understanding her disappointment and assuming that Jenny was a shrewd manager. If she had enough money over at the end of each week for a few personal gew-gaws, then she was welcome to them. Perhaps they compensated her for the situation in which she found herself, just as his trips to the Ring O' Bells compensated him.

But even when he was drunk, there was one subject on which Frank did not let himself dwell too closely, and that was Eve. Just the thought of her was like twisting a knife in his heart, and the pain had become increasingly acute as his marriage to Jenny soured. The suspicion that he had allowed himself to be hustled into wedlock without waiting for proof of Jenny's pregnancy, as an alternative to fighting for Eve, was rigorously suppressed, but still managed to raise its ugly head from time to time. On these occasions, Frank told himself that he had had no choice and therefore had nothing to reproach himself with. Jenny had panicked and now they were both paying for her mistake. But it had been a genuine error . . .

The Brownleas' old cottage was smaller than the one the Mailers occupied, with a cramped lean-to scullery and no living-room apart from the kitchen. There was no fire burning in the grate, and consequently no way of heating water for a cup of tea. The two wall-ovens, one on either side of the fireplace, were also cold, so Frank guessed that his evening meal would be the same. He was growing used to Jenny's rooted dislike of cooking, and hot food was fast becoming a luxury unless he went to his mother's for a meal.

Today, however, he did not care. He was still feeling far from well and all he wanted was a drink. He lifted down a cup from the dresser and went into the scullery to scoop some water from the butt in the corner nearest the door. When he had swallowed his fill, he dragged himself upstairs to the tiny front bedroom and sat down on the edge of the bed, his aching head clasped between his hands. In a moment or two, he would turn back the none-too-clean white cotton counterpane and have a rest.

His eyes wandered round the room, noting the smeared mirror which hung askew over the dusty chest-of-drawers. The bottom drawer of the chest was only half closed, with some of Jenny's clothing – a lace-edged petticoat, a pair of black silk stockings and a fine lawn, ribbon-threaded bust-bodice – spilling out over the rim. After staring vaguely for several seconds, Frank's attention sharpened. He had never seen his wife in any of these things, but that was not the point. The point was that his mother was right to question how Jenny could afford such finery on the money he was able to give her each week. Slowly he got to his feet and went across to kneel beside the drawer, pulling it wide open to see what else was inside.

The contents were in a mess, as though turned over by someone in a hurry to go out, and to be put to rights later when she returned. Apart from the things which Frank had already noted, there were several more pairs of silk stockings, a delicate fringed cream shawl, also made of silk, two ostrich feathers dyed crimson, a pair of brocade slippers, some more underwear and a yard or so of expensive Honiton lace. These had come from Warminster shops, not from the village. When had Jenny bought all this? And, more importantly, how had she managed to pay for it?

Frank stood up, and as he did so stubbed his toes against an object protruding from beneath the chest-of-drawers. Once again he squatted on his haunches, to discover a battered tin box which, he guessed, was normally pushed right back against the skirting-board and concealed from view. He opened the lid with trembling fingers to reveal a large wad of one-pound notes, held together by an elastic band.

Chapter Ten

He was waiting for her when she came home. Feeling like death, but buoyed up by his anger, Frank had made his way downstairs and sat facing the door. How long he had been there before the latch was lifted, he had no idea. Time had ceased to trouble him; his mind was too busy with other things.

It hadn't been difficult to work out the significance of that pile of notes — all eighty-five of them, for he had counted — nor to guess that there must have been others. A hundred probably, a nice round sum. Jenny had been paid, and handsomely paid, for her part in his seduction and subsequent shot-gun wedding. Her declared love for him, her claim to be pregnant, were both a pack of lies, and like a fool he had fallen for them hook, line and sinker.

But who had put her up to telling them? That, too, was not difficult to guess. Who else but Arthur Burfoot would have had an interest in preventing his marriage to Eve, except her parents? And Frank could not imagine either Doctor or Mrs Gilchrist soiling their hands with such a dirty trick. But the Squire would stoop to anything to get his own way; to do what he thought was right for his family.

Jenny was humming to herself as she entered the cottage, but stopped as soon as she saw her husband sitting at the table.

'Frank! What are you doing home this time of day?' She had a basket in one hand, and Frank could see that it contained several parcels.

'Never mind that. Where've you been? Shopping again, by the look of it. How do you afford all these little presents to yourself, Jenny? Because I don't make the mistake of supposing that it's food you have in there.'

She closed the door and put her basket down, defiantly, close to him on the green chenille cloth.

'Your Ma been getting at you again? Miserable old bag! She's jealous because she can't manage on what your Dad gives her.'

Frank's eyes had narrowed to slits, and Jenny was unable to see the red light of danger in them.

'She can manage all right, and makes sure he has a good hot meal every evening into the bargain. But clothes and suchlike have to be saved for, carefully, and then she's only ever been able to buy necessities. She's never owned silk stockings nor silk underwear.' Frank got up, supporting himself on his arms, hands flat on the table. 'But then, she never had cash stashed away, not like you have.'

The colour receded from Jenny's cheeks, leaving her very pale, and for a moment she looked frightened. Then she laughed.

'Been snooping, have you? Turning over my things?'

He shook his head. 'Sheer chance. I came home sick, touch of sunstroke, and went upstairs to lie down. You'd been careless — gone out in a hurry, I reckon. The bottom drawer of the chest was open and half the stuff spilling on to the floor. And you hadn't pushed your tin box back properly underneath it.' She was looking scared again and bit her lower lip as he pressed his advantage. 'Eighty-five quid in that box, Jenny. Eighty-five quid! And I'm willing to bet it was a hundred to begin with. I'm not even going to ask you how you got it, 'cos I know. From Arthur Burfoot. A bargain struck between you. "You get that poor, trusting sod, Frank Mailer, to marry you, and I'll give you a hundred pounds."'

Jenny hesitated, but knew it was no good denying things now that Frank had discovered the money. The only way was to brazen it out.

'All right, so what if we did strike a bargain? Squire didn't want you marrying his niece and I was sick of being poor. I wanted nice things. And now you know about the cash, we

can share it.' She smiled appeasingly. 'I'm sure there must be
lots of things that you'd like, too.'

The skin tightened across his cheekbones. 'I wouldn't
touch that money with a barge-pole! Not a single penny!'
His voice was harsh and filled with contempt. With a
suddenness that surprised her, he slapped her hard across the
face. 'You slut!'

Her fear gave place to anger as she drew back, hissing like
a snake.

'Don't you ever hit me again, Frank Mailer, or I'll leave
you!' But she knew, as he did, that they were empty words.
No woman could leave her husband without putting herself
beyond the pale. Her parents wouldn't shelter her or they too
might be ostracized. And where would she go if she left
Staple Abbots? She had no relatives or friends outside the
village.

Frank came round the table towards her. There was a look
in his eyes that made her grab for the door-latch, but he
moved swiftly to block her attempted escape.

'Oh, don't worry my girl, you won't have to leave me. I'll
leave *you*. But first, I think you owe me something. You've
never been a very loving wife, and now of course I
understand why. But I think I'm entitled to say goodbye
properly, don't you?'

'What do you mean?' Jenny asked, but she knew what he
meant all right, and was suddenly filled with a febrile
excitement. Years ago, when she had first walked out with
Frank, he had always aroused her, even though they had
never actually made love. She recalled the day when Eve had
discovered them together, with Frank's hand groping up her
skirts, and thought that perhaps something more might
have happened then if they hadn't been interrupted. Later
on, emotions had cooled between them and she had gone out
with other village lads, although she had submitted to none
of them. It was Donald Burfoot who had initiated her into
the pleasures of sex.

Looking back, she felt that whatever Frank claimed it was

not her fault that the marriage had been unsuccessful. Having tricked him into becoming her husband, she had been quite willing to behave like a wife. It was Frank himself who had proved indifferent, still half suspicious that she had lied. It occurred to Jenny, as he advanced purposefully towards her, that she didn't want to lose him; didn't want him to carry out his threat of going away. And he was offering her the chance to prove why he should stay. It never crossed her mind that his dislike of her was now so great that nothing she could say or do would alter his purpose by one iota; that he saw this simply as an act of revenge.

So when he grabbed her she did not, as he had expected, resist, but clamped her mouth on his, making no murmur of protest when he dragged her down with him to the floor.

*

Eve chewed the end of her pencil, a childish habit she was always being reprimanded for, while Miss Gerrish, forbidding in her grey flannel skirt and mannish white shirt, went step by step through the causes of the Peninsular War. Sitting beside Eve at their ink-stained desk, Rose stared out of the window and thought of Ernest Burfoot.

'And so,' Miss Gerrish said, 'we come to the emergence of Napoleon Buonaparte . . .'

The classroom door opened and Miss Flora Milward came in. The girls immediately stood, respectfully silent as the headmistress nodded at the teacher and then beckoned to Eve.

'There is someone to see you. He is waiting in the small sitting-room next to my study.' Once out in the corridor, Miss Milward permitted herself a frown of disapproval. 'As you well know, Eve, we do not encourage visits from anyone but relatives during term-time. Please make that quite clear to this young man and tell him it must not occur again. You may have fifteen minutes and not a second longer.'

Mystified, unable to think of any young man who might

wish to see her, Eve pushed open the door of the visitors'
sitting-room and entered, to be brought up short by the
sight of Frank standing, ill-at-ease, in the middle of the
flower-patterned carpet. He was wearing his best suit,
rubbed and shiny with age, the trousers a trifle too short in
the legs, and twisting his corduroy cap uneasily between
hands that trembled. She stared at him in astonishment.

'Frank? What ...? What are you doing here?' Her voice
shook, and a surge of love engulfed her. He looked miserably
unhappy, and she wanted to fold him in her arms and kiss
away all his pain. Angry with herself for such weakness, she
continued stiffly, 'Please sit down. You look so uncomfortable just standing there.'

'No. I won't sit down, thank you.' He swallowed. 'I'm
sorry, coming here like this, embarrassing you in front of
your friends, but I've enlisted. I went into Warminster last
week. I'm joining my regiment tomorrow, and I wanted to
say goodbye.'

Eve stared. 'I ... I don't understand. You're exempt from
fighting. Uncle Arthur arranged it with the War Office.'

'I volunteered. They're so desperate for men over there in
France, the Recruiting Offices'll take anyone who offers.
Under a certain age, of course. They knocked my exemption
on the head fast enough when I told 'em I wanted to go.'

'But ... your parents.' Eve forced herself to say the hated
name. 'Jenny ... What do they say about your volunteering?'

'Ma and Pa are none too happy, as you'd expect. And
Squire's livid. Cursed me uphill and down dale for half-
an-hour or more for being an ungrateful so-and-so. As for
Jenny —' He shrugged. 'I don't care what she thinks.' He
lifted his head and she saw that he was crying. 'I wish I'd had
the guts to wait for you, Auburn, like you wanted.'

She was in his arms, oblivious to the fact that one of the
mistresses might walk in at any moment. 'Frank! It's not too
late. We could still run away together.'

He laughed unsteadily and stroked her hair. 'What, and

have the law on our heels for the rest of my life? A deserter and the abductor of a minor!'

'I'm seventeen. A woman.'

'The law doesn't see it that way. And now I've enlisted, I'd be going absent without leave. I could be shot.'

'You might be shot anyway. Oh, Frank! Don't do it! Don't go!'

He held her tightly against him. 'I've no choice. Auburn! Auburn! I've made such a mess of our lives, haven't I? All because I couldn't wait for what was worth having. I let Jenny seduce me, and I let myself be pushed into marrying her. I *wanted* to believe she was pregnant. It made the decision easier. But now I know for sure she deliberately tricked me, pretending she was having a baby when she wasn't, I can't stay with her any longer.'

Eve tilted back her head. 'You say you know for sure that she tricked you? How did you find out?'

'It doesn't matter. Nothing matters now. I'm going, and I'm leaving you and I may never come back. Say you still love me, Auburn. I still love you.'

She kissed him passionately. 'I love you. Always and always. Oh, Frank, promise me you'll return safe and sound.'

He made a poor attempt at a grin. 'You're a one for wanting everything down in black and white. I can't make any promises like that, you know I can't. And I'd only mess up your life more than I have already.' He kissed her once more, then determinedly unclasped her hands from about his neck. 'Whatever happens, this is goodbye, Auburn. I must go. I've got to walk to Salisbury to catch my train. You've your whole life in front of you. Don't waste it wishing for what can never be.'

He was out of the door, his footsteps receding along the corridor, before Eve had time to pull herself together. She yelled, 'Frank!' at the top of her voice and wrenched at the door-handle, only to find Miss Milward barring her path. The headmistress had been hovering just inside her study, waiting for the unwelcome visitor to leave, and ready to

expel him at the end of fifteen minutes if he did not
voluntarily do so.

'Eve!' she exclaimed in scandalized accents. 'Young ladies
never shout.' She glanced shrewdly at her pupil's flushed
cheeks and suspiciously bright eyes before placing a restrain-
ing arm around Eve's shoulders. Flora Milward was even
more astute than her pupils credited her with being, and she
had no difficulty in sizing up the situation. Girls of Eve's age
often fell in love with totally inappropriate young men, and
no doubt in this case Dr Gilchrist had taken the necessary
steps to separate his daughter and the rather bucolic youth
who had just left in such a hurry. The headmistress sighed.
Social conventions were hard to accept when you were only
seventeen, and there was no point in telling Eve that one day
she would probably be grateful.

'You have my permission not to return to class this
afternoon. Go to your room and lie down for a while. I'll
inform Miss Gerrish. But you are not to leave the school
grounds, Eve. I put you on your honour.'

                                *

Donald came home on leave at Christmas. Ernest was home
for good, having been invalided out of the Army the
preceding month, after receiving terrible stomach wounds at
Passchendaele in September. He was skin and bone, a
skeletal wraith, eating spoonfuls of slop fed to him by his
mother. He cried very easily over nothing at all, but he was
alive and with a chance of at least partial recovery, not lying
dead in the mud around Ypres like three hundred thousand
of his contemporaries.

His appearance shocked Eve, as nothing else had been able
to do, into an awareness of what war was really like. At the
top of the stairs at Abbey Court hung a huge oil painting of
the battle of Waterloo: noble men dying in noble attitudes,
and not a wound nor a drop of blood in sight. But looking
at Ernest, listening to his stumbling words, made her realize

for the first time how false a representation it was.

Donald, too, was subdued, lacking his usual bombast, and Eve was genuinely pleased to sit with him after Christmas dinner quietly playing cribbage. Ernest was resting in his room, as he did for most of the day. Arthur and Mabel, Helena, Marcus and Hetty were huddled around a drawing-room fire only half its pre-war size, for even Arthur's source of black market coal was at last drying up. The two men were dozing, sated by their meal in spite of the fact that it had been a mere three courses instead of the customary five. Mabel was doing her beautiful needlepoint embroidery, while Helena and Hetty indulged in village gossip.

Inevitably, at some time during the afternoon, Jenny Mailer's pregnancy was mentioned.

'I heard the baby's due in March. That's what Mrs Kellaway told me.' Hetty sighed sympathetically. 'It'll give the poor girl something else to think about rather than worrying about Frank all the time.'

'It's his parents I feel sorry for,' Mabel gently intervened. 'Lizzie Mailer told me that he doesn't often write. They've only had two letters since he's been gone, and Jenny none at all, I believe.'

'Fancy leaving her like that, with a child on the way,' Helena was censorious. 'He needn't have volunteered. I was pleased to hear about the child, though; it shows that all's well between them.'

Eve knew by her mother's slightly raised voice that this remark was for her benefit. But Helena had no need to underline the obvious: the news of Jenny's pregnancy had come as a blinding shock. How could Frank have professed love for herself when he was still sleeping with his wife? It made a mockery of everything that he had said that afternoon last summer. She refused to mention his name or enquire about Jenny except in the most perfunctory way, shutting her ears to most of the gossip and thus remaining ignorant of the general opinion that Jenny was less than pleased to find herself expecting a child.

'Told me she didn't want the little so-and-so,' Mrs Crocker whispered in scandalized accents across the counter of the general store to anyone who would listen.

Hetty, who was one of the recipients of this confidence, did not refer to it at home. She wasn't the one to pass on unfounded rumours, she told herself virtuously. Nor did she mention it now.

Donald had won the game and seemed disinclined to start another. 'Let's take a turn round the garden,' he suggested, pushing back his chair. 'It's quite mild for the time of year. We can wrap up warmly.'

'Sensible idea, my boy,' boomed his father, who had woken up and overheard. 'Do you young people good to get away from us old fogeys for a bit. But mind Eve puts her coat and hat on. Can't have her catching a cold.'

The formal gardens, a riot of colour in spring and summer, looked unkempt and lifeless under the pale winter sun, the lawns uncut, the flower-beds frost-bound and the trees reaching skyward with leafless, twisted limbs. Only the evergreen shrubs and the skilfully shaped box hedges stood as they always did, a tribute to the skill and permanence of Jack Robbs, Arthur's head gardener, too old for call-up and working nowadays almost singlehanded to keep everything in trim.

Donald took Eve's arm as he guided her down the terrace steps and across the grass. Beyond the gap in the hedge was Mabel's rose garden, out of sight of the drawing-room windows. The high green walls had barely enclosed them from view before her cousin suddenly stopped and seized Eve in an embrace which seemed to crush the breath from her body.

'Marry me, Eve.'

She was so astonished that she was unable even to struggle. 'What?' she demanded unflatteringly.

'Marry me. I love you.'

'Donald, I . . . I don't know what to say. I mean, I had no idea . . . We're first cousins.'

'So? Lots of first cousins get married. Most of the royal couples of Europe are related to one another. Father and Aunt Helena would be delighted.'

Gently, Eve managed to free herself. 'Is that why you want to marry me? To please Uncle Arthur?'

'No, of course not. Not altogether. I've always been fond of you and this place needs an heir.' His eyes grew haunted. 'And if this war goes on much longer, God only knows if I'll survive it.'

'There's Ernest,' she reminded him.

He laughed, but there was no mirth in the sound. 'Ernest! He's in such a mess, I doubt if he'll ever have children.' He grabbed her once again, pressing her face to the rough tweed of his overcoat. 'We could get a special licence. We could be married before I have to go back next week!'

For the second time, Eve forced him away. 'I'm sorry, Donald,' she said a little breathlessly, 'but I can't. I'm very honoured and all that, but I don't love you, and I don't really believe that you love me. I want to go to university. I want to teach. These things are important to me.' She suppressed the knowledge that her ambitions would have counted for nothing at all had Frank ever asked her to marry him.

'You can't mean that!' he exclaimed angrily. 'You can't mean you'd rather be a schoolmarm than mistress of Abbey Court.'

Her contrition vanished. 'Yes, I do mean it. And if you loved me as you say you do, you'd try to understand. But you don't love me; you just want to please your father and provide this place with an heir. Well, there must be lots of other girls who'd be only too pleased to be your wife. Ask one of them instead.'

'I don't want to marry anyone else. I want to marry you. You're a Burfoot. Our family has owned the land hereabouts for generations. Staple Abbots means something to you. I believe in the blood-tie. At any rate, say you'll get engaged,' he pleaded. 'Knowing you're here waiting for me will be something to look forward to next time I come on leave.'

He looked so haggard, so desperate that, for a brief moment, Eve was almost persuaded to say 'Yes'. Everyone except her father and Aunt Josephine would be delighted, and life would be so straightforward. She was also as certain as she could be that, in time, Rose would become her sister-in-law; and Eve had a momentary vision of rose-scented summers and fire-warmed winters; leisurely, post-war, halcyon days. And Frank would be back in Staple Abbots, living with Jenny and his child . . .

'No, Donald,' she said. 'I'm sorry. I don't want to get engaged, either. Can we go in now, please? I'm getting cold.' And she made for the gap in the hedge.

Her cousin caught her by the arm and swung her round to face him.

'I've put it badly. You think I asked you to marry me because Father wants it. Well, all right, he does, but that's not the reason. I want it, too. More than anything. I mean it, Eve.'

He looked so much in earnest that she could no longer doubt his sincerity, and cast about in her mind for a way to turn him down without causing him too much pain.

'Donald, I really am fond of you. It's just that . . . I feel I'm too young yet to settle down. I . . . I need to spread my wings. Look!' She gave an encouraging smile and despised herself for raising hopes which she suspected would never be fulfilled. 'Ask me again in a few years' time, when I've had the chance to do the things I want.' She patted his hand with a forced optimism. 'You'll come through the war all right. I feel it in my bones.' What liars awkward situations made of people, she reflected guiltily. 'This isn't going to be our last meeting by any means.'

He stared hard at her before releasing her arm. 'You promise you'll think about it? And you'll go on writing to me at the Front?'

'Of course! I promise. So let's go in.'

He nodded, apparently satisfied, and they returned to the house. As they re-entered the drawing-room, Eve saw the exchange of glances between her cousin and uncle, and the disappointed frown on the latter's face at Donald's slight shake of the head.

*

The last two terms at Mayfields Academy passed like a dream, in which all the turmoil of Eve's mind was subjugated in work. Indeed, so hard did she apply herself that Miss Milward warned her against the danger of a nervous breakdown.

'You know what they say, my child, about all work and no play.' Eve was now chief prefect, and took tea each Sunday with the headmistress and her sister. Miss Milward thought for a moment before enquiring, somewhat diffidently for so forthright a woman, 'That young man who came to see you last year ... Is everything all right with him? I ask because you did mention later that he had enlisted.'

'As far as I know he is still unwounded,' Eve replied tranquilly, replacing the delicate bone china cup in its saucer. 'His wife gave birth to a baby daughter in March. I think she called her Virginia.'

'What a pretty name,' enthused Miss Emily. She heaved a sentimental sigh. 'All our young men! So brave. So brave.'

Her sister made no comment and changed the subject. The young man had been married, then! No wonder Dr and Mrs Gilchrist had nipped that particular romance in the bud. And her star pupil's apparent recovery, heart-whole and fancy-free, did not fool Miss Milward for a minute. All the hard work of these past three terms – hard work which had resulted in Eve matriculating not only in mathematics, English grammar and History but also in French, Latin, geography and English literature – had been her way of trying to forget. Ah, well! It was an ill wind that blew nobody any good. Eve was assured of a place at Bristol University and the Academy could chalk up its most spectacular success to date.

But Flora Milward was genuinely fond of Eve and hoped that no lasting scar had been left by the unfortunate affair. Young girls were so vulnerable; but she comforted herself with the knowledge that they were also extremely resilient. Nevertheless, she gave Eve an unprecedented hug when she said her final goodbye.

'My word, you are honoured,' Rose observed, as they climbed into the school carriage which would convey them into Salisbury and the station.

Eve did not answer. She was thinking that Frank must surely be due for some leave, and that she might get a glimpse of him when he came home.

It was a fortnight later when the village learned that Frank Mailer had been killed.

Part Two
1922–1935

Chapter Eleven

The dawn chorus woke Eve at four o'clock, when it was already light, and for the past two hours she had tossed restlessly, unable to sleep again. She heard the milkman arrive at Holly Lodge, the clash of churns, the rattle of wheels and the slow clip-clop of his horse's hooves as he made his way along the row of houses which fronted the wide, open spaces of the Downs. The paper boy delivered the dailies – the *Manchester Guardian* for Aunt Josie, the *Daily Sketch* for herself – at half-past-five, propping his bicycle against the wall and clumping up the garden path in his hobnailed boots, whistling one of Marie Lloyd's old music-hall tunes. As always, he left the gate open, and this morning a slight breeze blowing from the direction of the Avon Gorge made it swing on its hinges with an irritating squeak. The flow of traffic gradually increased, the ever-growing number of motor cars adding their noise to that of the carts and drays already on the road.

At six, abandoning all attempt at sleep, Eve got up, ran a comb through her still unbobbed hair, slipped her dressing-gown around her shoulders and went to perch on the broad window-sill. On the opposite side of the road the Downs, stretching in both directions, were dotted with trees and bushes, all wearing their tender summer green: a serenely beautiful picture, in stark contrast to the grime and chaos of the William Penn Road School where Eve would find herself in three hours' time, under the basilisk eye of Miss Hannah Perry.

Leaning back against one of the folded window shutters, Eve contemplated the present unsatisfactory state of her life, fighting off the memories of Frank which rose to haunt her

151

whenever she was alone. And not only alone; in a crowded
room, on a tramcar, in church, the sudden turn of a head, a
half-glimpsed profile, the echo of a laugh would recall him
vividly to mind. But she wouldn't think about him now or
she might cry and redden her eyes, inviting a rebuke from
the headmistress.

'Burning the candle at both ends, are we, Miss Gilchrist?'
the hated voice would snap. 'It won't do! It won't do at all.
We at the William Penn Road Junior School expect one
hundred per cent commitment from our teachers.'

Eve chewed her lower lip, twisting a strand of auburn hair
between her fingers. She would have liked to cut it, as was
fashionable, but Miss Perry had definite rules on hair style
and dress, and woe betide those teachers who contravened
them. If it wasn't for coming home every evening to Holly
Lodge and darling Aunt Josie, Eve believed that she would
have thrown in her hand long ago and returned to Staple
Abbots to marry her cousin Donald. What had happened to
all those wonderful plans she had made when she left
Mayfields Academy?'

'It's your own fault. You should have tried for Oxford,' her
aunt had told her. 'You have the brains for it. And don't start
making excuses. I know you, Eve. You lack confidence and
were afraid you'd be up against too much competition. You
thought that at Bristol you'd have a greater chance to shine,
and you could live with me rather than in Hall. But it was
a shortsighted policy, my dear, as things turned out. Oxford
would have given you contacts which, with the present
dearth of teaching jobs, would have ensured you a post at a
grammar school, which is where you ought to be.'

'Don't scold,' Eve had pleaded, close to tears. 'It's easy to
be wise after the event.' And Aunt Josie had at once
embraced her and apologized.

But she was right, of course. Eve had flouted Miss
Milward's advice to try for Oxford because she had funked
competing with girls who might prove to be much brighter
than herself. Moreover, after Frank's death she had craved the

warmth of familiar faces and lodgings. Bristol had not been a good choice, however. University life had proved disappointing, rather like an extension of school instead of the new and exciting experience that it should have been. To begin with, her year had boasted only four male students, all ex-servicemen and living at home, two with wives and children. Furthermore, three years ago the university was still recovering from the effects of the war, and although construction was now proceeding apace, most of the buildings which Eve and her fellows had to use were of necessity makeshift. The three lecture rooms of any dignity were borrowed from the nearby Baptist College; the rest were ex-Army huts, and the Students' Union functioned from a dilapidated church hall. The library was below ground level. No catering was available, and every meal meant either a journey home, sandwiches or a restaurant. So, all in all, she had spent three years of semi-frustration, but with the prospect of a decent post in a grammar school at the end of them.

Then, like mist on a mountain-top, the post-war economic boom had evaporated, leaving in its wake a slowly deepening depression and far more teachers than local authorities could afford to accommodate. Eve had applied for every grammar school vacancy in the Bristol area, but with so many candidates vying for each job on offer she had been unlucky. She had even tried as far afield as Manchester and Norwich in pursuit of jobs advertised in the *Times Educational Supplement*, but without success, losing out to local candidates. One sympathetic headmistress had advised her to make use of any influential contacts she might have among school governors, but Eve knew no one; and it was at that point that she almost threw in the towel and went home. However, the thought of her mother's and Aunt Hetty's spurious condolences, her father's disappointment and, above all, Uncle Arthur's gloating triumph at her failure, caused her to grit her teeth and go on.

'If it's money you're worrying about, don't,' Josephine

said. 'I'm quite happy for you to go on living here, rent-free, for as long as you need. I love having you. I don't want you to leave.'

Eve kissed her aunt gratefully. 'But I can't expect you and Papa to support me for ever. I've trained to be a teacher and I want to teach. What alternative is there for me, except marriage?'

'Ah! We're back to Donald Burfoot again.' Aunt Josie had shaken her head. 'Don't do it, Eve! Don't marry a man you're not in love with as a solution to any problem. Be patient. Something will turn up soon.'

And something had; a vacancy at the William Penn Road Elementary School.

'You can't apply for that!' her aunt had protested, horrified. 'Apart from the fact that you're over-qualified, William Penn Road is in a most insalubrious part of the city.'

'If I have to lower my sights in order to work, then I have to,' was the philosophical answer. And Eve had shut herself in her room to write out yet another interview application.

And this time, unfortunately, she had been successful; unfortunately because the martinet headmistress, Hannah Perry, had taken an even greater dislike to Eve than to the other members of her staff, and regarded her with deep suspicion.

'Don't think you're better than the rest of us, just because you've been to university,' she said on Eve's first morning. 'You won't find that cuts much ice at William Penn Road.'

Most of the teachers treated Eve with an equal contempt, partly because they were afraid of Miss Perry and terrified of losing their jobs, and partly because they too genuinely resented her. To add to her misery, Eve discovered that in the overcrowded school, where every class numbered over fifty pupils, they had run out of classrooms and Standard Three, to which she was assigned, had to use one half of the assembly hall, where the headmistress had her desk. This meant that she was constantly under Miss Perry's hostile gaze, and her discipline, as well as her teaching methods, was frequently called into question. The children, sensing that in this case misbehaviour did not necessarily earn them the cane, and that Miss Perry in fact quite enjoyed having a go at Miss Gilchrist, played up for all they were worth. Had it not been for a few bright pupils, genuinely anxious to learn, and one boy in particular, Arnold Bailey, Eve felt that she would surely have handed in her notice at the end of the first four weeks. As it was, she had now stuck it out for six months and fully intended to carry on at least until she had done her best to get Arnold into grammar school, where he eventually deserved to be. The obstacle to this was the boy's widowed mother, who wanted him out to work as soon as he left school in four years' time ...

'Miss Eve? What are you doing out of bed at this hour?' Clarrie Goodyear, Josephine's maid-of-all-work, came into the bedroom, balancing the early morning tea-tray on one arm and holding open the door with the opposite hand. 'Couldn't you sleep?'

Eve slid off the window-sill. 'The paper boy left the gate open. It creaks.'

'Dratted boy! I'll put some soap on its hinges.' And on this enigmatic note, Clarrie took herself off to her mistress's room, having first handed Eve her cup of tea. 'Breakfast at half-seven sharp,' she added over her shoulder.

This early start was necessary for Eve to catch the two tramcars which took her to William Penn Road. She had firmly rejected her aunt's generous offer to buy her one of the new little Austin Sevens.

'If I turned up in a car, that really would put the cat among the pigeons. No one would ever speak to me again. It would convince Miss Perry that I'm a fast hussy, unfit to teach in her school, and the rest of the staff would bitterly resent the fact that I could afford it. Darling Aunt Josie, keep your money for a rainy day.'

'I'm sixty-four,' Josephine had retorted drily. 'I've had all my rainy days. And I'm extremely comfortably off, thanks to the Mortons. My publishers have just started reprinting some of the earlier books, so the royalties will be rolling in yet awhile, and you're my only heir. You might as well let me spend some of the money on you now, while I'm alive to see you enjoy it.'

But Eve resolutely declined, still breakfasting at seven-thirty, still travelling to William Penn Road by tram. There were mornings such as this, however, feeling tired and depressed, when Eve wished she had the courage to accept the offer. She finished washing, brushed and pinned up the long auburn hair, dressed herself in the knee-length navy skirt and long-sleeved navy-and-white striped cotton blouse which she wore for school – bare arms were not permitted, however hot the day – and went downstairs to the kitchen, where she and Clarrie ate together. Later, she went to say goodbye to Aunt Josie, who did not get up until ten.

'I hope things are a little better today, my dear,' her aunt said, propped against her banked-up pillows. It was her usual morning wish.

Eve kissed the proffered cheek. 'I'm sure they will be.' It was her customary reply, but today it made Josephine chuckle.

'The English must drive other nations mad. All this stiff upper-lip nonsense. Why can't we show emotion? Why don't we rail against fate as any decent Frenchman or Italian would do? Why can't we lie on the ground, drum our heels and froth at the mouth like any right-minded Spaniard?'

Eve laughed, put on her hat and gloves and picked up her handbag. 'I suppose you and I could always start a trend.'

*

William Penn Road School stood at the end of a row of grimy terraced houses which abutted on to the main Bristol to South Wales railway line. On the other side of the street was a coalyard, and the narrow roadway was frequently blocked by the heavy carts and big Shire horses waiting for their loads. Coal-dust permeated everything, blackening the façade of every building and seeping into cracks caused by the constant vibration of passing trains. The school, like the houses, was badly in need of repair, and one of the chimney-pots tilted at a crazy angle on top of the gabled roof.

Eve pushed open the gate in the iron palings and made her way to the door marked 'Staff Entrance'. The playground was as yet only sparsely populated, most of the children living close enough to the school to postpone arrival until almost the final bell. But a dozen or more were playing hopscotch and giant-strides, or simply chasing one another, shrieking loudly, around the twenty or so square yards of concrete and gravel. She noted that she was not the first teacher to arrive, Bill Hutton's bicycle being already propped against the wall of the cycle-shed. A married man with a wife and five children, all of them crowded into a tiny two-bedroomed house, Eve suspected that he found marking and preparing lessons difficult at home, and came to school early for a bit of peace and quiet.

She was about to push open the door and go inside when she heard the clatter of boots across the playground and a hand grabbed her sleeve.

'Miss! Please, Miss, can I speak to you a moment?'

She turned to find Arnold Bailey at her elbow. He was a big, handsome boy of ten, with a thatch of light brown hair and widely spaced, very clear grey eyes. Even his much patched and too-small clothes could not detract from his general well-fed appearance. For unlike less fortunate classmates, Arnold's mother worked in a bakery and was able to bring home stale bread and cakes, sold to employees at greatly reduced prices. Moreover, Arnold was the only child, so there were no hungry brothers and sisters to share the pickings.

'Arnie!' Eve smiled encouragingly. 'What can I do for you?'

'I wanted to know when you were comin' round to speak to me Ma, Miss, like you said. You know, 'bout me trying for a grammar school place.'

Guiltily, Eve realized that it was some weeks now since she had made the promise, but had done no more about it, mainly because she was always so tired by the time four o'clock arrived. But she could not shirk her responsibilities for much longer. Suppressing a sigh, she asked, 'Would tonight be convenient?'

Arnie nodded. 'Ma's on late shift this week, so she'll be home teatime. Shall I wait for you after lessons then, Miss? By the gate? We only lives just down the road.'

'Yes. That'll be fine.'

A peremptory voice spoke from behind them. 'Arnold Bailey! What are you doing in the girls' playground? Get back to your own side immediately! Ah, Miss Gilchrist. I might have known you would have your finger in the pie somewhere.' Miss Perry, her ample form heavily encased in dark grey flannel in spite of the warmth of the day, looked coldly at Eve. 'School rules are not made to be broken, and I should have thought you would have better things to occupy your time than encouraging pupils to do so. A little more work preparation would not come amiss. Your geography lesson yesterday was very slapdash.'

The colour flooded Eve's cheeks. The woman was outrageous. She had no right to reprimand a member of staff in front of one of the children, and Eve could only be thankful that the child in question was Arnold Bailey. She could be fairly certain that he would say nothing, but there were many others who would be only too delighted to spread the story. Furthermore the reprimand was gratuitous, as Miss Perry must be fully aware, the class having been quiet for the entire forty minutes of the lesson, unexpectedly interested in what they were learning.

Biting back the angry retort which rose to her lips, Eve said quietly, 'I'll try to remember that, Headmistress.'

'Do so!' Miss Perry swept ahead of her, like a galleon in full sail. Eve followed.

The interior of the school smelled, as always, of chalk and drains, ink powder and unwashed clothes. There was also a strong scent of ammonia from the chemical works half a mile away. The corridor walls, divided by a horizontal black line into halves of dark and light green, showed peeling paint dimmed by the grime of years.

'What did Arnold Bailey want?' Miss Perry demanded, entering the staff cloakroom while Eve held open the door.

'I promised to have a word with his mother about him sitting the scholarship exam. He's a bright boy; he shouldn't have any difficulty getting a grammar school place.' Eve removed her hat thankfully; it was giving her a headache.

The headmistress's bosom swelled with anger. Her eyes were like flint.

'How *dare* you! You, a junior mistress here, to presume to take such a task upon yourself! What can you possibly know, after a mere six months, about the abilities and domestic circumstances of our pupils?' Miss Perry gave a mirthless snort. 'You know nothing! Nothing! And in this particular case, I first of all question your judgement of Arnold's capability. I have always found him a singularly obtuse and stubborn child. Secondly, it's obvious that you have no knowledge of his home affairs. Mrs Bailey is a widow who could not possibly afford to send her son to grammar school.'

'But if he won a scholarship—' Eve protested, but was ruthlessly interrupted.

'That's exactly the kind of remark I'd expect from someone like you, who has never known financial hardship.' The tone grew more sneering, more vindictive. 'Mayfields Academy, wasn't it? Flora and Emily Milward!' Miss Perry almost spat the words. 'Everything paid for by Papa! Let me tell you, my girl, that winning a scholarship is just the beginning. There's still uniform, books, travelling expenses. Oh, believe me, I know what I'm talking about!'

The little eyes in the puffy cheeks were, by now, mere slits, but Eve caught a gleam of pure hatred in them. Suddenly she felt sorry for Hannah Perry. She realized that all her life, she herself had taken for granted things that a lot

of other people had to struggle for. Nevertheless, she refused
to be intimidated. Arnold was a clever boy who deserved a
chance, and she was going to do everything in her power to
see that he got it. But she wasn't going to argue about it.

She answered submissively, 'Yes, Headmistress.'

*

'Ma, this is Miss Gilchrist. I told you she was coming. She
wants to speak to you.'

Fortunately for Eve, Miss Perry had been detained at the
final bell by Mr Hutton with some query concerning the
timetable, so she had been able to keep her tryst with Arnold
without being seen. It was only a few steps from the school
to his house, and within a couple of minutes Eve found
herself standing in a dark, stuffy passageway, such daylight
as there was filtering through the dirty glass panel above the
front door. Immediately ahead of her the staircase mounted
to the bedrooms, and a foot or two further on a door opened
into the kitchen where Mrs Bailey was waiting, having been
warned by her son at dinner-time to expect a visitor. She
smiled nervously and wiped one hand on her apron before
holding it out to Eve.

'How d'you do, Miss, I'm sure. Please . . . Sit down.'

She indicated one of the chairs standing beside a plain deal
table, over which hung a framed print of Holman Hunt's
'The Light of the World'. Eve did as she was bidden,
clutching her handbag and gloves, every bit as ill-at-ease as
her reluctant hostess.

'Mrs Bailey, I . . . I want to talk to you about Arnold.
About him sitting the scholarship examination to get a
grammar school place. He could, you know, easily. He's very
bright.'

'Say I can, Ma! Say I can!'

Mrs Bailey frowned at her son. 'You keep out o' this,
Arnie. Look, Miss, the boy knows as well as I do that I can't
afford to go sending him to one of these fancy schools. It

might've been different if 'is Pa were still alive, but he isn't, God rest him, so there we are. I earn enough to keep us both fed and clothed decent and pay the rent, without falling behind and getting dunned by the debt collectors, like some of the poor souls round here, and for that I'm thankful. But it's a struggle, and I don't deny I'm praying for the day when Arnie's fourteen and can get out to work.'

Eve was daunted by the argument, but not yet defeated. In response to an imploring look from Arnold, she tried again.

'Mrs Bailey, if you'll forgive me for saying so, I think that's very shortsighted. With a secondary education, Arnold can eventually get a much better job than he can without it. He's clever, he's very good at arithmetic. He deserves more than just working in the coal-yard.'

'Oh, I don't mean for 'im to go into the coal-yard.' Mrs Bailey was triumphant in her denial. 'I intend for him to have a job with prospects. Mr Wilbraham, round at the sweet-shop, he knows someone who'll get him an interview with the Post Office. Arnie'll have to start as a messenger boy, of course, but 'e'll get a good, serviceable uniform and a pair o' stout boots provided, five bob a week and an extra ha'penny for every telegram he delivers. And later on, he can sit an exam for promotion to postman or desk clerk.'

'But ...' Eve found herself floundering, then rallied gamely as she encountered yet another look of silent appeal from Arnold. 'He could do so much better than that, Mrs Bailey. He could go on to university; he could become a doctor or a teacher.'

But Eve knew at once that with the mention of university, she had said the wrong thing.

'No,' Mrs Bailey said flatly. 'It can't be done. it would cost money, Miss, with maybe another ten years before he's earning. It's out of the question.' She got to her feet, smoothing down her apron. 'And I'd be grateful if you'd stop filling up 'is head with all this nonsense. And if he's half as clever as you say he is, 'e won't have no trouble passing the

Post Office exams and getting on. Meanwhile, he'll be earning. Good afternoon to you. Arnie'll see you out.'

'Ma!' Arnold pleaded desperately, seizing his mother's arm. 'I don't want to work in the Post Office. I want to go to grammar school. Can't you understand? I want to learn more than they can teach me at William Penn Road.'

'Your son enjoys learning, Mrs Bailey,' Eve added in support, 'and it's not so common in a child of his age that we can afford to ignore it. On people like him depends the future greatness of this country.'

Mrs Bailey wavered momentarily, seeing her son in a new and visionary light, but common sense prevailed and she regretfully shook her head.

'No, Miss. I'm sorry, but there it is. I can't afford to send him, and that's all there is to it, I'm afraid.'

Eve stood up and pulled on her gloves, but she had one last card to play.

'If . . . if I could arrange for all Arnold's necessary expenses to be paid for – if he got to grammar school that is – so that it wouldn't cost you anything extra, would you be prepared to let him sit the scholarship then?'

'Ma?' Arnold breathed hopefully, after a pause.

'Charity, you mean?' Mrs Bailey was suspicious.

'No. Well, yes . . . no, not really.' Eve took a deep breath and began again. 'I have an aunt who, I feel sure, if I asked her, would be willing to help your son. She has no children of her own and she likes young people.' Eve was talking very fast now, trying to get the words out before she was interrupted. 'It would be a kind of loan. She could keep an account of all she spends on Arnold and . . . and he could pay her back in years to come, when he's earning. At least, before you say a final no, let me talk to my aunt about it and see what she says. If she doesn't agree, well, that's the end of the matter. But I feel sure she will, and in that case would you think about allowing him to sit the scholarship exam?'

There was another silence, while Eve and Arnold held their breath. At last, Mrs Bailey gave a defeated sigh.

'All right. As Arnie wants it so bad, you can ask your aunt. If she's got a hap'orth o' sense, she'll say no. But if she doesn't, I promise I'll think about it. Oh, get off, Arnie, do!' she added, as her son whooped with delight and flung his arms around her neck. 'And now you'll have to excuse me, Miss, or I'll be late for the evening shift, and if he's going to stay on at school for all them extra years, I can't afford to get the sack, now can I?'

Chapter Twelve

'So, if you could possibly see your way, Aunt Josie ... I mean, you did say you wanted to, well, spend some of your money on me now, and ... this is the way I'd ... like it spent, if it's all right by you.' Eve finished in a rush, staring down at the hands clasped in her lap and not daring to raise her eyes.

Supper – for it would have been over-dignifying Clarrie's homely evening meals to call them dinner – was finished and cleared away. Aunt and niece were sitting contentedly in front of the open drawing-room window, drinking coffee and watching the nightly parade of courting couples across the Downs, the girls in calf-length summer dresses, displaying more leg than had ever been shown before, clad in shiny stockings of artificial silk. A few of the young men had dared to remove their coats, and were enjoying the sunny June weather in their shirt-sleeves. If Aunt Josie were shocked, as surely her sister would have been, she was concealing it very well.

She put down her cup and saucer on the little marquetry-inlaid table beside her armchair. There was silence for a moment or two after Eve had come to the end of her stumbling request.

'Why do you especially wish me to help this young man?' she asked at last. 'I accept that he's probably a deserving case, but there are plenty of those. Is it that he reminds you of Frank?'

'He's nothing like Frank!' Eve protested quickly. 'Arnold Bailey's big and fair, whereas Frank was ... was ...'

'Small and dark,' her aunt concluded for her. 'Almost foreign-looking, I always thought. But I'd gathered that from your description. I meant in his situation in life: the bright boy who should be given a chance, instead of being

164

strait-jacketed by his circumstances.'

'Yes. Yes, I suppose so.'

Josephine regarded her niece speculatively. 'You're very reluctant to talk about Frank and your feelings for him. What are you afraid of?'

A young couple strolled by on the other side of the road, their arms entwined and gazing adoringly into one another's eyes. Eve swallowed the dregs of her coffee and put down her cup and saucer with a hand that shook.

'I'm not afraid,' she denied a shade too vehemently. 'There doesn't seem any point in talking about him. He's dead. As far as I'm concerned, there's nothing of him left. It's Jenny who has the only memento of him worth having, his child.'

'Ah!' Josephine nodded thoughtfully. 'You're still hurting. His death should have evened things out between you and Jenny, but he gave her his daughter, and you can't forgive him for that.'

The sun was sinking towards the west, enmeshing the tree-tops in a web of gold. The dying rays slanted in through the window, touching the room with fire.

'He came to Mayfields to see me,' Eve said in a low voice, 'after he'd volunteered to serve. He told me he loved me. I was ready to run away with him if only he'd agreed. Then, the first thing I heard when I arrived home for the summer vacation was that Jenny was pregnant. Do you know, for a long time I couldn't bring myself to believe that it was Frank's baby? I thought Jenny might have been with some other man. After all, she'd lied to him before. But the minute I saw Virginia, I knew she was his child. Even when she was tiny, she was the spitting image of Frank; small and dark and with great brown eyes. She's got nothing in her of Jenny at all.'

Josephine reached out a hand to smooth Eve's bowed head, then withdrew it, afraid that sympathy might be unwelcome.

'Marcus didn't tell me about the visit to Mayfields. Or didn't he know about it? No. I see. And you're still confused. You're not sure whether Frank really loved you or not.'

Eve raised her head at last and lay back in the chair, letting herself relax. She closed her eyes, watching great bursts of red and orange roll up under her lids.

'I don't think he knew, either, and that's what hurts most of all. Poor Frank. He didn't know whether he wanted me enough to risk the problems which would have followed our marriage, or a quiet life with a girl his parents and Uncle Arthur approved of, with a cottage and a secure job.'

There was yet another silence before Josephine said gently, 'I'm glad we've had this talk. At least I now understand, a little, your feelings about Frank Mailer.' This time she did reach out and give Eve's hand a squeeze. 'I could tell you you'll get over him, that someone else will undoubtedly come along, but I might be wrong. So I'll just quote Shakespeare, that man for all seasons, and remind you that "time and the hour run through the roughest day."' She drew a deep breath. 'So now, let's discuss this young lad you want to help. Are you sure his mother's really willing to accept my aid?'

*

Miss Perry was literally gibbering with fury. It did not matter to her in the least that fifty pairs of ears were listening at the other end of the room. From the moment she had crashed open the double doors leading into the assembly hall and mounted the rostrum to her desk, it was obvious that something out of the ordinary had happened to enrage her.

'Miss Gilchrist!'

Eve, who had paused in mid-sentence at the head-mistress's noisy entry, felt her heart sink. What on earth had she done now to be the target of such displeasure? She murmured to the class, 'Get on and read to the bottom of page three,' but without any hope of being attended to. Quaking, she approached the desk. 'Yes, Headmistress?'

There were red flecks in the steely blue eyes. You dare . . . You *dare* stand there and say , "Yes Headmistress?" as though butter wouldn't melt in your mouth! Do you know who I've just spoken to? *Do* you?' The voice had risen almost to a screech and Eve could only stare, too terrified to speak. 'Mrs Bailey! Arnold is to sit the scholarship exam, it seems, and if he passes, you—' here, just for a blessed moment, the voice became suspended while its owner fought with her emotions '—you are taking the burden of expense upon yourself! How *dared* you go behind my back? Just because you have the benefit of a university education' – spittle flecked Miss Perry's lips – 'you imagine that gives you the right to interfere! To usurp my prerogative as head of this school. Well, my girl, you'll soon learn differently, believe me. I am reporting you to the Board of Governors.'

Eve had stopped listening. Her concern was all for Arnold.

'But if Mrs Bailey wants her son to sit the exam, you can't prevent him.'

Miss Perry turned crimson. She seemed to swell until Eve was afraid that she was going to have a fit.

'No, I can't prevent him,' she hissed, 'but I can stop you behaving as if you run this school, and that's what I intend to do. I shall write a letter to the chairman of the Governors forthwith. This very morning! And until the hearing, you will be suspended. Collect your things and leave at once!'

'You can't do that,' Eve protested, but got no further.

'I am the headmistress. I am empowered to use my judgement if I consider a teacher to be unsuitable, and I consider you to be highly unsuitable, so go!'

Eve saw there was no point in arguing, but her legs were trembling so much that she could barely move. She forced herself, however, to walk to the other end of the hall where the children, white-faced and unnaturally silent, were sitting at their desks, hardly daring to breathe. Normally they would have been giggling and whispering and nudging one another, but Miss Perry's outburst had petrified them. Eve encountered Arnold's look of desperate enquiry and nodded reassuringly before gathering up her handbag and attaché case.

Once outside, she began to feel faint and paused for a moment by the gate, hanging on to the playground railings. A concerned voice spoke beside her. 'You all right, Miss Gilchrist?'

'Oh, Mrs Bailey. I didn't see you there. Yes, I'm fine now. I just felt dizzy for a moment.'

'Not surprised, dealing with that lot all day.' The other woman jerked her head towards the classroom windows. 'By the way, I've been to see Miss Perry. I told 'er I wanted our Arnie to sit the scholarship and that your aunt was kindly footing the bills.' Mrs Bailey chuckled. 'She wasn't best pleased, but I suppose you can't blame her.'

'Can't you?'

'Oh, no. It's her brother-in-law, you know, what's head of the Senior Boys' School, and he gets paid according to the number of pupils. Still,' was the cheerful rider, 'that's life, isn't it? Snakes and ladders. Ups and downs. Mind you thank your aunt again for all she's doing. Arnie's in his seventh heaven, though it beats me why. I never saw much to book learning, myself. I'll be seeing you then, Miss. Got to go now. I'm on afternoon shift at the bakery.'

And she was gone, more determinedly cheerful than Eve had previously seen her, finally reconciled to the fact that Arnold was going to stay on at school at least until the age of eighteen and then, maybe, try for a place at university. Still dubious when Eve had invited her and Arnold to tea at Holly Lodge to meet Josephine, she had arrived in a truculent mood, prepared to be the object of condescension; instead, she and her hostess had immediately taken to each other, and by the end of the afternoon were chatting away like long-lost friends. Arnold, too, had been delighted to discover that his benefactress was none other than the author of some of his favourite books, borrowed over and over again from the small school library. When they left, Mrs Bailey was happy to be accepting help from Josephine Gilchrist. Indeed, she had allowed herself to be persuaded that *she* was the one conferring the favour.

When Eve let herself into Holly Lodge shortly before lunch-time, Clarrie was just coming out of the kitchen.

'Lord, Miss Evie! What're you doing home this time of day? T'isn't a half-holiday, is it?'

Eve removed her hat and dropped her handbag and case on one of the hall chairs. 'Is my aunt about?'

'She's sat down in the dining-room, waiting for her lunch. You'd best join her. I'll lay another place.'

By the time Clarrie came back with the necessary cutlery and china, Eve had put her aunt in possession of the facts and the reason for her early return home. Josephine was out-raged.

'You're not going to take this lying down, Eve? You're going to fight it? You aren't thinking of tamely handing in your resignation, surely?'

Eve sighed, picking up her soup spoon as Clarrie set a bowl of home-made chicken broth in front of her.

'I must admit it had crossed my mind. Wouldn't it be the best solution all round? It will save a lot of aggravation, and at least I shall have left of my own accord, not been dismissed with ignominy.'

'Who says you're going to be dismissed?' Josephine demanded. 'You haven't done anything wrong. In fact, you haven't done anything at all except persuade a boy's mother to let him sit the scholarship exam. There's no crime in that. A good teacher must have the interests of her pupils at heart.'

'I don't suppose the School Governors will see it like that. I'm willing to bet they're all friends and supporters of Miss Perry. I know for a fact that the chairman is; I think he's her cousin.'

'Which is no doubt how she got the position in the first place.' Josephine frowned angrily. 'But they can't all be on her side; there has to be someone on the Board open to sense and reason. If you resign, it will be playing straight into that woman's hands. I'm willing to bet my last farthing that that's exactly what she's hoping you'll do, and then she won't have to appear vindictive and spiteful in front of anyone.'

Eve hesitated, suddenly feeling very tired as she began to relax after the trauma of the morning. It would be so simple just to resign. She would never have to return to William Penn Road Junior School, never have to face its Board of Governors. She could go home to Staple Abbots for a holiday: she could almost smell the scent of new-mown grass and the flowers in the cottage gardens, hear the birds singing in the trees and the jingle of harness. And Rose, she knew, was there at present, staying at Abbey Court. Helena's last letter had hinted excitedly at the news of a possible engagement. Dear Rose, how uncomplicated her life seemed compared with Eve's. She had known what she wanted from the age of fourteen, when she first set eyes on Ernest. Since leaving Mayfields Academy four years earlier she had been a lady of leisure, living at home with her parents in London or spending protracted holidays with the Burfoots. And although, initially, Arthur had been somewhat contemptuous of her connections with trade – even if Druitt's 'Famous Pork Pies' and 'Superior Pork Sausages' did grace his own table – his younger son's obvious fondness for Rose, coupled with Ernest's precarious state of health at the end of the war, had long ago predisposed him in her favour. So Eve, as well as everyone else, guessed that it was merely a matter of time and her cousin's fitness before the couple married.

'We could make it a double wedding,' Eve thought. 'Rose and Ernest, myself and Donald.' For Donald made it quite plain in his letters that he still wanted to marry her, and frequently reminded her of the promise she had made to reconsider his offer in a few years' time. It would so delight Mama and Uncle Arthur, and be the answer to all her problems.

It would also be the coward's way out and, in the long term, solve nothing. She did not love Donald and, furthermore, had discovered in herself a genuine ability for teaching. She had the knack of making lessons interesting, and so was able to hold the attention of a class. She liked her job. Was she going to throw everything away simply because she did not have the guts for a fight? And Aunt Josie was right. She had done nothing to be ashamed of.

She finished her chicken broth and laid down her spoon.

'There's no need to look so worried,' she smiled at Josephine. 'I'm not going to resign. I'll wait for my summons and then put my case to the Governors.'

*

'Come in, Miss Gilchrist. We're ready for you now.'

The disciplinary hearing was being held in the head-mistress's study at the Senior Girls' School, just round the corner from the Juniors' in William Penn Road. The same smell of chalk and ink powder permeated the corridors, and an air of depression had settled over the building like a pall. The headmistress's study was as grey and forbidding as all the other rooms Eve had passed on her way upstairs. Even the roses in the vase on the window-ledge had a defeated appearance, and the strip of carpet in front of the desk was a bilious yellowish-green.

The five members of the Board were ranged around the desk, three behind it, with the chairman in the centre and the remaining two seated one on either side. Facing them was a solitary upright chair, placed squarely in the middle of the rug. As Eve entered the room, Miss Perry left it, giving her a blazing look of triumph as she passed. Eve's heart sank. No doubt she was already judged and condemned. She glanced at the five men opposite, searching for a sympathetic face.

She found it almost immediately. The man to the left of the desk was younger than the others, who all looked to be somewhere in their mid-fifties. But this one she judged to be a little over thirty. He had thick, fair wavy hair, pale blue eyes, was very tall and thin, and the right sleeve of his beautifully tailored navy-blue suit was encircled by a black mourning band. Most important of all, his expression was distinctly friendly. Eve was seized by the oddest conviction that they had met before, and could not understand why the sight of him brought Frank so vividly to mind. He smiled encouragingly at her as she sat down.

'Now, Miss Gilchrist, let's hear what you have to say for yourself, then. And make it brief. We haven't got all day.' The chairman's hostile attitude made it plain whose side he was on.

Eve felt more flustered than ever. Memories of Frank jostled around in her head, blotting out her carefully rehearsed arguments. She had intended to be so lucid: instead, she was reduced to a gibbering wreck, mesmerized by the wart on the side of the chairman's nose.

'I ... er ... I ...' she began, then stopped, unable to continue.

The young man learned forward in his chair, willing her to look at him. 'Miss Gilchrist,' he said gently, and his voice was deep and musical, 'please take your time. There is no need whatever for you to be hurried.' He glanced reprovingly at the chairman as he spoke, then returned his level gaze to Eve. 'Now, in your own words, but only when you're ready.'

She felt soothed. All her agitation and apprehension drained away and her Mayfields Academy training came to her rescue. She could almost hear Miss Milward's voice, whenever any girl was called upon by the headmistress to explain her conduct. 'Begin at the beginning, say what you have to say as clearly and concisely as possible, and stop as soon as you have finished. Don't make excuses, don't elaborate. Above all, don't try to influence me.'

So she told her side of the story as lucidly and as briefly as she could, without any attempt to vilify Miss Perry or justify her own actions. She simply recounted what she had done and why, her hands folded quietly in her lap, her eyes meeting those of the various members of the Board without embarrassment, but also without challenge. When she came to the end of her story, she waited.

There was silence, broken at last by the chairman's heavy tones.

'Perhaps you'd step outside, Miss Gilchrist, while I discuss the case with my colleagues. We'll inform you of our decision in a few minutes.'

Eve stood up. She had chosen to wear a pale grey linen suit and white silk blouse for the occasion, and with her auburn hair confined beneath a deep-crowned hat, looked far cooler than she felt. Before the door was properly closed behind her, she heard the chairman snort, 'A very calculating young woman, wouldn't you say, gentlemen? We've all met her kind.'

Eve sat down on one of the chairs in the corridor, listening to the muffled sounds of lessons going on in the classrooms. So that was that: the chairman was definitely against her and would no doubt influence his fellow Governors, with the possible exception of the friendly young man. But four to one meant dismissal, for the local Education Department would certainly heed the findings of the Board. She should have resigned, she shouldn't have listened to Aunt Josie. Oh well, it was too late now to repine.

Her thoughts returned to the friendly young man and the puzzle as to why he seemed familiar. Whenever it was that they had met, it had been a long time ago. She had the impression that he had been much younger, and herself no more than a child. Frank and Aunt Josie were also a part of the memory, and she recalled, too, a pungent smell. But of what? Eve shrugged and gave it up. It occurred to her that she had been sitting on this hard chair for longer than a few minutes, and was suddenly aware of raised voices behind the study door. An argument was taking place, and although she could hear nothing of what was being said it was obviously quite heated. The altercation died down, but it was at least another five minutes before the door opened and she was invited back inside.

The first thing she noticed was the chairman's face, registering anger and defeat. Her champion, on the other hand, was smiling broadly, while of the other three Governors two looked satisfied and only one appeared to have any

reservations regarding their verdict. The chairman motioned
her peremptorily to a seat.

'Well, young woman,' he said truculently, 'we've decided
to give you another chance.'

The young man interrupted in his calm, deep voice. 'We
think you acted very properly, Miss Gilchrist, in the interests
of your pupil, and that your aunt is a very generous woman.
A great pity there aren't more like her.'

'Thank you.' Eve returned his smile. 'Does this mean I can
resume work tomorrow? I should like to get back to my class
as soon as possible . . . it's been over two weeks.'

'I see no reason at all why not, do you, chairman?' The
young man received a glare for his pains, but continued
unabashed, 'We shall be getting in touch with Miss Perry to
inform her of our decision this evening.'

The chairman slammed his hand down on the desk-top.
'May I remind you, Mr Prescott, that *I* am the chairman of
this Board? You take too much upon yourself, by God you
do!' He nodded at Eve. 'All right. You can go. Report at
William Penn Road sharp at nine tomorrow morning.'

'Thank you.' Eve smiled gratefully at the other members
of the Board, but particularly at the man addressed as Mr
Prescott. She guessed that without his active intervention,
she would be out of a job.

The early part of the day had been overcast, but now the sun
was shining. Even the smoke- and soot-blackened houses
seemed to have a more cheerful appearance, the net curtains
whiter, the paint less chipped than when Eve had passed them
two hours ago. She couldn't wait to give Aunt Josie the news,
and quickened her steps as she approached the bus-stop.

A large, open-topped car drew up beside her, and a
familiar, deep voice asked, 'Can I give you a ride home, Miss
Gilchrist?'

She paused and smiled. 'Mr Prescott! It's very kind of you
to offer, but I live near the Downs. It's a long way and I
wouldn't want to put you to any trouble. I suspect you've
already done more than enough for me this morning.'

'No trouble at all,' he assured her, opening the passenger door. 'I live on the other side of the Suspension Bridge. Leigh Woods. So the Downs are on my way. Please, get in.'

Thankfully, Eve sank into the soft leather upholstery and removed her hat, shaking loose the mane of auburn hair which had been pinned up beneath it. 'What a beautiful car,' she murmured.

'A Vauxhall E-type Velox,' he answered proudly. 'Two years old now, but still goes like a bird. Do you drive, Miss Gilchrist?'

She shook her head. 'My aunt does, though. She has a Ford at present, but she's keen to buy one of these new little Austin Sevens.'

'What age is your aunt?' he asked in amusement. 'She sounds like a very game old lady.'

Eve laughed. 'She's sixty-four, and she wouldn't thank you to hear herself described like that. But you're quite right, she is "game" as you call it. And she's very liberal-minded – always has been. In her twenties, she lived in London for a few years and was a member of the Fabian Society. She knew Wells and Shaw and Sidney and Beatrice Webb. Shaw still writes to her occasionally, and so does Ramsay MacDonald. She's a writer herself. Children's books. Some of them are about a family called the Mortons.'

'Good God!' Eve's companion was so impressed that he failed to notice a dog in the road until it was almost too late, and had to swerve to avoid it. 'You mean she's *that* Josephine Gilchrist? I loved her books when I was young, and now they're a great favourite with my daughters.'

'You're married, then?' Eve was conscious of the note of surprise in her voice, and blushed. Why shouldn't he be married? It was just that there was something in his general attitude that suggested the single man.

'I'm a widower,' he answered quietly. 'My wife died last March.'

Eve felt her colour deepen. 'I—I'm so sorry,' she stammered. 'I didn't know...'

'Of course you didn't. How could you?' There was silence before he went on, as though in answer to her unspoken questions, 'My daughters, Justine and Olivia, are ten and six years old. We live with my mother.' He added, in a carefully neutral tone which it was difficult for Eve to interpret, 'I've always lived with my mother, even when I was married.'

Chapter Thirteen

'Aunt Josie, this is Mr Prescott, one of the Governors of William Penn Juniors', and thanks to him I still have a job.'

Josephine had been on the watch for Eve's return, and as soon as the Velox drew up in front of Holly Lodge and she saw her niece in the passenger seat, she had hurried to open the front door. Five minutes was sufficient to acquaint her with all the facts; she turned a glowing face towards her unexpected guest.

'Mr Prescott, I can't thank you enough. It's almost lunchtime. Won't you honour us by staying?'

'Please, you must call me Lawrence. And, thank you, I should like to stay very much, but I ought to let my mother know. Do you by any chance have a telephone?'

'Behind you, on the hall table. Dial eight for the operator.' Josephine turned to Eve. 'I'll just go and let Clarrie know that we shall be three instead of two.'

Eve, not wishing to eavesdrop, went into the dining-room. It was too warm, however, to close the heavy oaken door, and scraps of Lawrence Prescott's dialogue with his mother could plainly be overheard.

'Yes ... Yes, I know I promised ... I couldn't let you know earlier ... No ... no, I didn't know myself until just now ... I appreciate you're on your own, but I'll be home by three at the— I'm sorry, Mother, but ... Would you rather I picked up Justine and Livvy from school, on my way ...? Yes, I realize that would make me later. I just thought it would save you sending Harold with the car. No, all right, I'll come straight home.' The receiver was replaced on its stand and there was a momentary silence; then Lawrence Prescott appeared in the doorway, wearing a rather forced smile.

'Everything all right?' Eve asked, turning. She had moved to the far end of the room as soon as she heard him hang up and seemed to be gazing intently out of one of the windows.

'Yes, thank you.' He came to stand beside her. 'What a beautiful view.'

'I'm sure you have equally beautiful views on the other side of the Gorge.' What a banal remark: she had done a lot better during the journey home. But Eve could think of nothing to say, being preoccupied with the disparity between the self-assurance with which her guest had stood up to the rest of the William Penn Board of Governors, and his almost subservient approach to his mother. She was relieved when Josephine returned to take charge of the conversation.

Over the main course of steamed fish, with new potatoes, beans and fresh peas from the garden, Lawrence Prescott repeated his admiration for the Morton books.

'I read and re-read them as a child, and now they're great favourites with both my daughters.'

Before her aunt could ask the inevitable question, Eve interposed, 'Mr Prescott's wife died last March, Aunt Josie.'

Josephine was all concern. 'How terrible for you. She wasn't ... I mean, surely she couldn't have been all that old?'

'The same age as myself, thirty-one. Bel – Belinda, that is – caught a bad cold in February and it turned to double pneumonia.'

'But you say you have two little girls.' Once Josephine's interest was aroused, no consideration of sensibilities could prevent her from satisfying her curiosity. 'How on earth do you manage? Who looks after then while you're out at work?'

A faint colour stained Lawrence Prescott's thin cheeks. 'I don't work. I have a weak heart caused by rheumatic fever when I was young. My mother' – the colour deepened – 'is over-protective of me. I think she exaggerates the seriousness of my condition.'

'And you and your daughters live with her now?'

'We always have done.'

'And your wife didn't object?' Josephine was intrigued. Nothing, not even Eve's shocked exclamation of 'Aunt Josie!' could stop her probing further.

Lawrence Prescott's eyes were fixed on his plate as he chased an elusive bean with his fork. 'No. Bel was my cousin, you see: my father's sister's daughter. She had known my mother all her life and they understood one another.'

'And you don't have to work?'

Eve decided it was time to intervene. 'Aunt Josie,' she protested, 'this is getting like the Spanish Inquisition. It's all right, Mr Prescott, we don't have a torture chamber in the cellar should you give the wrong answer.'

He laughed at that. 'I don't mind, really. Before her marriage,' he went on, addressing Josephine, 'my mother was Calanthe Robartes. You know – Robartes's Surgical Boots and Shoes. Grandfather Robartes was a very wealthy man and Mother was his only child. She inherited everything when he died. Does that answer your question?'

Josephine laid her knife and fork together on her empty plate, frowning. 'But what on earth do you do with yourself all day?'

Eve devoutly wished that the floor would open and swallow her up. Lawrence Prescott, however, seemed not to resent Josephine's interrogation, and it occurred to her that he was used to such cross-examinations from his mother, accounting for his movements, always apologetic. She wanted to shake him. How was it that he could stand up for other people, but not for himself?

'You don't have to answer, Mr Prescott,' she told him, looking daggers at Josephine.

Her aunt had the grace to blush. 'I'm behaving extremely badly, Mr Prescott. Unfortunately, there's a belief amongst my generation that advancing years are an excuse for every kind of rudeness. Tell me to mind my own business.'

He laughed, and his pleasant features became almost

handsome. Eve thought, 'He doesn't laugh enough.'

'Oh, I'm used to it,' he said, confirming Eve's suspicions.
'I'm on the Boards of several local charities and two schools;
William Penn Road Juniors, as you know, and Longhurst, a
privately endowed school on the other side of the Downs,
near Stoke Hill. My elder daughter, Justine, will be going to
Longhurst next year, I hope, if she passes the entrance
examination. And I also paint.'

'You paint! What do you paint?' Josephine was delighted
at this evidence of an artistic bent.

Lawrence Prescott smiled his thanks at Clarrie, who was
removing the dirty dishes, then gave a self-conscious
grimace. 'Trains. They're the great love of my life. My
mother thinks it childish; she thinks I should have outgrown
my enthusiasm for being an engine-driver by now.' The pale
eyes lit with amusement. 'But men, as you must be aware,
Miss Gilchrist, are always children at heart.'

Eve laughed, but Josephine was only half-listening.
'That's it!' she exclaimed, with the air of one making a great
discovery. 'From the moment you arrived, I was sure that I'd
seen you somewhere before. You won't remember – it was
years and years ago – but Eve and I and a young friend were
on Temple Meads station, watching the trains. The friend,
whose name was Frank, had chosen it as the afternoon's
entertainment. I don't recall that Eve and I were too taken
with the idea to begin with, but in the event we enjoyed
ourselves, thanks to you. You were very helpful and
informative.'

Lawrence Prescott shook his head incredulously. 'Really?
I'm afraid I can't remember the incident at all. But I'm so
pleased to think we've met before and that I was useful to
you. And, of course, to the other Miss Gilchrist.' He glanced
shyly at Eve.

'Oh, Eve won't remember the occasion, either,' Josephine
said. 'She couldn't have been more than eight years old at the
time.'

'But I do,' Eve smiled. 'I've been trying to think, all

morning, why you seemed familiar. You must have made a deep impression on me, Mr Prescott.'

Her remark, meant innocently enough, seemed to throw him into confusion, and he spent the remainder of the meal addressing himself almost exclusively to Josephine. It appeared he had held two exhibitions of his work at a Bristol art dealer's shop in Wine Street, and on each occasion sold all that was on display. But his mother, he said, was not keen on this commercialization of his talent, preferring him to paint in an entirely amateur capacity.

'A thoroughly domineering woman, I should imagine,' Josephine remarked to Eve when, just before three o'clock, they watched the Velox speed away across the Downs. 'A bit of a monster.' They withdrew into the shade of the house and closed the front door. 'What a coincidence, though, your Mr Prescott turning out to be the same young man that we met on the station, all those years ago.'

'He's not my Mr Prescott,' Eve disclaimed, pouring herself another cup of coffee from the pot on the sideboard. 'And from all I've heard and seen this afternoon, I don't think he'll ever be anyone's except his mother's.'

'He liked you,' Josephine urged, but Eve shook her head. 'I'll be very surprised if I ever hear from him again.'

*

Eve spent the four-week summer holiday at Staple Abbots. Josephine had wanted her niece to accompany her to France, but Eve's conscience was troubling her.

'I'd love to, but I ought to go home. I don't see nearly enough of Mama and Papa nowadays, and they're growing older. Papa's sixty-two, he'll be retiring soon. Besides, I've had a letter from Rose. She and Ernest are getting engaged on her birthday and I must be there.'

And Marcus's obvious delight at seeing his daughter for the first time since Easter made the sacrifice worthwhile. He met her at Warminster station, and they drove slowly home across the sun-dappled Plain, past once grassy tracks now worn threadbare by innumerable Army manoeuvres. Although it was four years since the end of the war, Eve was more aware than ever of the ubiquitous military presence around Salisbury.

'Do you remember how we weren't allowed out of the village for days on end?' she asked her father, but Marcus needed no reminding.

'Thank God those times are over and will never come again. The League of Nations will see to that. People have at last come to their senses and realized how futile war really is.'

It seemed like fate that, as the open-topped tourer drove past the first few straggling cottages of the village High Street, Jenny Mailer should be coming out of one of them, holding her four-year-old daughter by the hand. Marcus hesitated for a second before pulling into the side of the road and offering them a lift.

'I can let Eve off at Rosemary Villa and take you and Ginny on to your mother's.'

It was very hot and Jenny accepted gratefully. She climbed into the back seat, dragging the reluctant child after her.

'Oh, stop your whining, do! You've been in a car before. Sorry, Doctor, but she can't abide the smell of the leather.' Her eyes strayed to Eve, half-slewed round in her seat. 'You've had your hair bobbed,' she said enviously.

Marcus turned to look at his daughter. 'I knew there was something different about you.' He sounded pained. 'I thought you said your headmistress didn't approve of her women teachers having short hair?'

Eve smiled tranquilly. 'Miss Perry and I have reached an understanding. Although I still have to hold class in the hall, she doesn't interfere like she used to. You see, I now have a friend at court. I'll tell you all about it when we get home.'

Since the day of the disciplinary hearing Hannah Perry had barely spoken to her, except when absolutely necessary, leaving Eve very much to her own devices; but that at least was preferable to the former malicious sniping. Eve had plucked up courage to have her hair cut, and even that had provoked no reaction beyond a tightening of the lips. The headmistress had obviously been warned of Lawrence Prescott's interest in Miss Gilchrist. Not that the interest had led to anything, Eve reflected, as Marcus got out to re-crank the engine. She had neither seen nor heard from him in the intervening two months. But had she expected to? Not really.

Marcus resumed his seat behind the wheel and they started off again, a royal progress, waving to friends and returning greetings. Yet all the time, Eve was sharply aware of the two in the back seat: Frank's wife and child. And it was of little Virginia Mailer that she was most conscious. As she had told her aunt, the girl was the image of her father – small, wiry and dark-complexioned, with almost black hair and enormous brown eyes. She didn't take after the Slades at all.

The first evening at Rosemary Villa was spent in catching up on one another's news. As always, Helena and Hetty were brimming over with village gossip, while Marcus was quietly absorbed in anything his daughter might have to tell him. His indignation at Hannah Perry's conduct was equalled by that of his wife and sister-in-law, although the two women's interest in the story was only really engaged when Eve revealed that Lawrence Prescott's mother was Franklin Robartes's heir.

'Not the Surgical Boot and Shoe Company man?' Hetty demanded. 'He must have been worth a pretty penny when he died. Have you ... er ... seen this Lawrence Prescott since?' She tried to sound casual, without quite succeeding.

'I'm afraid not, Aunt Hetty.' Eve changed the subject. 'What's happened to Jenny Mailer? Is she still helping out at the general store?'

Helena nodded. 'But Mrs Slade tells me she's not happy. Jenny's always moaning, she says, about there being nothing to do in the country.'

'Not enough men,' Hetty put in waspishly. 'That's what she means by nothing to do. Mrs Crocker was complaining to me only the other day about the disgraceful way Jenny flirts with all the travelling salesmen who come into the shop. It would never surprise me, you know, if one day she just took off and abandoned that poor child to her mother.'

'Do you really think so?' Helena was disturbed. 'Maggie Slade couldn't cope; she's crippled with rheumatism.'

'For goodness' sake!' Marcus reproved them. 'Jenny's devoted to Virginia. That child is all she has left of Frank. So, let's talk about something else,' he went on more cheerfully, aware of Eve's sudden stillness. He cast around in his mind for anything which might divert Helena's and Hetty's thoughts from village scandal. 'Have you told Eve about the arrangements for Rose's and Ernest's engagement party?'

*

It was a quiet affair, mainly family and a few close friends. Ernest, although much better than he was, had still not fully recovered from his experiences in the war. Mr Druitt, who was a week-end guest at Abbey Court, plainly had reservations concerning his daughter's choice of husband, even though Mrs Druitt was just as plainly delighted. She and Mabel formed a determined alliance against their husbands, whose doubts were mutual if for varying reasons. Donald seemed indifferent to his brother's concerns, holding aloof from the proceedings and only showing any animation when Eve arrived with her parents and Hetty.

His six-foot frame had fleshed out in the past four years: he was going to be a heavy man, like his father. Although only twenty-six years of age, his sandy hair already had a salting of grey, the result of all he had suffered in the trenches. The blue eyes, so similar in colour to Mabel's, sometimes had a faraway expression as if he were lost in a world of his own. Unlike his brother, however, he was able to appear jovial and carefree on the surface, whatever the turmoil of his mind. He still rode to hounds and played an excellent game of cricket, being captain of the village team.

By contrast, Ernest was a mere shadow of his pre-war self, clinging to Rose and his parents, and rarely venturing beyond the village pale. Marcus assured Arthur and Mabel that he would improve with time, meanwhile encouraging his younger nephew in the latter's passion for working on the farm.

'Let him do whatever he likes,' Marcus advised Arthur, 'even the most menial jobs, if that's what he wants. He's always loved the land, and I've spoken to some of the men. They say he's more himself when he's out in the fields with them.'

Rose confirmed this fact as she and Eve stood together on the little balcony outside the drawing-room window, sipping champagne.

'He's happy here,' Rose said, indicating with a sweep of her arm the broad acres of tree and meadow surrounding the house.

'And you won't mind living with your in-laws?' Eve asked, the words finding an echo in the recesses of her mind.

Her friend shrugged. 'If it's what Ernest needs, then I'll have to put up with it. I love him, Eve. I'll do anything that's necessary.' There was a moment's silence, while a skylark soared high above them, singing its pure, sweet song. 'And you? Has there been anyone else since Frank?'

Eve shook her head. 'No, there's been no one but him. We both fell in love too young, Rose, but you're lucky. Your dreams have come true.'

The lark had ceased its calling, and apart from the low-voiced buzz of conversation at their backs the August afternoon lay hot and quiet all about them. Presently, Rose said, 'But then, you see, Ernest loves me, too.'

Their friendship was too deeply rooted for Eve to take offence, but that she was hurt sounded in her voice. 'And you think Frank didn't love me?'

Rose turned quickly, laying a comforting hand on her friend's arm. 'I think Frank Mailer didn't know his own mind, and I don't know that we can blame him for that. The circumstances were ... well, difficult, to say the least. But – forgive me – I do think, have always thought, that you deserve better.'

'Better than a farmhand, do you mean?'

'Better than someone who doesn't love you enough to overcome all the difficulties strewn in his path.'

Eve felt herself near to tears, and to disguise her feelings exclaimed impatiently, 'Oh, Rose! I don't want Christian from *Pilgrim's Progress*, for God's sake! I want a normal man with faults and shortcomings, like everybody else.'

Rose's arm slid up and around her friend's shoulders. 'I'm sorry. It was thoughtless of me. I'm so happy myself, I want you to be happy as well.'

A voice spoke from behind them. 'What are you two doing, whispering secrets?' It was Donald, emerging from the French doors on to the balcony, holding a plate of sandwiches. 'Want one?'

Both girls declined. 'I must go in to Ernest,' Rose said. 'He'll be missing me. He doesn't like me to be too long away. Give me the sandwiches, Donald, and I'll take them indoors. You stay and talk to Eve.'

She took the plate with an ostentatious flash of her engagement ring, a circle of diamonds set round a central emerald, which Eve recognized as having once belonged to Grandmother Burfoot. Then she was gone, and Eve found herself left alone with her cousin. Donald immediately possessed himself of her hands.

'Eve,' he said urgently, 'four years ago you promised to think over my proposal of marriage. You said to ask you again in a few years' time, when you'd done all the things you wanted to do. Well, now I'm asking you. Will you marry me?'

'Oh Don! I'm only twenty-two. I haven't done very much yet with my life. It's still too soon.' She reached up and kissed his cheek. 'I truly am sorry, but you've taken me by surprise.'

'In that case,' he told her eagerly, 'think it over. Give yourself time to get used to the idea. How long are you home for? Another two weeks, isn't it? I'll ask you again before you leave.'

Eve wanted to deter him, but she didn't know how. She suddenly felt sorry for him. As a schoolboy, Donald had always seemed so armoured in conceit, so self-absorbed, that it had been easy to dislike him and she had rarely, in his absence, given him a second thought. But the war had altered him, as it had so many others. He had lost the bombast of his youth and, although he did his best to conceal the fact, Eve realized that he was far more vulnerable to rejection than in the past. So instead of saying, 'No, I'm sorry, Donald, I don't want to marry you,' the words which rose instinctively to her lips, she merely returned the pressure of his hands and made her escape inside.

Arthur was just beginning a speech, toasting the engaged couple and wishing them happiness, but it was subdued in tone for him, as were the congratulations which Rose and Ernest later received. There was an uneasiness, Eve reflected, in this post-war world more noticeable in the country than the town. In the city, life was lived at a more frenetic pace. Short skirts and bobbed hair had liberated women to a degree undreamed of in the old days, and the increasing prevalence of motorized vehicles meant that people could get from place to place faster than ever before, generating a climate of excitement. There was less sense of a way of life lost and gone for ever, along with a whole generation of young men in the mud and carnage of Flanders.

This feeling of depression remained with Eve for the rest of her stay at home. On the surface, the village seemed almost the same as it had always been. Most of the cottages in Staple Abbots now had water on tap, but pipes had not yet been laid as far as Lower and Upper Abbots. And although Abbey Court had been wired for electricity,

elsewhere gas was still the main source of illumination, with
many upper storeys still relying on candle-power. The
general store, with its long wooden counter, sacks of sugar,
beans and bran, its boxes of dried fruit and canisters of tea,
had not changed at all, but there was a new war memorial
in the churchyard to those half-dozen local boys who had lost
their lives. Bert Naysmith's stables were half their original
size, and the garage once dreamed of by young Jim
Naysmith had finally been opened by strangers.

During the rest of her holiday Eve went for long walks on
her own, visiting all those places in and around the village
where she had been with Frank. She wasn't sure why she did
so; whether it was an attempt to exorcize his ghost once and
for all, or to bring him more vividly to mind, conscious that
of late his image had been fading.

'You're very restless,' her father complained. 'We hardly
see you.'

Eve excused herself on the grounds that it was a shame to
waste the marvellous weather.

'I thought you'd want to be with Rose,' Helena reproa-
ched her, 'discussing wedding plans.'

'It's a bit early for that,' Eve said hurriedly, not wishing
to reveal that she was deliberately keeping away from Abbey
Court.

She had somehow managed to avoid Donald since the
engagement party, and was tempted to return to Bristol a
few days early in the hope that she might escape seeing him
altogether. She upbraided herself for cowardice, but had a
foreboding that another confrontation could trap her into
giving a promise she would regret. The more she thought
about him, the more he aroused her pity; and pity was no
basis for marriage, as Aunt Josie would be the first to point
out.

But it was with a sense of fatality that she discovered he
had invited himself to supper at Rosemary Villa the evening
before she was due to leave.

'He telephoned this afternoon while you were out, and

asked if he could come,' Helena informed her daughter, her eyes sparkling with anticipation. 'He said to tell you he expected the answer to his question. Now, what can that mean, Eve?'

'Go and tidy up, child,' Aunt Hetty scolded, 'and put on a longer skirt. That one shows far too much leg.'

Marcus said nothing until his wife and sister-in-law had left the room to consult with Doris in the kitchen. Then he got up from his favourite armchair and put an arm around Eve's shoulders.

'You know,' he pleaded gently, 'it would be very nice to have you home again permanently; to be able to see you whenever I liked. I miss you, my dear, more than I can say.'

Chapter Fourteen

'For heaven's sake!' Josephine exclaimed, irritably for her when addressing her niece. 'You've been engaged to Donald for nearly two years. It's high time you either married him or broke off the engagement. This state of indecision is doing you no good. You're drifting along at William Penn Road Juniors' like a soul in limbo because you can't make up your mind about the future. For your own sake, Eve, as well as everyone else's, decide one way or the other – and do it soon.'

Eve grimaced and laid aside Aldous Huxley's most recent novel, *Antic Hay*, which she was reading. It was Saturday, and beyond the big bay window the rain poured down relentlessly, flattening the grass of Downs and gardens alike and making the leaves on the trees bounce to its rhythm. Every car which passed had its hood raised against the inclement weather, and the tyres sent up fountains of spray from the puddles at the sides of the road. The grey monotony of the sky had not lifted, it seemed, for weeks during this summer of 1924.

'I know,' she admitted. 'You're right, Aunt Josie. I just need a little more time.'

Josephine snorted and turned back to her desk, where she was finishing her accounts. She put ten pounds in one-pound notes into an envelope, which she sealed.

'Don't forget to take that with you on Monday morning and give it to Mrs Bailey. It's Arnold's expenses for the coming quarter. Say how delighted we are with his progress at the grammar school. So far, he's certainly justified the faith you had in him.' She swivelled round in her chair until she was once more facing Eve. 'As for you, my dear, you don't need time – you need courage; courage to tell Donald that you never really wanted to marry him in the first place; that you allowed circumstances to force your hand.'

'Oh, that's not . . .' Eve began and then stopped, unable to continue.

'Not true?' Josephine rose ponderously from her chair. At sixty-five, she was far more overweight than her height suggested. She tired easily these days, and when she went upstairs, always had to pause on the half-landing to regain her breath. She sank down beside Eve on the blue velvet sofa.

'Nonsense! Of course it is, and what's more you know it. Do you think I'm so stupid that I haven't been able to piece together what really happened, by talking to you and Marcus? Not to mention Helena and Hetty, who are both as transparent as a couple of bubbles. First of all, there was the general approbation: what a good, sensible girl you'd finally been. And your father was missing you, he told me so. What's more to the point, he told you so as well. Then Rose was delighted to think you'd be living in the same house, her sister-in-law, and because she was pleased, Ernest was also. And contentment is so vital to his recovery. I don't know what stipulations or conditions you laid down when you accepted Donald's proposal, but I can guess that once you'd said "Yes", you found yourself boxed in by the general atmosphere of euphoria. Since when, you've been wondering how you can extricate yourself from an impossible situation without hurting Donald and disappointing everyone else. Well, the short answer, my dear, is that you can't.'

Eve stared ahead of her, twisting the solitaire diamond engagement ring – a ring which, like the one Ernest had given Rose, had belonged to Grandmother Burfoot – round and round on her finger. Every word Josephine had uttered was true, but once she admitted it openly she would be forced to do something about it, and just for the moment she could not bring herself to face the consequences of those actions. All the same, time was running out. After two years of stalling on one pretext and another, her family – not to mention Donald – were growing impatient. She wouldn't be able to put them off for much longer.

Eve sighed and turned her head to smile at her aunt. 'I promise I'll go down to Stable Abbots some week-end soon and . . . and sort things out one way or the other.'

Josephine looked sceptical, but said merely, 'Make sure you do. I shall hold you to that, my child.'

*

A month later, Eve had still done nothing to redeem her promise, despite the fact that Donald had telephoned her half a dozen times during the intervening weeks, pressing her to set a date for the wedding. She had also received letters from both her mother and Aunt Hetty, the latter's containing a veiled threat that she was about to descend on Holly Lodge and force a decision from her.

'Let her try,' Josephine remarked grimly when apprised of the fact. 'I'll make Hetty's visit so uncomfortable, she'll be off back to Staple Abbots before she can open her mouth on the subject. But Donald, now, or your parents, that would be different. They have a right to know what's going on. And don't forget, school breaks up soon and you've no excuse then for not going home. You can't run away for ever.'

Eve knew her aunt was right, and it was a prospect she dreaded. However she decided, she foresaw an end to her peace of mind. On the last Saturday before term finished, and because for once the sun was shining, she decided on a shopping expedition to raise her spirits. She managed each month to save a little from her salary, after paying Josephine for her board and keep, and a survey of her summer wardrobe convinced her that another cotton frock was a necessity rather than an extravagance. So, after lunch, she caught the bus to the Tramways Centre and walked as far as Wine Street. It was while she was looking in the window of Baker Baker's that she felt a hand brush her shoulder and a voice said tentatively, 'Miss Gilchrist?'

She turned to find Lawrence Prescott beside her. He raised his hat.

'Mr Prescott,' Eve was astonished by the pleasure she felt at seeing him. 'How ... how are you after all this time?'

Her first impression was that he looked even paler and thinner than at their last meeting two years earlier, but he answered so emphatically, 'Extremely well, thank you,' that she decided after a few moments that she had been mistaken. 'And you?' he continued. 'Although I need hardly ask. You look ... wonderful.' He smiled shyly, but the blue eyes expressed an unashamed admiration.

'Thank you.' Eve was taken aback, not knowing what else to say. She was not used to receiving such delicately expressed compliments; or compliments at all, for that matter. Donald took it for granted that as he had asked her to marry him, she must know she was a good-looking woman and therefore did not need to be told. 'I was ... just thinking of buying a new dress for the summer.'

'Oh. Well, in that case ...' Neither of them seemed capable of uttering a sentence without floundering in a sea of hesitation. 'I was – er – wondering if you'd care to ... to have a cup of tea with me. But if you're in a hurry ...'

Eve thought: 'This is ridiculous.' Aloud, she said firmly, 'Yes, please, I should like to very much. The dress isn't urgent. There's a Cadena Café near here; we could go to that.'

Her companion seemed to find nothing strange in the decisive way in which she had taken the lead, and Eve remembered his mother. What was she called? Something odd. Ah yes, Calanthe. And his daughters? Justine and Olivia. Eve was amazed at what she was able to recollect about Lawrence Prescott, just as she could recall their first meeting all those years ago.

It was when they were seated at a corner table in the café and Eve was about to remove her gloves, that she remembered her engagement ring. Before she was even aware of what she intended doing, she had pulled off the solitaire

with the left-hand glove and concealed it in her handbag.
She regarded her bare finger with detached curiosity,
noticing the paler band of flesh where the ring had been.

Lawrence gave the order for tea and cakes with a quiet
competence which regained him the initiative.

'That's a very fetching hat,' he said of her wide-brimmed
green straw with its trimming of artificial lilies-of-the-
valley. He removed his bowler and laid it on the empty chair
beside him, along with his grey suede gloves. He was a bit
of a dandy, Eve decided. There was a moment's silence before
he continued with a rush, 'It is so nice to meet you again,
Miss Gilchrist.'

It was on the tip of Eve's tongue to ask why, if he was
really that pleased to see her, he had not contacted her
during the past two years. Then she remembered guiltily
that the last time they met he was in mourning for his wife,
who had been dead for only a few months. It was customary
to observe a year's full and six months' half mourning, and
she guessed that by both upbringing and inclination
Lawrence Prescott was a conventional man.

'And I'm equally delighted to renew our acquaintance,'
she answered with her warmest smile. 'It gives me another
chance to thank you again for all you did for me with the
Board of Governors. Incidentally the boy, Arnold Bailey, is
doing exceptionally well at Bristol Grammar. I think we
may have a future Prime Minister in the making.'

They both laughed, and her words led them naturally into a
discussion of the first Labour Government, which had been
elected in January, and the current difficulties Ramsay
MacDonald was now facing. Eve was hardly surprised to
discover that her own liberal views, inherited from Marcus and
fostered by Josephine, found no echo in Lawrence Prescott's
way of thinking; but he was a gentle, caring man, eager to help
those less well-off than himself, and she could not but admire
him. By the time they had finished their tea and cakes, she was
thoroughly at ease in his company. Reluctantly, she picked up
her handbag and gloves preparatory to leaving.

Lawrence came back from the cash-desk after paying the bill, but instead of making a move to go he sat down again. Eve glanced at him enquiringly.

'I ... was wondering,' he began haltingly, then stopped.

'Yes?' she encouraged him.

'Well ... The school term finishes next Friday, and I was wondering ...'

'Yes?' she said again, when he seemed incapable of continuing.

'If you'd come with me to Paris?' He saw her startled face and went on hurriedly, 'I – I don't mean it quite as it sounds. Not the way you're thinking. I'm sorry, I put it badly.' He drew a deep breath which appeared to steady him. 'Mother and I promised to take the girls to Paris for the week-end, to see the closing of the Olympic Games on Sunday. But Mother's broken her ankle and can't go; however, we don't want to disappoint Justine and Livvy, so she's ... agreed that we can go without her. But her cross-Channel ticket and her hotel room have been booked and paid for in advance. I was going to cancel them, and then ... then I ran into you, and I wondered ... It will,' he added earnestly, 'be separate hotel rooms – you do understand that?'

'Oh, I do.' Eve suppressed a desire to laugh. 'Will your mother approve, though?'

He flushed with embarrassment and avoided her eyes. 'I don't expect I'll say anything to her,' he admitted after a moment. 'She's disappointed enough already, and ... and it might upset her to know that ... well, that someone was taking her place.'

'But your daughters? Won't they be bound to tell her?'

Lawrence shook his head. 'Oh no! They're used to keeping secrets.'

A warning sounded at the back of Eve's mind: common sense told her that acceptance of the invitation would land her in a situation fraught with potential difficulties. She was engaged to someone else, a fact that she had concealed, while he was dominated by his dragon of a mother. Both of them were reduced to subterfuges, and both were trapped in prisons of their own making. Well, she at least could free herself. If she went with Lawrence Prescott to Paris, even though under the most innocuous of circumstances and chaperoned by his daughters, she must break her engagement to her cousin. Her actions of this afternoon had told her something about her emotions, and she would ignore that knowledge at her peril. Not only was she not in love with Donald, but she did not even like him. She had never liked him, only felt pity for what he had suffered in the war. But that, plus a desire to make her parents – particularly her father – happy was no basis for a marriage. She had only ever wanted to be married to one man, and that was Frank. What she felt for Lawrence Prescott was still a mystery to her, but an intriguing mystery nevertheless.

'I'll come,' she agreed, 'on one condition: that you tell your mother about me. Otherwise, I'm sorry, but no. And so that there are no secrets between us' – she felt in her handbag and extracted her gloves, shaking the engagement ring free from the left one – 'I am at present engaged to my cousin, but I intend to end it. Not,' she added quickly, in case he got the wrong idea, 'because of anything that's happened this afternoon, but because I don't love him. I've known for a long time that our marriage could never work.'

Lawrence blinked rapidly, then smiled, his eyes alight with pleasure, 'I'm glad,' he said. 'No, I don't mean that, not altogether anyway. I'm just happy that there's nobody else.'

*

Eve had been abroad only once before in her life, the war having curtailed all such trips until she was almost nineteen. For her twenty-first birthday present, however, Josephine had taken her on a fortnight's holiday to her beloved Provence, but a stop-over in Paris had not been on the itinerary. Seeing it now for the first time, Eve was enchanted by its beauty and elegance – so different from noisy, bustling, chaotic London, which she had been introduced to at Rose's wedding.

Lawrence had picked her up in the Velox immediately school finished on Friday evening; Justine and Olivia, together with the luggage, were riding in the back. They had driven to Dover, caught the night ferry to Calais, arriving in the small hours of Saturday morning, and proceeded from there not to the inexpensive pension of Eve's imagination, but to the exclusive L'Hotel in the Rue des Beaux Arts. It was her first real indication of Calanthe Prescott's wealth; for she had no doubt in her own mind who controlled the money. Lawrence was at liberty to spend as much as he liked, provided he abided by his mother's rules, but he did not hold the purse-strings.

During the journey, Eve had enquired how the news that she was joining the party had been received. Lawrence hesitated just long enough to allow eight-year-old Olivia to pipe up from the back, 'Grandma doesn't know, does she, Daddy?'

Justine made a hurried attempt to hush her sister, but her intervention was not swift enough. It occurred fleetingly to Eve that the child bore too great a burden of secrecy for someone only twelve years old.

As the wind-blown darkness fled by on either side of the car, Eve turned her face towards Lawrence. 'You promised,' she accused him. 'It was my condition for coming with you.'

'I know, and I'm ashamed. But my nerve failed at the very last minute.'

Eve sighed. 'That makes two of us,' she admitted. 'I haven't told my fiancé yet, either.'

'Truly?' Lawrence sounded relieved. 'I'm glad I'm not the only coward. But ... but you are going to break your engagement?'

'Oh, yes. For my own sake.' She wanted suddenly to make that crystal-clear. 'I'm going home when this week-end is over. I shall tell Donald then.'

She did not ask if he, similarly, would tell his mother about her presence on this trip. That was something he must sort out for himself. As Josephine had pointed out to her, any other attitude on Eve's part might be misconstrued.

'Finish with Donald first, and enjoy your freedom before you decide if you want to embark on another relationship quite so soon.'

On reflection, Eve realized that this was good advice. Her reaction in the café had been scrupulous, but unnecessary. No one, surely, could have doubts about this week-end in Paris: she and Lawrence were sleeping in separate rooms and were chaperoned by his two daughters.

Eve had hit it off with Justine and Olivia at once. They were naturally charming, well-mannered little girls, but they were also friendly, eager to chat and confide in her. Eve suspected that it was a relief to both of them to be able to talk without reserve, after the secretive atmosphere of home. Justine was very like her father, with the same fair, wavy hair and pale blue eyes. Olivia, the darker of the two, had straight brown hair cut in a Dutch doll fringe above a pair of long-lashed hazel eyes. Both were small-boned and delicate, but it was a well-nourished fragility, not the painfully underfed thinness of some of the William Penn Road children.

The week-end was over all too soon, even though it was Wednesday morning before they finally returned to Bristol. Eve thoroughly enjoyed the closing ceremony of the Olympic Games, but it was Paris itself which gave her the greatest thrill. The Louvre, the Invalides and the Arc de Triomphe, the Champs Elysées, the shops, and the cars blaring impatiently on their horns in a totally Gallic way; all these things fascinated her and made her wish the time was twice as long. Lawrence proved to be an interesting and well-read companion, anxious for her comfort and entertainment, as well as that of his daughters. When Eve asked him, as they were standing in front of the 'Mona Lisa', if he wouldn't rather be at the Gare du Nord spotting trains, he laughed and said, 'Not if it means being parted from you.'

'Daddy thinks you're nice. He told me so,' Olivia put in with youthful candour.

Justine kicked her sister's ankle, but Lawrence managed to conceal any embarrassment he might have felt by announcing that it was time for lunch. 'And in France, I must remind you, eating takes second place to nothing, not even Great Art.'

Yes, Eve thought as the Velox drew up outside Holly Lodge and Lawrence got out to unload her case, the last few days had been exciting and extremely worthwhile. They had shown her that the last thing she wanted was to bury herself in Staple Abbots before she had seen more of the world. But on top of that, she had thoroughly enjoyed Lawrence's company and that of his daughters. She turned a glowing face towards him as she said goodbye.

'Thank you. It was lovely. I enjoyed every single moment.'

'Good. I'm so pleased.' He cradled her hand in his for longer than was strictly necessary, and it was only when she made to withdraw it that, with a slight flush, he let it go. 'We shall see one another again, I hope?'

'I'm going to Wiltshire,' she reminded him, 'for the next few weeks, until the start of term. I'll telephone you when I get back.'

'Let me telephone you,' he suggested quickly. 'I – I have more free time than you do.'

It was a lame excuse and they both knew it, but Eve gave no hint that she understood. 'Yes, all right,' she agreed. 'You get in touch with me. And now, I must go and see how Aunt Josie is. You're sure you and the girls won't come in? She'd be delighted to see you.'

But in spite of Justine's and Olivia's chorus of, 'Oh, Daddy, can't we?' he remained adamant. 'Another time,' he told them.

Eve waited on the pavement until the car was out of sight, then picked up her case and went indoors to be met by her aunt, just emerging from the drawing-room.

'I thought I heard a car. Oh, Eve, while you've been away, something terrible has happened.'

Eve's immediate thought was that someone had died.

'Is it Papa?' she demanded.

'No, no! Nothing to do with your father.'

'Mama? Aunt Hetty? Donald? Uncle Arthur? For goodness' sake, tell me!'

Josephine waved her to silence with an imperious hand. 'No, no! I'm sorry. Perhaps I was exaggerating, but it seems terrible to me. Come and sit down, you must be exhausted after that journey. I'll ring for coffee.' She ushered Eve into the drawing-room and tugged on the bell-rope. 'But before Clarrie brings it, there's something you must know. She's leaving us at Christmas. After all these years – at her age, mark you – she's getting married!'

Eve laughed with relief. 'Is that all? Thank God! I thought there'd been a serious accident, at the very least. And Clarrie isn't that old, you know. I'm sure she can't be a day over forty.'

Josephine lowered herself into her usual armchair. 'You can be very set in your ways by that time of life,' she retorted grimly. 'Besides, I thought she was happy here. She's been with me for over ten years; she came to me the summer before the war and we got on well from the start. Clarrie understands me, she knows all my odd little ways.'

'You'll find someone else,' Eve reassured her, 'and in the meantime, I shall be here to help out. We'll manage.'

But Josephine was in an uncharacteristically pettish mood. 'I'm too old to start training a new girl. It's a nuisance at my age.' There was the chink of crockery just outside the door. 'Shush, shush!' She put a warning finger to her lips. 'I wouldn't want to appear upset at all.'

'Of course not. Perish the thought!' Eve gave her aunt a conspiratorial grin. 'Clarrie!' she exclaimed as the door opened. 'Congratulations! Who's the lucky man?'

Clarrie flushed self-consciously as she placed the tray with the coffee things on an occasional table close to Josephine's chair.

'Thank you, Miss Eve. It's Mr Soloway from the greengrocer's shop near the top of Blackboy Hill. And did you have a good week-end? Although it's been more like a week really, hasn't it?'

Josephine groaned and clapped a hand to her forehead. 'Eve, dear, forgive me. What a selfish old woman I've become! Did you enjoy yourself? Tell me all about it while I pour the coffee.'

Eve did as she was bidden but later, while she was unpacking in her room, her thoughts returned to Josephine's dilemma. If her aunt was able to engage someone soon, then Clarrie could train the newcomer in the ways of the household before she left in December. A solution had suggested itself to Eve, but she was not sure that her aunt would agree to her proposal; nor was she certain that it was what she herself really wanted. But being in the company of Lawrence's children these past few days had reminded her of Frank's daughter, Virginia. She remembered the little girl who had been dragged into Marcus's car, and Jenny's obvious impatience with her. Ginny's misery had stuck in her mind for weeks afterwards and haunted her dreams. Perhaps if Jenny were happier, then her daughter would be also. And Jenny was fed up with life in the country, Mama and Aunt Hetty had said so. A taste of city life might be just what she needed.

'And she's been well trained in domestic work at Abbey Court,' Eve urged over luncheon. 'What do you think?'

Josephine looked doubtful. 'I can see the advantages, of course. Someone we know. No need to chase after references. But a child in the house – I don't know that my nerves could stand it.'

'Virginia's six years old,' Eve pointed out. 'She'll be at school all day. And when she's home, I'll be here as well to help look after her.'

Josephine glanced suspiciously at her niece. 'Frank's child. Is that what this is about? She'll still belong to Jenny, you know, my dear.'

There was a pause before Eve said in a subdued tone, 'I know that, Aunt Josie, and I promise I won't forget. It's just that ... I don't want his child to be unhappy, if I can do anything to prevent it. A young person about the house will do us both good. New life, new hopes.'

'And new responsibilities,' her aunt added dourly. Then she smiled. 'You may be right,' she conceded. 'Very well, you have my permission to ask Jenny Mailer if she'd like the position. Unless, that is, you change your mind first.'

Chapter Fifteen

Donald glanced up from the solitaire ring lying in the palm of his hand, and said fiercely, 'I won't let you go.'

He and Eve were in Mabel's rose garden, where he had first asked her to marry him almost seven years before. Then it had been winter, with everything bare and brown. Today the garden was a riot of colour, the pride and joy of old Jack Robbs, who had now been joined by young Jack Robbs, one of the lucky ones who had come through the war unscathed. Velvety dark reds vied with peaches and pinks, yellow and white petals starred the grassy paths and the warm sunshine was filled with the mingled scents of the flowers. A dove was cooing in the ancient elms, and from the terrace beyond the wall of yew Eve could hear Ernest calling querulously for Rose.

She had been at home three days and had decided last night, after a family dinner at Rosemary Villa which included Donald and his parents, that she must put an end to her engagement as soon as possible. Conversation throughout the meal had consisted mainly of pressure on her from all sides finally to set a wedding date, and a discussion between Helena and Arthur on the form the village celebration should take. Mabel had patted Eve's hand and whispered that they were having Donald's bedroom redecorated, while the room next to it was being converted into a sitting-room.

'It will look even nicer than the suite we had done for Rose and Ernest.'

Aunt Hetty had added her mite. 'If you can't make up your mind, Eve, we shall have to do it for you. You can't be allowed to shilly-shally any longer; it isn't fair to Donald. What about the first week in October? The weather is often beautiful at that time of year. And you can post your resignation to the Education Authority right away, then you won't even have to bother about the new term.'

It was when her father had endorsed this idea that Eve knew she must do something quickly, and do it without consulting anyone first. She had hoped that she might discuss her feelings with Marcus — explain how the engagement, on her side at least, had come about, and why she now felt that she must end it. She had also hoped that he would understand; but she had come to realize that her father was growing selfish and sometimes wondered, with hindsight, if he might not always have been so. Maybe when he was younger, he had simply been able to disguise the fact better. Whatever the truth of the matter, he certainly wanted her to return to Staple Abbots to live. He was soon to retire and needed her close at hand. She was to provide the companionship and stimulus for his old age which he could not find in his younger sister or in Helena and her family.

Eve had been tempted to speak out last night while they were all together, but had decided that Donald had a right to be told before the others, so she had walked up to Abbey Court this morning.

'Come for a stroll with me, Don. There's something I have to say to you. It's important.'

How they had ended up in the rose garden she had no idea, nor did the significance of the location strike her until afterwards. She just wanted to get matters straight between them. She drew off the diamond ring that had belonged to Grandmother Burfoot and pressed it into her cousin's hand.

'I'm sorry, Donald, but I can't marry you. I should never have agreed to it in the first place. I'm so very, *very* sorry. It's all my fault, I know, but I can't make bad worse by going through with it.'

He stared at her, thoroughly bewildered. 'What are you talking about? Of course you want to marry me.'

'No,' Eve said. 'No, I don't. I never did. Please, Donald, try to understand. We couldn't be happy.'

'I won't let you go! I won't! I've waited years. This time you're not going to escape me.'

She felt her temper rising, and was glad. Anger might help to convince him.

'You haven't any choice but to let me go. And there's no question of "escaping". I'm twenty-four years old and my own mistress. You can't force me to marry you.'

For answer he lunged at her, but she was too quick for him and side-stepped. He went sprawling on the grass path in an undignified heap. When he had scrambled to his feet, he asked murderously, 'Are you keeping something from me? Is there someone else?'

'No, not really. Not in the way you mean. I did go to Paris for a few days with a friend of mine, a widower, but—'

She was now allowed to finish. 'You went to Paris – *Paris!* With another man while you were engaged to me? You . . . you slut!'

Eve opened her mouth to defend herself, to explain how things had really been, but changed her mind. Disgust might do the trick where other means had failed. Perhaps it would persuade her cousin that he didn't want to marry her. So, 'I'm sorry,' she said again and left it there.

She thought for a moment that he was going to strike her: she saw his right hand balled into a fist, and he was breathing deeply. But he contented himself with hurling the ring into a clump of rose-bushes, a gesture which seemed to relieve his feelings slightly. The red light died out of his eyes and he looked as though he were about to cry. At last he opened his mouth and she braced herself to accept meekly, without answering back, anything he might have to say. She owed him that much. The fault was hers for having allowed herself to be pressured into an engagement she had never wanted.

But instead of the personal abuse she was expecting, he said with a venomous snarl, 'I'm sick of this bloody country! I'm sick of Staple Abbots and everyone in it. There's nothing here for me now!' He swung on his heel and disappeared through the gap in the hedge.

*

Marcus, Helena and Hetty celebrated New Year and Eve's
twenty-fifth birthday at Holly Lodge, Eve having resolutely
refused to return to Staple Abbots since her precipitate
departure in August.

Donald had salvaged his wounded pride by letting it be
known that *he* had broken off the engagement after Eve's
disclosure of her trip to Paris with another man. She had not
contradicted him. Only to her parents and Aunt Hetty had she
disclosed the truth, but still they had been shocked by her
behaviour, even though they accepted her version of events.

'You may know that you and Mr Prescott slept in separate
rooms,' her mother chided, 'and that ... well ... nothing
happened. But how can other people be sure you're not lying
in order to protect yourself?'

'Quite so,' Hetty had nodded. 'There are such things as
communicating doors. Not,' she had added hastily, 'that I
know personally about such things, but one reads of them in
the *Daily Sketch*.'

Aunt Hetty and Mama, however, had not been as
disapproving as they might have been had Eve been to Paris
with anyone but Lawrence Prescott. The Robartes inheritance mitigated the impropriety of conduct which would
otherwise have been roundly condemned. Marcus, however,
was less forgiving. He was deeply disappointed at the
overturning of his plans to have his daughter near him. Even
now, after a lapse of over four months, his manner towards
Eve was constrained.

They shared an early breakfast together on New Year's
Day, her birthday morning. The three older women had
decided to eat in bed, and Jenny Mailer was preparing their
trays in the kitchen. For Jenny had jumped at the chance of
moving to Bristol and, so far, had been at great pains to
convince Josephine that she had made the right decision by
employing her. She had listened with unwonted humility to
everything Clarrie had told her, meticulously following

instructions, and had given Clarrie a small gift when the
latter finally left, just before Christmas, to get married. She
had even expressed gratitude towards Eve for recommending
her for the position; but Eve suspected Jenny still harboured
a grudge, still resented her inferior status.

Virginia, too, had settled in well, soon getting over her
uprooting from Staple Abbots and the village school, and
making new friends at the local Primary. She was a little
afraid of Josephine to begin with, but quickly realized that
the rather forbidding manner concealed a tender heart and a
genuine love of children. As for Eve, she was drawn to her
from the first, discovering that this pretty young woman
with the red hair was not only happy to play with her,
entering readily into all her games, but also to listen to her,
sharing her small joys and sorrows – something her mother
never had the patience to do.

'Do you think it wise to pay so much attention to that
child?' Marcus asked after Virginia had left the dining-room.
She had come to say good morning to Eve before they both
set out for school.

'Why not?' But Eve didn't really need her father to tell her
the reason. She knew perfectly well that it wasn't simply
Virginia's natural sweetness of nature which attracted her,
but the fact that she was also so palpably Frank's daughter.
However, Eve was in no mood to argue. Besides being her
birthday, she had a long day ahead of her at William Penn
Road, so she changed the subject by asking, 'Is Aunt Mabel
very upset? I really don't care about Uncle Arthur, but I'd
hate to think I'd hurt Aunt Mabs.'

'Naturally she's upset, what do you expect?' Marcus
buttered a piece of toast with unnecessary vigour. 'And even
more so now that there's a prospect of losing Donald
altogether.'

Eve frowned. 'Whatever do you mean, Papa? Donald's not
ill, is he? Mama hasn't said anything.'

'He's talking of going to Australia. To live ... permanently. Your mother doesn't believe he's serious, that's why

she hasn't mentioned it to you. But Arthur and Mabel think
he means it.'

'But why? He has everything to stay here for. When Uncle
Arthur dies, Abbey Court, the farm and the village will all
belong to him. He can't mean to be an absentee landlord,
surely?'

Marcus bit into his toast. 'I don't know what Donald's
intentions are, and I don't think he does either. It's all
speculation at the moment. Besides, there's no entail on the
property. Arthur could as easily leave everything to Ernest.'

Eve shook her head. 'He won't, though. Uncle Arthur is
very conventional; he believes in the rule of primogeniture.
He'll persuade Donald to stay here, somehow.'

Marcus looked hopeful. 'You sound almost as if you care
whether or not Donald stays or goes.'

Eve sighed and drained her coffee cup. Replacing it in its
saucer, she wiped her mouth on her napkin and got to her
feet.

'I must go or I shall miss my bus.' She kissed her father's
cheek. 'Don't mistake me, Papa. I'm interested in what
Donald does only in so far as it affects the village . . . and you
and Aunt Hetty and Mama. Tell Aunt Josie I'll be home as
soon as I can this evening, because I'm sure she has a birthday
treat planned.' She added in mock horror, '1925. Twenty-
five years old! I'm getting on; I'll soon be on the shelf. How
do you fancy an old maid for a daughter?'

She whisked out of the room before Marcus could answer
and ran upstairs to get her hat and coat. It was a bitterly cold
morning, with a hint of snow in the air, so she added a scarf
and found her woollen gloves. The bedroom windows were
still patterned with frost — 'Jack Frost's been painting
pictures during the night!' Virginia had informed her
excitedly — and icicles hung from the eaves. Eve hurriedly
made her bed, a chore which in the past she had always left
for Clarrie but with which she hesitated to burden Jenny.
Then she went to say goodbye to her mother and aunts, but
found them still asleep. She returned downstairs and let

herself out quietly, so as not to disturb them.

It was even colder than it had felt indoors and her feet slipped on the icy path, making her glad of her sensible leather brogues and thick lisle stockings. Every blade of grass in the small front garden was stiff with rime, the borders of shrubs and bushes white and ghostly. A few doors away, the milkman's horse snorted out great clouds of steaming breath, and two cars, Josephine's Austin Seven and Marcus's black Ford saloon, stood in the roadway silent and empty, a couple of old blankets draping their bonnets. On the opposite side of the road, drawn up on the grass verge of the Downs, a third car had its engine running, but it was only when the horn was sounded that Eve glanced across and recognized Lawrence's Vauxhall.

He opened the off-side door and called, 'I thought you might be glad not to have to wait for buses and trams this morning.'

She hurried over and he got out, punctilious as always, to usher her into the passenger seat, covering her knees with a car-rug. She was deeply touched by this consideration for her comfort from someone who did not have to be out and about so early in such treacherous weather.

'Lawrence, how kind of you. But what about the girls? How are they going to get to school?'

'The chauffeur will take them later, in Mother's car,' he answered lightly. 'By the way, many happy returns of the day. You see, I remembered. Not,' he added, 'that I deserve much credit. New Year's Day isn't an easy date to forget.' He reached over and took a package from the back seat, laying it in her lap. 'This is for you. I hope you like it.'

'Oh, you shouldn't have troubled,' Eve protested. 'What is it? Can I open it now?'

'If you like.' He looked suddenly shy. 'It's nothing much. I mean, they're not real stones . . . just paste.'

By this time, Eve had untied the ribbon and removed the pink tissue paper. Lifting the lid of a little box, she stared enraptured at its contents.

'Oh, Lawrence, thank you. It's beautiful.'

The brooch was indeed a work of art. Set with coloured brilliants, it was fashioned in the form of a peacock, each feather in its spread tail mounted on a tiny spring which made it quiver and shimmer with reflected light at every vibration.

'I – I'm glad you're pleased.'

'It's exquisite! Of course I'm pleased.'

'Good.' He put the car into gear and they moved forward to join the steady stream of traffic heading for the top of Blackboy Hill. As he carefully negotiated the steep descent, Lawrence went on, 'On Saturday, could you – I mean would you – come to tea? I want to introduce you to my mother.'

*

'If you don't want to go, telephone Lawrence now and make some excuse,' Josephine advised her.

'I can't. It's too late. He's calling for me at half-past three. Besides, I couldn't possibly hurt his feelings.'

'Also, you're curious,' her aunt added drily. 'But meeting his mother does have certain connotations: it suggests to me that Lawrence is getting serious. Think carefully, Eve. Do you want to take on a widower and two stepdaughters? I noted that you didn't mention the invitation to either your parents or Hetty while they were here.'

'There wasn't much time. I was only asked the day before yesterday, and they were gone first thing this morning.' Eve encountered her aunt's ironic smile and said, 'All right. More than enough time, I admit, to have told them if I'd really wanted to. But you know what Mama and Aunt Hetty are like. They would have been choosing wedding dresses by now.'

Josephine laughed. 'True. But I don't believe that's the real reason you didn't tell them. You haven't made up your mind yet about Lawrence.'

Eve grimaced. She and her aunt had finished lunch and were huddled now over the drawing-room fire. The leaping flames scorched her face and the fronts of her legs, but her back and feet were freezing in spite of the draught-excluder along the bottom of the door.

'What's wrong with me, Aunt Josie?' she asked. 'First Donald, now Lawrence. Why am I so frightened of committing myself to anyone? Of trying to make things work?'

'I can answer that in two words,' Josephine said briskly. 'Frank Mailer. You're scared of a second betrayal.'

'Perhaps. Or am I still in love with Frank?'

Her aunt shrugged. 'Only you can answer that question, my dear. So, you intend going this afternoon?'

'I can't possibly get out of it this late in the day. Besides, as you guessed, I'm curious. I'm longing to see the dragon for myself. The only question now is, what do I wear?'

Josephine laughed. 'The perennial cry of womankind! But a sensible one. You will feel much more confident if you know that you look your best. You can borrow my fur coat if you want.'

So when Lawrence arrived punctually at three-thirty, Eve was waiting for him, arrayed in Josephine's sable coat and with one of the new cloche hats in brown felt framing her face. Beneath the coat, and in defiance of the weather, she wore her beige silk afternoon tea-dress, not only because it was flattering to her complexion and figure but also because it was two years old and had a mid-calf-length skirt. In the past twelve months skirts had risen to an immodest height, and the fashion magazines all forecast that they would rise above the knee before the year was out; a prediction which had already elicited an angry response from churchmen and other self-appointed guardians of morals.

Lawrence greeted her shyly, twisting his bowler hat between nervous hands.

'I . . . I was afraid you'd change your mind,' he said.

'Of course not.' Eve made her smile as convincing as she could. 'I promised.' She carefully avoided Josephine's eyes as her aunt emerged from the drawing-room just in time to overhear this exchange.

'Miss Gilchrist.' Lawrence shook Josephine's hand. 'I'll make sure Eve's home in time for dinner.'

'My dear boy, she's twenty-five. She could stay out all night and I shouldn't be able to stop her.'

'That'll do, Aunt Josie.' Eve kissed Josephine's cheek. 'Not everyone has your broadminded approach to life.'

Her aunt laughed and whispered in her ear, 'I shall look forward eagerly to hearing all about it.'

Eve frowned her down and was relieved when the front door finally closed behind her. Aunt Josie could be an embarrassment at times.

The journey across the Suspension Bridge to Leigh Woods was a short one, but seemed longer than it was on account of the unaccustomed silence between them. Eve made one or two efforts at conversation, but Lawrence's replies were monosyllabic, preoccupied. She could feel her own apprehension rising.

Robartes House was not as large as she had expected: an early Victorian mansion set well back from the road in a tree-lined side street of this affluent suburb. Nevertheless, it was big enough, as Eve learned later, to accommodate comfortably not only Calanthe Prescott, her son and grand-daughters, but also a number of servants including a cook, chauffeur and housekeeper, three kitchen- and four parlour-maids. An acre of garden required the services of only one full-time and one part-time gardener, neither of whom slept on the premises. The interior of the house, particularly the entrance hall and staircase, struck Eve as being extremely dark, panelled from floor to ceiling in oak, the only source of light being the stained-glass windows surrounding the front door and on the landing. The furnishings, too, were made of a solid and heavy walnut, while the floor was marble tiling which echoed unnervingly to every footfall.

However, the room into which Lawrence presently led the way, after Eve had been divested of her hat and coat, was altogether brighter, with tall French windows, cream-papered walls and deep sofas and armchairs upholstered in a floral cretonne. A huge log-fire burned in the grate, and the mantelpiece above displayed a row of four Dresden china shepherdesses, two on either side of an ormolu clock. A further collection of Dresden china occupied a glass-fronted cabinet, lined with green watered silk, in one corner of the room. The pale blue carpet was deep-piled and soft to tread on – like walking on cotton wool, Eve thought.

'Mother.' Lawrence spoke softly, almost reverentially. 'This is Eve Gilchrist.'

Calanthe Prescott rose gracefully from her armchair and held out one soft, white, well-manicured hand.

'Miss Gilchrist. My son has spoken to me about you. I am so happy to meet you at last.'

Eve found herself looking into a pair of eyes the same pale shade of blue as Lawrence's. The fair wavy hair was also his, not just bobbed but fashionably shingled. Lawrence had told Eve that his mother was fifty-six, but had she not known Eve would have judged Calanthe to be at least ten years younger. The peach-bloom skin showed no sign of wrinkles, just as the hair showed no speck of grey. And the low-waisted, short-skirted dress of fine grey wool revealed shapely legs in pure silk stockings and breasts flattened, not with complete success, to the new androgynous look which was currently all the rage. Beside Calanthe Eve felt positively dowdy, and wished that she had worn her shortest frock. She also wished that she had followed her impulse to have her hair at least semi-shingled, in defiance of what her family or Miss Perry might have said.

At Calanthe's invitation, she sat down in a corner of the sofa facing the hearth, but when Lawrence would have sat beside her his mother asked sharply, 'Darling, why are you sitting there? You know you prefer your own chair.' She gave a tinkling laugh. 'You wouldn't believe, Miss Gilchrist, how grouchy my dearest gets if everything doesn't go exactly as he likes it. And naturally, the girls and I indulge him. His heart isn't strong, but I expect you know that.'

'Mother!' Lawrence protested, a faint tinge of red staining

his pale skin, 'you know I'm much better than I was. Doctor Massey told me so only last week.'

Calanthe leaned across and squeezed his hand. 'Darling, of course. Of course!' But her words conveyed, as they were intended to do, the opposite meaning. 'Forgive me, I'm just a fussy old mother hen.' Again came the tinkle of laughter. 'You know what we old ladies are!'

'Dearest! You're not old, you know you're not.' But the denial was made half-heartedly, with an uncomfortable glance in Eve's direction.

Out of the corner of one eye, Eve saw her hostess's expression harden into surprised disbelief. Calanthe was obviously used to unreserved homage from her son. Before she could say anything, however, the door opened to admit Justine and Olivia, who greeted Eve with delight.

'Miss Gilchrist.' Justine held out her hand, smiling broadly, while her younger sister kissed Eve's cheek. Calanthe's carefully darkened eyebrows shot up.

'You seem remarkably familiar with our guest, my darlings. Have you met her before?'

Lawrence hurried into speech. 'Yes. Yes . . . they have, Mother. They were – er – in the car one day when we . . . we saw Miss Gilchrist waiting at a bus stop and – and offered her a ride into the Tramways Centre.'

Justine nodded. 'That's right, Grandmama.' And she nudged Olivia in the ribs.

'I see.' And it was plain to Eve that Calanthe Prescott did indeed see, and a great deal more than she was meant to. Eve presumed that when Lawrence's wife was alive, there had been no need for lies and subterfuge: the two women had been hand in glove, he had as good as said so. But why on earth didn't Lawrence stand up to his mother? He was thirty-three, for heaven's sake! A grown man. But he was also financially dependent on her; he had never earned his own living and probably did not even know how to do so.

A uniformed maid entered, wheeling the tea-trolley, and the awkward moment passed.

'Sit down, girls,' Calanthe said, 'and look after Miss Gilchrist.' She added with deceptive sweetness, 'After all, you appear to know her better than I do.'

Chapter Sixteen

The teachers of William Penn Road Junior School were crowded together in the staff-room. Standing next to Bill Hutton, Eve noticed the frayed edges of his shirt cuffs, and how far his bony wrists protruded from his sleeves. The elbows of his jacket had been patched, and patched again. The narrow face was gaunt, as if he did not get enough to eat; which, with a wife and five children to support on his meagre wages, he probably didn't. And, as so often happened in the company of her fellow workers, Eve felt ashamed of the privileged life she led. The post-war cycle of industrial decline, spiralling unemployment and social bitterness had barely touched her, except that five years after leaving university she was still here, at William Penn Road, instead of teaching at a grammar school; a small hardship compared with those of others.

'What's the meeting about?' Rita Gurney asked uneasily.

But no one knew, and they had to wait for Miss Perry's arrival to find out. The headmistress marched in twenty minutes later, her expression even more pugnacious than usual, carrying an afternoon edition of the evening paper which she slapped down on the table in the middle of the room.

'It's official,' she said. 'There is going to be a General Strike, starting tomorrow. So, let me make it quite clear that I expect every one of you to get here somehow, even if you have to walk all the way. Nor do I expect unpunctuality. You will have to leave home earlier than usual, that's all. Lack of transport will be no excuse. Is that understood?'

There was a murmur of assent. It was left to Eve to enquire with apparent innocence, 'But if we do that, Headmistress, aren't we helping to defeat the object of the strike?'

Miss Perry spun round to glare at her. 'Certainly. Do you want this country held to ransom, Miss Gilchrist, by a lot of Bolshie miners and their friends?' Without waiting for an answer, she continued, 'We're British! King, Country and Empire! Those are our watchwords.'

'Hear, hear,' volunteered Bill Hutton, and Eve stared at him helplessly.

'You're the very one who ought to be fighting for better wages and conditions,' she told him, as they filtered out of the staff room.

'If I did that, I'd lose my job, and then where would Gladys and the children be?' He sniffed. 'You'll be all right. Mr Prescott'll be driving you to and from school, no doubt.'

Rita Gurney, a large, jolly spinster whose optimistic spirit not even Miss Perry and William Penn Road could break, spoke from behind them.

'I was pleased as punch you spoke up, Eve. No one else would have dared. I thought La Perry was going to choke on her own bile. But she daren't try sacking you again, not while you're such friends with one of the school Governors.' Bill Hutton had by now moved ahead, anxious to ensure that his class was behaving itself in his absence, so Rita drew abreast and linked her arm through Eve's. 'When's the wedding to be, then? You've been going out with Mr Prescott for more than two years.'

'He has to propose marriage before we can fix a wedding date,' Eve responded drily. Had it been anyone but Rita Gurney who asked the question, she would have snubbed the impertinence; but she was fond of Rita, who had never shown her any animosity, and who never complained about her own drab life looking after an invalid mother. But Rita's obvious curiosity made Eve clam up. 'I must get back to the hall,' she added, 'before Miss Perry arrives. My little darlings will be taking every advantage of this summons to the staff-room. It's arithmetic this afternoon and they hate it.'

But Eve herself found it difficult to concentrate for the

remaining hour before the four o'clock bell. Rita Gurney's
question had merely echoed those of her mother and Aunt
Hetty, whose recent letters had grown increasingly clamor-
ous for information on the subject of her friendship with
Lawrence. Even Uncle Arthur had hinted, during her last
visit home at Easter, that he just might be able to forgive her
rejection of Donald, and Donald's consequent emigration to
Australia, were she to marry Calanthe Robartes's son. It
would demonstrate, he had intimated, that she was neither
as stupid nor as feckless as her early infatuation for Frank
Mailer had led him to believe. Only Aunt Josie kept quiet,
although it was often plainly an effort for her to do so.

The trouble was, Eve thought, as she chalked up multi-
plication and division sums on the blackboard, that she could
give no one a definite answer concerning either Lawrence's
intentions or her own. During the last two years, their
relationship had developed from a semi-secret into an open
one. Eve was a regular visitor to Robartes House, just as
Lawrence and his daughters were to Holly Lodge, where Olivia
and Virginia Mailer, with a mere two years difference in their
ages, had become fast friends. Calanthe, once she had satisfied
herself as to Eve's background – daughter of a professional
man, niece of a wealthy landowner – had put no obstacle in
their path, always impeccably polite if not exactly welcoming.

But what did it all amount to? Eve wondered, frowning
fiercely at Johnnie Gaukroger, who was craning over his
neighbour's shoulder in an effort to copy his answers.
Flowers and expensive presents on her birthday, boxes of
chocolates and the best theatre seats, holding hands in one
of the new moving picture houses now springing up all over
Bristol, sedate good-night kisses: in short, deep and genuine
affection on both sides, but seemingly without an ounce of
passion between them. Did she, however, want passion from
Lawrence? Eve rapped on her desk with a ruler to draw
Johnnie's attention to her displeasure, before lapsing once
more into thought whilst supposedly marking some exercise
books.

She had a suspicion that she was the one who dictated the speed at which their relationship developed, Lawrence being too much of a gentleman to force the pace. She was extremely fond of him, so what inhibited her? The reasons were always the same: Calanthe Prescott, Lawrence's dependence on his mother, his two children and his state of health. No, not the girls; Eve got on too well with both Justine and Olivia for them to be considered as anything of a problem. But Lawrence's heart was undoubtedly weak, although probably in nothing like as serious a condition as his mother would have him believe. The Prescotts, of course, had never been panel patients, and Calanthe's doctor was only too willing to encourage a rich client's concern about her son. Eve wondered if she could ever persuade Lawrence to abandon his mother's roof, and had doubts concerning her own ability to fit in at Robartes House.

Stalemate, then, she thought with a sigh, as Miss Perry reluctantly reached down beside her chair and rang the last bell of the day.

'Hand in your papers, please, before you go!' Eve shouted, above the babel which succeeded this eagerly awaited signal of release. 'And John Gaukroger! Next time I see you trying to cheat, you'll be kept in after school.'

There was an unrepentant 'Yes, Miss', as Johnnie headed for the hall's double doors and disappeared from view. Eve grinned to herself as she put the rest of the books to be marked, together with the arithmetic tests, into her attaché case and went off to the staff-room to collect her hat and coat. Once outside in the warm May sunshine, she took a deep breath, the daily sense of freedom washing over her as she stepped through the playground gate and into the street. The Vauxhall Velox was waiting for her, drawn up to the kerb, and Lawrence as always got out of the car at her approach. This afternoon, however, there was a look of concern on his face.

'Is something wrong?' she asked, returning his chaste peck on the cheek.

He took both her hands and held them sustainingly. 'It's your uncle,' he said. 'Miss Gilchrist had a telephone call from Staple Abbots about two hours ago.'

'Uncle Arthur? Why, what's happened?'

'He had a very severe stroke this morning and died almost immediately. Miss Gilchrist asked if I would drive you both down to Wiltshire tonight and stay until you return. Because of course, with this strike, there won't be any trains running.'

*

Uncle Arthur dead! It seemed impossible. He had been so much a part of her life ever since she was born. Like Josephine and Marcus, Eve could not pretend to any great depth of grief; she had never really cared for her uncle, but she did experience a shocked sense of loss. The villagers, too, mourned the passing of a man born in the old Queen's reign and bred in the proud tradition of the British Empire on which the sun never set; the representative of solid Victorian virtues which appeared to be increasingly under threat in this age of the Charleston and the flapper in knee-high skirts. Arthur Burfoot had been, according to his lights, a good landlord and a respected employer. And now Staple Abbots, village and farm, belonged to Donald, thousands of miles away on the other side of the world.

'Why didn't Father-in-law leave everything to Ernest?' Rose complained fretfully after the reading of the will. 'We could have managed. Ernest is so much better.'

This was obvious. In the two years since his brother's departure, Ernest had improved almost beyond recognition, from the shattered creature who had returned from the war to a man busy and fulfilled, contentedly married and helping his father to run the estate and farm. Rose was as much in her element as her husband, never happier than when she was out in the fields assisting the men, or tinkering with farm machinery.

'What will happen, now?' Eve asked. 'Will Donald come home?'

Rose snorted in disgust. 'Oh, no! He's never coming back. He's written to Mother-in-law, making that plain. So Ernest and I will continue to run the estate for him – with the hope, I suppose, that he might one day make it over legally to us.'

This information, retailed to Marcus that evening, evoked only a shake of the head.

'If that's what Rose and Ernest are hoping, I think they're being over-optimistic, unless they can afford to buy the property from Donald, which I very much doubt. I have an uneasy feeling that he'll want to capitalize on his inheritance; make as much money out of it as he can. Don't you agree, Mr Prescott?'

Lawrence was staying as a guest at Rosemary Villa until such time as Eve and Josephine were ready to return to Bristol, all public transport still being paralysed by the General Strike. He had proved himself invaluable in his own quiet way, telephoning Miss Perry and apprising her of events, offering comfort to Helena and lending a sympathetic ear to Hetty's round condemnation of the strikers.

'Oh, I don't know, sir,' he said, in answer to Marcus's question, leaning forward in his chair with his hands clasped loosely between his knees. 'I don't believe any decent man would sell his birthright to a stranger.'

'Then you have more faith in human nature than I have,' Marcus retorted grimly.

'But who,' Eve demanded, 'would want an isolated estate in the wilds of Salisbury Plain?'

Her father laughed, but there was no comfort in the sound.

'Donald will have no trouble selling Staple Abbots, believe you me! There's been a potential buyer eagerly waiting in the wings for years.' And in answer to the puzzled look on her face, Marcus added in exasperation, 'The War Office! They're simply longing to snap up Staple Abbots. It's slap in the middle of one of their biggest military reservations.'

'Donald would never sell to the War Office!' Helena protested, appalled. 'The village, the Court, the farm have all belonged to the Burfoots for generations.'

'Of course he wouldn't!' Hetty declared, while even Eve thought her father for once completely mistaken.

'No Burfoot could bring himself to do such a thing,' she said to Lawrence, when they went for a walk after supper. 'By the way, Aunt Josie and I are ready to leave as early as you want tomorrow morning.'

They had crossed the village street and taken one of the roads to Upper Abbots, passing St Peter's Church on the corner. Its ancient stones were weathered and peaceful in the evening sun, just visible behind the elms which screened the building. The wall enclosing the graveyard was bright with stonecrop coming into flower, and in the long grass at its foot cowslips lifted their golden heads, nodding in a gentle breeze. A rook cawed in the trees high above them, and further on they passed a cottage, the garden thick with the scent of lilac blossom, its well-stocked beds overflowing with grape hyacinths, tulips and wallflowers. The woman standing in the cottage doorway wished them 'Good evening.'

'Sometimes, it all seems a bit too good to be true,' Eve said. 'Like an illustration on a biscuit tin or a box of chocolates. Mind you, Papa would tell you differently. He sees only bad drains and rotting timbers.'

'Doctor Gilchrist's a practical man.' Lawrence smiled ruefully. 'I don't think he likes me very much.'

'What nonsense! Of course he does!'

Lawrence shook his head. 'We don't see eye to eye politically. He's all for Socialism and the "Brave New World." And I suspect that you are too, Eve. You're very like your father in your way of thinking.'

They had reached Staple Round, a circle of beech trees cresting the rising ground. Beyond, the road wound downhill to a broad, treeless horizon, where Upper Abbots showed as a distant smudge against a glorious sunset. Eve paused in the shadow of the Round and looked consideringly at him.

'Does it worry you? That we don't always think alike, I mean?'

He returned her look without dropping his eyes. 'No, I love you just as you are. If I tried to change you in any particular, you wouldn't be Eve. I wondered ... I mean, I hoped that you might feel the same way about me.'

He had told her that he loved her, but there was no surge of elation, no breathless quickening of the heart such as she had experienced with Frank. Nevertheless a warm, satisfying glow of contentment filled her, a feeling of having come safely into harbour, and just for the moment she forgot everything else. She held out her hands.

'Dear Lawrence. I love you, too ... just as you are. No strings.'

He gave that wide joyous grin which transformed his normally serious features, but was so rarely seen. Then he took her in his arms and kissed her, his body suddenly hard and urgent against hers. His passion took her by surprise and she responded immediately, aware how long it was since she had experienced any desire for a man. She was twenty-six years old and had never had a man make love to her in the fullest sense of the expression. A century, even half a century, ago she would have been regarded as an old maid, fit only to look after elderly parents or chaperone young nieces. Nowadays, however, women married and had children much later in life, and women over thirty even had the right to vote.

This unexpected need for Lawrence made her light-headed and unwary. She pressed closer to him. Her lips opened under his and she felt the strange, rough texture of his tongue. Her arms tightened round him until she was aware of nothing except the accelerated beating of her heart ...

He pushed her away almost roughly, and she saw the slightly shocked expression in his eyes. He had not expected this reaction from her. It was not the mark of a well-brought-up young woman to display such a positive response to male advances. Nice girls, as Aunt Hetty was never tired of repeating, held men at arm's length until after the wedding. It was only women of a 'certain sort', generally from the lower classes, who led men on and got themselves into trouble. Even post-war emancipation had not permitted a lowering of sexual standards.

Eve defiantly raised her chin. 'I've embarrassed you. I'm sorry.'

'No ... Of course you haven't.'

'Lawrence,' she said quietly, 'I can't help the way I'm made, and you said yourself that you wouldn't want to change me. I'm a passionate woman. You'll have to accept that if ...' She hesitated; women – those same nice, well-brought-up, conventional women – never mentioned the word marriage before it passed the lips of a man. But she had already shocked Lawrence once, so she might as well be hung for a sheep as a lamb. 'If,' she finished, 'you want to marry me. Do you?'

Just for a moment he looked as though he might turn tail and run, then he smiled shyly.

'Yes,' he said. 'I want to marry you, Eve. If you'll have me, that is.'

'I should be honoured, Lawrence dear.' Her demure formality staunched his disapproval and made him laugh. 'Do you think,' she added provocatively, 'that we should risk another kiss?'

It was only later, as they walked slowly back to the village arm-in-arm, that she remembered Calanthe Prescott and wondered what on earth she had done.

*

'Of course you must have a white wedding,' Calanthe said. 'You mustn't be selfish, Lawrence darling, just because you've been married before. This is Eve's first time and naturally she wants to do the thing properly.' She smiled graciously at her future daughter-in-law. 'Leave everything to me. I'll organize it.'

Eve recruited her strength with a sip of Earl Grey tea from

a Royal Worcester bone china cup. This would be the first trial of strength between them.

'That's very kind of you, Mrs Prescott, but I shall be married at home in Staple Abbots. My parents will make all the arrangements.'

'Ah! How silly of me.' A look of displeasure momentarily shadowed the perfectly made-up features. 'I was forgetting.'

Eve wondered what exactly it was that Calanthe had forgotten. That Eve had relations of her own? That they could possibly be of any importance? That a retired country doctor and his wife could afford to marry off their daughter in a style befitting her wedding to Jacob Robartes's grandson? It was on the tip of her tongue to enquire, but she saw the distress on Lawrence's face and said nothing.

Calanthe got her second wind after this initial setback. Eve had been invited to Sunday tea at Robartes House in order to discuss her and Lawrence's plans for the future, and there was to be no reprieve.

'You'll be making your home here, that goes without saying, and after tea you must come and see the suite of rooms I'm having prepared for you both.'

A stray shaft of sunlight struck sparks from the square-cut emerald on Eve's left hand, and she glanced thoughtfully at the ring which had once belonged to Lawrence's Grandmother Robartes. She had a sudden sense of déjà vu; of Donald giving her the diamond solitaire which had been Grandmother Burfoot's; of Aunt Mabel whispering that they were having his bedroom redecorated and the room next to it turned into a sitting-room. The phrase 'out of the frying-pan into the fire' occurred to her; but of course the present situation wasn't at all the same as her engagement to her cousin. She was extremely fond of Lawrence, whereas she had never really liked Donald, only felt sorry for him. All the same there were similarities, as Aunt Josie had been the first to point out.

'You must put your foot down,' she had advised her niece. 'Start as you mean to go on.'

So, with a jutting chin, Eve said, 'Lawrence and I were thinking of buying a house of our own. After all' — she blushed slightly — 'if Justine and Olivia should have a little half-brother or -sister, we should need the extra room.'

There was a silence so profound that the ticking of the ormolu clock on the drawing-room mantelpiece sounded like the chiming of Big Ben. Out of the corner of one eye Eve could see Lawrence frozen into stillness, his fingers gripping the arms of his chair until his knuckles showed bone-white against the gaily flowered cretonne. Then the hush was broken by Calanthe's tinkling laugh.

'My dear child! Do you know what houses cost these days? Even a modest four-bedroomed one could be two or three hundred pounds. Where would you find the money? I don't imagine your salary as a teacher at William Penn Road has allowed you to make any savings. Lawrence has his quarterly allowance, and what he makes from selling his paintings, such as it is, but he's used to spending all that on himself. I make myself responsible for the girls — so long as they're under my roof. So I do think, Eve, my dear, you're being just the tiniest bit irresponsible. Lawrence's heart is not strong, as you know, a burden I shall now be able to share with you. He needs rest and care and attention. In those circumstances, Doctor Callender assures me he can live a normal life, but the last thing he needs is worry and aggravation. Finding a house, raising the money, buying furniture, curtains and carpets would involve both those things, wouldn't you agree? No, be quiet, Lawrence dearest, let me finish. As for space, Robartes House has as much as — probably more than — you will ever need. Besides, what of Justine and Olivia? They have lived here since they were born; it would be most upsetting for them to be uprooted.'

Eve looked at Lawrence, waiting for his support, but still he said nothing. Later, during the drive across the Suspension Bridge to Holly Lodge, he explained, 'Mama's used to having me and the girls around, my darling. For the moment she's still coming to terms with the fact that I'm getting married again, and I don't want to upset her more than I have to. And she's right about one thing. We simply haven't the money at present to live independently in the style to which we're both accustomed. But I promise that once we're married, I really will settle down and paint in earnest. I know I can sell my pictures. It's just a matter of producing them in sufficient numbers.'

Eve asked quietly, 'Don't my wishes count for anything?'

Lawrence raised one hand from the steering-wheel and laid it placatingly on her arm.

'You know they do. And if there were only you and me to think about, I'd gladly risk a little hardship. But there are Justine and Olivia to consider. We can't expect them to suffer just because we want to be on our own. I give you my solemn promise that it will only be until I've made enough money to buy us all a proper home.'

Eve felt trapped. She knew the provisions of the late Jacob Robartes's will; Calanthe had made it her business to inform her. The huge fortune had been left exclusively to his only child for her sole use during her lifetime, and to be disposed of by her, as she wished, at her death. Several watertight clauses had prevented Calanthe's husband having any say in the use of the money, and had reduced him, like his son, to the status of a mere dependant. Perhaps it was fortunate, Eve reflected, that he had died young, when Lawrence was only a few years old. Life with Calanthe must have become an increasingly intolerable burden.

Should she see that as a warning? But she had her affection for Lawrence and the prospect of eventual escape to sustain her. As long as she had his promise that sharing his mother's roof was only a temporary arrangement, surely it wouldn't hurt her, for Justine's and Olivia's sakes, to do as he asked for a little while at least. A small, chill voice whispered that she was being naïve, but she chose to ignore it. Life was rushing by and she wanted a man of her own to take care of her and, more importantly, go to bed with; and for a woman like herself, only marriage brought that freedom. Love, in its

deepest sense, had died with Frank: she neither needed nor
expected another such experience. But she felt, in some
obscure way, that she was cheating Lawrence, therefore she
owed him something.

She pressed the hand lying on her arm. 'All right,' she
agreed. 'Just to begin with we'll live at Robartes House. But
darling, you *must* give me your word that it's simply a
temporary measure.'

Chapter Seventeen

Eve sat up in bed, hugging her knees, and glanced around the old familiar room. Nothing much had changed over the years. The curtains were of a thicker material, but still rose-patterned, and the white crocheted bedspread had been lined with pink silk. But the strawberry-coloured carpet, the walnut furniture, the jug and basin with roses round the rim, the shelves of books and dolls and the dolls' house were all exactly as she had left them when she went away to university, and just as they had been waiting for her each time she returned. She couldn't count the number of occasions on which she had sat up in bed, as she was doing now, and listened to the birds singing in the lilac tree outside the window.

This morning, however, was different. Today was her wedding day, and in a few hours she would marry Lawrence in St Peter's Church. She didn't know whether to be glad or sorry that the long months of preparation were nearing their end. In one way, she was happy to be done with the endless fussing by her mother and Aunt Hetty who, in the past four months, had spent more time at Holly Lodge than in Staple Abbots, severely trying the patience of both Eve and Josephine with their protracted shopping expeditions and discussion of wedding plans. In addition, there had been the disagreement with Calanthe; a disagreement which stemmed from the older woman's discovery that the third bridesmaid who, along with Justine and Olivia, would follow Eve down the aisle, was the daughter of Josephine's housekeeper.

'For heaven's sake, my dear girl,' she had expostulated, 'we can't possibly have that. If your aunt is pushing you into asking this Virginia what's-her-name for some reason of her own, let me speak to Miss Gilchrist. I'll soon rid

229

her of any such quixotic notion.'

'It has nothing whatsoever to do with my aunt,' Eve had replied, coldly furious. 'I want Virginia to be my bridesmaid, and I intend having her no matter what you say. And her mother is also being invited to the wedding.'

She did not think it wise to mention then, or at any subsequent time, the friendship existing between Olivia and Ginny; nor did she offer the slightest explanation as to why she wanted the child to be her bridesmaid. She had simply continued with her plans, ignoring all her future mother-in-law's attempts to make her change her mind, and quite enjoying herself in the process. But the barely concealed antagonism between the two women had the effect of making Lawrence ill; he grew short of breath and at least twice, while he and Eve were sitting together in Calanthe's drawing-room, she had felt the whole sofa shake with the pounding of his heart.

Eve had remained firm, but how often could she do so in the years ahead? Lawrence's delicate health would always be there like the big stick in the corner, threatening to beat her into submission. And it was this worry, nagging away at her throughout the months of her engagement, which had woken her this morning long before anyone else was stirring. It was only just daylight, the pale September sun gleaming like an aureole around the edges of the curtains. Not even the maid, Vera, Doris Hosier's successor, was up yet. Eve lay back once more against her pillows, straightening her legs and closing her eyes in an effort to go back to sleep.

But sleep was elusive. Her unquiet thoughts chased one another around inside her head, like squirrels in a cage. Common sense told her that even now, at this eleventh hour, it was not too late to call off the wedding if she had any doubts about it. But she couldn't do that to Lawrence. And anyway, she didn't want to. She was fond of him, and had grown even fonder over the intervening months since their engagement. She was necessary to him and the girls in a way she had never been necessary to anyone else in her life before. Perhaps

Lawrence did not realize it yet, but he needed to free himself from Calanthe; to become a person in his own right, on his own merit, instead of living always in the shadow of his mother. He was a talented artist, but he wanted encouragement, something he had never been given because success would mean independence. It would be an uphill battle, but Eve had become increasingly aware lately of her inherited strength of will and purpose.

Suddenly, she was unable to stay in bed any longer. She felt restless, longing for the day to be over, to be Lawrence's wife, to take care of him. She wondered if he, too, was awake in his bed at Abbey Court, where Rose and Ernest were putting up all the bridegroom's friends and relations. Getting out of bed, she padded across the room and poured some cold water from the jug into the basin. She rinsed her face, shivering as the icy drops splashed her skin. Then she brushed her hair and dressed quickly in the tweed skirt and silky, handknitted jumper, the lisle stockings and brogues which she had worn yesterday for the journey to Staple Abbots. Her wedding dress – ankle-length white georgette with a deep border of pearl-encrusted silver lace – hung like a ghost from the picture-rail. The filmy veil, with its coronet of orange blossom, was still shrouded in tissue paper. Eve put on her coat, found her gloves, for the September mornings were growing chilly, and tiptoed downstairs, letting herself out silently through the back door.

Dew lay heavy on the grass, and a lingering memory of yesterday's garden bonfire scented the air. Spiders' webs draped the bushes with an iridescent pall, and the smell of apples drifted in from the orchard. Chrysanthemums, asters and early Michaelmas daisies filled Aunt Hetty's carefully tended borders; autumn crocus and cyclamen made gay patches of colour under the trees. Beyond the front gate the village street stretched still and silent, with one or two lights, paling now in the brightening day, showing in the bakery behind the Jenks's shop and in the dairy on the opposite side of the roadway. A clatter of churns suggested that the milk cart was already being loaded, and Eve heard the old horse whinny as it was harnessed between the shafts.

She began walking briskly in the direction of Abbey Court, then turned off along the footpath beside the Ring O' Bells. Five minutes later, she had reached Long Meadow and the track leading to the rickyard. She paused, staring over the gate into the hayfield, already partially mown. A ghost, pale and insubstantial, came towards her, hand held out in greeting. A voice, faint but familiar, called: 'Auburn!' She answered joyously: 'Frank!' but there was no one there, only a faint breeze whispering amongst the stubble. Eve turned away, her eyes blind with tears, scrabbling in her coat pocket for a handkerchief. Frank was dead; gone along with all those halcyon pre-war days when it always seemed to be high summer; lost in the mud and agony of Flanders. Her future now lay with Lawrence and his daughters.

'And with his mother,' persisted that nagging voice at the back of her mind, but she ignored it. Nothing could be allowed to spoil today. She must get back to Rosemary Villa before she was missed by the ever-vigilant Aunt Hetty. Besides, by the time she had bathed and dressed the bridesmaids would be arriving: Justine and Olivia from the Court, Virginia from her grandmother's house, where she was staying with Jenny. As she regained the High Street, Eve passed the village postman with his sack of mail.

''Morning, Miss Eve. This is the big day, then! Missus and I have bin invited to the wedding.'

'I hope you both enjoy it.'

'We shall. Missus loves a good cry, an' you'll be a bride worth looking at.'

She thanked him and moved on, almost running now in her anxiety to reach home before Aunt Hetty woke up. But it was Josephine who sat at the scrubbed kitchen table, sharing an early morning pot of tea with Vera.

'I've been out,' Eve said unnecessarily. 'I couldn't sleep.'

Her aunt nodded understandingly and, picking up the teapot, filled another cup with the scalding-hot, dark brown liquid. They talked at random for a while, but when Vera had clattered off to the dining-room to lay the breakfast, Josephine leaned across and gripped Eve's free hand.

'Darling, you're certain about this marriage? It won't all be a bed of roses, you know.' She grimaced. 'Ugh! What a nasty little cliché. Why don't I just come out with the truth? You'll have trouble with Calanthe.'

Eve smiled and put down her cup. Raising herself from her chair, she reached over and kissed her aunt's cheek.

'I know. But I think I'm strong enough to cope. And now, I must go upstairs and run my bath. That geyser takes such a time to heat the water.'

Josephine glanced out of the kitchen window. 'It looks as though it's going to be another beautiful day. Let's pray nothing happens to spoil it.'

'Pessimist,' Eve said; and had cause to remember her reproach an hour or so later.

They were still at breakfast, her parents, her aunts and herself, animatedly discussing last-minute preparations, when they heard the front door open and voices raised in the hall. Then Vera popped her head around the door and announced, 'It's Mrs Ernest, m'am,' but Rose was already inside the room. She was waving a letter.

'Oh, Marcus,' she wailed, 'you were quite right! This has come this morning, from Australia. It's Donald; he's instructed his solicitors to sell everything, lock, stock and barrel, to the War Office. He says they've offered him a price he can't refuse!'

*

The wedding breakfast was held at Abbey Court, with a Warminster firm hired to do the catering. Everyone did their best to be cheerful, but inevitably uneasiness clouded the enjoyment. Rumours of Donald's decision to sell to the War Office were already circulating among the villagers; and throughout the service in St Peter's, Eve was conscious of the sibilant whispers behind her. Later, during the reception, she was aware of people sidling up to Rose and Ernest, faces creased with anxiety.

Lawrence asked, 'Is something wrong?'

They were waiting to cut the four-tiered cake, decorated with silver bells and horseshoes, and made for the occasion by Mrs Jenks to one of her special recipes.

'I'll tell you presently,' Eve whispered. She could see Calanthe trying to engage her mother in conversation, but it was obvious that Helena's mind was elsewhere. Suddenly the day seemed spoilt and she wanted it to be over; to be away with Lawrence to London, where they were spending the night before catching the boat train from Victoria Station to Dover.

'We'll go to Switzerland,' Lawrence had said. 'Just the two of us for a fortnight. It'll be wonderful.'

Eve had kissed him. 'We'll have a lot longer than two weeks by ourselves, darling, once we've saved enough money for a place of our own. It needn't be a house to begin with; a flat would do, so long as it's big enough for four. Your paintings will sell, I know they will. You just have to make yourself settle down and work.'

He had returned her kiss but made no answer, a significant omission which she failed to notice at the time but which had since returned to haunt her. She consoled herself with the belief that things would be different after they were married; then her influence must surely be stronger than Calanthe's.

Was she deluding herself? she wondered as, with Lawrence's hand covering hers, she sliced into the bottom tier of the cake, the other three sections having been removed. There was a cheer, led by the best man – a thin, cadaverous middle-aged individual who had been introduced to Eve by Calanthe.

'The brother-in-law of a cousin of my late husband.' Yet again, Eve had felt uneasy. Didn't Lawrence have a friend he could have asked?

But it was far too late now for doubts. She had had her chance to withdraw, had she wished to. For good or ill she was Mrs Lawrence Prescott, nervously twisting the heavy, plain gold band on the third finger of her left hand. 'Auburn! Sweet

Auburn.' The words echoed inside her head. Hastily she suppressed them.

'Is something wrong?' Lawrence asked yet again. 'You looked for a moment as though you were crying.'

Eve blinked quickly, horrified to realize that there were tears in her eyes.

'No, of course not. The sun's a bit strong. It's making my eyes water, that's all.' The meal, the toasts, the cake-cutting were over and she got to her feet. 'We'd better go and and circulate among our guests.'

Calanthe, resplendent in a pale blue satin dress and coat, with an organdie hat weighted down by matching pale blue roses, was the first to reach her. Rising from her own place two seats distant, she overwhelmed Eve in a scented embrace.

'Eve, dear! Welcome to the family!' She turned to her grand-daughters. 'Darlings, say hello to Stepmamma!'

Ten-year-old Olivia giggled and Justine flushed with embarrassment. Eve said quietly, 'I hope they'll both call me Mother. I don't want to sound like the wicked witch in "Snow White and the Seven Dwarfs".'

Calanthe said nothing, but a flush of anger was discernible beneath her make-up. She was unused to public rebuke of any sort, however lightly given. Fortunately she had no time to reply, as Eve was surrounded at that moment by members of her family, and villagers anxious to shake her hand. Of the latter, Rose and Ernest had been at pains to ensure that as many as possible were invited to the reception, and Eve had expected to see people like the Vicar and his sister, the Jenks, her old schoolteacher, Miss Jillard, Albert and Edith Naysmith, Ellen and Jeb Marston. But it was a shock to see George and Lizzie Mailer among the guests, until she recollected that Virginia was of course their grand-daughter.

George, Eve reckoned, was by now in his middle fifties, his wife some years younger. But in appearance they could both have been well over sixty, their faces pinched and lined, Lizzie's shoulders rounded with constant stooping, her husband thin and narrow-chested, emaciated by his annual winter battle

against bronchitis. When he wished her happiness, his voice
was hoarse and rasping, the hand which gripped hers rough
and calloused.

'Good of you to ask Ginny to be your bridesmaid, Miss Evie.
Lizzie and I appreciates it, don't we, girl?' But the glance
accompanying the words was sly and knowing. Eve recalled
that she had never cared for George Mailer very much. It had
always seemed to her that Frank's endearing qualities came
from his mother.

'We do that.' Lizzie smiled, a defeated curling of the lips, as
though life had proved too much for her, and kindness was
something she was uncertain how to deal with. Her face
creased into a worried frown. 'Is it true, Miss Eve, what
everyone's saying? Mr Donald, has he sold all the land to the
War Office?'

Eve hesitated, reluctant to be the dispenser of bad news on
her wedding day. 'I think you must ask Mr Ernest about that.
He knows more than I do.' She looked for Rose. 'I must go and
change now. We ought to leave within the hour if we're to
reach London in time for dinner.'

Accompanied by her friend, she made her way upstairs to
the big first-floor front bedroom once occupied by Alfred and
Mabel, now the private domain of Rose and Ernest. Her
suitcase lay packed and ready on the bed, her going-away dress
and coat of pale, peach-coloured shantung were spread out on
the counterpane beside it. White silk stockings, gloves and
pigskin handbag, together with a smart black cloche hat sport-
ing a diamanté buckle, completed an outfit chosen largely by
Aunt Hetty from one of Clifton's most expensive dress shops.
With a sigh of relief, Eve removed her veil and the band of
artificial orange blossom which, during the last half-hour, had
begun to give her a headache. She turned her back to Rose.

'Undo the hooks for me, there's a dear. I'm too tired to make
the effort.'

Rose complied. 'I know what you mean.' She added
viciously, 'Why, oh why did that damn letter have to come
today of all days?'

Eve said wearily, 'Donald wasn't to know.' Then she grimaced. 'But he couldn't have timed it better if he'd planned it! Do you think it's his way of taking revenge on me, Rose? Do you think it's my fault? There are bound to be some people who'll blame me. Mama and Aunt Mabel have already given me some very reproachful looks, and Aunt Hetty has as good as said so. Even Papa hinted that the situation might have been avoided.'

'Take no notice of them!' Rose retorted with spirit. But she could not resist adding, 'It was a great pity you ever got engaged to Donald, though, feeling the way you did about him.'

Eve made no answer. She and Rose had been friends for far too long for them to quarrel on her wedding day. Instead, she slipped a silk kimono over her underwear, and sat down at the dressing-table to powder her nose and repair her lipstick.

There was a knock on the bedroom door and Eve called, 'Come in!' expecting it to be Justine or Olivia. She was totally unprepared for the sight of Jenny Mailer.

Jenny, at twenty-nine, had put on weight; not altogether surprising, Eve reflected, when she thought of Jenny's mother. Mrs Slade had always had a tendency to fat and was now, in middle age, a very heavy woman. Jenny, however, was unlikely to let herself go in quite the same way; not, at least, as long as she retained her looks and was attractive to the opposite sex. She was very well corseted.

'Jenny.' Eve swivelled round on her stool. 'Is something the matter?'

The older woman advanced half-way into the room, across the stained floorboard surround and patterned square of Wilton carpet.

'I'm sorry to bother you, Eve, today of all days.' Her broad, bland smile gave the lie to her words. Eve noted the absence of the deferential prefix to her name and wondered what was coming. 'But the fact is it won't wait until you return from honeymoon. I shall be gone by then.'

'Gone?' Eve frowned. 'Gone where?'

'To America. New York. My gentleman friend is going to emigrate and he wants me to go with him. I've said yes, of course.'

'America?' Eve couldn't seem to get her thoughts together. She tightened the sash of the kimono and stood up. 'Does my aunt know about this?'

'Not yet. I wanted to speak to you first.' Jenny displayed uncertainty for the first time since entering the bedroom. 'My friend and I will be leaving at the end of next week. All the formalities are completed.' Once more she showed symptoms of nervousness, but Eve hardly noticed. She had suddenly realized that she would be losing Frank's daughter.

'But Virginia!' she exclaimed. 'How does she feel about going? She hasn't said a word to me, nor to Miss Gilchrist.'

'Well . . . that's just it. Ginny doesn't know anything about it.'

'*What?*' Eve and Rose spoke simultaneously.

Jenny took a deep breath and seemed to regain her composure.

'I haven't said anything to Ginny. Stanley – that's my gentleman friend, Stanley Millman: manager of a chemist's shop in Whiteladies Road – he doesn't like children. He doesn't want Ginny to go with us. And she doesn't like him, so it wouldn't have worked out, anyway. So I'm leaving her behind.'

Eve was horrified and relieved, both at once. 'But your mother, what does she say to all this? What does she feel about being saddled with Ginny?'

Jenny lowered her eyes and stared at the intricate whorls and lines of the carpet, before raising her head again defiantly.

'That's just it. Ma won't want Ginny. She doesn't like her, says Ginny reminds her too much of her father.' Jenny looked Eve full in the eyes, smiling a little. 'Ma never did like Frank Mailer. Didn't like the way he treated me. Thought he was two-timing and sly.'

Eve ignored this. 'But what's going to happen to Virginia? For heaven's sake! She's only eight years old. No woman can just abandon her child like that!'

The older woman's face hardened, flattening out the softening contours until she appeared almost ugly.

'Oh yes, she can!' came back the vicious answer. 'If the child's been forced on her, like Ginny was forced on me by Frank! Oh, yes! Didn't you know that?' The angry sneer was pronounced. Jenny had dropped all pretence of friendliness, and the years of pent-up resentment and envy showed plainly in the bitter lines around her mouth. 'Thought Ginny was intended, did you, Eve? Well, think again! Frank knew I never wanted a child, but he didn't care. Forced his attentions on me. Made me think he loved me, when all he really wanted was revenge. Joined up, though he didn't have to. Hardly ever wrote. Never came home on leave, even when he knew about the baby. So, if he didn't want her, why should I? I've done my duty by her up till now. This is the chance I've been waiting for; a man who's fond of me and the start of a brand-new life. Why shouldn't I take it? You tell me that!'

'If you don't know,' Rose interposed, her face contorted with fury, her eyes bright with unshed tears, 'you don't deserve to be a mother. You're a heartless bitch!' Such an expression from one normally so mild-tempered made it doubly insulting and Jenny flushed angrily.

'Just because you're sterile—' she began hotly, but Eve cut her short.

'So what's going to happen to Ginny, if your mother refuses to have her? Let's keep to the point.'

'I was wondering if . . . for the time being . . . she could stay with Miss Gilchrist at Holly Lodge. She likes it there. It's become her home. And she's no trouble; she's very quiet and well-behaved.'

'But my aunt is seventy! She can't be expected to look after a child of eight.'

Jenny lifted her chin. 'She'll get a new housekeeper easily. There won't be any difficulty, not these days. People are falling over themselves for work. And with her money, she could afford to employ a maid as well. She and Ginny are very fond of one another. I thought you might ask her for me. She'd listen to you.'

'And if she says no?'

Jenny shrugged. 'Then Ginny'll just have to live with my mother or the Mailers. Because I'm not passing up this opportunity. No one and nothing is going to stop me.'

Eve's mind was reeling under this second unexpected blow of the day. She should be getting dressed. Lawrence and the guests would be wondering what had become of her, but she was unable to concentrate on anything but this present problem. She heard Rose trying to argue with Jenny, to provoke her into a sense of guilt. But Eve knew it was useless. She believed Jenny when she said that she had made up her mind. This was the woman who had invented a pregnancy in order to trap Frank into marriage; a woman without compunction when it came to her own desires.

Virginia, of course, ought to be the responsibility of her grandparents, but there were other things to consider. She was a bright, intelligent child who had benefited considerably from Josephine's company and conversation. If she was sent back to Staple Abbots she would be trapped in the poverty and ignorance of a country village, with no one to take an interest in her education. She would be unhappy and frustrated, just as her father had been. Moreover, Eve would lose track of her; of this child who, now more than ever, she felt should really have been hers. The knowledge that Virginia had not been the result of Frank's love for Jenny had come as a profound shock, overturning all her beliefs of the past eight years and leaving her bewildered. She needed time to rearrange her ideas, but time was something she was short of at the moment. Through the confusion, however, one certainty stood out like a beacon light. She could not lose track of Ginny; she would not contribute to her unhappiness if she could possibly prevent it. She looked at Jenny.

'I'll speak to my aunt,' she said. 'Now. Before I go away. Go and ask her if she'll come up here. Immediately.'

Chapter Eighteen

'Donald's letter was a bad augury,' said Eve. 'I can see that now.'

'Nonsense!' Josephine exclaimed robustly. 'And after all this time, nothing has happened. No one's been turned out of hearth and home. Your parents and Hetty are still at Rosemary Villa; Rose, Ernest and Mabel still at the Court. Life in the village goes on absolutely as normal. At least, it was doing so when I was there last week. In fact, the War Office has probably turned out to be a better landlord than Donald would ever have been thousands of miles away on the other side of the world.' She paused, then asked, 'Or were you not referring to Staple Abbots, but to more personal problems?'

She and Eve were sitting on a seat on Brandon Hill, the city laid like a carpet at their feet, the Cabot Tower behind them soaring skyward, a permanent reminder of Bristol's part in the discovery of North America. It was nearly four years since Eve and Lawrence had been married in St Peter's Church; four years during which the voting age for women had been reduced to twenty-one, the 'wireless' had become an integral part of many homes, Lindbergh had flown the Atlantic, the Wall Street Stock Exchange had crashed and the planet Pluto had been discovered. Ras Tafari had become Emperor Haile Selassie of Abyssinia, the kingdom of Serbs, Croats and Slovenes had had its name changed to Yugoslavia, and only two months ago, on the 24th of May 1930, Amy Johnson had completed her solo flight from London to Australia in less than twenty days. The world was changing, and changing fast, but to Eve the past four years felt more like a lifetime of stagnation and frustration.

If she had had a baby things might have been different, but she seemed incapable of conceiving; a source of bitter disappointment to her mother, and of great satisfaction to Calanthe to whom it appeared to prove something immensely significant. Even Marcus expressed a certain sadness at his lack of a grandchild, while Hetty bombarded her niece with a succession of old wives' remedies for infertility. Only Lawrence himself remained unperturbed, saying simply that they already had a family in Justine and Olivia, and taking her away on holiday to France and Italy, or Switzerland where they had spent their honeymoon.

That had been an idyllic fortnight, in spite of the worry over Ginny and how she would manage at Holly Lodge without her mother. They had stayed at Engelburg, high in the mountains above Lake Lucerne, taking long walks each day, quietly contented in one another's company. Lawrence had proved himself to be a considerate and satisfying lover, the only cloud on the horizon being the necessity for Eve to keep her passionate nature in check. She had soon discovered that any attempt by her to take the lead, or the suggestion of any variation in their lovemaking, embarrassed her husband. But that apart, they had enjoyed a peace of mind, a mutual optimism in their future which had lasted until they returned to Bristol.

It had become apparent almost at once that Lawrence would never be able to paint in a professional capacity while they remained at Robartes House. The moment he settled down to work in his garden studio, Calanthe would just 'happen' to need him for this or that little thing; jobs she wanted done and done immediately. Not that she ever put it in quite those words.

'Darling, don't let me disturb you. I know I'm being a nuisance, but I'm such a silly about these little things' – changing a plug, mending a fuse, finding her reading glasses – 'and I hate bothering the domestics for such trifles.'

Then there were all the charitable committees of which she was a member. Suddenly Calanthe decided that she was getting too old; she needed Lawrence to help her shoulder the burden.

'Darling, I'm sixty-six' – or -seven or -eight or -nine as the years rolled by – 'and I can't manage as well as I used to do. But you know how I hate to disappoint people. If you could take on one or two of the committees for me, I'd be so grateful.'

Eve noted, angrily at first but with an increasingly cynical detachment, that on such occasions Lawrence's health was never a problem. It was only when *she* wanted anything done, or reminded her husband of his promise to apply himself to his painting in order to become financially independent of Robartes House, that Calanthe grew over-solicitous. Doctor Callender would be sent for, and he would earnestly advise Lawrence to 'take it easy. You can't be too careful now that you're approaching forty. A dangerous age.'

And there was no doubt that pressure of any kind *did* upset Lawrence, making his heart race and his breathing difficult. In the first two years of their marriage, Eve had done her best to foster the inclination which she was sure he had to escape from his mother's domination. She had taken him to look at houses, none of which they could afford, but in the hope that it would inspire his will to work, because it was certain that he could earn his own living. All his completed canvases were snapped up at once by various small art galleries, both in Bristol and London, but there were so few of them and he sold them at giveaway prices. When Eve remonstrated with him, he would shrug and say, 'But, darling, it's just a hobby.'

'That's the whole point!' she would protest in exasperation. 'It shouldn't be. You're good, Lawrence! Too damn good to waste your talent in this dilettante fashion.'

But such vehemence upset him. He would be forced to lie down while his heart recovered its equilibrium, and although no word of reproach ever passed his lips Eve nonetheless felt desperately guilty at making him suffer.

Half-way through the third year of her marriage, she

reached the conclusion that Lawrence was incapable of standing up to his mother, of changing the familiar pattern of his days. She would have to do it for him. Like their father, Justine and Olivia were perfectly willing to deceive Calanthe in small matters, such as Eve's inclusion in the trip to Paris all those years ago, but they knew no other life than that of Robartes House, and to begin with they were too young to feel rebellious. Lately, however, Eve thought that she detected signs of resentment on Justine's part at her grandmother's domineering ways, and she suspected that if she ever did succeed in extricating herself and Lawrence from Calanthe's clutches, she might well have an ally in her elder stepdaughter.

Josephine's voice cut into her thoughts. 'You've gone very quiet. Is something bothering you, my dear? Your mother-in-law, for example?'

Eve replied as cheerfully as she could, 'Not more than usual,' having no wish to burden Aunt Josie with her troubles. She considered that Josephine was looking far from well these days, overweight and frequently breathless. True, she was seventy-two and had moved with difficulty for a long time, but until recent months she had displayed an upright carriage and a sprightliness of mind which nowadays seemed to be lacking. She walked bent over, leaning heavily on her ebony cane, and although still interested in what went on around her she wanted only good news; she could no longer be bothered with other people's problems.

So now, instead of probing deeper as once she would have done, she was happy to accept her niece's assurance that all was well. She looked forward to these Tuesday afternoon excursions, when Eve drove them to wherever took their fancy: the seaside, deep into the surrounding country or, as today, much nearer to home. She wanted nothing to spoil these outings. Suddenly recollecting some good news of her own, she opened her handbag and triumphantly produced a letter.

'From Arnold Bailey. I received it this morning. He's won a scholarship to Cambridge.'

Eve was delighted. 'What's he reading, does he say?'

'English literature is all he mentions. You were right about that boy. He's clever and it's been a privilege to help him – he'll probably become Prime Minister.'

Eve laughed. 'Don't set your sights too high for him, Aunt Josie. He's more likely to end up a teacher.' She grew serious. 'Maybe he'll be lucky to be that. Unemployment's getting really serious.'

But again Josephine did not want to know. She rose unsteadily to her feet.

'I think we'll go home now, my dear, if you don't mind. The sun's a bit strong and it's given me a headache. Let me take your arm.'

Eve had parked the car in Great George Street and they made their way downhill, along the paths threading the ornamental gardens. She noticed how heavily her aunt leaned on her, forcing her to take almost all her weight, and also how restricted was her breathing.

'When we get back to Holly Lodge,' Eve said, 'you must lie down. I shall tell Martha to give you your dinner in bed this evening.'

'Stuff and nonsense!' Josephine snapped, with something like a return of her old spirit. 'You leave my domestic arrangements alone. Neither Martha nor I appreciate interference.'

'I shall instruct Ginny, then. She's quite capable of putting you both in your place.'

Eve smiled fondly as she spoke. At twelve years old, Virginia Mailer resembled her father even more than she had done as a baby. The dark hair, the brown eyes with their lurking gleam of laughter, were Frank's to the life, as were the small, wiry frame and the thin arms and legs which always seemed slightly out of control. Ginny also had the same devil-may-care charm which concealed an underlying seriousness. But there she and her father parted company. The single-minded determination which turned anything she set her heart on into reality was Jenny's. The battles of will between her and Martha Carpenter, Josephine's present housekeeper, were titanic, and it was usually Ginny who won.

'Martha calls her "a right little Tartar",' Josephine chuckled. 'I think she finds her more than she can handle on occasions.'

'And what about you? Do you and Ginny still get on?'

'Of course. We always have done. It's good at my age to have young blood about the place. I admit that I was more than doubtful when you first proposed the arrangement, but it's worked out far better than I could have imagined.'

'Does Ginny miss her mother, do you think?'

Josephine shook her head. 'Not one iota. Never did, even in the beginning. I don't think she liked Jenny very much; they were more like polite strangers than mother and daughter. It struck me as a difficult relationship from the time they first came to live at Holly Lodge.'

'Does Jenny ever write?'

'Very, very occasionally. Birthdays, Christmas, but that's all. Only cards. Never any letters, and never any address.'

'And Virginia honestly doesn't mind?'

'I can't see any sign of it. Her only worry is that she might have to return to Staple Abbots to live, with either the Mailers or Mrs Slade. Now she's at grammar school, she wouldn't want to leave. She's a bright child, enjoys learning. Ah! Here's the car, thank goodness.'

She climbed with difficulty into the front passenger seat, settling herself with a sigh of relief. Eve cranked the engine into life and got in beside her, but did not immediately take the steering wheel.

'You really should rest more, Aunt Josie. I'm serious.'

'Mind your own business. And I'm serious, too.' Eve laughed, but her aunt did not join in. Instead, she turned her head to look at her niece. 'Eve, what's going to happen to Ginny when I die?'

'That's not going to happen for ages yet,' Eve declared stoutly. 'Especially not if you take greater care of yourself.

All the Gilchrists are long-lived, I've heard Papa say so many a time.'

'I have to go some time. It's inevitable.'

'But not yet. And by then, Lawrence and I will have a place of our own. We're not going to stay at Robartes House for ever.'

Josephine half-opened her mouth as though to query this assertion, but thought better of it. It was comforting to believe her niece, to let the situation ride from day to day, to pretend that there was no cause for concern.

'Right,' she said. 'Now, take me home. This headache is getting worse by the minute. I think I might have my dinner in bed tonight, after all. But only this once, mark you! Don't imagine you've achieved some kind of permanent victory.'

Eve grinned and manoeuvred the corner into Park Street, heading up towards the University. As they passed, she cast envious eyes at the new complex of buildings. It was all so different now from those makeshift days just after the war. By the time they reached Queen's Road Josephine was sound asleep, and remained so for the rest of the journey. As Eve pulled up in front of Holly Lodge, she nudged her.

'Aunt Josie! Wake up, we're home.' There was no response, so she spoke more loudly. 'Aunt Josie! Wake up! It's time to get out.' And when there was still no answer, she shook her aunt's arm.

Martha Carpenter, having heard them arrive, appeared on the doorstep.

Eve wound down her window. 'Martha, come and see if you can rouse Miss Gilchrist, will you? I can't seem to wake her.'

Martha walked down the garden path and rounded the bonnet to the passenger side of the car. Opening the door, she said, 'Miss Gilchrist!' very loudly, at the same time putting a hand on Josephine's shoulder. Suddenly, she stiffened.

'What is it?' Eve demanded shrilly, but she had already guessed the answer.

Slowly, the other woman straightened her body. 'I think we'd better send for the doctor, Mrs Prescott. I can't hear any heartbeat. I think Miss Gilchrist's dead.'

*

In accordance with Josephine's wishes, the funeral was a simple ceremony, with an interment afterwards at Canford cemetery, where she had reserved herself a plot. Until the day of the funeral the July weather had been reasonably fine, but – appropriately, Eve felt – on July 22nd it poured with rain. A tearful Martha had insisted on preparing a meal at Holly Lodge in time for the mourners' return, and the party from Staple Abbots – Marcus, Helena, Hetty and Mabel – was staying there overnight.

Virginia looked like a frightened ghost, her thin face white with grief and shock. She had refused to go to school since Josephine's death, and for the past week Eve had been living in the house to keep an eye on her. Last night, after Ginny was in bed, Martha had requested a word.

'She's sick with worry, Mrs Prescott, and that's a fact. Doesn't know what's to become of her, now that Miss Gilchrist is dead. She doesn't want to go to either of her grandparents; I did get that much out of her, and I don't s'pose they've got a claim on her – not legal, that is, her mother still being alive, although God knows where! A proper no-good piece she seems to be, abandoning the child like that.'

'It's all right, Martha.' Eve had spoken with more assurance than she felt. 'I shall make myself responsible for Virginia. She will come and live with my husband and me.'

'Well, that's a relief and no mistake. Miss Olivia will be pleased. She and Ginny seem such friends whenever you bring your daughters over here.'

But Eve, spending another wakeful night in her old bedroom, listening to an owl hooting somewhere among the trees of the Downs, could not foresee Virginia being happy at Robartes House – faced, as almost certainly she would be, with the scarcely veiled animosity of Calanthe.

'My dear girl, this child is not your responsibility.' Eve could hear her mother-in-law's intonation of weary incredulity. 'She's nothing to you; she must be sent back to her people in the village.' And although, in this instance, Lawrence would undoubtedly stand up to his mother, the subsequent atmosphere in the house would be tense and uncomfortable. Eve's day-to-day existence would be even more fraught than at present, as she tried to keep Virginia out of Calanthe's way; to shield her from the barbed sallies which could undermine the confidence of a sensitive adolescent.

The problem of Virginia had loomed so large in her mind since Josephine's death that Eve had not had time as yet to grieve properly for her aunt. She was aware of a raw and gaping wound, of a great hole torn in her life, but for now there were more important things to think about. Lawrence and the girls supported her at the funeral and returned to Holly Lodge afterwards, but, blessedly, Calanthe did not accompany them; she sent her condolences, an impossibly large and showy wreath of arum lilies and the excuse that obsequies depressed her. She preferred, she said grandly, to remember people as they were in life.

Martha welcomed them back with sherry, set out on Josephine's best silver tray in the dining-room, and had lit fires both there and in the drawing-room.

'Such a nasty day, Mrs Prescott, I took the liberty while you were gone. I thought of you all getting soaked and decided you might like a bit of warmth. I hope I did right.'

'Quite right, Martha. Thank you.'

The funeral party was augmented by the presence of Josephine's solicitor, Mr Edward Murray of Murray and Johnson, Commissioners for Oaths. A true gentleman in the literal sense of the word, he devoted himself to Hetty, whose depth of grief at her sister's death had taken everyone, not least herself, by surprise. She and Josephine had never been close, even as girls. 'Chalk and cheese' was the way Marcus had always described them. The twelve years' disparity in their ages had also been a barrier to greater intimacy; but over the past decade they had ceased to argue quite so vehemently, content to accept that they would never agree and allowing their differences to sink into a calmer kind of goodwill.

'Josie was only seventy-two,' Hetty mourned, dabbing at her eyes with a lace-bordered handkerchief. 'She didn't look after herself properly, you know. She smoked those horrible little cigars. I'm sure it wasn't good for her.'

'Oh, nonsense, Hetty!' Marcus spoke impatiently to hide his own grief. 'There's no harm in smoking. Everyone does it nowadays, including women. Josie was just ahead of her time in that respect.'

Edward Murray nodded his support. 'Indeed, my doctor maintains that smoking is extremely efficacious. He says it helps to kill germs.'

Hetty sniffed and subsided once more into the folds of her handkerchief, refusing to be consoled.

Lawrence slipped an arm around Eve's shoulders. 'Darling, you look exhausted. As soon as your parents and the aunts leave tomorrow morning, you must come home, where we can see that you get some rest.'

Eve's hackles rose at the description of Robartes House as 'home'. How could Lawrence be so obtuse? And the realization that *he* still thought of it as such frightened her, suggesting that her four years' hard work to prise him loose from Calanthe's clutches had been in vain. But how else should he think of it, when he had lived there all his life? She was being unfair. She smiled, kissed his cheek and went to talk to Aunt Mabel, who was sitting on her own wearing a rather neglected air. But Eve found it difficult to concentrate on the older woman's expressions of sympathy, when all she could think about was Ginny. The child was making a pretence of eating, but the contents of her plate were almost untouched. Her face looked bloodless and there were dark smudges around her eyes. Her safe little world had been brutally torn apart, and she was mature and sensible enough to know that even if Eve insisted on 'adopting' her, living under someone else's roof could never be the same as living at Holly Lodge where, over the years, she had come to regard herself as the daughter of the house.

The meal was over at last and it was time for the reading of the will. Justine and Olivia, together with Virginia, began collecting up the dirty plates and glasses, ignoring Martha's protests that she could manage. The adults followed Edward Murray into the drawing-room, where Martha had already set out the coffee things. Eve, doing the duty of hostess, poured out and handed round the cups. The solicitor produced a buff envelope from his inside waistcoat pocket, from which he extracted some sheets of stiff, legal-looking paper.

'It's not a complicated document,' he said, seating himself on an upright chair near one of the windows. 'There are several bequests to past servants, the largest being one thousand pounds to Mrs Clarissa Soloway who, I understand, was Miss Gilchrist's housekeeper for a number of years. A hundred pounds is willed to Miss Martha Carpenter, the present domestic.' Mr Murray paused for an appreciative sip of his coffee before continuing: 'One of the sources of my late client's annual income was from shares in a Provençal hotel business. These will, of course, now be sold and the money is to be invested by me and my partners as we see fit, the income therefrom being for the use of a Mr Arnold Bailey until such time as he graduates from Cambridge University.' Glancing around the room, Mr Murray saw bewilderment on every face but Eve's. She obviously understood what was behind that particular clause, so he could proceed without further explanation.

'I now come to the final and main bequest of Miss Gilchrist's last will and testament. When the aforementioned legacies have been paid and the funeral expenses met, the residue of the estate – this house, the royalties from her books, all other monies – is left solely and entirely to her niece, Mrs Eve Prescott of Robartes House, Leigh Woods, Bristol.'

There was a momentary silence. Then: 'Well!' breathed Hetty, uncertain if she were upset or not at being left out of her sister's will. 'I suppose,' she added, a little piqued, 'we ought to have seen that coming.'

Marcus's reaction was unequivocal. He got up, went across the room to his daughter and kissed her. 'Congratulations, my dear. Josie's income from her books was substantial. You'll be quite a wealthy woman, won't she, Mr Murray?'

'Mrs Prescott will certainly be comfortably off,' the solicitor admitted primly.

But Eve heard neither of them. She sat as though rooted to her chair, her mind racing. It had never occurred to her, obvious though it was on reflection, that Josephine would make her the main legatee. When she thought of it at all, she had assumed that she might get something, but had anticipated that her father and Aunt Hetty would inherit the bulk of whatever Aunt Josie had to leave. She glanced across the room at Lawrence, wondering if the full significance of her inheritance had yet hit him. More important even than the money, Holly Lodge was hers. All at once, they had a house of their own and the means to maintain it. They could take up residence tomorrow! There was nothing to stop them. The will would not be proved for a week or two, perhaps longer, but Mr Murray was unlikely to raise objections.

And Ginny! That problem was solved as well. She would continue at Holly Lodge as she had done for the past six years, only now she would also have Justine and Olivia for company. Eve must ask Martha to stay on, too. She suspected that the housekeeper would be only too willing; only yesterday, she had been tearfully bemoaning the fact that she would have to look for another place. 'But I shan't easily find one as good as this, Mrs Prescott, and that's a fact. Since Miss

Gilchrist had that new Aga cooker put in in the kitchen, cooking's been a real treat. And what with the Hoover and the electric iron instead of them old things you have to heat up on the stove, well, I never knew housework could be so easy.'

Oh yes, Martha would be glad to stay all right, and surely Lawrence would be bound to see the advantages. And the girls? Eve didn't really believe they would object, once they got used to the idea. The only opposition would be from Calanthe, but how could she prevent them leaving? She would try, of course, but there was nothing she could do.

Eve squared her shoulders and stood up. She must speak to Lawrence as soon as possible; make him fully aware of what Aunt Josie's legacy meant to them both. She had set them free.

Chapter Nineteen

Calanthe leaned back in her armchair and smiled wearily, but it was a smile which held a suggestion of gritted teeth.

'My dearest' – she addressed Lawrence, ignoring Eve – 'if you want to go and live at Holly Lodge, of course I can't stop you.'

All the windows of the house were wide open, the weather having once again turned hot. An occasional breeze blowing up from the river now and then stirred the curtains, but for the most part the air was static. Calanthe's perfume was overpowering, a heavy, musky scent that assaulted the olfactory nerves and made Eve sneeze. Lawrence looked unhappy as he got up from his chair and crouched down beside his mother's, taking one of her hands in his.

'Mama, it makes sense. And Eve wants to live there so that she can look after Virginia. She feels the child is now her responsibility.'

Eve, perched on the window-seat, was conscious of her nails biting into her palms. She wanted to yell, 'Stop blaming me! Stop pretending I'm the only one who wants to leave here.'

But wasn't she? If she were honest, had Lawrence shown any real enthusiasm for the move? When she had first explained what her inheritance could mean to them, she had not imagined the look of consternation on his face. It had not occurred to him that this was the answer to their problem, because he had never seen any problem in living at Robartes House. Perhaps if she had been able to have his child, he might have felt differently, but after four years of marriage there was still no sign of a baby. And she was thirty now; soon she would be too old.

Calanthe opened eyes flashing with indignation and glanced venomously at her daughter-in-law.

'As far as I can see, Eve has absolutely no reason to make herself responsible for this child. She's not even a relative. Why doesn't she try to trace the girl's mother, if she's that concerned?'

Eve's patience snapped. 'If you want an answer to your question, why don't you try asking me directly, instead of addressing Lawrence as though I'm not here?'

Tears welled up in Calanthe's eyes and she pressed a hand to her chest. 'Darling, I didn't mean to be rude.' Her clasp tightened on Lawrence's hand. 'I'm not feeling very well today . . . one of my nervous spasms.'

'It's all right, Mama,' Lawrence said, stroking her wrist. 'We'll discuss it when you're feeling better.'

'No.' Eve left her seat to stand belligerently in the middle of the room. 'I'm sorry, Lawrence, but this has to be decided as soon as possible. It isn't fair to Martha, leaving her on her own with Ginny. And neither is it fair for the girls to be in such a state of uncertainty. This is Justine's last term at school, and now she's decided against going to university she'll have all the worry and strain of finding and starting a job. She'll want the stability of a settled home. The same applies to Livvy; the next four years will be vital ones for her and she needs peace and quiet. We can give her that at Holly Lodge, where we'll be a family, not lodgers under your mother's roof.'

Calanthe's mouth thinned to a nearly invisible line; her nostrils flared. She seemed to have forgotten about her nervous spasm. Certainly she had recovered her voice, which came out strongly in spite of the fact that it was shaking with temper.

'My son and grandchildren have never been lodgers! This is their home and always has been ever since they were born. You're the only one, Eve, who isn't happy here, who has stirred things up, who has tried to turn my dear ones against me.'

Eve felt a small stab of conscience, but she stood her ground.

'I married Lawrence on the understanding that we would one day have our own house. I don't think that's an unreasonable demand for a wife to make of her husband; it's what most women expect when they get married. Now at last, thanks to the generosity of my aunt, we have that chance without overtaxing Lawrence's strength.' Eve heard the note of impatience, almost of sarcasm, in her voice and immediately regretted it, but she kept her eyes fixed on Calanthe. 'You aren't going to stop us.'

'Eve!' Lawrence had straightened up and was regarding her in astonishment. She had never heard him sound so hostile. 'Can't you see that Mama isn't well? You're upsetting her. We'll discuss the matter this evening when the girls are home. Now, please, drop the subject.'

The barely concealed smile on her mother-in-law's face was the last straw as far as Eve was concerned. In the days since Josephine's funeral and the reading of the will, she had thought of little else except her impending freedom. Lawrence had always known her feelings about living at Robartes House; she had made them crystal clear. And although she had never actually extracted a firm promise from him, he had nonetheless married her under false pretences if it had never been his intention to move.

It came to her suddenly that she had to leave Lawrence. Now, today, this minute. He might follow her, he might not – in which case Calanthe would have won. But she had won anyway as long as Eve allowed herself to drift along, waiting for Lawrence to make up his mind, letting herself be blackmailed into submission by her husband's delicate state of health and her mother-in-law's trumped-up illnesses. For Eve had no belief in Calanthe's migraines, nervous spasms and dizzy spells: they were always too convenient. Calanthe might be over seventy, but it was Eve's opinion that she was as strong as a horse. There was even a possibility that she could outlive her son; that Eve would never know any life with Lawrence away from his mother. Better to make a break now than be forced to sell Holly Lodge, lose Virginia and regret it for the rest of her life. Better to try to goad Lawrence into action and fail, rather than grow into an embittered and frustrated woman. She was deeply attached to him, but surely it was preferable to live apart rather than have that affection turn to dislike.

She raised her head and looked at her husband. 'No, Lawrence, we won't talk about it later because as far as I'm concerned, there's nothing left to discuss. I'm going upstairs to pack and then I'm going to phone for a taxi to take me to Clifton. What you decide to do is entirely up to you. I only know that I can't stay here a moment longer, not now that I have somewhere else to go.'

Lawrence gave a nervous laugh. 'You don't mean it, darling, you know you don't. So please don't make a scene. I've told you, we'll talk it over this evening.'

'No.' She moved past him to the door. 'I'm leaving and I'm not coming back.'

Calanthe's eyes glittered with triumph. 'I always told you, darling, that she was selfish and hardhearted. Perhaps now you'll believe me. We don't need her here, we never have. Let her go. It'll be like the old days again; just you and me and the girls.'

*

'Oh, I do so enjoy a good historical film,' Hetty said, surreptitiously blowing her nose as she and Eve emerged from the darkness of the Embassy Cinema and turned towards Queen's Road. 'And Garbo is so beautiful.'

Eve laughed. 'Don't you mean that you enjoy a good cry and that John Gilbert is so handsome?'

Hetty looked momentarily affronted, then gave a little giggle. 'And why not? Sixty-four isn't too old, you know, to appreciate a good-looking man.'

'Then why haven't you married again?' Eve wanted to know. 'You've been a widow since before I was born.'

Her aunt flushed. 'Well, I never really cared for *that* side of marriage, if you know what I mean. But it doesn't stop me liking men.'

Eve smiled. 'You always were a flirt, Aunt Hetty.' She took the older woman's arm. 'Let's have a cup of tea at Bright's before we go home.'

Over the past four years Hetty had taken to visiting Holly Lodge with increasing frequency, sometimes accompanied by Marcus and Helena but more often than not on her own. To begin with, she had seen it as her mission in life to reunite Eve with her husband, her conventional soul having been shocked to the core by their continued separation. Unknown to Eve she had, on one occasion, visited Robartes House, but Lawrence had been out and her reception by Calanthe had been so frosty that her sympathies had somersaulted in favour of her niece, and she had made no further attempt to contact the Prescotts. But this setback had not stopped her hoping that things would work out eventually.

'Has Lawrence still made no effort to get in touch with you?' she asked, as they settled themselves at a table in Bright's restaurant and ordered anchovy toast and a pot of tea.

Eve shook her head. 'No. I used to phone him a lot in the early days, but he was never the one who answered and I was always told that he wasn't in. I suppose I deserved it, but it hurt. I didn't imagine he could be so adamant. And to be fair, he's never prevented the girls from visiting me, nor let Calanthe stop them coming. I see both of them at least once a week, though Livvy won't be able to keep it up, of course, once she goes up to Oxford.'

Hetty pursed her lips. 'Well, you know, while I can't blame you for wanting to get away from that horrible mother of his, it can't have been pleasant for Lawrence, knowing that you put Virginia's interests before his.'

'I put my *own* interests before his, Aunt Hetty. They just happened to coincide with Ginny's, that's all.' But she avoided looking at her aunt, not entirely certain that she believed this. She added defiantly, 'Anyway, if Lawrence had

had any sense, he would have left as well. He could have done so much more with his life if it hadn't been for Calanthe.'

'Perhaps he didn't want to do anything with his life,' Hetty observed shrewdly. 'There are people like that, you know, quite content to live from day to day without making too much of a song and dance about it. I should know – I'm one of them!'

Eve laughed. Either her aunt had changed as she grew older, or she had failed to appreciate her properly in the past. Maybe she had never taken the time to try. Certainly Eve enjoyed Hetty's visits to Bristol far more than she had done when Josephine was alive, and only wished that she could say the same for her mother. But she had never been able to persuade herself that Helena's apparent helplessness was anything other than a self-centred, iron-willed determination to be cosseted by family and friends.

'You think I'm wrong, don't you, Aunt Hetty? You think I should have sold Holly Lodge, sent Virginia back to her grandparents at Staple Abbots and stayed at Robartes House.'

Hetty finished her anchovy toast and cast covetous eyes at the cake trolley, groaning under its weight of pastries, iced sponges and chocolate éclairs. She smiled invitingly at the waitress, and when she had eventually made the difficult choice of a cream slice, she settled back on her small gilt-painted chair.

'I think a wife's place is with her husband, yes, if that's what you're asking me. But then, I'm old-fashioned. As for Virginia Mailer, I've always thought she was the responsibility of her own family once that mother of hers had abandoned her. But you and Josephine disagreed and now you're stuck with the consequences.'

Eve said quietly, 'Ginny's like a daughter to me. The one I've never had.'

Hetty sniffed. 'Yes. Well ... I suppose I can guess why that is. Perhaps we'd better change the subject. Do you know the young fellow at that table over there? He keeps staring at you.'

260 · Brenda Clarke

Turning her head to peer across the restaurant in the direction of her aunt's pointing finger, Eve saw a man in his early twenties whose large, loosely-knit frame overflowed the delicate chair on which he was sitting and threatened to upset the small glass-topped table in front of him each time he moved. His big, good-natured face beneath a thatch of light brown hair was wreathed in smiles, and as she stared he lifted a hand in greeting. For a moment she was nonplussed, then she recognized him.

'Arnold! It's Arnold Bailey!'

'Who?' Hetty wrinkled her brow. 'Oh, you mean that boy whose expenses Josephine paid so that he could go to grammar school. She always did have more money than sense. And then she made the arrangement in her will to put him through Cambridge. Incidentally, and I've been meaning to ask you this for some time, how on earth did she come to have shares in a Provençal hotel?'

'She used to go there a lot on holiday. Arnold!' Eve held out her hand as, having threaded his way between the tables to the imminent danger of the other customers, he arrived beside her chair. 'How lovely to see you!'

'Hello, Mrs Prescott. I was so sorry to hear of Miss Gilchrist's death. I did write to you at the time – I hope you received my letter?'

'Yes, I did, and thank you. This is my other aunt, Mrs Jardine, Miss Gilchrist's sister.'

'Younger sister,' Hetty murmured as her little hand was crushed in Arnold's large one. She fluttered her eyelashes. 'Surely you must have graduated from Cambridge by now?'

Arnold reached for a chair at a nearby empty table, picked it up and dropped it down beside theirs with a studied nonchalance. 'Last year,' he said. 'Nowadays, I teach English literature at a private boarding-school in Hampstead. At the moment, I'm home on special leave for my mother's wedding.' He grinned at Eve. 'She's marrying Sam Atherton who used to keep the greengrocer's shop on the corner of William Penn Road. You must remember him, Mrs Prescott? A little bald-headed chap, very much under the thumb of his wife. She died eighteen months ago and Ma was sorry for him. Took him under her wing. Now they're getting married.' The grin broadened. 'Out of the frying-pan into the fire, poor man, but he doesn't know that yet. The big day's tomorrow.'

'Well, mind you give your mother my warmest congratulations,' Eve told him. 'She deserves a little happiness; she's worked hard all her life. I knew you'd graduated, of course, because the money set aside under Aunt Josie's will has reverted to me, but I had no idea what you'd been doing since. What's this school you're at? And how did you come to get the post there?'

'It's the Wentworth School for Boys near Hampstead Heath, and the headmaster is the father of a friend of mine, Keith Ingram, whom I met at Cambridge. Fees thirty guineas a term. A far cry from William Penn Road, eh, Mrs Prescott?'

'It is indeed,' Eve responded a trifle grimly. 'And does this friend of yours teach there as well?'

'Keith? No. He's gone as Parliamentary Private Secretary to one of his uncles who's a junior Minister in the present Coalition Government. Lucky devil! Politics is something I'd like to get into someday.'

Eve laughed. 'Aunt Josie always had you down as a future Prime Minister. Who knows? Perhaps you'll fulfil her ambitions for you after all.'

If she had expected him to deny it with a modest shake of the head, she was disappointed. 'It's entirely possible,' he answered cheerfully. He indicated the two cardboard boxes which he had placed on the floor near his feet. 'Look, I've finished my shopping – a new shirt for me and a wedding present for Ma and Sam Atherton – so can I run you anywhere? My car's just round the corner.'

'That's very kind of you,' Hetty said quickly before Eve could refuse. 'It will save us catching the bus.' She began gathering her things together. 'When did you learn to drive? Have you had to take one of these newfangled driving tests?'

Arnold gallantly helped her on with her coat. 'No. Happily, they're not compulsory yet, though I understand they soon will be.' His eyes slid appreciatively over Eve as she stood up. 'That's a spiffing frock, if you'll allow me to say so.'

Eve was well aware that the currently fashionable, cut-on-the-bias, almost ankle-length dresses suited her slender figure, and that the one she was wearing – in steel-blue crêpe de Chine with an inset of beige chiffon at the neck and a diamanté clip on the shoulder – was particularly becoming to her. Nevertheless she found herself taken aback by the compliment – mainly, she supposed, because it came from Arnold Bailey. It made her realize how long it was since she had last seen him. This was not the gauche, working-class boy with the broad Bristol accent that she remembered; this was a suave, well-spoken, polished young man who had learned all the lessons, both academic and social, which education had offered him, and turned them to his advantage. He had come a long way from William Penn Road, and she was relieved to note that he spoke of his mother and future stepfather with affection. She would have felt unbearably guilty had he shown contempt for his roots.

'Thank you, Arnold.' She did her best to sound gracious instead of awkward. 'I'm living at Holly Lodge, by the way. I'm . . . living apart from my husband at present.'

He made no comment, merely inclining his head as if to indicate that most of his acquaintances were either separated or divorced; as they probably were in an increasingly permissive society, which churchmen and others blamed on the growing influence of the cinema and the proliferation of film magazines detailing the complicated lives of the Hollywood stars. Eve sensed that Arnold was viewing her with a new respect as a woman of the world, and the idea made her uncomfortable.

His car, a four-year-old Morris Minor Tourer, was parked near the university, and was obviously his pride and joy from the loving way he handled it. As they pulled out from the kerb, he asked, 'Can you drive, Eve?'

Yet again, she was taken aback. What had she either said or done to merit such informality? When had she ceased to be Mrs Prescott in his estimation and become Eve? She was twelve years his senior, had once been his teacher and was therefore entitled to be treated with the respect accorded to an older person. She saw Aunt Hetty raise her eyebrows. But she could hardly protest, riding in his car, so she simply answered, 'Yes. I used to drive my husband's, but I've never bought one of my own.'

Arnold smiled over his shoulder at her, almost knocking down a cyclist in the process. 'You should, then you could motor up to town to see me.'

Eve was beginning to feel a little alarmed by such overt and persistent advances until she noticed how his eye was taken with every pretty girl or good-looking woman who passed by on the pavement. Indeed as the journey progressed, she became worried for her and Hetty's safety, so frequently did Arnold allow his attention to wander.

'He likes the ladies,' her aunt mouthed silently, and Eve nodded.

It was nearly half-past four by the time they reached Holly Lodge, and as Arnold assisted his passengers to alight Virginia appeared round the corner, swinging her school satchel by its straps.

'Hello, Aunt Eve. Mrs Jardine.' She had greeted both women and glanced curiously at the car before suddenly becoming aware of Arnold. A deep blush, starting at the base of her throat and rising to her forehead, suffused her thin features in a painful tide. She stared as though mesmerized at the broad, handsome face with the smiling eyes and mouth. Stiffly, she jerked out a hand. 'Hello. I'm Virginia Mailer.'

'And this is Arnold Bailey,' said Eve, noting with misgivings all the symptoms of instant hero-worship. 'I used to be his teacher more years ago than I care to remember.'

'Doesn't look old enough, does she?' Arnold asked easily, returning the handshake. You're Eve's . . .?'

'Adopted niece,' Ginny said, adding breathlessly, 'Would

you like to come in, Mr Bailey, and have tea? It's Martha's baking day and we always have fresh scones and cakes on a Friday.'

'Arnold has already had tea, in Brights's,' Eve put in smoothly. 'That's where we met him.'

'I should be delighted,' Arnold replied, smiling at Ginny. 'I don't call a fancy cake and two miniscule cups of weak brown liquid having tea. They give you such small portions in a restaurant.'

There was nothing for it but to endorse Ginny's invitation and lead the way indoors. She liked Arnold, Eve told herself as she directed him where to hang his overcoat and explained the location of the bathroom. She just wished that he didn't make her so uneasy, and that Ginny hadn't taken such an obvious and immediate shine to him. Never mind; they weren't likely to see him again after today. She went to the kitchen to warn Martha that there was a visitor for tea.

'Oh, well, that makes two,' the housekeeper said cheerfully. 'Miss Olivia phoned to say she'd be coming to say goodbye. She's off to that Oxford in a few days' time.' Even as she spoke, the doorbell rang. 'What did I tell you? I reckon that'll be her now.'

Eve found her stepdaughter standing in the hall, having been admitted by Ginny. The two girls, as always, were delighted to see one another and were already chatting. Their friendship, which had survived the years, seemed to Eve an unlikely one. Virginia was inclined by nature to be reserved, which had been one of the problems between her and her mother. Jenny had found her daughter too like Frank; she had never been sure what she was really thinking. Olivia, on the other hand, was vivacious, outgoing and impulsive. The only person with whom she was at all secretive was Calanthe, but even so she was able to treat her grandmother with a good-humoured tolerance which eluded her elder sister. Justine, who had taken a commercial language course after leaving school, and was now working as secretary to the manager of a Bristol hotel, was finding it increasingly difficult as the years went by to live at Robartes House, and only stayed for the sake of her father.

The September weather was still too warm to permit of tea being eaten round the drawing-room fire, and it was therefore laid out on the table in the dining-room. When Eve and the two girls entered, Hetty and Arnold were already seated at the laden table, engaged in conversation. Her aunt, Eve noted, was giggling as coyly as a schoolgirl, obviously falling under the spell of Arnold Bailey's charm. She introduced Olivia.

'My younger stepdaughter. She's going up to Oxford the day after tomorrow. Arnold was at Cambridge, Livvy.'

If she had thought to drive a wedge between them with this information, the ploy was foredoomed to failure. Arnold's eyes had widened with pleasure the moment Olivia entered the room, and they continued to register appreciation as she took her seat beside him. And Eve had to concede that, at eighteen, Olivia was well worth looking at. The hazel eyes were ringed with thick dark, spiky lashes; the Dutch-doll fringe had gone and the straight brown hair had been treated to one of the newest permanent waves, which softened the somewhat angular face. Livvy's figure, too, was all that a woman's body should be, perfectly proportioned, with curves in all the right places; and the two or three inches of leg, visible beneath the long summer skirt, showed neatly turned ankles and small, slender feet. The girl had grown into a beauty, there was no doubt about it. As soon as he saw her, Arnold Bailey had eyes for nobody else. And Olivia liked him. She listened with a flattering air of absorption to everything he said, oblivious to all Ginny's efforts to claim her attention. Eve, watching from her seat at the head of the table, felt her heart bleed for Ginny, and devoutly wished that she and Hetty had come straight home after the cinema. She willed Arnold Bailey to eat his tea and go. Much as she liked him – and she did, in spite of his blatant desire to charm – she felt that the sooner he was out of their lives, the better it would be for all of them.

Chapter Twenty

Bristol, like everywhere else in the United Kingdom, was a riot of flowers and Union Jacks. On the corner of Victoria and Bath Street, Georges' Brewery was draped in red, white and blue, with flags hanging from every window. In Colston Avenue the statue of Edmund Burke was banked with pots of flowering shrubs, while at the entrance to the Avenue one of the new neon signs flashed Bristol's greetings. The cathedral and the church of St Mary Redcliffe were floodlit after dark; the Coliseum in Park Row was garlanded in lights. Outside the Victoria Rooms, the statue of Edward VII had almost disappeared beneath a mass of foliage; and the long descent from the Downs to the Tramway Centre – Blackboy Hill, Whiteladies' Road, Queen's Road, Park Street – was strung with bunting which supported shields and placards, all bearing the same message of congratulation on Their Majesties' Silver Jubilee. King George V and his consort, Queen Mary, had – on this Monday morning of May 6th 1935 – reigned for twenty-five years.

At ten o'clock there was to be a Service of Thanksgiving in Bristol Cathedral, attended by all the civic dignitaries, and by nine the city centre was awash with sightseers. Later on, Justine reflected, it would be even worse. The schools were to close for the day once a sweet-filled mug, decorated with the royal likenesses, had been distributed to every child, along with a free pair of boots, the gift of the Council, for those who needed them. Unfortunately, with the city so crowded hotel personnel found themselves having to work, including the staff of the Dorset.

The Dorset Family Hotel, tucked away in the medieval St Mary-le-Port Street, had no need to advertise its presence. It

266

was sufficiently well-known to a select and discriminating clientele – whether for full-board accommodation or simply for meals – never to have a vacant room nor an empty table. Justine considered herself extremely fortunate to have obtained the post as the manager's secretary, and not for a moment did she envy Olivia her life at Oxford.

'I'm not clever, never have been,' she would say with the happy confidence of one who knew that she could give her words the lie at any time she wished. For unlike the majority of her countrymen, she not only found foreign languages easy to assimilate but also had no inhibitions when it came to pronunciation. (Her schoolmates had dissolved into embarrassed giggles whenever the French teacher had exhorted them to move their lips; it was so unnatural and un-English.) On the strength of this talent, both Lawrence and Calanthe had expected her to go to university and had been deeply disappointed when Justine had declined. For a while she herself had worried that she might have made the wrong decision, and she compromised by taking a two-year course at a commercial college. But once she had started her job at the Dorset Hotel, she had no more doubts. The academic life was not for her; she much preferred the cut and thrust of business.

She was at her desk in the manager's office bright and early this Monday morning, having beaten the Jubilee rush by leaving home at half-past-seven. Now, at eight-thirty, with the hotel's guests only just beginning to filter down to breakfast, she was already typing up the notes left for her by Mr Raymond yesterday evening. As she reached for the telephone in an effort to find accommodation for one of their regular customers elsewhere in the city, she spared a thought for her counterparts in London. The capital must be absolutely seething.

The thought of London reminded her of Arnold Bailey, Eve's protégé, whom she had met first during the Christmas holiday, and again at Easter. His mother, it appeared, had emigrated to New Zealand shortly after marrying for the

second time last autumn. As a result, whenever he returned
to Bristol Arnold now stayed at Holly Lodge, a semi-
permanent member of the household. It was Olivia who had
explained to her Arnold's background and his connection
with their stepmother; and it was immediately obvious to
Justine that her sister had fallen under his spell. To begin
with the knowledge had amused her, Olivia having so far
seemed impervious to the charms of the opposite sex. But it
did not take her long to realize that Virginia had also fallen
heavily for Arnold Bailey, and that the relationship between
her and Olivia was suffering as a consequence.

'It's so foolish to let a man break up an old friendship,' she
had protested when they returned to Robartes House late on
Boxing Day evening. 'Especially one like Arnold.'

'What do you mean?' Olivia had demanded belligerently.
'He's the nicest man I've ever met, and Ginny's far too young
for him.'

'Rubbish! She's only two years younger than you are.'

'She's sixteen. I'm eighteen. That makes a big difference
to a man of twenty-two. She's just a child where Arnold's
concerned, and he's too kind to tell her that she bores him.
But anyone can see that she does.'

Justine pulled down the corners of her mouth. 'I don't
think Arnold Bailey's bored by anyone in skirts. He's a born
philanderer; he even made a set at me.'

But Olivia had refused to accept this. 'He was just being
pleasant because you're my sister.'

At Easter things had gone from bad to worse, with Olivia
deeply envious of a situation which decreed that Virginia and
Arnold should share the same roof for a month. She had
started nagging her father about moving to Holly Lodge.

'Mother's right, Papa. It isn't good for us to be living here
with Grandmama.'

Bewildered, Lawrence had stood his ground. 'I can't leave
her, she isn't well. She needs me.'

He had never mentioned Eve by name since she left
Robartes House, although he never forbade his daughters to

speak of her and listened intently to everything they said.
Justine sensed that Lawrence felt bitterly betrayed by Eve's
disaffection, but at the same time found it difficult to blame
her. He was a man torn apart by his sense of duty towards
his mother and his affection for his wife. His health was
deteriorating, and only last week Justine had warned her
stepmother of the fact. But Eve had only shaken her head.

'I can't go back, darling. Calanthe wouldn't let me; it's her
house and she'd simply say no. There's room enough if you
and Livvy want to move in here, and you know I'd love to
have you, but I can't encourage you to leave your father. Oh
dear! What a mess it all is.'

It *was* a mess, but Justine realized that there was very
little anyone could do about it. It would need a fundamental
change in her father's character – an ability to make
decisions for himself, instead of relying on his mother –
which was unlikely to happen at this late stage. He was
forty-four, he wouldn't alter now. She sighed and inserted a
sheet of hotel notepaper into her typewriter.

The glass partition door between the outer and inner
offices opened, and her boss Harold Raymond entered with
a young man in tow.

'Justine, my dear, this is our new recruit, Jules Denon. I
told you about him, remember? His parents run a hotel in
Marseilles, and he's come to learn the English side of the
business. I'm going to leave him in your capable hands, if I
may. It's chaos out there this morning.' The manager gave a
jerk of his shiny, bald head in the general direction of the
hotel lobby. 'The place is packed with visitors for the
dancing and firework display on the Downs this evening.
Leave what you're doing.' He waved a plump, beautifully
manicured hand at the letters on her desk. 'There's nothing
there that's desperately important. Show Jules around
instead; find out from the housekeeper which is his room and
see him settled in. Happy staff, happy hotel! You know my
motto.'

He bustled out, blowing Justine a kiss. When the door

had closed on his ample form, she permitted herself a smile.

'As you may have gathered, Mr Raymond's in his element when the hotel's overflowing and the dining-room's fully booked.' She spoke French almost without thinking, and saw Jules Denon raise his eyebrows. 'I'm sorry,' she added in English. 'I'm afraid my accent isn't very good. Maybe you can help improve it?'

'No, no! Please, I did not intend to criticize! You speak French remarkably well for an Englishwoman.'

She laughed. 'Now there's a backhanded compliment if ever I heard one. Let's go and find out where Mrs Gregory has put you and then you can unpack. Where have you left your cases? At the desk in the lobby?'

By the end of a hectic morning, they had become firm friends. Jules Denon was not handsome by conventional standards – his face, beneath an unruly thatch of dark hair, being too round for the matinée idol good looks of Hollywood or the West End stage. His height, too, was just a little over five foot five, barely an inch more than Justine's own. Furthermore he could, if he were not careful, run to fat in middle age. He was already slightly overweight for his years, which she judged to be, like her own, somewhere in the early twenties. She also discovered that they shared a sense of humour and liked many of the same things, including good food. He told her that the Hotel Denon was famous for its cuisine, one of the reasons why he had chosen the Dorset Family Hotel in which to do his foreign training.

'My parents are anxious to attract English visitors, therefore it is necessary that I understand what English people like.'

'Fish and chips and a glass of mild and bitter,' Justine said, laughing. 'You have to educate the English palate. We're not a nation naturally obsessed by eating. Something to do with our Puritan heritage. Anything that gives pleasure is suspect and regarded as probably sinful.'

Jules nodded understandingly. 'Like sex,' he agreed.

Justine blushed furiously. Sex was not a word usually

mentioned in the presence of women, but he seemed to find it perfectly natural, a fact which made him even more deliciously different from the Englishmen of her acquaintance. He insisted on treating her to lunch, and as the hotel dining-room was full, they ate at the Prince's Restaurant above Stead and Simpson's shoe shop, on the corner of St Mary-le-Port and High Street. And if he found steak pie, boiled cabbage, stewed prunes and custard not quite to his taste, he was far too polite to say so, and sent his compliments to the chef by a waitress who stared at him as though he were mad. Giggling helplessly, he and Justine made their way back along the narrow street to the Dorset, beneath the ancient houses' overhanging eaves.

*

Eve had been hoping that her parents and Aunt Hetty would come to Bristol for the Silver Jubilee celebrations, but Staple Abbots was offering too many attractions of its own. Nor, naturally enough, was Arnold to be lured from the processions and displays of the capital, with their great central service in St Paul's. Besides, he had written, Olivia was coming down from Oxford to see the sights and he had promised to squire her around.

Eve made the mistake of reading out the letter to Virginia without first discovering its contents for herself, the result being that Ginny had grown very quiet and withdrawn over the past few days, refusing to take any interest whatsoever in the Jubilee. Or, indeed, in anything else. At first Eve had been sympathetic, but she was fast losing her patience as the 6th of May dawned. She had tried to persuade Ginny to accompany her to the Cathedral service in the morning and on a tour of the city in the afternoon, but both suggestions had been turned down flat.

'Well then, what about the band concert on the Downs this evening? They're relaying the King's broadcast message to the crowds. And afterwards, there's dancing and fireworks. You'd enjoy that.'

Ginny shook her head. 'I'm tired,' she answered sullenly. 'I can't be bothered.'

'Oh, for heaven's sake! Stop behaving like a child! All this nonsense just because Livvy's meeting Arnold in London! Can't you see that he's not serious about either of you?'

But Virginia merely grew more sullen and spent the holiday in her room, only coming downstairs for meals. Eve decided with a sigh that she must be getting old. Had she forgotten so soon how she used to feel about Frank? But there was nothing she could do for Ginny except leave her to enjoy her misery in peace.

She found the Cathedral service more moving than she had expected. It brought back memories of the coronation celebrations in Staple Abbots, the trestle tables set up in the High Street and Uncle Arthur's patriotic speech. She had worn blue kid boots and a frilled lace dress, and Old Tom Ormes, long since dead, had played his fiddle for everyone to dance to. She remembered dancing with Frank . . .

How long was it since anyone had called her Auburn? She put up a hand to touch a strand of hair escaping from beneath the brim of her green felt hat. Nowadays no one remarked on its colour, and she suspected that its brightness was beginning to fade. Only yesterday morning she had found two grey hairs clinging to the teeth of her comb. It came to her suddenly, standing there in the chill of the nave, listening to the soaring music of organ and choir, that she was lonely. Her life was full of people, but she had no close friend. She and Rose had drifted apart after they were married, each wrapped up in her own concerns. Rose had the village and Abbey Court and, above all, Ernest; and she had had Aunt Josie and Lawrence . . . But she was conscious of the significant difference in tense. Hers was in the past.

Martha insisted on cooking lunch in spite of Eve's offer to eat out.

'I'll have to cook for Miss Ginny, so why not you? Besides, they charge too much in them rest'rants.'

After the meal, when Ginny had once more retired to her

room, Eve gave herself the promised tour of the city streets, comforted by the beauty and scent of the massed banks of flowers. But once again her enjoyment was marred by an awareness of being alone. Everyone else seemed to be in couples, arms entwined. Her sense of isolation grew as the afternoon wore on.

'Martha,' she said, when the tea-trolley was wheeled into the drawing-room, 'do you still intend going to the concert and firework display this evening? If so, why don't we go together? I don't think Ginny's going to change her mind.'

Martha made a face. 'Oh, Mrs Prescott, I wish you'd asked me sooner. As it is, I've promised a friend. I could put her off, I suppose.'

Eve was horrified. 'I wouldn't hear of it! It was just that I thought it silly if we were both going on our own. I shall be all right.'

Martha seemed convinced by her hearty tones and trotted away, satisfied, to the kitchen. Eve ate her solitary tea, then went upstairs for a bath before walking the few hundred yards from her front door to the newly erected bandstand. There were already hundreds of people milling around, and more were arriving every minute by bus and tramcar. Excited children – allowed to stay up late for this special occasion – chased one another, shrieking with laughter, across the grass, while their parents unpacked flasks of tea and packets of sandwiches from the baskets they carried with them. The band, competing bravely against the crescendo of human voices, had already started to play selections from *Merrie England*, *The Yeomen of the Guard* and other patriotic pieces. A rousing finale of 'Land of Hope and Glory', in which everyone joined with gusto, was the prelude to a sudden hush as the Lord Mayor called out: 'Ladies and gentlemen, pray silence for His Majesty the King!' And then the voice of George V, a little ragged with emotion, came over the loudspeakers specially wired up for the occasion.

The dancing began almost as soon as the broadcast ended. Light operatic numbers gave way to 'Red Sails in the Sunset' and 'The Isle of Capri'. Complete strangers were partnering one another across the boards laid down by the Corporation, or, if they could find no space on this makeshift floor, stumbling, hysterical with laughter, over the uneven grass. It was a night for happiness, for putting aside cares and worries and irksome responsibilities and joining in the fun. But Eve, who had moved after the concert to stand withdrawn beneath the shelter of a spreading oak, felt close to tears.

Someone touched her arm. She turned her head and there, miraculously, was Lawrence, immaculately dressed as always, even thinner than she remembered him, the fair, wavy hair now a little sparse on top. But otherwise he had not changed; he looked just as he had done the first time they met. She stared, so pleased to see him that she could think of nothing to say.

'I've been watching you for some time,' he said. 'You looked so lonely, I felt I had to speak. I hope you don't mind.'

'Mind? Why on earth should I mind?' She smiled.

There was no answering smile. 'After you left, I assumed you never wished to hear from me again.'

'How could you possibly think that? I wanted you to come with me, for heaven's sake!' Exasperation surfaced. 'It was *you* who didn't want to speak to *me*. You never made any attempt to answer my telephone calls.'

She felt rather than saw his sudden stillness. 'What telephone calls?'

A young couple, trying to foxtrot over the rough and uneven ground, stumbled and cannoned into them before moving on with laughing apologies. It was getting dark, almost time for the fireworks, and the dancing was coming to an end. The evening was growing chilly and people were buttoning up coats and pulling on gloves, rounding up children before they strayed too far in the gathering dusk. But Eve was barely conscious of anyone except herself and Lawrence.

'In the early days I telephoned Robartes House on many occasions, but you were never there. At least, I was always told that you were out. And once Aunt Hetty called on your mother in an effort to talk things over, but Calanthe was so rude to her that she didn't stop. Didn't . . . didn't you know about any of this?'

'No.' Lawrence took a deep breath. 'No one told me.' There was another silence, then he said painfully, 'I suppose, if I'd had any sense, I should have guessed. I should have tried to contact you. But I was hurt . . . desperately hurt. I thought you must have grown to hate me when you put Virginia's interests in front of mine.'

He was twisting the truth as, Eve could see now, he always had done in order to avoid blaming himself for his actions. Over the past five years, encouraged by his mother, he had constructed a version of events that placed the onus for what had happened squarely on her shoulders and left him in the clear. So what, she wondered, would he make of the fact that Calanthe had deliberately kept from him Eve's attempts at reconciliation? Which of them would he believe? For she had no doubt that her mother-in-law would vigorously deny all knowledge of the matter. Eve wished now that she had told Justine and Olivia, but at the time she had considered it unfair to involve them in the quarrel more than was strictly necessary. She had also suffered from a misplaced sense of pride. She should have persisted in trying to get in touch with Lawrence. Knowing Calanthe as she did, it should have occurred to her that he might be kept in the dark. Instead, she had assumed his silence to mean that he no longer cared what happened to her. Yet he had filed for neither an official separation nor a divorce. That, surely, should have told her something. She had been so blind! So stupid!

She slipped a hand through his arm and he made no move to rebuff her. 'The fireworks are starting,' she said quietly. 'Shall we get a bit closer? People seem to be gathering mainly over there.' The music had stopped at last, but the babel of voices was as loud as ever and as the first rockets ascended into the sky, bursting into a shower of multi-coloured stars, there was a satisfied chorus of 'oohs' and 'ahs'. Eve continued, 'Virginia Mailer means a great deal to me, but it was never my intention to put her interests before yours. It just seemed to me that both your interests coincided with the move to Holly Lodge. I've never made any secret of the fact that I think you live too much in your mother's shadow.'

More rockets hissed into the air and spangled the night sky amber and green, pink and gold. Children, some still clutching the jubilee mugs given to them at school that morning and from which they refused to be parted, jumped up and down with excitement.

After a long pause, Lawrence answered in a subdued tone which Eve had to strain her ears to catch, 'I know that's what you've always thought. But I'm fond of her, Eve. I realize you might find that hard to believe because you don't like her. Oh, I don't blame you! I'm well aware she's not an easy woman to like; she's selfish and self-centred and wants her own way. But she makes me feel safe, and that's very important to me.'

'Don't I make you feel safe?'

Lawrence hesitated before replying. 'No. You ... You frighten me, rather.'

'*Frighten* you?' Eve was incredulous. 'For heaven's sake, in what way?' She added impatiently, 'We can't talk here. Will you come back to Holly Lodge? We can have a drink if you'd like one.'

He nodded, and they pushed their way out of the crowd. Holly Lodge was a haven of peace and quiet after the noise and turmoil of the Downs. Eve led her husband into the drawing-room, shadowed and empty, with the remains of the evening's fire smouldering in the grate. She switched on the lamps and drew the heavy curtains across the windows, islanding them in a little sea of light. Lawrence refused all offers of refreshment, but sat down in one of the armchairs near the hearth, holding out his long, bony hands to the dying embers. Eve removed her hat and coat, tossing them on to the settee, then sat opposite him, putting a few more pieces of coal on the fire as she did so. An orange flame spurted, licked across one of the lumps and caught. In moments, there was a friendly blaze.

'What did you mean,' she asked, 'when you said I frightened you? How could I possibly do that?'

He avoided looking at her, staring instead into the fire. 'You're ... well, you're very demanding. Physically, I mean. I suppose you're what the books would call a passionate woman.'

'What books?' Eve was confused.

Lawrence looked uncomfortable. 'You know ... Books on ... on marriage. My mother has a couple. She gave them to me to read before I married Bel. They both warn against ... well, against women with ... strong sexual appetites. They warn against men overtaxing themselves. And, of course, that would be even more important for someone like myself who has a weak heart.'

There was a long silence, unbroken except for the crackling of the flames. At last, however, Eve said slowly, 'I expect those books are quite old by now. Ideas have changed since they were written. But, oh, Lawrence, I wish you'd said something.' Hadn't she suspected, though, that he felt like that? Hadn't she known, deep down, that sexually she made him uneasy? And hadn't she ignored the knowledge because of her own needs? She got up quickly and knelt down beside his chair, taking one of his hands in hers and stroking it gently. 'Darling, I'm sorry. I didn't properly understand. Things will be different in the future, I promise.'

He turned his head then, smiling wryly. 'Is there going to be a future? You can't come back to Robartes House. It wouldn't be fair to ask you.'

No, he was right; she couldn't do it. But Calanthe was only sixty-six; she might live for years yet. Eve raised his hand and pressed it against her cheek. 'You wouldn't think of leaving your mother?'

Lawrence shook his head. 'No. She needs me as much as I need her.' He sighed. 'I should have told you that years ago, shouldn't I, before we were married? I ought to have been honest with you. I just hoped that things would work out somehow.'

'Yes. But I think I understand why you didn't.' Eve released his hand and sat back on her heels. 'Promise me one thing.'

'What?' He reached out and gently pushed a stray lock of hair away from her eyes.

'That when anything happens to your mother – when she dies, I mean – you'll come and live here and let me look after you.'

Lawrence kissed her tenderly. 'I don't deserve you, I know that. And yes, I promise, if you're sure it will make you happy.'

Part Three
1939-1945

Chapter Twenty-one

'So we want to get married,' Justine said defiantly, holding tightly to Jules's hand. 'No one can stop us, we're both well over twenty-one. But we'd prefer to have your blessing if we could.'

The hot June sunshine spilled in through the drawing-room windows of Holly Lodge, the stained-glass lights making jewelled patterns on the carpet and drawing Eve's attention to the fact that, in places, it was almost threadbare. She ought to think about buying a new one, but there seemed no opportunity at present. There were so many other calls on her time. The past eighteen months, since Lawrence had come to live with her following his mother's unexpected death, had been busy ones: adjusting to her husband and elder stepdaughter residing permanently at the Lodge; helping Lawrence with the business of selling Robartes House; nursing him through a bout of pneumonia which had still further undermined his health; travelling at a moment's notice to Staple Abbots on at least three occasions when her father, now nearing eighty years of age, had been seriously ill with bronchitis. In addition there had been Olivia's graduation, then seeing her safely installed in a flat in London, where she was at present working as assistant fiction editor for one of the proliferating women's magazines; and visiting Virginia who was in her last term at Oxford.

There had been other worries, too, as the prospect of yet another war loomed in Europe. The previous September, Prime Minister Neville Chamberlain had returned from Munich declaring it was 'peace in our time', but except for the most hardened optimists few had really believed in the agreement signed by himself and the German Chancellor,

Adolf Hitler. Three months earlier, in March, after German troops had occupied Czechoslovakia, Britain and France had agreed to support Poland if that country were similarly invaded. In Bristol, air-raid shelters were already being dug beneath Queen's Square and College Green, and there had been a demonstration of barrage balloons on Durdham Downs. The population at large was introduced to the mysteries of the Anderson shelter, for providing cover in back gardens, and both local and national newspapers carried instructions on how to make blackout curtains. Small wonder, therefore, that there had been no time to think of replacing worn-out carpets; and now, here was Justine adding to their worries by announcing her intention of marrying a Frenchman and going to live in France.

Not that Eve had anything against Jules Denon, and at any other time would have wished him and Justine every happiness. She liked the young Frenchman very much and had welcomed him with pleasure whenever her stepdaughter had brought him home. This had happened with increasing frequency during the past twelve months, but as the European political situation deteriorated she had begun to pray that the friendship between the couple was no more than that. Common sense, however, warned her that this was a false hope. Jules had originally come to Bristol in the spring of 1935 with the intention of remaining two years; he had now been here for four. Justine had been taken on several occasions to meet his parents in Marseilles; although it seemed to Eve that, after the first visit, there was a little reluctance to invite her back. No doubt Monsieur and Madame Denon had seen the way things were between their son and Justine, and were uneasy about his marriage to a foreigner. The young people themselves had shown no hurry to formalize the relationship, content until now to let it take its course; waiting, presumably, until they had saved enough money to feel secure and not be a burden to Jules's parents. But all that had changed with the headlong descent into a war which everyone now accepted as inevitable; no longer a question of 'if' but 'when'.

'We shall be at war by Christmas,' Jules said, sitting tensely on the edge of the settee, clutching Justine's hand. 'When that happens, I must be at home in my own country, ready to fight if need be. And I want Justine there as my wife. I love her, Mr Prescott, very much indeed.'

'So you might,' Lawrence retorted angrily, 'but that's an entirely selfish point of view. What if you are called up? How will that affect Justine? A stranger in a strange country suddenly left all alone.'

There was a strained, pettish note to his voice which Eve had noticed with growing frequency since his mother's death. Calanthe had never regained consciousness after a bad fall down the main staircase of Robartes House just after Christmas, 1937; she died two weeks later, and Lawrence still had not recovered from the shock. It showed in his inability to resume his painting, in little bouts of petulance of which he was afterwards ashamed, in the ease with which he fell prey to innumerable coughs and colds. His heart, too, beat even more erratically than it used to do, shaking the entire bed at night, when he was asleep. He clung to his family as to a lifeline, relying on them for some semblance of normality in a world which seemed to him to be disintegrating. And at the centre of that world were Eve and Justine. They and Martha were always present or near at hand, the fixed and stable points in a shifting existence which had replaced the quiet, well-ordered life he had previously led. And now Justine was proposing to go away, not just to a different city but to a foreign country – and one, moreover, which could be engulfed any day in another terrible war.

'But I want to go, Papa.' Justine tightened her grip on Jules's hand. 'I love France and I speak French well; Jules says so. I shan't be lonely. Jules has three brothers and a sister all living at home, and his parents run a hotel – a business which, thanks to Harold Raymond, I know all about. We love each other and nothing's going to stop us getting

married. We'd just prefer it was with your consent. We can't
wait any longer; time's running out. For one thing,
Monsieur and Madame Denon are insisting that Jules goes
home whatever else happens. They think, quite rightly, that
he's been here far too long already. They've been extremely
patient, but now they want his help in running the Hotel
Châtain. After all, that is what he has trained for. While his
parents were prepared to let him stay in Bristol, there wasn't
any hurry. We weren't even sure of our feelings for one
another.' Here she and Jules exchanged incredulous glances,
plainly amazed that they could both have been so blind.
Justine continued, 'But once we knew he had to go back to
France, there was no question in either of our minds. We
want to be together for the rest of our lives.'

'But not at a time like this!' Lawrence's voice grew
shriller. 'Not with another war imminent. It's madness! You
must see that.'

Justine's level gaze met his. 'I can't see anything, Papa,
except that I have to go with Jules. I'm sorry, but he's the
most important person in my life and I have to put him
first.'

Lawrence flung himself back in his chair, defeated by an
emotion that was as old as time. Young people never
believed that love could dim and fade. They always thought
it would last for ever. And sometimes, of course, it did.

Later when they were both in bed, watching the moon rise
behind the trees, rimming each leaf with a silver thread, Eve
said gently, 'You might as well accept it, darling. Justine's
right, we can't stop them marrying. She's twenty-seven; so's
he. More than old enough to know their own minds.'

Lawrence tossed restlessly, shifting from side to side, his
heart thudding irregularly. 'I know, I know. I'm being
selfish, you don't have to tell me. But I don't want to lose
her. She'll be living amongst strangers! If it were Paris it
wouldn't be quite so bad; she's familiar with Paris. But
Marseilles! All those foreign sailors! It's no good you
laughing like that. I daresay I am being over-protective and

fussy. But we know nothing about Jules's parents or this hotel of theirs. It might be the most frightful place.'

Eve propped herself on one elbow and kissed him gently. 'Darling, calm down. It's not good for you to get so excited. And as far as the hotel is concerned, at least I can set your mind at rest on that score. Apart from the fact that I can't imagine Jules's mother and father running anything other than a highly respectable establishment, as soon as he mentioned the Hotel Châtain this afternoon I recognized the name. I suppose I must have heard him talk about it before, but for some reason it was only today that I made the connection.'

'What are you saying?' Lawrence demanded, trying to suppress a note of peevishness. He was sweating and there was a familiar pain in his chest which frightened him, and nowadays there was no Calanthe to soothe and reassure. Kind as Eve was, gentle as she could be, she still lacked the sympathy of his mother. She was, after all, a doctor's daughter. Her general approach to illness was based firmly in common sense – obey the rules, follow the medical advice and you're bound to feel better – when all Lawrence wanted was to be petted and spoilt and told how bad he was feeling.

Eve settled herself more comfortably and took his hand. 'You remember that Aunt Josie had shares in a Provençal hotel? The income from them put Arnie through Cambridge, and afterwards they reverted to me as part of her general estate. I decided to sell them, and they made quite a tidy sum. Well, it was the Hotel Châtain in Marseilles. It suddenly came back to me when Jules mentioned it today. So, you see, your fears are groundless. It's a very thriving business. How's that for the long arm of coincidence?'

'You didn't say anything,' Lawrence complained. 'Why didn't you tell Jules and Justine? They'd have been interested. And how on earth did your aunt come to have shares in a French hotel in the first place?'

'She was always going on holiday to Provence; she adored it there. As to how she acquired the shares, goodness only knows! I had no idea they existed until after she was dead. Anyway, that's one thing less for you to worry over. All you have to do now is accept that Justine will marry with or without your consent and decide which you'd rather she did. And as Jules doesn't think his parents will be coming over for the wedding, it would be nice if we could be there.'

There was a moment's silence, then Lawrence nodded. 'All right,' he murmured wearily. 'You win.'

*

It was a very quiet, Register Office wedding, the denominational difference between bride and groom making it difficult for them to marry in church.

'She'll convert to Rome, mark my words,' Lawrence prophesied gloomily over breakfast, and Eve, irritated, asked, 'What on earth does it matter if she does?'

It was not the happiest of notes on which to start the morning, and indeed a sour undercurrent seemed to mar the whole day. Apart from themselves and Martha, the only other guests invited to the ceremony were Olivia and Virginia, and it was unfortunate that Olivia should arrive from London with Arnold Bailey in tow.

'Justine, darling, I knew you and Jules wouldn't mind. I do so hate travelling alone, and as Arnie was coming home anyway it seemed sensible to bring him along.'

Eve said abruptly, 'I thought the schools didn't break up for another three weeks?'

Arnold grinned unrepentantly. 'Outbreak of measles. Quite a severe one, so as it's so close to the end of term the Head decided it was better to shut up shop altogether. Sorry to muscle in on the wedding, but I didn't know anything about it until Livvy mentioned it last night, when I telephoned to find out if she were coming down for the weekend.'

Eve said no more. It was obvious that neither Justine nor Jules cared who was at the ceremony apart from each other; and she herself would have been delighted to see Arnold three weeks earlier than expected had it not been for the effect it must have on Virginia, who was forced to watch him dance assiduous attendance on her friend. She had arrived from Oxford the previous evening, her final exams behind her and only a couple of weeks to go before she came down for good. She had been looking forward to the wedding as a quiet family affair – for she regarded herself now as a family member – but here was Arnold to disturb her peace of mind. To be fair, Eve conceded, he did not ignore Virginia, but in many ways that only made things worse, because then Olivia grew jealous. He played off one girl against the other with such practised ease that Eve found herself almost disliking him. The trouble was that she found it impossible to be cross with Arnold for any length of time, particularly when he greeted her with such genuine and flattering affection.

'Just as young and pretty as when you used to be my teacher!' he exclaimed, and insisted on sitting next to her in the taxi which took them to the Register Office.

The wedding ceremony itself was brief, and almost before she knew it Eve found herself in the foyer of the Dorset Hotel, shaking hands with Harold Raymond, who had insisted not only on hosting the reception but on paying for it as well.

'My wedding present to the happy couple,' he beamed. 'The very least I could do, considering what a wonderful secretary Justine's been to me all these years. Heaven alone knows how I'm going to replace her!' With a flourish, he seized one of Justine's hands and kissed it, at the same time making a bow. 'My dear Madame Denon, I salute you! The best, the fairest, the fastest shorthand writer in the West of England! *Je vous remercie.*'

'Is he always like this?' Arnold asked *sotto voce*, and was frowned down by Eve.

'Behave yourself,' she admonished, but he only grinned and escorted both Olivia and Virginia into the manager's private dining-room, where a substantial buffet was accompanied by half a dozen bottles of the Dorset's best champagne.

Eve shook her head, smiling ruefully, before turning her attention to Lawrence. He was looking extremely pale and more than a little fragile, but when she would have urged him to a chair he pulled his arm free, like a fractious child.

'I'm all right.' His eyes turned towards his elder daughter. 'Justine . . . She looks lovely, doesn't she?'

Eve slipped an arm through his and gave it a gentle squeeze. 'Lovely,' she agreed. Which was no more than the truth. But it was not just the smart, belted two-piece of white shantung, nor the small veiled hat perched rakishly on the fair, wavy hair that made Justine appear to such advantage. Rather it was the sparkling blue eyes, the glow of contentment, the radiant happiness which transformed prettiness into beauty. Whatever doubts her father and stepmother might harbour about her marriage, Justine obviously did not share them.

Beside her sister, Olivia, who had always been considered the slightly more attractive of the two, today looked plain. Her floral frock and edge-to-edge navy-blue coat, her high-heeled navy kid shoes and pure silk, flesh-coloured stockings all shouted 'London', as did the wide-brimmed navy organdie hat with its matching band of floral silk swathing the crown. But the hazel eyes were discontented, the full red mouth pulled down at the corners, giving her a sullen, pouting look which was echoed by Virginia. 'Damn Arnold,' Eve thought viciously, her goodwill towards him suddenly evaporating. Why did he always have to play Lothario? He fancied himself too much, that was the trouble.

Harold Raymond was beside her, gallantly complimenting her on her own appearance.

'Blue suits you delightfully, Mrs Prescott. It brings out the colour of your eyes and complements that gorgeous auburn hair. And what a superb fur, if you'll pardon my saying so.' He reached out a hand and lovingly stroked the silver fox stole flung across Eve's left shoulder. 'My father was a furrier, you know. Had a shop in Castle Street. I learned a lot about furs from him, and that, believe me, is a splendid one.'

Eve laughed. 'A present from my husband and particularly hot on a day like this.' She slipped it off and draped it over the back of a chair. 'You'll miss Justine, Mr Raymond.'

The small, womanish hands were raised despairingly. 'Ah, my dear madam! "Miss" is too poor a word to describe my feelings on this occasion. Justine has been my good right arm. I have no idea what I shall do without her. Although what will happen in the months ahead, who can say? I am very much afraid that life is about to be turned upside down for all of us. War will no longer be something remote from these blessed islands. The aeroplane, I fear, will bring it right to our own doorsteps.'

Eve frowned. 'In London and the east, perhaps. But will German planes be able to reach as far as Bristol, do you think?'

'Oh lord, yes!' Arnold's voice cut in cheerfully. He was holding a plate piled high with food from the buffet, and while Eve and Harold Raymond watched, fascinated, he stuffed a whole chicken vol-au-vent into his mouth, chomping steadily until it was gone. When at last he could speak, he continued, 'Don't take any notice of all the propaganda our lot are handing out. Damned efficient chaps, the Jerries. In devious ways, they've been breaking the disarmament clause of the Versailles Treaty ever since the mid-twenties. As far as bombers go, they've got the Dornier, the Heinkel . . .'

'You seem to know a lot about it,' Eve murmured suspiciously.

'Yes, well . . .' He demolished a canapé. 'Been taking flying lessons out at Croydon. Very knowledgeable bloke, my instructor. When the balloon goes up, which it will very soon, I shall volunteer for the RAF.'

Eve cast a scared glance over her shoulder to where her husband was sitting, talking to Justine and Jules. 'For heaven's sake, lower your voice, Arnie. Lawrence is unhappy enough as it is at the prospect of Justine going to France. It's only by dint of persuading him that war isn't inevitable that I'm keeping him sane. Are you so certain it can't be avoided?'

Arnold helped himself to a large portion of chicken salad. 'As certain as God made little green apples, as an American friend of mine puts it. And it isn't all going to be over by Christmas, either! In fact, unless the Yanks eventually come in on our side we could well go under.'

Eve and Harold Raymond stared at him in horror. Before either of them could protest at this heresy, however, Jules walked over to join them. He also kissed Eve's hand, but without any of the little manager's flamboyance.

'*Belle mère*.' His eyes twinkled. 'You must allow me to call you that, now that Justine and I are married. My wife ...' he smiled joyously at the words and repeated them with relish, 'my wife tells me that your aunt, Miss Josephine Gilchrist, was once a shareholder in my parents' hotel. What a very small world! I must ask Papa about it when I get home.'

'Yes. Please do. I should love to know how he came to meet her.' She reached up and kissed Jules on the cheek. 'You'll take care of Justine, won't you?'

The smile faded. 'With my life. You mustn't worry. I love her.'

Eve nodded. 'Yes, I know.' She closed her eyes for a moment, and Frank's face swam up out of the darkness: small, dark, olive-skinned. His voice sounded in her ears. 'Auburn ... Sweet, sweet Auburn.' How foolish it was that she still thought of him after all these years. Would she never get over the pain of losing him, first to Jenny Slade and then, even more finally, to the war?

At last everyone had finished eating. Lawrence and Jules both spoke briefly, the former obviously labouring under a great weight of suppressed emotion; the cake was cut, the toasts drunk and then it was time to leave for Temple Meads station and the London train. As Eve stood on the draughty platform, waving goodbye to Justine and Jules on the first leg of their cross-Channel journey, she recalled that day long, long ago, when on this very spot she had encountered Lawrence spotting trains. It was odd how well she could remember him, considering that she had never expected to see him again: tall and thin and pale, in a grey cashmere overcoat over a darker grey suit, and a bowler hat tilted rakishly on the fair, wavy hair. He had imparted all sorts of information about the railways to her and Frank, his eyes shining with excitement, until the chauffeur arrived to tell him that his mother was waiting. Prophetic words! Calanthe had always been waiting somewhere in the background. Even in death, she still exerted power over her son.

Eve sighed and linked her arm through her husband's, giving it an affectionate squeeze. His expression was bleak as he stared after the departing train. As the tail-end carriage disappeared from view, he shivered violently as though someone had just walked over his grave.

'We'll go and spend a holiday with them as soon as they're settled,' Eve told him bracingly, but Lawrence shook his head.

'No,' he said quietly, 'it's too late. There won't be time. Both our countries will soon be at war, do you think I don't know that?' He gave a little snort of mirthless laughter. 'Twenty-one years since the carnage and destruction of the last one. Just long enough for another generation of cannon-fodder to grow to manhood, and here we go again! Can't we ever learn?'

Arnold, overhearing, spoke cheerfully from behind them, where he was walking between Virginia and Olivia.

'Oh, there'll be none of that slogging through the mud this time, Mr Prescott. This war will be lost or won in the air.'

Olivia shuddered eloquently. 'I wish you wouldn't talk like that Arnie! You know nothing about it, really. I'm sure the Germans won't drop bombs on us when it comes to the point, because we should only retaliate and drop bombs on them.'

Virginia saw a chance to score and took it. 'What very naïve, not to say positively childish, ideas you have some-times, Livvy!' she remarked loftily. 'People like us are just so many statistics to the men in power. As long as they can provide for their own safety, they don't care twopence what happens to us.'

'When I want a lecture,' was the furious retort, 'I'll let you know. Until then, Virginia, please keep your censorious utterances to yourself!' They had reached the station fore-court, and Olivia suddenly swung on her heel. 'I think I'd better go back to Town this afternoon, after all, instead of waiting until tomorrow. I've a pile of work to get through before Monday. My overnight case can stay at Holly Lodge until I come home next time; there's only a nightdress and a sponge-bag in it.'

'But why?' her father demanded, deeply distressed. 'It's gone three o'clock now, and surely you aren't expected to work on a Sunday?'

'I've work at the flat I can do.' Olivia seemed determined; and although Eve added her protests to Lawrence's she knew that they would do no good. Her stepdaughter was bent on teaching Arnold a lesson by depriving him of her company. She either couldn't or wouldn't see that he truly didn't care whether she was there or not. He would simply transfer all his attention to Virginia, whose eyes were already sparkling at the prospect. 'I'm sorry, Papa.' Olivia kissed her father's cheek and then was gone, plunging back into the station without vouchsafing a word to anyone else.

In one way, Eve was thankful to be rid of her; at least now they would not be subject to foolish rivalry for the next twenty-four hours. But for Lawrence's sake, and because he had already been emotionally scarred by the day's events, she forced herself to go after her younger stepdaughter and persuade her to return.

'For his sake, Livvy, please! Ignore Ginny if you must. But you and she used to be such good friends.'

Olivia stared sullenly at her smart kid shoes. 'Not any more. She's grown into a conceited little baggage. Who does she think she is, anyway? She's only the abandoned daughter of one of your aunt's housekeepers, whom you've been kind enough to educate. A mistake, if you ask me. It's given her ideas above her station.' She saw the glimmer of anger in Eve's blue eyes and added hastily, 'All right, I'll stay, for Papa's sake and because you've asked me so sweetly.' And having taken the wind completely out of her stepmother's sails, she once more walked off the platform to join the others.

For a moment or two Eve remained where she was. She felt tired and dispirited, now that the main action of the day was over and only the long evening stretched ahead. She thought again of Frank ... 'Auburn. Sweet, sweet Auburn.' The words went round and round in her head ... With a tremendous effort she pinned a smile in place, settled her fur stole more securely on her shoulder and followed Olivia through the booking-hall and out on to the station forecourt.

Chapter Twenty-two

'So we're moving out of Rosemary Villa after all these years and coming to live here, at the Court, with Rose and Ernest.' Helena settled back in her chair with the satisfied air of one who has managed to get in first with a startling piece of news.

'*You're leaving Rosemary Villa?*' Eve's reaction was all that her mother and aunt had hoped for. 'But you can't! It's your home.'

Hetty took over from her sister-in-law, determined not to be left out of the conversation. 'Marcus will be eighty this year, and as you know his health is not what it was. And all this food rationing is making things very difficult. At least, this way, we can pool our allowances with Rose and Ernest. Now that Mabel's dead, they'll be glad of the extra company; they said so.' Hetty smoothed the skirt of the black woollen dress which she had worn to this morning's funeral in St Peter's Church and continued plaintively, 'And since the outbreak of war, you can't get domestic help for love or money. All the young girls are either joining the women's services or going off to work in munitions factories. It really is most thoughtless of them ... I don't know what you're snorting about, Marcus — it isn't funny.'

The doctor lit his pipe and exhaled a cloud of smoke, smiling with ironic affection at his sister. 'Oh, but it is, Hetty, if you think about it. Here we are fighting for our lives, maybe for our very survival as an independent nation, and all you can talk about is the lack of servants. You're thoroughly selfish, my dear; always were, always will be. It doesn't matter to you in the least that half of Europe is overrun, or that our army has just been thrown out of France lock, stock and barrel. All you know is that your comfort's threatened!'

'Well, really—!' Hetty was beginning indignantly when they were joined by Rose and Ernest, who had been busy until now talking to some of the other funeral guests and seeing that they had enough to eat from the buffet table.

'Darling!' Rose stooped to kiss Eve's cheek. She had lost the plumpness of her youth, and the toffee-brown eyes looked enormous in the pale, thin face. In this first spring of the war she was almost forty and had a harassed look about her, as though years of devoting herself to Ernest, and overseeing the efficient running of the Court and Home Farm, had taken their toll. Which, Eve reflected, they probably had. She herself knew something about the strain of nursing a sickly husband, but she had no other responsibilities, unlike poor Rose. 'Have Aunt Helena and Uncle Marcus told you that they're coming to live with us here?'

'Just this minute.' Eve shifted along the sofa to make room for Rose to sit beside her. 'What will happen to Rosemary Villa, I wonder, once it's empty?'

Ernest lowered himself into a neighbouring armchair with a sigh of relief. Standing for any length of time always exhausted him. 'It won't remain empty for long, don't you worry. People are getting out of the cities before the air-raids begin. The War Office could let all the village houses ten times over. Mind you, a lot of the villagers have evacuees billeted on them. Plenty of vacant rooms, now that the men have been called up. We're expecting a couple of kids ourselves, one of the reasons we want to get the place as full as possible. The more bedrooms occupied, the less space for outsiders. I tell you what!' His eyes brightened, and he ran an emaciated hand through the greying red hair. 'Why don't you two come and live here, as well? You want to get out of Bristol, you know. What with the docks at Avonmouth and the aeroplane works at Filton, it'll be high on the Germans' target list.'

Afraid that Lawrence might seize on the offer, Eve answered quickly, 'And leave Holly Lodge empty? No, I couldn't possibly – thanks all the same, Ernest. And besides, I'm working as from next Monday.'

'Working?' Helena was appalled. 'But you're a married woman with a husband to look after. I hope it's not in one of those Forces' canteens or a factory, for heaven's sake! And anyway, I should have thought you were much too old.'

Eve responded irritably, 'Mother, there's a war on. Every able-bodied person is needed to do his or her bit. And I'm only the same age as Rose! How can I possibly sit idly at home while the young people are risking their lives? Arnold's in the RAF, Ginny's a "Wren" and Livvy's in the WAAF. I should feel as though I were letting them down if I didn't do something. As it is, it's only a desk job in Censorship, although it does mean working Saturdays and Sundays. But Martha looks after Lawrence.'

'Censorship?' Hetty wrinkled her brow. 'What are you censoring?'

'The Irish mail. There are thousands of Irish workers in this country, all writing home or being written to two or three times a week.'

'And you open their letters and read them?' Marcus was horrified. 'Isn't that a violation of their rights?'

'No, Papa, not in wartime. Not under the Defence of the Realm Act, you must be aware of that.'

'But surely,' Rose put in, 'men away from home must write . . . well, you know' – the colour mounted in her cheeks – 'all sorts of . . . of intimate things.'

Eve laughed. 'It helps to be broad-minded, if that's what you mean.'

'Lawrence!' Helena spoke sharply. 'What do you think of this job of Eve's? Surely you can't approve of it?'

Lawrence hesitated, torn between telling the truth and taking sides against his wife. Loyalty won. 'I'd rather she was home with me, of course, but as Eve pointed out, every able person is expected to do something. It's just unfortunate that I'm in no fit state to make a contribution. I feel sometimes that I'm rather a coward.'

'Nonsense, darling!' Eve protested, amidst general disclaimer. 'You wouldn't be accepted for anything even if you volunteered; you're not strong enough.' And she tried to still the voice in her head which murmured that Lawrence really would be useless because he was so frightened – for Olivia, for Justine in far-off France, of the possibility of a German invasion. But most of all, he was terrified at the prospect of air-raids which, with every passing day of this final week of May 1940, as the ill-fated British Expeditionary Force was rescued from the Dunkirk beaches, seemed an increasing hazard. The German army was within a few miles of Paris, and the Luftwaffe would soon be able to establish air bases along the coast of northern France.

A few of the funeral guests were leaving, and Rose and Ernest got up to say goodbye and accompany them as far as the front door. Aunt Mabel had been ill with cancer for some time, so Eve found it inevitable that phrases such as 'blessed relief', 'better where she is now' and 'what she would have wished' should drift in hushed tones across the room to where she was sitting. One glance at her father's face told her that such unthinking platitudes upset Marcus, and in order to divert his attention she said quickly, 'We had another letter from Justine yesterday. She's expecting her first baby in the autumn and is bubbling over with excitement, in spite of Jules being away in the Army.'

'Oh, how splendid!' It was Hetty who answered, while Marcus did his best to look interested without quite succeeding.

For the truth was, as Eve was forced to admit to herself, that while he accused his sister of being selfish and egotistical, Papa was equally as self-engrossed as Aunt Hetty, and had been for a good many years past. Perhaps, as Aunt Josie had once suggested to her, he always had been – or why else would he have abandoned so easily his youthful aspiration to work among the Bristol poor for the comforts and security of Staple Abbots? But Eve shied away uneasily from such reflections.

She noticed how tired Lawrence was looking and decided it was time that they, too, were leaving. She wanted to get back to Bristol while it was still light; driving in the blackout was dangerous. Moreover, although she did her best to reassure her husband, she was convinced that air-raids were now a definite probability but had no idea what to expect. At the end of March, one-legged, green-painted wooden 'tables' had appeared in the streets, which would change colour in the presence of gas; a circumstance which had suddenly alerted the population to the horrifying possibility of such attacks. Anyone who remembered the terrible effects of gas warfare in the Flanders trenches could not help but be apprehensive. Gas masks had been issued at the outbreak of hostilities and were now carried everywhere by everyone, even to the bathroom and lavatory. Eve reached for hers from under her chair and stood up.

'Darling,' she smiled at Lawrence, 'it's time we went.' She kissed her parents and Aunt Hetty. 'Well, I suppose when I come home next you'll be living here. When exactly are you moving?'

'As soon as possible,' Marcus answered, struggling to rise. 'Now the decision's made, there's no point in dragging our feet. Maybe sometime next week. It depends on Rose and Ernest.' He squeezed Eve's arm. 'Look after yourself, my dear. Don't take any pointless risks. And try to come to see us more often.'

'I don't think that will be possible, Papa. Petrol's just gone up to 1/11½d a gallon to discourage people from using too much. I suspect that the next step will be all-out rationing. But we'll keep in touch by phone. Lawrence, darling, are you ready?'

They said their goodbyes; but as they drove away from Abbey Court, back through the village and on to the Warminster road, Eve felt a sense of relief. In these wartime days Staple Abbots seemed locked in the past, a place where nothing materially altered. Every house had blackout curtains, it was true, and people like Aunt Hetty complained of rationing, lack of domestic staff and evacuees, but the younger faces missing from the village were largely unknown to Eve while all the remembered ones were still there, their owners going about their customary business. She had to admit that it would be strange not to go back to Rosemary Villa any more, but such a change was a natural one given the passage of time and the fact that she had elderly parents.

Martha was on the front doorstep of Holly Lodge to welcome them home.

'Did you have a good journey, Mrs Prescott? Mr Prescott, dear, you look all in. Come and have some supper. I've put hot-water bottles in your bed. It's a chilly evening.'

Eve removed her hat and followed Martha and Lawrence indoors. War or no war, it was good to be home.

*

On the 22nd of June France concluded an armistice with Germany, dividing the country into two – the northern part being under the control of Berlin, the southern ruled by a puppet government from Vichy. Lawrence was beside himself with worry, watching every post, hoping for a letter from Justine. Three days later, at a quarter past midnight, Bristol had its first air-raid warning, and when the 'All Clear' sounded two and a half hours later the first bombs had been dropped in the centre of the city. It was the beginning of what was to become a way of life for the next twelve months.

By mid-November, Eve was used to getting up in the middle of the night, donning slacks, jumper and coat over her pyjamas and taking refuge in the cupboard under the stairs. She and Lawrence had voted against having a shelter in the garden and, instead, had cleared the 'glory hole', as Martha called it, of all unnecessary junk, set up three small camp chairs swathed in blankets, and made themselves as comfortable as possible until the 'All Clear' sounded. Then they climbed wearily back to bed for an hour or two's sleep, before the alarm reminded Eve that it was time to get up again and set out for the office. Fortunately she had only a short distance to go, which enabled her to snatch a few extra moments with Lawrence.

These moments were important for both of them, clinging together after the disturbance of the night, Eve holding her husband closely in her arms and murmuring words of comfort and reassurance. Since the fall of France he had suddenly grown weaker and frailer, worn down by anxiety, waiting for a letter which never came ... and would not come now, Eve thought, until the war was over. She willed Lawrence to survive at least until then, but who could tell when it would be? Or what would be the outcome? But the successful air battles, fought during the late summer in the skies over the south-east of England, had lessened the threat of a German invasion. If only the Americans would come in on Britain's side, all might yet be well, and Eve did everything in her power to keep up Lawrence's spirits.

'Justine and Jules will be all right,' she would urge, 'now that the French have stopped fighting. They'll be safe in Marseilles, you'll see.'

He was like her child, the one she had never had. They had ceased to make love many years ago, and even had his health permitted it he seemed to have lost the urge. Eve suspected that he had never really forgiven her desertion of him. She did her best to make reparation by trying to take Calanthe's place, but doubted if she could ever truly succeed. His mother had occupied a unique niche in his life which no one else could fill.

Arnold, Virginia and Olivia came home at different times on leave, all looking very smart in their officers' uniforms. Occasionally two of them would be home together, but so far – to Eve's great relief – the explosive mixture of all three at once had been avoided. That Arnold was fond of both girls, she had no doubt, but whether he favoured one more than the other she had no way of telling. He seemed to act in exactly the same manner towards each, and when alone with Eve talked of other girl-friends. With all the weddings going on, with comparative strangers marrying at the drop of a hat, Eve could not help wishing that Arnold would make a similarly impulsive decision and announce that he had a wife. Olivia and Virginia might then resume their friendship and start looking for someone else. But until that happened, she resigned herself to an arctic climate whenever they were beneath the same roof.

Sunday the 24th of November was cold and dank, and the lights had to be kept on all day in the office. Eve, for whom it was no longer a penance to work at weekends, was nevertheless thankful when the hands of the clock finally showed five-thirty. She put aside her blue pencil and the pile of letters she had been reading.

'Praise be!' said the woman sitting next to her, and there was a general murmur of assent from the room's other occupants. Some of the women reached for soap and towels, heading for the ladies' cloakroom, but Eve felt too tired to bother. She was only half a mile from Holly Lodge and would have a bath as soon as she reached home. No one was supposed to use more than four inches of water, but even that was enough to wash away the grime of the day. She suddenly felt hungry and wondered what Martha had prepared for supper. Thank God that so far they had been able to keep her; that Lawrence's state of health demanded that he have someone constantly in attendance. Eve stretched her arms luxuriously before gathering up her unread pile of letters and handing them to the table supervisor, to be put under lock and key for the night.

As she hurried home through the blacked-out streets, she remembered how the church bells used to ring out on a Sunday evening, breaking the sabbath hush. Now such a sound would mean a German invasion, followed by the inevitable panic and fear. The windows of the houses which in the past were so bright and welcoming, stared blindly back at her, with only here and there the tiniest chink of light. In Pembroke Road an air-raid warden passed her, running, probably late for duty. Eve thanked her lucky stars that it was not her night for firewatching, although so far the night-time raids had not done a great deal of damage. Some bombs had been dropped, a few people had been killed, barrage balloons had caught fire, but to date Bristol had not suffered anything like London. This, together with the fact that many civil service ministries, plus the B.B.C., had moved into the city, reinforced the idea that it was beyond the range of heavily laden German bombers.

Eve let herself in at the front door of Holly Lodge, and the familiar smell of the house came to greet her. It conjured up, as always, memories of Aunt Josie, of the large, comfortable figure writing at her desk, or having one of her little naps in front of the drawing-room fire. And tonight, for some reason, it also brought back vivid memories of Frank, of those few days he had spent there more than thirty years ago, his small dark face alight with wonder and excitement.

Eve made sure that the blackout curtains were properly drawn before switching on the hall light. Martha popped her head round the kitchen door.

'I thought I heard you, Mrs Prescott. You go and tidy up, dear, and have a word with Mr Prescott, and by then the meal'll be ready. I managed to get a couple of pork chops from the butcher. Big ones . . . they'll go between three of us. I had to queue, mind. Queues everywhere nowadays.'

Eve followed her into the kitchen, where the chops were sizzling loudly under the grill.

'How's Mr Prescott been today?'

Martha wrinkled her nose. 'We-ell, it ain't been one of his better days, and that's a fact, but on the other hand I've known him worse. Difficult to say whether or not he's really feelin' bad, or just a bit depressed and lonely. Worries a lot about Miss Justine – more, I'd say, than he does about Miss Livvy.'

Eve nodded. 'He gets letters from Olivia, I suppose that's the difference. He has some idea of where she is and what she's doing. I'll go and see him before I clean up. Is he in the drawing-room, as usual?'

Martha nodded. 'Doing one of those jigsaws of his. I'd be willing to give him a hand now and then, but they're always the same ... all trains. Why doesn't he try a nice picture of a cottage garden? Or that one I gave him last Christmas? Errol Flynn and that there Olivia de what's-her-name in *Robin Hood*. Lovely film, that was. I saw it three times when it was on at the Triangle Cinema.'

Eve laughed. 'He prefers trains, Martha.' She sighed. 'I wish he'd show some interest in painting them again. It might take his mind off other things.'

Lawrence was sitting in his usual armchair to the left of the fireplace, the abandoned jigsaw on a small table beside him. Although it was less than a quarter complete, Eve recognized it immediately as a picture of the Cheltenham Flyer. She had helped Lawrence to make it many times.

'Darling.' She knelt in front of him, taking his hands in hers, and was astonished at how cold they were. The warmth from the fire was quite considerable and was scorching her face. 'Martha says you haven't had a very good day.'

He smiled wearily. 'I'll be all right now you're home.'

At once she felt guilty. With an invalid husband to look after, she didn't *have* to go out to work; she would have been granted exemption had she applied for it. But the thought of being cooped up all day long at home, while all around her people were doing their bit to help win the war, would have driven her mad. Ever since her marriage she had been confined to a domestic existence, simply because it was not considered acceptable for married women to work; it was judged to be taking bread out of the mouths of married men and their families. But now, suddenly, women were in demand everywhere. It was too good an opportunity to miss. And Lawrence had Martha, kind, devoted Martha, who liked nothing better than cooking and cleaning and looking after them both.

Was she being selfish? Eve wondered. Wasn't it true that Lawrence had always been second best? That she had treated him shabbily? That it was a woman's duty, a part of the marriage contract, to subjugate her wishes to those of her husband? The trouble was, of course, that her father had instilled too many liberal notions into her head when she was young. Perhaps Mama and Aunt Hetty had been right when they said such ideas were unbecoming in a female. Aunt Josie wouldn't have agreed, but then Aunt Josie had never been married.

Eve rose from her knees and, leaning forward, kissed her husband gently on the lips. 'I'm going to wash and change, then we'll have supper. I shan't be long. Give me twenty minutes. Here.' She moved the table with the jigsaw nearer to him. 'Do a bit more of your puzzle.'

He waved it away petulantly and shook his head. 'I'll finish it after we've eaten, when you can help me.'

Eve mounted the stairs to her room, the Grandfather clock on the landing striking six o'clock as she did so. She stepped out of her sensible, low-heeled shoes, stripped off her dark woollen dress and beige lisle stockings and went into the freezing bathroom, where she lit the gas jet beneath the geyser and waited for the water to heat. When it was drawn, four inches looked such a little drop and lost its warmth so quickly. She thought longingly of pre-war days when she had soaked in deep baths of hot soapy water scented with bath-salts, and when the bathroom could be heated with an electric fire. Dismissing such yearnings as unpatriotic, Eve climbed out again, towelled herself down and put on clean underwear, a pair of dark brown slacks and a fawn, roll-neck pullover. She felt better and ready for the evening ahead. After supper, she and Lawrence would have a quiet time together, finish the jigsaw and either listen to the wireless or play some Mozart on the gramophone. She would make up to him for the lack of her company during the day.

Eve opened her bedroom door and started downstairs. As she reached the bottom, the clock struck the quarter hour. Martha appeared in the kitchen doorway, holding a soup tureen.

'It's all ready,' she said, but her voice was drowned out by the sudden wail of the siren. 'Dratted old thing!' she exclaimed irritably as soon as she could make herself heard. 'Do you want to carry on, or get under the stairs for a while until we see how bad it is?'

'Carry on,' Eve said. 'We can always make a dash for it if anything happens. I'll fetch Mr Prescott into the dining-room.' But as she crossed the hall she stopped to listen, suddenly conscious of the drone of planes overhead. She had never before heard them in such concentrated numbers. She glanced uneasily over her shoulder at Martha, who had also paused in the dining-room doorway and was looking rather white. 'Dear God! There must be hundreds of them.'

At that moment, the whole house shook with the crash of gunfire as the anti-aircraft batteries opened fire. Seconds later, the screech of the first bombs falling on the city could be plainly heard. Martha dumped the tureen on the dining table.

'Get Mr Prescott, quick! This is the real thing. Those buggers up there mean business.'

Eve wrenched open the drawing-room door. 'Lawrence! Quickly, darling, under the stairs!'

But the room was in darkness, save for the glow of the fire, and he was not in his chair. Her heart missed a beat. Where was he? What had happened? Then she saw him standing by the window with the curtains slightly open, staring out. The sky was blood-red with the light from dropping flares. Panic-stricken, Eve ran through to the kitchen at the back of the house, switched off the light and peered through the window, down over the heights of Clifton to the densely packed heart of the city, which seemed to be ablaze from end to end. More tremendous explosions tore it apart even as she watched.

'God in heaven,' she breathed. And the Downs lay directly across the route to Avonmouth and the docks. Even as the thought formed in her mind, she heard the whistle of a descending bomb, immediately overhead.

Chapter Twenty-three

Eve thought: 'This is it!' Then her mind went blank. Afterwards, when people asked, 'How did you feel at that moment?' she could never remember. She was only conscious of the whine of the bomb, the splintering of tiles, followed by a burst of light somewhere above her. There was no time to feel fear or even relief that she was still alive; she just knew that the house had been hit and that she must do something about it.

She ran half-way up the stairs and, by standing on tiptoe and peering through the banister rails, saw the blackened hole on the landing, out of which issued clouds of acrid smoke and spurts of yellow flame. She yelled down to Martha, 'It's an incendiary, outside the bathroom door.'

The bathroom! Dear God! She had just been using the geyser and the gas-pipe which fed it ran under the landing floorboards. If the heat melted the lead there would be an almighty explosion. She tore downstairs and wrenched open the door of the hall cupboard which concealed the meters, her fingers trembling as she turned off both gas and electricity supplies. Then she rushed into the front garden and screamed at the top of her voice: 'Stirrup-pump needed here! Quickly!'

Did she have the remotest chance of getting one? The stench of smoke and the dust of falling masonry assailed her nostrils. Air-raid wardens and fire-fighters were scurrying about like ants trying to protect their anthill. Flares dropped from the German bombers made everything as bright as day, and the drone of engines filled the night sky. Afterwards, it was rumoured that only sixty planes were actually involved, but at the time it sounded like hundreds.

Eve ran back indoors, vaguely aware as she passed of Lawrence standing in the drawing-room doorway, but she had no time to give him. Martha was struggling through from the kitchen with two buckets of water, one of which she handed to Eve. Together they carried them upstairs, not even conscious of the weight as they concentrated all their attention on not spilling any of their precious burden. The landing was well alight by now, the flames licking merrily up the wallpaper. A mere two pails of water could not begin to douse them, and only produced clouds of evil-smelling steam. They raced downstairs again, and while Martha refilled the buckets at the kitchen sink Eve, without much hope, ran to the front door and tugged it open.

'Dear God,' she prayed, 'please let someone have brought a stirrup-pump.'

And there it was, a miracle, on the doorstep. She couldn't believe her eyes. The departing warden called over his shoulder, 'Leave it outside as soon as you've finished with it. Good luck! And just keep your fingers crossed that Jerry doesn't cut the water mains.'

Eve's heart seemed to stop. She hadn't considered the possibility of the water supply failing and it became doubly urgent to save Holly Lodge before that happened. Until this moment, when she was in danger of losing it, she had not realized how much the house meant to her; how many memories were enshrined in its bricks and mortar. It was more her home than Rosemary Villa had ever been.

Martha reappeared with the pails of water. Eve seized one from her and plunged the pump into it, then unwound the hose and nozzle.

'One of us must work the pump and the other go upstairs to douse the flames. And we want a third person to keep the bucket topped up. Lawrence! Come here, darling! You'll have to help. Lawrence! Quickly!'

For a moment she thought he wasn't going to move, petrified as he was by fear. But something in the urgency of her voice finally galvanized him into life and he came slowly across to join them. Eve said desperately, 'Darling, it would be best if you went upstairs and directed the water at the fire. It won't require so much physical effort. I'll work the pump and Martha can keep filling the bucket.'

She held out the hose but he backed away, shaking his head. 'No,' he said. 'No, I'll see to the bucket. I'd rather.'

There was no time to argue. Eve could smell scorching wood as the bathroom door was set alight. 'Start pumping!' she screamed at Martha and dashed up the stairs two at a time, flinging herself flat on her stomach on the landing carpet and pointing the nozzle at the flames. It seemed like an eternity before the first jet of water came through, but in reality it was a matter of seconds. And it kept coming, in a pure, bright stream, with only momentary hiccups when Lawrence was not quite swift enough refilling the bucket. In half an hour the blaze was under control, and by the time the Grandfather clock struck eight the last persistent flame had finally been quenched, and there was nothing left to do but assess the damage.

That, however, could wait until morning. Outside, death and destruction still rained down, but Eve was too emotionally and physically exhausted to care. Her face and clothes blackened with smoke, the acrid stench of burning filling her nostrils, she carried the stirrup-pump into the front garden and left it outside the gate. Almost immediately, someone grabbed it and bore it off, shouting triumphantly, 'I've got one!' Martha had protested that they ought to hang on to it in case they needed it again, but Eve refused to entertain the possibility.

'Lightning never strikes in the same place twice,' she declared optimistically. 'And just at present, other people need the pump more than we do.' If there was one thing war taught you, it was not to be selfish. 'What we all want now is a cup of tea.'

Martha shook her head. 'There's no gas. You turned it off, remember? And until we find out what damage that thing's done up there, we daren't turn it on again. So we can't boil a kettle.'

'Damn!' Eve muttered. 'But you're absolutely right.' She glanced anxiously towards Lawrence, who was slumped on the bottom stair, leaning with eyes closed against the newel post. She went over to him. 'Darling, if Martha and I help you, can you get as far as the drawing-room and lie down on the settee?' He made a little movement of his head which she took for assent, and between them she and the housekeeper managed to hoist him to his feet, dragging him almost bodily across the hall. When at last they had seen him comfortably settled, Eve kissed his cheek. 'You were wonderful, darling. We couldn't have managed without you.'

As they left the room, there was another explosion which made the whole house shake and Martha whispered, 'That was close!'

Eve pushed back her hair, leaving fresh smudges on her already blackened forehead. 'I know, but Mr Prescott's in no fit state to get under the stairs. I wonder,' she added thoughtfully, 'if the electricity's still working?' She opened the cupboard, pulled down the main switch, and immediately all the lights in the house sprang to life. 'Good God! It is. We're in luck. But first thing in the morning, we go out and buy three big thermos flasks, which we fill every teatime, and one of those camp stoves that Boy Scouts use. If there are any shops left standing tomorrow, that is! Meantime, we'll use the electric fire in the kitchen, lay it on its back and heat the water on the bars. We'd better hurry.' This as yet more violent explosions rent the air. 'I'll plug it in while you fill the kettle.'

Boiling the water in this way was a laborious process, and while they waited the two women sat at the kitchen table, too tired to chatter. Eve found that the noise going on outside no longer worried her; the experiences of the past hour and a half had deadened all feeling. She put milk and sugar in the cups and made tea like a sleep-walker. When it had brewed, she poured out a cup and pushed it across the table to Martha, then carried a second one into the drawing-room for Lawrence.

He was lying in the same position in which she had left him, on his back, with his head supported by an arm of the settee, one leg crooked at the knee and the other dangling over the side. She put the cup and saucer down on the little table, on top of the partially finished jigsaw, and gently pressed his shoulder.

'Lawrence! I've brought you some tea, darling. Martha and I are having ours in the kitchen.' When there was no response, she shook him again.'Lawrence! Wake up! You need something hot and sweet inside you to counteract the shock. We all do.' There was still no answer, but one of his arms slipped off his chest, hanging slackly, and it was only then that Eve realized quite how still he really was; that, in fact, she could detect no sign of breathing.

*

'Hetty and I can stay with you as long as you want us,' her mother said after the funeral. 'I know Olivia has to get back to her unit. She told me she only has a forty-eight-hour pass.' A slight frown creased Helena's still smooth forehead. 'I should have thought Ginny might have been here.'

'She tried.' Eve, as always, was irritated by her mother's barely concealed animosity towards Virginia, for no better reason than that the girl was Frank Mailer's daughter, a constant reminder of an episode Helena would far rather forget. 'She phoned last night. She's extremely upset that she couldn't get home, but Lawrence wasn't a blood relation, and her C.O. wouldn't release her for anything less.' Eve stared round the drawing-room, suddenly aware how empty it felt. The unfinished jigsaw was exactly as Lawrence had left it, the pieces scattered across the table, forlorn scraps of blue and green and brown. Martha had offered to put it away in its box, but Eve had said, 'No, not yet. I'll do it myself when I'm ready.'

The last few days, since the night of the bomb, were lost in a sort of dream. There had been so much to do, to organize, so many people to get in touch with, hampered by the fact that half the time the telephone lines were down. And the mess on the landing and in the bathroom had had to be cleared up. The damage was not quite as bad as she and Martha had at first imagined, thanks to the promptness with which their request for a stirrup-pump had been answered; but there was a large hole in the landing floorboards, and it had taken both of them the best part of a day to wash down the bathroom walls. The door and its surround were badly charred and the landing carpet a sodden mess, singed black along the edges. A local builder had fixed a tarpaulin over the hole in the roof until something more permanent could be arranged. Worst of all, however, was the stench of burning which permeated the entire house, clinging to skin and hair and rising from their clothes whenever they moved. Eve had said to Aunt Hetty only that morning, 'I don't think I'll ever forget this smell as long as I live. I'll never be able to smoke another cigarette.'

Her mother and aunt had arrived from Staple Abbots the previous day.

'Your father sends his love, but he isn't really fit enough at present to leave the Court. He's suffering from another bad bout of bronchitis; it's always the same, every November.' Helena had given her daughter a sympathetic hug; but after the crowded train journey, the long delays, due to troop movements, at every wayside halt, and being forced to stand in the corridor because there were no vacant seats in the carriages, she was more inclined to dwell on her own ills than Eve's. And her affection for Lawrence had never gone deep. Secretly, she thought of his death as something of a blessing. She added matter-of-factly, 'Rose and Ernest send their condolences, of course.'

It was Hetty who was inclined to be tearful, worrying about what Eve would do now. 'You ought to come back with us, you know, dear, and have a good rest.'

But Eve found this approach as irritating as her mother's
near-indifference. 'There's a war on, Aunt Hetty. People are
dying all the time. There's no time for grief.'

Politely, she refused Helena's offer that she and Hetty
should stay on beyond tomorrow. 'I'm starting work again in
the morning, Mama. I've arranged for a taxi to take you both
to the station.' The drawing-room door opened and Olivia
came in, wearing her WAAF uniform. The peaked cap sat
squarely on her short dark hair, and she had her greatcoat on
over her skirt and tunic.

'I've come to say goodbye. My train goes at four o'clock.'
She held out her hand to Helena, then stooped to kiss Eve's
cheek. 'This *is* still my home, isn't it?' she asked.

Eve was on her feet immediately, clasping her stepdaughter in a fierce embrace. 'Darling Livvy! You know it is!
Always! *Always!*' She looked into the small face so close to
hers and noted the dark circles under the hazel eyes. 'Try not
to be too sad, my dear. He wouldn't have wanted that.'

Olivia made a brave attempt to smile. 'All right, I'll try.
I promise.'

Eve went with her to the front door, where a taxi was
waiting drawn up to the kerb outside the gate. It was a rare,
late November afternoon of needle-sharp sunlight, the sky a
delicate eggshell blue, free of even the smallest cloud, the
light as clear and pure as running water. It was hard to
believe that tonight the same horror might engulf them once
again; that there were people alive and healthy at this very
minute who, by tomorrow, could be dead or maimed. Eve
gave herself a little shake. She mustn't think like that, she
must just take every day as it came. She was conscious of
Olivia asking her a question.

'I'm sorry, Livvy. What did you say?'

'I said, have you heard anything from Arnie lately? I don't
seem to have had a letter in months.'

Eve, who had received two in the last three weeks, tried
to reassure her stepdaughter without mentioning the
fact. 'Darling, I expect he's busy. You know yourself how

difficult it is to find the time to write.'

Olivia nodded, wanting to be convinced, then kissed Eve once again. 'Take care, Mama. You're all I've got at present. Oh, God! I wish we could get in touch with Justine! Papa's death is going to be such a shock for her when this rotten war is finally over.'

It was a thought which had been exercising Eve's mind ever since that terrible moment, five nights ago, when she had realized that Lawrence was dead. A heart attack, the doctor had confirmed, brought on by the strains and stresses of the night and the physical effort of humping buckets of water.

'Why on earth didn't I insist that he used the hose?' Eve had agonized to Martha, but she received short shrift.

'Don't go blaming yourself, Mrs Prescott. That's just plain self-indulgence. There was no time to stand and argue, or we'd all be dead, burned to a cinder.'

Eve knew it was true, but she could not avoid some feelings of guilt, nevertheless. And bound up with the guilt was the knowledge that she had never loved Lawrence in the way that she had loved Frank Mailer. She had been fond of him, cared for him, looked after him to the best of her ability. But the figure of his mother, living or dead, had always stood between them, as had the years of separation for which, with some justification, he had held her responsible. She could not exonerate herself completely.

But as she turned back into the house after waving goodbye to Olivia, she remembered Martha's accusation of self-indulgence. There was no time for introspection. This was all-out war in a sense that even her parents' generation had not known it. There was no 'front line' for the troops any more, while the civilians sat safely at home, carping and criticizing and handing out white feathers. On Tuesday morning she had walked all the way from Clifton, down through the city streets to the Tramways Centre and beyond. She found the scale of destruction unbelievable. The Great Hall of the University, built since her own time there, was

nothing but a burned-out shell, as was a part of the Art
Gallery and Museum; the Prince's Theatre in Park Row,
where she had spent so many enjoyable hours, had been
reduced to a pile of rubble; Bristol Grammar had lost its
prep school building. She descended Park Street, where
hardly a shop was left standing, into the old medieval heart
of the city. The Cathedral had survived, but all around it was
devastation. St Nicholas's Church was just four walls and the
crypt; Bridge Street and St Mary-le-Port Street had disappeared completely; the Old Dutch House was in ruins. St
Peter's Hospital, a unique and beautiful Elizabethan building, had been demolished; the Fish Market, the Upper
Arcade, Wine Street, Castle Street, scenes of so much late-
night Saturday shopping, had been wiped off the face of the
earth. And every so often, she was turned back by the police
while the Bomb Disposal Units detonated an unexploded
bomb.

She had been standing, close to tears, near what had been
the entrance to St Mary-le-Port Street, when someone
touched her on the arm. Turning, she found Harold
Raymond at her elbow.

'Mr Raymond!' she exclaimed with pleasure. 'How nice to
see you.' Then the realization had dawned. 'Oh, my God!
The Dorset! Of course, it's . . . it's gone!'

He nodded sadly. 'Yes. Completely flattened. All my hard
work, all the years of effort I've put into that place, and now,
nothing!' He drew a deep, shuddering breath and gripped
her arm. 'Well, there you are! Mustn't complain. Plenty in
the same boat as me, and there were no lives lost. We got
everyone to shelter in time. I suppose you haven't heard from
Justine?'

'No,' Eve said, but told him the rest of her news. He had
patted her hand sympathetically and expressed his condolences, but was too wrapped up in his own troubles to be
able to spare much attention for hers.

Afterwards she had toiled home, again on foot, although
there were some buses running, wanting to tire herself out. She

needed to sleep that night, to escape the horror all around her and the endless self-questioning. She had stopped for coffee at a little basement restaurant in Clifton, run by a Frenchman and decorated with Tricolours and posters of exhortation '*à tous les Français*' from General Charles de Gaulle. The coffee had been hot, fragrant and delicious, insensibly lifting her spirits and making her feel that all might yet be well. '*La France a perdu une bataille! Mais la France n'a pas perdu la guerre!*' she read, and wondered why both battle and war should be feminine gender when men were the cause of so much trouble in the world. When she had finished, she thanked the proprietor and went home feeling far better than she would have thought possible an hour or two earlier.

This mood of greater optimism had lasted until today, the day of the funeral; but now, as she went back into the house, she was once more filled with despondency. She felt that she had made a mess of her life, taken all the wrong turnings, made bad decisions. She confided as much to Aunt Hetty that evening, after her mother had gone upstairs to bed.

'Nonsense!' Hetty declared as stoutly as she was able in the circumstances. Yesterday's train journey had tired her, and today had been emotionally exhausting. The warmth of the drawing-room fire, combined with the glass of whisky which Eve had persuaded her to take as a nightcap, had made her pleasantly drowsy. She was already half-asleep, wishing herself in bed and praying that there would be no air-raid tonight to disturb her slumbers. She longed to be back safe and sound in Staple Abbots, where, although there were constant troop movements around and through the village, the wail of the siren was unknown. She sipped her whisky again and added dozily, 'After all, what happened with Frank Mailer wasn't your fault. That was your father's and Uncle Arthur's doing.'

A lump of coal caught and flared, the flames leaping chimneyward with a noise like torn silk. There was a moment's silence before Eve demanded harshly, 'What on earth are you talking about?'

The staccato rattle of words shook Hetty wide awake to a dismayed realization of what she had said. She sat up straight, blinking owlishly, and made a desperate bid at concealment.

'Nothing, dear, nothing! I mean,' she babbled, 'Marcus and Arthur wouldn't have let you marry Frank, now would they? You must have known that.'

'They couldn't have stopped me once I was twenty-one. Oh, I knew you and Mama and Uncle Arthur would have prevented the marriage if you could, but Papa was never against us.' Her aunt made no comment. 'He wasn't, was he? I accept he probably wished I'd fallen in love with somebody more suitable, but he would never actively have tried to oppose us.'

'No, no!' Hetty agreed, anxious to protect her brother but still confused by the whisky and the heat from the fire. 'That was why he left it to Arthur. It was Arthur who arranged it all; it was nothing to do with Marcus.'

'Arranged what?' Eve asked, rigid with suspicion. 'What was it that Uncle Arthur arranged, Aunt Hetty? Jenny Slade and her fake pregnancy, was that it? It was, wasn't it? I can see the truth in your face.' Things long past, half-forgotten, suddenly began to make sense. 'It was a put-up job, as they say in those gangster films. Uncle Arthur persuaded Jenny ... No, there must have been more to it than that; Jenny never did anything from pure disinterest. Of course! He paid her, didn't he? He paid her to set her cap at Frank. Paid her to seduce him and then pretend that she was having a baby. And afterwards, when she and Frank were safely married, she could say it was all a mistake.' Another thought piled in on top of the others. 'That's why she didn't want Ginny. She never intended having a baby at all. Dear God! Now I can see everything – and you say that Papa knew about this?'

Hetty went on the offensive, recollecting that attack was the best form of defence. 'He did what he thought was right for you. You're his only child, for heaven's sake! He didn't want to see you throw your life away for a nobody like Frank

Mailer! A farmhand, who would never be anything else! And don't forget, my girl, that it couldn't have worked if your precious Frank hadn't been the lecherous little so-and-so that he was.' Hetty was suddenly furious — with her unguarded tongue, with her niece for daring to sit in judgement on her father, with having to live through the privations of another war and, above all, with the long-dead Frank Mailer, the cause of all the trouble in the first place. She spat, 'It must be obvious, even to you, that he had to *screw* Jenny Slade before she could convince him she was pregnant!'

There was a shocked silence. Hetty's hand went up to her mouth and she stared at Eve, wide-eyed with dismay, like a naughty child who has said a naughty word. In spite of everything, the turmoil of discovery and bitterness at her father's betrayal, Eve had to laugh. 'Aunt Hetty! You of all people! I never thought I'd hear you use a word like that.'

Hetty gathered the rags of her dignity about her and rose, a trifle unsteadily, to her feet.

'I'm going to bed,' she announced. 'I suppose we'll see you in the morning before you leave for work? And remember! Whatever we did, we did for your own good. I never intended telling you. It just slipped out because I'm tired and that whisky has made me a little tipsy.' She wove an uncertain pathway to the door, where she paused and looked over her shoulder. 'And I'd be obliged if you wouldn't let on to Marcus and Helena that I've said anything to you on the subject.' She went out, closing the door carefully behind her.

Eve sat on, staring unseeingly into the heart of the dying fire. She should have guessed the truth long ago, at least where her mother and Uncle Arthur were concerned. She just hadn't believed them capable of such deviousness. Such cunning . . . such under-handedness. But it was finding out that her father had been a party to the conspiracy which really upset her; the realization that all his fine talk about equality and the classless society had been so much hot air when it came to his daughter and her choice of a husband.

Her happiness had come a poor second to his desire for
respectability, both hers and his own. She wondered if she
would ever be able to forgive him.

Slowly, Eve got to her feet and put the fire-guard in front
of the fire, then climbed the stairs to bed. On the landing,
she could hear the tarpaulin on the roof flapping in the wind.
She was dog-tired and every bone in her body ached. She
couldn't do any more tonight. Like Scarlett O'Hara, she
would think about things tomorrow. Tomorrow, after all,
was another day.

Chapter Twenty-four

Arnold's was the first letter to arrive, announcing that he had managed to get leave for Christmas. When it dropped through the letter-box of her Pembroke Road flat, Eve was glued to her radio listening to the early morning news. The Japanese had destroyed the United States fleet at Pearl Harbor the previous day, and while the tally of dead and the loss of ships were appalling, it was nevertheless good tidings for a beleaguered Britain. In this December of 1941 the Americans were finally in the war, and the sense of relief was enormous. Even the normally impassive broadcasters sounded as though they could cheer.

It would be nice to have Arnie home for Christmas, Eve decided, glancing disparagingly round the rather cheerless little furnished flat. He could have the spare bedroom. She thought longingly of Holly Lodge, now requisitioned and turned into offices by the Ministry of Aircraft Production. She had guessed – after Lawrence's death and Martha's departure to work in a Forces canteen somewhere in the south of England – that this was bound to happen sooner or later; and she had it in writing that, all things being equal, she would get the house back at the end of the war. And she had been fortunate. It had survived intact the five months of intensive bombing, from that first attack in November 1940 to the final Good Friday raid on April 11th of this year, without any further damage. The roof was repaired, her furniture in store, and she had been lucky in finding alternative accommodation quickly. One of the younger members of Censorship had volunteered for the WRNS, and Eve had been able to take over her basement flat. This comprised a living-room-cum-kitchen, two tiny bedrooms and the share of a bathroom on the first floor.

Virginia's letter came two days later. She had also managed to get a week's leave and would be in Bristol just before Christmas. Oh well, thought Eve, there was only one thing for it; Ginny would have to share her bed. It would be cramped, but not too uncomfortable. She decided not to tell Olivia that the others would be home together; but that same evening, her stepdaughter telephoned.

'Mama? How are you? Good news! I've some leave due to me, so I shall be with you for Christmas. Isn't that marvellous? Actually Christmas! You haven't made any plans to go to Staple Abbots, have you?'

'Not until this moment,' Eve said drily. 'But now, I think we shall have to. I must try to get leave myself and then contact Rose and Ernest.'

'I don't understand,' Olivia protested, so Eve explained the situation.

'Isn't it absolutely extraordinary? All three of you at once. It's never happened before; not even two of you together.'

There was silence at the other end of the line before Olivia remarked in an altered voice, 'Arnie and Ginny will be home as well?' She gave a brittle laugh. 'They're both quite strangers. I haven't heard from either of them in ages.' There was another pause, then she added, 'I used to think that Arnie was fond of me. We were good friends at one time, but that seems to have changed. He never bothers to write any more.'

Eve said as bracingly as she could, 'But you haven't seen one another since you both joined up – at least two years – and in those circumstances people tend to drift apart. It's inevitable. And don't forget that he has other, far more important things on his mind. These young men are living all the time on the edge of death. I don't suppose it makes them over-sensitive to other people's feelings.'

Olivia snorted derisively. 'Mama, some girls on the station get letters every day from their boyfriends, many of whom are pilots.'

'Was . . .? I mean, *did* Arnie consider himself your boy-friend?' Eve enquired cautiously, trying to be tactful. 'He . . . well, he never gave me the impression that he thought so, but I could have been mistaken of course.'

'Perhaps it wasn't quite as definite as that,' Olivia conceded grudgingly, 'but we were certainly close. We used to go out a lot together in London, especially that summer before the outbreak of war.'

'Then you'll be able to sort things out with him at Christmas,' Eve encouraged her. 'But I'll try to arrange for the four of us to go down to Staple Abbots, to the Court. There's not enough room here for all of us.'

When she explained the problem at work the following morning, one of the other women offered to forgo her leave so that Eve might spend Christmas with her family. Someone else made a gift of some unused petrol coupons to assist with the journey, and Rose and Ernest, when approached, were genuinely delighted at the prospect of seeing them.

'As long as you all bring your ration cards with you, it will be lovely,' Rose enthused over the phone. 'And Uncle Marcus will be absolutely thrilled to see you again, Eve. He was only complaining the other day that you don't get in touch as often as you used to.'

Eve grimaced to herself as she hung up. She guessed that her father must find it strange that she no longer wrote to him personally, but simply included him in her general letters to Mama and Aunt Hetty. She found it difficult, however, since her aunt's revelations of a year ago, to know what to write to him without revealing that she knew the truth. She wanted to ask him why he had betrayed not just her and Frank, but himself as well. And how had he reconciled it with his conscience? But without telling tales on Aunt Hetty, her hands were tied. She must keep silent. Maybe she would understand better when she saw him, face to face.

*

But the only thing Eve really understood, when she saw her father again, was that he had grown old and frail and bad-tempered, and that his ill-humour was not improved by the fact that Helena and Hetty and even Rose allowed themselves to be bullied by him.

'He's over eighty,' they argued, when Eve protested at his tyrannical ways. 'He probably won't be with us much longer.'

'And don't you go upsetting your father,' Hetty whispered fiercely, when she and Eve were alone together. 'And don't pretend you don't understand me.'

'I wasn't going to,' Eve assured her. 'But surely age shouldn't be an excuse for bad manners.'

She was not enjoying the holiday as much as she had expected. The first disappointment had been the journey down, fraught with tension. The pre-war Citroën, which Eve normally kept in a rented lock-up garage, had been overhauled for her by the man in one of the upstairs flats, and filled with petrol. She had been a little wary of driving it again after such along while, but it had behaved very well; which was more than could be said for her passengers. After a certain amount of bickering, Olivia had been forced to sit beside Eve in the front while Arnold and Virginia sat in the back. And it had been as apparent to Olivia as it was to Eve that, from the first moment of seeing Ginny again after a lapse of some time, Arnold found her extremely attractive. For at twenty-three, Frank's daughter had grown, somewhat surprisingly, into a beautiful woman.

She was still small, with the same dark, almost black hair and deep brown eyes, but the thin, wiry frame had fleshed out, giving it a new maturity. The slender legs looked stunning in the black stockings of a WRNS uniform, while the young, firm breasts only served to emphasize the narrowness of her waist. Even Eve, who had seen her not that long ago, had to admit that Virginia had suddenly blossomed. Nor could she help noticing that Ernest was very impressed when, after an hour and a half of almost non-stop flirtation in the back seat and a stony silence in the front, the Citroën finally drew up before Abbey Court's front door and he welcomed them in.

'Of course, her mother was a stunner,' he said later after supper, when he and Eve were washing up in the stone-flagged kitchen. He grinned reminiscently. 'At least, Donald and I always thought so. Mind you, Virginia isn't much like Jenny in appearance. I wonder if she's as good in bed.'

Eve stared, then finished wiping a dinner plate which she placed carefully on the kitchen table. 'Are you saying that you and she . . .? She and Donald . . .?'

Ernest glanced hurriedly over his shoulder to make sure that Rose was out of earshot. 'Oh, not me, no! She wouldn't look at me. Donald was the heir-apparent. That girl had ideas above her station, but the Old Man was too smart for her . . . killed two birds there with one stone.' An expression of consternation crept over his face. 'What . . . What I mean is . . .'

'It's all right, Ernest. You don't have to tell me what you mean.' Eve, who was wiping another of the heavy Crown Derby dinner plates, felt suddenly tempted to drop it, quite deliberately, on the flags and watch it smash into smithereens. Instead, she changed the subject by asking, 'Do you hear anything much from Donald?'

Her cousin emptied the washing-up water into the sink and slammed his mop down on the draining-board with such a vicious crack that the wooden handle broke in the middle. 'That bastard! I wouldn't give him the time of day after the dirty trick he played on Rose and me, selling out to the War Office. We offered him a fair price, but he just wasn't interested. All he was concerned with was making as much money as possible.' He stared blankly at the broken mop before throwing the lower part of the handle into the sink tidy, along with a mess of cold tea-leaves and vegetable peelings. 'Of course, it would never have happened if you hadn't turned him down,' he added reproachfully. 'Still, I suppose things haven't turned out too badly. The War Office are decent enough landlords. Well, that's our chores done for the day. Let's go and join the others for coffee. If you can call this horrible chicory mixture we get nowadays by that name!'

Eve went to bed with a great deal to think about and the firm conviction that she would never get to sleep, but the next thing she knew after her head touched the pillow was that it was Christmas morning. Sitting up in bed, sipping the cup of tea which Rose had brought her, she thought: 'This time next week, I'll be forty-two.' Once again the sense of something lost, some opportunity missed, took hold of her. The ghost of Frank Mailer, never very far away when she was in Staple Abbots, seemed even closer to her than usual. The paralysing spectre of what-might-have-been returned with yet greater force, now she knew that others beside herself and Frank had had a hand in shaping their future.

It had been arranged the previous evening that, with the exception of Rose and Hetty who would stay home to cook Christmas lunch, the rest of them would go to church for the morning service. But when it came to the point Marcus did not feel well enough, Helena elected to stay with him, Ernest decided that he too was unequal to one of the new vicar's rather long-winded sermons, while Arnold and Virginia announced that they preferred to go for a walk around the village.

'I ought to visit Granny Slade and Grandfather and Grandmother Mailer,' Ginny said defiantly. 'Grandfather's over eighty.'

'You have at least three more days in which to do that,' Olivia pointed out in a tight little voice. 'There's surely no necessity for you to rush off immediately.'

'The truth is,' Arnold put in, 'I'm a bit of an agnostic, so it's no use me going to Matins. And Ginny's promised to show me all her childhood haunts. So you'll have to excuse us.'

Olivia made no comment, but her face was a mask of unhappiness. Eve wanted to beg her stepdaughter not to make her pain at Arnold's rejection so obvious; she wanted to say, 'Don't give him the satisfaction of knowing that you care.' She liked Arnold but, as on previous occasions, was forced to recognize that there was a callous, egotistical streak in his otherwise sunny and extrovert nature. Whoever else he loved, he would always love himself best. He couldn't help it, it was the way he was made.

'It's just you and me, then, Livvy,' she remarked briskly, rising from the table. 'We'll have to represent the family. We might as well go early, then we can have a walk before the service begins.'

*

For some reason, standing there in the church singing the familiar carols, Eve's mind went back to that Easter of 1916 when the old vicar, the Reverend Ellice, had given out the news that James Naysmith had been killed, the first casualty of the last war from Staple Abbots. Then, it had been a morning of bright sunshine, redolent with the scent of lilies. Narcissi, rhododendrons and tulips, daffodils and wall-flowers had adorned every available niche, and there had been a huge copper vase full of bluebells to the right of the altar steps. People had worn their Sunday-best clothes and looked bright and neat. Now, in the murky light filtering through the windows, robbing the stained glass of all its vibrant colour, there was an air of shabbiness about the place, a feeling of despair that after only twenty-one years of peace, war should have happened yet again. There was, besides, an undercurrent of unease, a sense of tension which Eve found it hard to explain. Surely, now that America was coming in on their side, people should be more optimistic, more inclined to look towards a successful outcome to the conflict.

After the service, she stopped to speak to old friends: Bert Crocker and his wife, who had come out of retirement to run the village store while their son and daughter-in-law were in the Forces; Mrs Jenks, who had given up the bakery business some years before but who still helped, rheumatic and partially deaf as she was, behind the counter while the present assistant was away; Miss Jillard, the ex-schoolmistress, who travelled into Salisbury three times a week to serve with the WVS. Eve introduced Olivia to them, asked all the right questions about their families and listened understandingly to their doubts and fears, which not even a determined optimism could disguise successfully.

'But there was something else, too,' she remarked during lunch, doing justice – as they all were – to one of the Home Farm chickens which had been killed specially for the occasion. 'There was a sort of uneasiness even amongst those who haven't anyone in the Forces. I don't know why, but Livvy sensed it as well, didn't you, darling?'

'They listen to too much gossip and rumour,' Ernest answered impatiently. 'Now, you youngsters can do the washing-up while the rest of us turn on the wireless and catch the news. Then we'll unwrap our presents.'

The news was gloomy: Hong Kong had surrendered to the Japanese. Eve asked Rose, 'What did Ernest mean when he said that the villagers listen to too much gossip and rumour?'

'Oh, there are all sorts of stories flying about in a military zone like this. The soldiers come into the Ring O' Bells in the evenings and find it amusing, I suppose, to rattle the civilians. The last tale I heard was that some of the houses might be requisitioned as Army billets. I don't take any notice. There have been so many rumours of one kind and another, but so far nothing's happened. Shall we go and give a hand with the washing-up? It doesn't seem fair to leave it all to Arnold and the girls.'

As soon as they walked into the kitchen, however, it was plain to both women that there was an unfriendly atmosphere. 'Is something the matter?' Eve asked.

'Arnie and I are engaged to be married,' Virginia said, slipping a hand through his arm. 'He asked me this morning while we were at Granny Slade's. We were going to tell you all after the present-giving, but I – *we* wanted Livvy to be the first to know. I thought she'd be pleased for us ... but she isn't. She's been horrid.'

'I simply said you deserved one another.' Olivia flung her wet teacloth down on the kitchen table. 'I don't see anything wrong with that.'

'It's the *way* you said it.' Virginia was obviously upset. Happy herself, she wanted everyone else to be happy for her; particularly Olivia. She didn't want her pleasure to be the cause of someone else's pain.

Eve went over to her stepdaughter and put an arm about her shoulders, giving her a squeeze.

'I'm sure Olivia is just as delighted as we all are at the news. Many congratulations, darling! You, too, Arnie; I hope you and Ginny will be extremely happy. When is the wedding to be? Or haven't you decided?'

'As soon as we can both get special leave.' Arnold smiled at Virginia; but Eve, watching closely, considered that there was something proprietorial in his manner, more like a man contemplating a new possession than his future wife. She recalled that in the days when Ginny had been a thin and awkward teenager, he had barely had a word to spare for her except in a teasing, elder-brotherly way. Now, however, she was a very desirable woman, one who would turn heads in any company, and Arnold had always had a hankering for the best. Ever since he had been plucked from the ruck of William Penn Road Junior School, he had been determined to make the most of his chances. He made no secret of the fact that, if he survived the war, he hoped to go into Parliament; and Virginia, with her looks and brains – she had gained a Double First in Modern History and English Literature at Oxford – would be an asset to any young, aspiring politician. But Eve was unsure if it were a sufficient basis for a happy marriage, and during the remaining days of the holiday she searched desperately for some genuine signs of love on Arnold's part.

On the last morning of their leave, he and Virginia borrowed the car and drove into Salisbury to buy a ring; a cluster of small diamonds in a platinum setting. Virginia, showing it off to her friends and family, was ecstatically happy, while Arnold looked on smiling complacently. Olivia said little beyond informing Eve that she would be thankful to get back to camp.

When the engaged couple visited George and Lizzie Mailer that afternoon, Eve decided to go with them. She felt a sudden urge to see Frank's parents and the cottage again after so many years. But the visit depressed her. In her mind, people and place were enshrined, changeless, in what now seemed to her to be the permanently halcyon summer days before the First World War. And she was surprised by alterations which common sense should have told her must surely have been made: gas-light instead of paraffin lamps and candles; a gas-stove in the kitchen and the old wall-ovens bricked up; running water downstairs, instead of having to rely on the neighbour's well; her father's old surgery converted into a bathroom. Improvements, every one of them, but changes for which she had been unprepared.

George Mailer was eighty-one, Lizzie seventy-five. They still managed to rent their cottage from the War Office, getting by on the old-age pension and a small sum paid weekly to George from Home Farm profits. But it was a desperate struggle, and it showed. Lizzie could no longer keep the place as clean as she once had; dust lay thick in corners and along ledges where her impaired eyesight had failed to spot it. The second-hand carpet and cheap three-piece suite, which had replaced the rag rugs and settle, were stained and in several places torn, but were items too expensive to be replaced. The only touch of luxury in the room was a silver picture-frame enclosing a faded sepia photograph of Frank, stiff and awkward in his Army uniform.

'Glad to see you again, Miss Evie,' Lizzie said, shaking her hand. 'Forgive me if I don't get up, but my screws are playing me up today. Ginny, run and put the kettle on and make us all a nice cup of tea. And there's some seed cake in the orange tin.' When Virginia, followed by Arnold, had gone to do her grandmother's bidding, Lizzie lowered her voice a fraction. 'You've done a good job on her, Miss Evie. You've given her a chance in the world. Who's this chap she's set on marrying?'

George butted in before Eve could reply. 'Education!' he spat. 'I don't hold with it! Leastways, not for women. We'd've been a sight better off if we'd had Frank's daughter to look after us in our old age.'

'Shut up, you silly old fool!' his wife exclaimed disgustedly. 'Girls don't stay at home nowadays. She'd have left the village long ago, even if her mother hadn't taken her away in the first place. There was nothing for her in the Abbots. I'm grateful, Miss Evie, even if George ain't.' She followed the direction of Eve's eyes with her own, and nodded. 'Nice picture of our Frank, that, isn't it? Had it taken in Southampton day before he embarked. Paid for it and left the photographer our address.' She hesitated, then asked, 'Would you like to have it?'

'What? No, no! I couldn't possibly...' Eve was embarrassed. 'It's the only one you have, surely?'

Lizzie shrugged. 'We're both old. We'll soon be joining him, wherever he is. I'm serious. You can have it.'

Eve shook her head. 'If you want to give it away, you must give it to Ginny.'

George Mailer cackled. 'She don't want it – offered it to her the other day. Never knew her father – don't mean nothing to her, do 'e?'

'Here, you take it.' Lizzie moved with sudden determination and struggled to her feet, making her laborious and painful way across the room to the window-sill. 'It's a good frame, mind. None of your rubbish. George and I bought it in Salisbury the summer of 1919. Cost us five-and-six.' She held out the photograph with one hand while supporting herself against the wall with the other, so that Eve was forced to rise and take it from her before Lizzie could return to her

chair. When she was settled once more, she added, 'You were
fond of our Frank, I haven't forgotten that. I know we were
against you both at the time, but you'd've done better by
him than that Jenny Slade!' Lizzie spat the name with
contempt. 'It's you who've done right by his child, and all.
That photo and its frame's all we've got of value to leave
anyone, so I want you to have it, Miss Evie. And I'll take it
amiss if you refuse.'

'In that case, thank you. Of course I'd be pleased to have
it, if it's all right with Mr Mailer.'

'He'll do what he's told,' Lizzie informed Eve grimly.

Virginia and Arnold returned, the latter carrying a tin
tray on which reposed cups and saucers and the teapot. Eve
said uncomfortably, 'Your grandmother's given me this
photograph of your father, Ginny. I hope you don't mind?'

'Why on earth should I? I don't want it.'

It occurred to Eve then that Virginia had never evinced
any great interest in Frank; had never asked questions about
him, never wanted to know what he was like as a boy. Nor
had she ever pined for her mother, apparently indifferent to
Jenny's desertion. She lived for the present and those people
who showed her kindness. If they abandoned her or let her
down, she dismissed them from her thoughts. But it might
be different with Arnold. He was the first real love of
Virginia's life; to him belonged the first true flowering of her
affection. The phrase 'putting all your eggs in one basket'
flitted into Eve's mind, but she prayed that she was wrong.
Nevertheless, the relationship troubled her: Virginia was
plainly so much more in love with him than he was with her.
It was too one-sided.

Eve sighed and drank her tea. There was nothing she or
anyone else could do except hope for the best, but she wanted
happiness for Frank's daughter. She glanced down at the
photograph in her lap, at the thin, dark face, unnaturally
solemn, frozen by the photographer's lens for a solitary
moment. It wasn't really like Frank, the expression was too
withdrawn and wooden, but it brought memories flooding

back and, with them, the old yearnings. Sometimes she felt as though all her life, since that moment when she first heard that Frank was dead, had been a dream; that one day she would wake up and discover that for the last twenty-three years she had been sleepwalking.

At last, it was time to go. They said their goodbyes and began the long walk back to Staple Abbots. As they turned the corner into Lower Lane, Eve paused for a moment and glanced back at the row of cottages. They looked still and peaceful in the fragile winter sunlight, smoke rising from the chimneys and a powdering of frost across the roofs. Then she ran after the others.

Chapter Twenty-five

Eve was staring in the window of a baker's shop when she first met Jeff Hamilton.

The Censorship offices had moved to the West of England Academy, which meant that lunch-hours could be spent shopping in Queen's Road or Park Street. Not that there was a great deal to be had anywhere these days, and what there was was rationed. Next week, Arnold and Virginia were getting married in the church at Staple Abbots, and Eve had volunteered to make the wedding cake. By dint of doing without herself, and help from working colleagues, she had scraped together sufficient ingredients to bake a single tier and, by means of some under-the-counter assistance from her local grocer, had marzipanned and iced it. But it looked rather sad by pre-war standards. What the bakery displayed in its window was a three-tier cardboard wedding-cake mock-up, suitably decorated with silver flowers and horse-shoes, which was placed over the real thing and removed before cutting. Would it be worth buying one? Eve wondered. It would certainly make more of a showing on the table at Abbey Court, but on the other hand people's expectations might be raised unduly. She took a pace backwards in order to get a better view, and stepped heavily on someone's foot.

'I'm sorry!' she exclaimed, whirling round and stretching out an apologetic hand. 'So clumsy of me.'

'Think nothing of it, ma'am,' said a pleasant American voice, and Eve found herself looking into the face of a US Army officer.

American troops had been flooding into Bristol during the past few months until, in this May of 1942, they seemed to have taken over the city. The female population was in its seventh heaven. Here, at last, were soldiers smartly dressed; men who were polite and deferential to women; men with money; men who could conjure up almost unattainable luxuries, like nylon stockings and expensive perfume. The male population, on the other hand, looked on in growing resentment and frustration while transatlantic mania gripped wives, sisters and daughters.

So far Eve had had no personal contact with Americans, simply admiring them from a distance. This was partly because she went nowhere where she might meet them; and only the previous evening she had realized that her social life had become practically non-existent. Of recent years Lawrence had absorbed all her time and attention, and after his death she had found it difficult to resume old friendships. So many people were away or working unsociable hours – and besides, she quite liked her own company. After a long day scrutinizing letters, deciphering some almost illegible writing, watching carefully for any unguarded slip of the pen which could be of value to the enemy, any phrase or sentence which might have a hidden meaning, all she wanted to do was to get back to the flat, have a wash, eat and then curl up with a book or the wireless. *ITMA*, the *Brains Trust*, drama, *Hi, Gang!* and, more recently, *Desert Island Discs* – she enjoyed them all, but she was in danger of becoming a recluse, too lazy to get out and meet people. She relied on letters and telephone calls from Staple Abbots or the children for her contact with the larger world. And just at present, all her attention was concentrated on preparing for the wedding.

It was five months since the engagement, and only now had Arnold and Virginia been able to arrange leave together. Ginny had decided that she wanted to marry in Staple Abbots, and Rose had offered the Court for the reception. Arnold had jumped at the chance, although he confided to Eve that Ginny would have preferred the Ring O' Bells.

'She's afraid her grandparents will feel uncomfortable, but

I told her not to worry. We can hide the old folk away somewhere in a corner. I've invited my C.O. and a couple of the lads, and I could tell they were very impressed by "and afterwards at Abbey Court".'

Eve had hung up after this telephone conversation with a thoughtful expression, but had refused to dwell on it unnecessarily. Nevertheless, she wished Arnie was not quite so much of a snob, and the thought had been chasing around inside her head as she stared at the cardboard wedding-cake. Perhaps if she had been less absorbed, she might have been more careful.

'I – I hope I haven't done any damage,' she said feebly. 'I really am most terribly sorry.'

The American smiled. 'I told you, there's no need to apologize. I'm not hurt. It was an accident. Look, just to show there's no ill feeling, let me buy you a cup of coffee.' And he indicated a nearby ice cream parlour.

Eve hesitated, but she still had half an hour of her lunch hour remaining and she liked what she saw; a tall, lean man in his middle forties with smiling, deep blue eyes that crinkled endearingly at the corners, a wide, mobile mouth and dark hair greying slightly at the temples. 'Thank you,' she said, 'that would be very pleasant.'

At the glass-topped counter they bought coffee and sandwiches for Eve and an ice-cream soda for her escort. When they had settled themselves in two of the gold-painted, basketwork chairs at one of the little tables, Eve asked, grinning, 'Couldn't you face our English coffee?'

The American laughed. ''Fraid not. What's it made from?'

'Chicory mixed with coffee beans. There's a war on – er, Captain?'

'Major.' He touched the single gold oak leaf on his shoulder. 'A Captain has two silver bars.'

'Sorry.' Eve picked up a sandwich. 'I'm very ignorant about military insignia.'

'Will you stop saying sorry all the time! It makes me uneasy.'

They both laughed this time and were soon chatting away like old friends. Eve learned that his name was Jeff Hamilton, that he came from Philadelphia, was forty-five years old, married with a wife called Linda and two boys, Drew aged eleven, and Jeff junior who was twelve. With very little encouragement he produced photographs of them all, and Eve found herself looking at an attractive, plumpish blonde, considerably younger than her husband, her arms around the shoulders of two boys with close-cropped hair and full-length denim trousers, who could only be American. English boys of that age would still be wearing short flannels and long grey woollen socks.

In return, she sketched a brief outline of her life to date, dwelling only on the happier moments. He was intrigued by the name William Penn Road Junior School, and recollected that Philadelphia's founder had had connections with Bristol.

'His father's buried in St Mary Redcliffe Church, and he married Hannah Callowhill in the Friends' Meeting House in Broadmead. If you like,' Eve found herself volunteering, 'I'll show them to you one day.'

'Hey, thanks. Look, give me your phone number. I'll give you a call sometime and we'll arrange a date. I'm billeted in a house near what you people call the Downs. We've just taken it over from your Ministry of Aircraft Production. It's called Holly Lodge ... Now, why do you find that so amusing?'

Eve shook her head and glanced at her watch. 'I'll tell you another time, but take it from me that coincidences do happen. Now I really must go. I'm late already. Thank you for the coffee and sandwiches.'

He rose with her. 'I shall call you, you know. That's a promise.'

Eve nodded, only half believing him. The following day he telephoned.

*

By the end of the month, when she drove down to Staple Abbots for the wedding, Eve found herself plunging head-long into an affair. She and Jeff had not yet slept together, but she knew as well as he did that it was merely a matter of time. They saw one another as often as their respective jobs allowed and, with the permission of his Colonel, he had arranged for her to visit Holly Lodge.

'You see how well we're keeping it for you,' he said, as he conducted her round. 'We've cleaned it up quite a lot. Those Ministry people had left it in a goddam mess.'

Eve expressed her gratitude, but had been glad when the visit was over. Seeing her old home in the hands of others was deeply upsetting, and she declined all invitations to repeat the experience. So Jeff came to the flat instead, bringing her presents of whisky and nylons and sharing, not without protest, her meagre rations.

'God! No wonder you're all so thin. How does anyone expect you to survive on this lot?'

'Nonsense!' Eve declared stoutly, serving scrambled dried egg on toast. 'We're probably healthier as a nation than we've ever been. Half of us aren't over-eating, and the other half have enough to eat for the first time in their lives.'

To begin with, they talked a lot; about their families, books, films, plays. But never about the future. From the start that subject was taboo, as though they both knew that what happened after the war had nothing to do with their relationship. That was strictly for the here and now, living for the moment. As the weeks went by, Jeff mentioned his wife and sons less and less, pushing them into a compart-ment of his mind labelled 'If I get back'. Ahead lay uncertainty, hardship and possibly death. Linda and the boys had nothing to do with that, cocooned in a land flowing with milk and honey where there were no food queues, bomb-sites or dispossessed.

He and Eve also walked a lot and laughed a great deal, finding amusement in the most ridiculous things. One evening, passing a fish-and-chip shop, they paused to read the notice outside. 'Owing to Hitler, chips will be littler. Owing to Hess, fish will be less.' For some reason this piece of doggerel struck them both as excruciatingly funny, and they kept repeating it all the way back to the flat, staggering about the pavement like a couple of drunks. On another occasion, strolling across the Downs in the warm spring dusk, Eve tripped over a loose stone and went sprawling flat on her face. Once Jeff had assured himself that she wasn't hurt, they giggled uncontrollably – behaving, as Eve tearfully pointed out, like silly schoolchildren rather than responsible middle-aged adults.

'You speak for yourself,' he protested, gasping. 'I haven't felt so young in years.'

The night he kissed her for the first time, she knew it was going to happen. It was two days before she was due in Staple Abbots for the wedding, and they were in the flat, listening to a concert being relayed on the radio from the Royal Albert Hall: Dame Myra Hess giving a recital of the music of Schumann and Bach. They were sitting side by side on the badly sprung black leather sofa, not quite touching, their shoulders within an inch of one another's. As Dame Myra began the chorale, 'Jesu, joy of man's desiring', from one of Bach's church cantatas, they turned towards each other, smiling with pleasure – and the next moment were locked in a passionate embrace. Had there not been an interruption, they would probably have gone to bed there and then, but just at that moment the flat's front-door bell sounded.

Cursing under her breath, Even went to answer it. Olivia was standing at the bottom of the area steps, her case on the ground beside her.

'Hello, Mama. I've managed to wangle a couple of days' extra leave, so instead of going straight to Staple Abbots I decided to come home and travel down with you on Tuesday.' She kissed Eve's cheek. 'I hope I'm not being a nuisance.'

'No ... No, of course not, darling. Come inside. I've a friend here, an American officer, but you won't mind that.

He's . . . very nice,' Eve added lamely.

For a moment Olivia looked intrigued, but she had other things on her mind.

'Oh! Well . . . I hope it's not going to be inconvenient, Mama, but . . . I've brought someone with me.' She turned and called up the area steps: 'Andy, darling, come on down.' A tall man in the uniform of a naval lieutenant descended and facing her stepmother once more, Olivia said defiantly, 'Mama, I want you to be the first to meet my husband, Andrew Bridges.'

*

Eve couldn't remember anything very much for a while after that. She must have introduced Jeff and seen him off the premises, cooked supper, changed the sheets on her double bed, made up the single one in the spare room for herself, poured out tots of whisky; because the first thing she could recall with any clarity was drinking a toast to the newly-married couple. It was dark, and the clock on the mantel-piece showed a quarter past eleven. She said, 'Livvy, darling, if you don't mind, I think you'd better explain everything again. My head's in such a whirl, my brain's not functioning properly.'

'Poor Mama, it's been a shock. I'm not surprised. It was a bit of a shock to us as well, wasn't it, Andy?'

Andrew Bridges nodded. Able to take stock of him properly at last, Eve decided that she liked him. She was usually wary of making up her mind about people too quickly, but there was something in his face which struck her as essentially kind and gentle. He was not handsome; indeed, his features were undistinguished, and but for his height — over six feet, Eve judged, in his stockinged feet — he might easily have been overlooked in a crowd. His eyes were bluish-grey in colour, his hair blond, curly and extremely fine, the sort that falls out early; it was already receding from his broad, high forehead, and Eve guessed that he would lose the bulk of it before he was forty. His disposition seemed retiring, and she was surprised to learn that he was a regular officer in the Royal Navy.

'Father was in the Navy. Grandfather, too,' he explained almost apologetically. 'Never really wanted to do anything else.'

He and Olivia had met six weeks ago, at a dance in Portsmouth, he had proposed three weeks later and they had been married by special licence only that morning.

'We didn't want all the fuss of an engagement,' Olivia said a shade defiantly, 'or a big church wedding. I'm leaving all that to Virginia and Arnie. After all, it isn't as though I've any family apart from you, Mama, who would have been able to attend, and I knew you couldn't just drop everything and come down to Portsmouth. Andy's parents were there, and a few of his friends, but that was all. It was a very quiet affair.'

'I might not have been able to come to the wedding,' Eve retorted, 'but I should have appreciated being told what was happening.' She was hurt, but trying not to show it.

Olivia gave her a fleeting smile and lit a cigarette. 'Sorry. I ought to have said something, I know. Andy kept telling me to phone you. But it's all been such a rush.' She blew out a cloud of smoke. 'I wonder what Ginny will say when she finds out I've beaten her to it.'

'Well, you'll certainly steal her thunder,' Eve said drily, and saw a hard little smile lift the corners of Olivia's mouth. Alarm bells were ringing in her head as she looked at her stepdaughter. This was no love match – not, at least, on one side. This was a jealous woman cocking a snook at her more fortunate rival. If she couldn't have Arnold herself, Olivia would prove to him that he wasn't the only pebble on the beach; that she had very quickly found consolation elsewhere. Eve doubted if she even saw Andrew Bridges as a person. He had asked her to marry him, and Olivia had recognized a chance to undermine what she considered to be Virginia's triumph. Eve suddenly felt sure that Olivia had

arranged her own wedding so that the honeymoon would
coincide with the other ceremony at Staple Abbots. Not a
sound basis for a lasting marriage. She wondered if Andrew
had any idea what he had let himself in for.

Eve had still not made up her mind on this point when
she and her two passengers drove into Staple Abbots early on
Tuesday morning. As the Citroën drew up before the front
door of Abbey Court, Hetty emerged to make them
welcome.

'Aunt Hetty,' Olivia said, getting out of the car, 'this is
my husband, Andrew Bridges. Andy, darling, this is Mama's
aunt, Mrs Jardine.'

Hetty's reaction – a startled scream, a babble of non-stop
questions – was all that Olivia could have wished for; and
once indoors, Rose and Helena were equally as excited. Even
Marcus and Ernest expressed surprise and interest. But this
was not enough for Olivia.

'Where are the happy couple?' she wanted to know. 'I
thought they were arriving yesterday.'

'Arnold's gone for a walk to calm his nerves and Ginny's
upstairs getting ready. Where do you expect a bride to be on
her wedding morning?' Rose scolded.

'I'll give her a hand,' Olivia said casually. 'Mama, you'll
look after Andrew for me, won't you?'

But Virginia, disappointingly, was genuinely delighted
for her friend, and came rushing downstairs wrapped in a silk
kimono, her hair still wet from washing, to shake Andrew's
hand and kiss his cheek.

'I'm so pleased for you and Livvy. I just hope you and she
will be as happy as Arnie and I intend being. And Navy, too.
I expect Livvy's told you I'm in the Wrens. Long live the
Senior Service!'

Her stepdaughter's face, Eve thought with grim amusement, was a study. Having followed Virginia downstairs
again, she stood framed in the dining-room doorway, the
picture of frustration. What had she hoped for? Jealousy,
annoyance, indignation? Anything, probably, except this

wholehearted and disinterested approval. But then, as Arnold's voice sounded from the back hall, Olivia's expression lightened. After all, her marriage was really for his benefit.

Virginia gave a shriek and headed for the stairs. 'Don't let him see me! It's unlucky! I've been avoiding him all morning.'

Arnold came in looking, Eve considered, handsomer than ever in his carefully pressed Flight Lieutenant's uniform, colour whipped into his cheeks by the chill spring wind. Three other men were with him, two the same rank as himself, the third a Group Captain who was introduced to Eve as 'my Commanding Officer'. Then it was Olivia's turn to make introductions and drop her bombshell.

'My husband, Andrew Bridges.'

'Your—? Well, this is a surprise, indeed.' Arnold held out his hand, smiling broadly, but there was sufficient edge to his voice to give Olivia some small satisfaction. And Eve detected enough irritation in his manner during his subsequent barrage of questioning, for her to corner him in the drawing-room just before she left for the church.

'What's the matter, Arnie? Aren't you pleased for Olivia?'

'I'm neither pleased nor otherwise,' he snapped. 'Livvy's affairs are nothing to do with me. I'm a bit annoyed, though, that she's chosen today to spring her little surprise. It isn't fair on Ginny. Oh, by the way, did I tell you that I've had a telegram of congratulation from my mother and stepfather in New Zealand?'

'Someone did mention it,' Eve replied shortly. 'Don't change the subject, Arnie. Why does it bother you, Olivia being married? You could have had her yourself, but you didn't want her; you preferred Virginia.'

'You're completely wrong. It doesn't bother me in the slightest.' He gave an unconvincing laugh. 'I'm just a bit taken aback, I suppose, after the way she acted when I got engaged to Ginny. I thought ... I mean, she gave me to understand that ...'

'That she was in love with you,' Eve supplied for him.

'Well, yes. I suppose so.'

'And now she's married Andrew.'

Arnold nodded. 'And such an odd-looking fellow.'

'Andrew Bridges is a very nice man,' Eve replied tartly. 'None of your tricks, mind, Arnie! You've made your choice. See that you stick to it. You'll have me to answer to if you make Virginia unhappy.'

It was an empty threat, and she knew it. What could she possibly do to Arnold nowadays that could hurt him? She saw the gleam of derision in his eyes as he came to the same conclusion, and was relieved to hear her mother calling.

'Eve! It's time we were going! Come along, dear!'

She glanced uncertainly at Arnold, who suddenly relented and kissed her.

'Don't worry. I'll look after Ginny . . . if I survive the war.'

And with that, Eve had to be content for the moment. She went to join the others.

*

There were quite a few people at the reception. Most of the villagers had turned up at the church, and many who were not official wedding guests had been invited back to Abbey Court by Rose and Ernest. Contrary to Ginny's fears, neither the Mailers nor old Mrs Slade were at all intimidated by their surroundings. Arnold's plan to hide the grandparents away in some obscure corner was frustrated by their willingness to mix and chat with all and sundry. At one point Lizzie Mailer, to Arnold's acute embarrassment, buttonholed Group Captain the Honourable Peter Chester to tell him the story of her son, killed in the First World War. Eve saw Arnold whisper a few words to Virginia who, after staring at her new husband for several seconds in astonished indignation, resolutely shook her head. She had, Eve realized with deep satisfaction, refused to obey Arnold's instruction to break up the conversation, and turned away to cut the cake. This was just as Eve had made it. Acting on Jeff Hamilton's advice, she had decided against the cardboard mock-up.

'What's the point?' he had asked when she consulted him. 'Everyone knows it's just a fake, so what purpose does it serve? Goddammit! Tell 'em what you're always telling me. There's a war on!'

Virginia was looking extremely pretty in a pale blue crêpe-de-Chine dress, with puff sleeves and padded shoulders, bought with carefully hoarded clothing coupons. She had also managed to get a pair of nylons from somewhere, making her legs look even more sensational than usual, and her dark hair, recently permed, curled from beneath a small blue hat. Frank would have been proud of her, Eve reflected, blinking back the tears.

The cake was cut, the toasts drunk, speeches made. The reception was all but over as the guests made their way towards the front door, to wave the newly-married couple off on their four-day honeymoon. Virginia had gone upstairs to fetch her coat and Eve found herself standing beside Arnold, who had come to wish her goodbye and thank her for all she had done for him over the years.

'I'm very sensible of what I owe you and the late Miss Gilchrist,' he said, 'even if I don't always show it. Thank God you turned up at William Penn Road Junior School!'

As always, Eve was mollified by his charm. Whatever displeasure she had been harbouring against him was instantly dispelled when he smiled in that particular fashion.

'That's enough soft soap,' she admonished, giving him a little push. 'Off you go. Just make Ginny happy, that's all the thanks I want.'

He grinned and nodded towards Olivia and her husband. 'You're right, I've made my choice and I don't regret it. Besides, Livvy seems to have fallen on her feet. Andrew's a very nice bloke when you get to know him. Pretty well-off too, I gather, from what he was saying about his parents.'

Eve laughed. 'You know more about him than I do,

already. I haven't liked to be too inquisitive. Not that money's a consideration with Livvy, I imagine. After all, she was co-heiress to the Robartes fortune.'

Arnold's face suddenly had an arrested expression. 'I thought ... I mean, I assumed ... I assumed that *you* had inherited all your husband's money.'

'Good heavens, no! Lawrence left me something, of course, but naturally the bulk of it went to the girls. Justine's half is being held for her until she can be contacted after the war. Why? What difference can it make to you?'

'Mmm?' Arnold stared at her vacantly for a moment, then shook his head as though trying to clear his mind. 'Oh, nothing! Nothing at all! As you say, what possible difference could it make to me? Ah, here's Ginny at last. Now we can be on our way.'

He went out into the hall to join his bride, leaving Eve staring after him feeling suddenly desperately uneasy.

Chapter Twenty-six

Jeff Hamilton sat up and reached for the packet of Lucky Strikes on the bedside table.

'Do you mind?' he asked Eve. 'It won't upset you?'

She raised herself on one elbow, shaking her head. 'Of course not. It's just the taste of smoke in my mouth I can't stand; it reminds me of the night of the bomb. Sorry to be such a wet blanket.'

He put out a hand and stroked her hair, its rich auburn dulled by time and the inevitable streaks of grey. 'You're never that,' he said softly. 'I love you, Evie.'

As she sat up beside him the pale September sunlight, easing its way through the bars of the basement window set high in the bedroom wall, laid a faint patina of gold across her still smooth skin. 'You're married,' she reminded him, as she had continually reminded him for the past eighteen months, ever since they had first slept together a week after Arnold's and Ginny's wedding. 'You have a pretty wife and two fine sons.'

He took a long pull on his cigarette and blew out a cloud of smoke. 'I can't think about them. They're not real to me any more; they're something that happened in another life.'

Eve sighed and rested her chin on his shoulder. He smelled good, of soap and tobacco and leather. 'You might feel that way now, but it'll be all different when you get home again. Then it will be me and England that will be the past, the other life, the life you've left behind.'

He stubbed out his half-finished cigarette in the ashtray and turned to kiss her, folding her in his arms. 'I may never get back to the States. You and this war may be the only things left to me. That's why I need you.'

'You mustn't think like that,' she said, pausing between each word to return his kisses. She drew her head back, looking deep into his eyes. 'Or do you know something the rest of us don't?'

'You're not allowed to ask that – you know I can't answer. But the war's hotting up. We're into Italy. The B.B.C. said last night that it's only a matter of days before the Italian Government surrenders. Russia's yelling for the Allies to start a Second Front and it must come soon. Hell! It's ten months since the Russkies turned the tide at Stalingrad.' His body grew more urgent as he kissed her lips, her throat, her breasts, pushing her down in the bed and making love again.

Later, while he was dressing and she was percolating coffee – proper coffee which he had brought her – she told herself: 'I mustn't be deceived into thinking that I really mean anything to him. I must keep my head, realize that I'm just part of this nightmare he's living through: this strange, cracked, disjointed existence which has brought him thousands of miles from normality and home. He's lonely, lost, frightened, like millions of his compatriots. And, also like them, he won't admit to, or show it.'

Jeff came out of the bedroom and took her in his arms once more. 'I'll try to see you tomorrow,' he whispered. 'Walt Morello said he might swap evening duty with me.' He was almost suffocating her with the intensity of his embrace. 'Evie! Evie!' We've got to spend every moment that we can together. We may not have much longer.'

She fought him off. 'You do know something,' she accused.

He shook his head. 'It's only rumours at the moment. But we're moving out soon, I'm sure of that. It stands to reason. There's a lot of training to be done before most of our troops are ready for Europe.'

He kissed her then as though he would never stop, but in the end, with the mantelpiece clock already showing nine-thirty and being on duty at ten, time itself forced him to let her go. Eve accompanied him to the front door and watched him ascend the area steps. When he reached the top, he turned and ran down again. 'I love you,' he whispered, and then was gone, his footsteps echoing along the street. Eve bolted the door and drew the blackout curtains. She threw his untasted coffee down the sink and poured herself another cup, savouring the aroma.

The electricity supply was low, so she drew her chair closer to the standard lamp and picked up the sea-boot stocking she was knitting. The wool was rough and oily as it slid through her fingers, but out in the storm-ravaged waters of the Atlantic it would eventually provide warmth and protection for some poor sailor. If she worked hard tonight she could finish it, and tomorrow she would take it and its fellow, and the other two pairs she had recently completed, to the WVS Centre on her way to work. She would, of course, be inveigled into taking more wool, but this time she would choose Air Force blue or khaki. Ordinary socks didn't take so long to knit, nor were they so hard on the skin.

She had just turned the heel when the phone rang. One of the children probably — it couldn't be Jeff: he never telephoned while on duty. Eve laid down her knitting and went across to the ugly little bamboo-cane table just inside the door. It was an inconvenient and draughty place to keep a phone, but it had been there when Eve took over the flat's tenancy and she had never bothered to move it. She lifted the receiver. 'Eve Prescott speaking.'

'Eve! Is that you? Thank heavens I've caught you. I was afraid you might be out, firewatching or something.' It was her mother's voice, high-pitched and agitated.

'Mama? What's the matter? Is it Papa?' At eighty-three, Marcus's health continued to be fragile.

'No, it's Hetty. She has pneumonia. Rose and Doctor Allen are upstairs with her now. The doctor says her condition's very grave. Oh, dear! I never thought anything would happen to Hetty before your father. She's only two years older than I am, and always seemed so strong.'

'Mama! Calm down!' Eve strove to sound cheerful. 'Aunt Hetty isn't dead. As you've just said, she's very strong. She'll get over it.'

Helena refused to be comforted. 'But how are we going to nurse her? Ernest and Rose are busy all day around the farm, and I'm not fit enough to do it.'

Eve's heart sank. She understood perfectly what her mother was hinting at, but there was nothing she could do. Mama must surely know that. 'Let me speak to Papa,' she urged gently.

But when Marcus finally came to the phone, he also was too upset to be rational. 'You ought to be here, Eve,' he kept saying. 'You ought to be here.'

'I can't drop everything just like that, Papa. I've a job to do. Look, let's see what happens first, what arrangements Mama and Rose are able to make between them. I'll come if it's absolutely necessary, but Aunt Hetty might not be as bad as you think. She might recover quite quickly.'

'Your aunt's old,' Marcus snapped. 'She's quite likely to develop emphysema. She's been ill for several days, and this morning there was blood in the sputum.'

Eve said, 'I'm sorry, Papa, but I still don't think I can ask for leave right now. I'd have to come by train, anyway. I've used nearly all my petrol coupons.' She felt a rising tide of panic, she wanted to be free of this situation, not to have to think about it. At the same time she felt guilty because they were her parents, her aunt, and all the responsibility for them had been shouldered by Rose and Ernest; Rose who was no relation except by marriage, and Ernest who was only a nephew. She went on hurriedly, 'I'll ring you in the morning before I leave for work, and you can tell me how Aunt Hetty is then.'

She hung up quickly to forestall any argument, and stood staring at the silent instrument. 'Damn!' she said out loud, then returned to her seat and picked up the sea-boot stocking. But she could no longer concentrate, and after making two mistakes in as many minutes she threw it down in disgust. She supposed that she could ask for leave tomorrow, and if she were refused that would be the end of the matter. But the truth was that she did not want to ask, in case her request was granted. She wanted to be near Jeff for as long as he needed her, and what he had said this evening about moving soon had frightened her. She had no doubt that he was right; the expectation of a European front being opened by the Allies was prevalent everywhere this autumn. The newspapers and even the radio news bulletins were full of speculation about a possible date.

Eve linked her hands behind her head, leaned back against the cushions and closed her eyes. Why was it so important for her not to let Jeff down? Was she in love? She was certainly very fond of him. She wished she could make up her mind. Did she feel about him as she had once felt about Frank? As she still felt about Frank in those quiet moments when she had time to consider the past? Her affection for Lawrence, she had long ago realized, had been largely maternal: ironic, really, in the circumstances. But Frank Mailer was the yardstick by which she judged her affection for other men.

She went to bed early, hoping that a good night's rest would resolve the question for her, but her sleep was broken by dreams and she awoke unrefreshed, with a nagging headache at the back of her eyes. She got up and made herself a strong, sweet cup of tea which she drank scalding hot, standing at the kitchen sink and staring at the blank wall beyond the tiny window. Normally, the fact of living in a basement didn't bother her, but this morning the atmosphere was claustrophobic and she felt unable to breathe. The tea calmed her a little, and she considered breakfast. She had finished her bacon ration two days earlier, and she couldn't face scrambled dried-egg powder again. There was a packet of oats somewhere in the cupboard, but the thought of lumpy porridge – and hers was always lumpy – was unappealing. Toast, then, and marmalade.

The telephone bell broke the silence. Eve jumped and spilled tea in her saucer. Her father or mother for certain.

Just for a second she was tempted to ignore it; to run into the bedroom and pull one of the pillows about her ears, to blot out that shrill, insistent ringing. Then, disgusted with herself, she picked up the receiver.

'Eve!' With a leap of the heart, she recognized Jeff's voice. He barely waited for her to answer, sounding urgent and slightly breathless. 'Listen, honey! I've managed to get this evening off. Walt Morello came up trumps. I'll be at the apartment around seven. Promise me you'll be there! Promise me, Evie!'

'Yes. Yes, of course, I promise. Jeff, what's the matter? What's up?'

'Honey, I've got to go. Seven o'clock! Be there!'

He rang off. The line hummed quietly until she too replaced the handset. She stared blankly at the opposite wall, with its faded paper and gloomy Landseer print of the Scottish Highlands. Her heart was thumping unpleasantly. The telephone rang again, and once more Eve grabbed the receiver.

'Jeff? What's hap——?' She got no further.

'Eve, it's me, Rose. I think you ought to come down, dear, if you possibly can. I really do! Aunt Hetty's a great deal worse.'

'What?' Eve strove to adjust her thoughts. 'Oh ... oh, Rose. Yes. O.K. I'll try to come. But it'll only be for an hour or two. I have to be back by this evening.'

*

Rose met her at Warminster. Eve descended from the train with her mind still in a whirl. The last few hours had been full ones; hunting for her supervisor's home number, telephoning to let her know what had happened; ringing the station to find out the times of trains; dressing and catching the bus to Temple Meads; standing in the corridor of the Southampton train, crushed between an RAF corporal and a black-bearded lieutenant in the Navy. And the journey had taken twice as long as in pre-war days; it was gone eleven before she climbed into Rose's old Morris Minor.

'You haven't brought any luggage,' her friend protested.

'I told you on the phone – I have to be back in Bristol by seven this evening. I've only asked for a day's leave. I can't be spared for longer.' It was a lie, but only a very little one.

'You might have to be,' Rose answered, changing gear noisily as she took the Staple Abbots turning. 'I don't think you realize quite how ill Aunt Hetty is.'

Eve made no reply, but her heart sank. She had made a deliberate decision not to contact Jeff before she left home; not to let him know what was happening. That way, she reasoned, she would force herself to be ruthless about returning; not allow herself to be talked into staying. Rose and her parents were panicking about nothing, she decided. Once she had seen Aunt Hetty, she would be able to reassure them.

Her mother met her at the front door, looking reproachful and careworn. Helena's soft prettiness had not aged well. The abundant copper-coloured hair of her youth was now white and inclined to be wispy, the blue eyes behind their wire-framed spectacles were faded, and the contours of her face had lost definition, the once delicate chin now puffy. She clung to her daughter with frail but determinedly clutching hands.

'You've come just in time!' she said. 'Doctor Allen doesn't think poor Hetty will last the night.'

Rose got out and slammed the car door. 'Eve isn't staying that long,' she told Helena wearily. 'She has to be back in Bristol by this evening.'

Helena was appalled. 'No, no! You have to stay! We need you, Papa and I. Surely there's someone you can phone? The people who run your department, whoever they are, surely they would understand that this is an emergency?'

Eve looked past her mother to Rose, noting the tired lines around the eyes and mouth, the sallowness of the skin beneath its weatherbeaten tan, the calloused hands and the dirt under the fingernails. And she thought of her friend as she had first seen her at Mayfields Academy; plump and bright-eyed, bursting with energy. Marrying Ernest might have been what Rose wanted, but life had not been easy for her. Moreover, her own and Ernest's parents had died when they were both comparatively young, so they might have expected a peaceful middle age together. Instead, they had willingly shouldered the burden of Helena, Marcus and Hetty. Eve suddenly felt desperately guilty. She couldn't possibly run out on Rose now; nor could she leave her aunt if she were indeed dying. Somehow or other she must get a message to Jeff at Holly Lodge and explain why she could not be at the flat that evening.

'It's all right Mama,' she said gently, kissing her mother's cheek, but nodding at Rose, 'I'll be staying as long as you need me.'

Helena smiled tremulously. 'Of course you will. I knew you wouldn't fail me, darling.'

*

Hetty died at two o'clock the following morning, with Eve sitting by her bedside holding her hand.

When she first saw her aunt the previous day, she had been shocked, unprepared for the painfully laboured breathing and the way the flesh seemed to have fallen away from the bones. Never a big woman like her sister, Hetty looked so tiny beneath the mound of bedclothes. Her face was bloodless, her eyes shut and she seemed unaware of her surroundings. The progress of the illness had been unexpectedly rapid, and there had been no time to send to Salisbury in an effort to hire a private nurse. Rose and Doctor Allen had done what was necessary between them, shooing Marcus from the sick-room where he hung around offering unwanted advice.

'Linseed and mustard poultice was good enough in my time,' he grumbled to Eve the moment he saw her. 'But no!

Allen orders up antiphlogistine! Thinks we're made of money!'

'It's lighter than home-made poultices,' Rose argued, overhearing. 'It holds the heat longer and doesn't need such frequent changing.'

Marcus snorted angrily, unconvinced. 'Unnecessary and bloody expensive!'

'Oh, come on, Papa,' Eve coaxed. 'To listen to you, anyone would think that you're down to your last penny.' And then, when her father still seemed anxious to continue the argument, she had gone upstairs to see Aunt Hetty, after which all other considerations had been swept from her mind.

As a child she had not been fond of Hetty, finding her a stickler for the proprieties and over-bossy. But after Josephine's death, and in the years when she and Lawrence were separated, Eve and her younger aunt had drawn closer together and she had come to value Hetty's advice and company. She found it hard to accept that Rose and her parents had spoken no more than the truth when they said that Hetty was dying. So she sat by the bed, taking one of the skeletal hands in hers, and tried to will some of her own vitality and strength into her aunt's emaciated little body.

Rose brought up her meals on a tray, and Eve only left the room every now and then to go to the bathroom. She lost track of time, failing to notice when the pale September sunshine gave way first to the encroaching shadows of early evening, and then to total darkness. Her mother and father came to share her vigil and Rose, followed later by Ernest, arrived to draw the blackout curtains and switch on a heavily shaded lamp, set well back in a corner of the room where its light could not disturb the patient. Close to midnight Hetty seemed to take a turn for the worse, the difficult breathing growing ever more stertorous. Rose telephoned the doctor, who arrived within fifteen minutes, to shake his head gravely.

'I'm afraid you must all prepare yourselves for the worst,'

he told them solemnly. 'I did warn you that Mrs Jardine might not live through the night. It can only be a matter of hours now. I'll stay for a time, but there is nothing I can do.'

'No!' Eve exclaimed fiercely, tightening her grip on her aunt's hand. 'She can't die. I won't let her.'

She knew how foolish her words must sound as soon as she had spoken, but she would not retract them. Too much of her childhood and early life was already lost to her – Frank, Aunt Josie, Aunt Mabel and Uncle Arthur, Rosemary Villa – for her not to feel a momentary sense of panic. She could not afford to lose Aunt Hetty too.

Eve must have dozed off for a minute, because she was suddenly aware that Hetty had recovered consciousness and was struggling to prop herself on one elbow. Then she began to expel the air from her lungs in great racking gasps. Seconds later, she fell back against the pillows. Doctor Allen felt for her pulse before saying quietly, 'It's over. She's gone.'

Eve couldn't believe it. The end had come so swiftly, with so little warning, that she found it hard to accept that it had actually happened. She leaned forward, shaking her aunt by the shoulder in an effort to rouse her.

'Aunt Hetty? Can you hear me? Wake up!'

The doctor gently removed her hand. 'It's no good, Eve, my dear. She can't hear you.'

Rose got stiffly to her feet. 'I'll go down and put the kettle on,' she said practically. 'I'm sure we could all do with a cup of tea. You can help me, Ernest. Eve will see to Uncle Marcus and Aunt Helena. I'll come back later and do what's necessary.'

Greatly to her surprise, Eve discovered that her own grief went deeper than that of either of her parents. Her mother and father were certainly upset, but their sorrow had a selfish element to it. Even after their removal from Rosemary Villa to the Court, Hetty had continued in her role of major-domo, organizing all their meals, amusements and general pleasure, assisting Rose to run a house which had been designed for an army of servants and now had to function with only three. Indeed, it was largely thanks to her that Rose had been free to help on the farm.

'I don't know how we shall go on without her,' Helena declared tearfully. 'I can't do things in the house like poor Hetty did. My health won't permit it. It's as much as I can do to look after your father, and I'm sure he isn't really as bad as he pretends. I'm the one who needs cosseting. Eve, darling, I really do wonder if . . .'

Eve gave Aunt Hetty a final kiss on the cold forehead and got up from her chair, stretching her cramped limbs.

'Not now, Mother, please.' She drew a deep breath, but the air in the bedroom was fetid and stifling. She needed to get out of doors, even if it were the middle of the night . . .

The middle of the night! She glanced disbelievingly at the clock on the mantelpiece. Half-past two! Jeff! She hadn't contacted him. Once she had seen Aunt Hetty, everything else seemed to have been driven from her mind. How on earth could she possibly have been so forgetful? He would have gone round to the flat at seven to find no one in. He might have gone back several times, only to discover the place still shuttered and silent. And she had promised to be there. She had *promised*! Eve raced downstairs, almost falling over the last two steps. Thank God she knew the Holly Lodge number without having to waste more time trying to discover it.

The night duty switchboard operator was a Sergeant Luke Briccuss. Eve had met him on two or three occasions and recognized his voice.

'Sergeant Briccuss, it's Eve Prescott. Look, I know this is irregular, but could you possibly put me through to Major Hamilton? I know it's the middle of the night, but it's terribly important.'

'Sorry, ma'am,' came back the answer in Sergeant Briccuss's southern drawl. 'I surely hate to be disobliging, but—'

'I *must* speak to him,' Eve interrupted desperately. '*Please*, Sergeant, just this once!'

'I would if I could, ma'am, that's what I'm trying to tell

you. But Major Hamilton left this evening at twenty hundred hours, along with Captain Morello and half a dozen others.'

'Left?' The hand gripping the receiver was suddenly slippery with sweat. 'Left Holly Lodge? How long for?'

'Left Bristol, ma'am. Permanent.' The clipped tones told her that Sergeant Briccuss would say no more, and had probably bent the rules already in telling her this much.

'He won't be coming back,' Eve said flatly, and Luke Briccuss made a little noise indicative of confirmation. 'Thank you, Sergeant. You've been very kind.' She hung up.

'Eve?' It was Rose standing beside her, looking concerned. 'Come and have a cup of tea in the kitchen. You could do with it. Aunt Hetty's death seems to have hit you hard. Where are Aunt Helena and Uncle Marcus?'

'What? Oh . . . still upstairs, I think.' Eve pushed her hair back from her forehead, barely conscious of what she was saying. 'I'll . . . I'll go up and get them.'

'No, I'll go. You stay here. Are you all right? Were you phoning somebody?'

'Yes . . . they weren't there.'

Rose smiled. 'Asleep, more like. Do you realize it's a quarter to three in the morning? Go and get that tea inside you. It'll make you feel better.' And with one lingering, curious glance, Rose vanished upstairs.

Like a woman in a dream, Eve made her way to the kitchen where Ernest and Doctor Allen were talking in low voices, discussing the events of the night. As she poured herself a cup of tea with an unsteady hand, Ernest cleared his throat and said gruffly, 'Nothing's changed, you know, Eve. Uncle Marcus and Aunt Helena will stay here with us. Staple Abbot's their home; they wouldn't be happy anywhere else.'

With a tremendous effort of will, Eve forced herself to concentrate on what her cousin was saying, and to thank him. 'It's very good of you.'

But she was relieved when the two men resumed their conversation, leaving her to her thoughts. And now, at last, she had the answer to her question: she *was* in love with Jeff, she loved him as she had loved Frank Mailer, all those years ago. She had known it for certain the moment Sergeant Briccuss said that Jeff had gone, and would not be coming back.

Chapter Twenty-seven

He didn't write, nor did he telephone: total silence. He had vanished from her life as suddenly as he had entered it, and Eve felt bereft.

She lived in a kind of limbo for those first few weeks after Aunt Hetty's death, going through the motions like an automaton. Afterwards, she could only just remember going home, returning to work, visiting Staple Abbots the following Monday for the funeral, her parents silently reproachful when, once again, she left. It was like looking at pictures through a thick fog, knowing that what was happening was happening to her but unable to connect with any of it. Each time the phone rang she would pick up the receiver with trembling hands, convinced that this time it must be Jeff calling from 'somewhere in England'. But it was always either Ginny or Olivia or one of her friends; most often, her parents.

After a week or two, she grew a kind of protective shell. Inside she hurt just as much as ever, but on the surface she managed to resume a normal life, to accept the inevitable, to tell herself that was that; an episode which was over. 'You're forty-three,' she admonished her reflection in the mirror. 'High time you were past this sort of nonsense. Besides, Jeff's a married man.'

The autumn weather continued fine. As predicted, Italy surrendered to the Allies and, on the 13th of October, declared war on Germany. The Axis partnership was broken and, although no one doubted that there was a long, hard struggle ahead, the end of the war – if not actually in sight – at least could be thought of as round the corner. Everyone talked about a Second Front, an invasion of Europe, some time next year.

Scrutiny of the Irish mail intensified, as the censors searched for the merest hint of a suggestion that the letter-writer knew something he or she wasn't supposed to. All correspondence from people on the 'black list' was sent to London.

Olivia came home on a forty-eight-hour pass and talked about everything except her marriage. 'Andy?' she queried vaguely when Eve asked after his welfare. 'At sea, darling, last I heard, but God only knows where. All very hush-hush. You know how it is nowadays.'

'I wasn't asking *where* he is,' Eve retorted. 'Of course you can't know that. I'm just enquiring *how* he is, that's all.'

But Olivia seemed uninterested. 'Oh, he sounded OK when he wrote.' She changed the subject, saying off-handedly, 'I've been posted to the same station as Arnie, did I tell you?'

'No. How is he?'

'Fine. Sends his love. Hopes to get a pass and come home some time to see you.'

Olivia tried to sound as casual speaking of Arnold as she did when talking about her husband, but Eve was not deceived. There was an undertone of excitement surrounding his name which was absent when Andrew's was mentioned. Moreover, Olivia avoided looking directly at Eve whenever the subject of Arnold cropped up in conversation.

'How's Ginny?' Eve demanded sharply.

'Don't know. Haven't heard from her lately.' Her step-daughter lit a cigarette.

'But surely Arnie must have. Hasn't he mentioned her?'

Olivia inhaled deeply before replying. 'We don't see that much of each other.' She blew the smoke down her nostrils. 'But I think he said she was OK.'

She was lying. Eve couldn't say positively how she knew, but some slight inflexion of the voice gave Olivia away. She was seeing quite a lot of Arnold, Eve was certain of it. Could Livvy somehow have wangled her present posting? Impossible, surely! But whatever the truth of the matter, she and

Arnold were together and in contact far too much for Eve's liking. A sudden recollection of the wedding, and the expression on Arnold's face when he learned that Olivia had inherited half of the Robartes fortune, came unbidden into her mind.

But there was nothing she could say without proof – and anyway, who was she to cast a stone? Hadn't she been having an affair with a married man? Hadn't she seriously contemplated taking Jeff away from his wife and children? Wasn't the idea of following him to the States after the war her fondest dream? Relationships became fragmented in the maelstrom of emotions surrounding sudden parting and death. It was an unreal time, in which normal standards and patterns of behaviour had no place. So she held her tongue and hoped that everything would sort itself out when peace was restored. Or perhaps if Arnold came home, she might pluck up courage to have a word with him.

But Arnold did not come and his brief letters made no mention of any hope of leave. Then Virginia phoned from Portsmouth, complaining of a seventy-two-hour pass cancelled without explanation at the last minute. 'It was sickening,' she said, 'because I was meeting Arnie in London. He had tickets for Covent Garden and a lunch-time concert with Myra Hess. Luckily, they weren't wasted. Livvy managed to get some time off and went with him.'

'But she had a forty-eight-hour pass only the other week,' Eve protested. 'She came home, to the flat.'

'Did she? Oh . . .' Ginny sounded vague. 'Well, I don't know how she managed it then, but she did somehow.'

By telling a few lies – a dangerously ill relative, probably – Eve thought grimly, but once again she held her tongue. When Virginia had rung off, she made herself a cup of tea and sat down to think, but tiredness overcame her. She had been working hard since nine o'clock that morning, and it was now half-past seven at night. She put her cup and saucer on the little table beside her chair and closed her eyes. Only for a moment, she told herself; then I'll make a proper meal and really give some thought to Arnold and Olivia. The cushion was soft behind her head, and for once her neck was resting at a comfortable angle. In less than five minutes, she was asleep . . .

*

Eve was suddenly awake, and the clock on the mantelpiece told her it was a quarter-past-nine. She had been asleep for almost two hours.

'Damn!' she exclaimed, sitting forward in her chair. But at least she hadn't missed the 'Sunday Night Postscript' after the news, and tonight the speaker was one of her favourites, Emlyn Williams. She was half out of her chair, reaching for the radio's on-switch, when she realized that the telephone was ringing. She stared at it stupidly, as always trying to calm the beating of her heart. 'It won't be Jeff,' she told herself, 'it never is. It will most likely be Mother.'

She was wrong, but not by much. When she picked up the receiver, Rose's voice hummed down the wire.

'Oh, Eve! Thank God! I thought you must be out. I've been ringing for simply ages.'

'I was dozing. Rosie? What is it?' She didn't ask if anything were the matter with her father; she had made that assumption so often in the past and was nearly always wrong. And she would have been wrong this time, also.

'Oh, Eve, I don't know, but I think something terrible is about to happen.' Rose sounded distraught.

Eve was puzzled. 'Whatever do you mean? What terrible thing could possibly happen in Staple Abbots? You didn't even have air-raids at the height of the blitz.' She made a poor attempt at a joke. 'Don't tell me Papa's mislaid his hearing-aid again.'

'It's no laughing matter.' Rose's voice was choked and Eve could guess that she was holding back a flood of tears with difficulty. Rose, who never cried!

'I'm sorry, I didn't mean to be flippant. For God's sake,

tell me what's wrong! I'm standing here in the most dreadful suspense. Rose, darling, get a grip on yourself.'

She heard her friend swallow hard and take a deep, calming breath. When she spoke again, Rose had her voice almost under control.

'Yesterday morning every house in the village, including Upper and Lower Abbots, had a formal notice from the War Office requesting – no, ordering, really – that someone from each household be at the school on Tuesday morning at ten sharp, for a meeting with the Land Agent of Southern Command. All lessons have been cancelled for the day, and we've been told that we must be there.'

'Well,' Eve interrupted bracingly, 'the War Office do own the village, with the exception of St Peter's and the Methodist Chapel. It's probably some new regulation about limits; how far you can stray off the main roads, or something of that nature. I mean, preparations for the Second Front must be well under way by now. The papers are full of it. And remember, during the First War, how the Army authorities used to seal off Staple Abbots for days at a time? No, of course you don't; you didn't live there then. But ask Mama and Papa. They'll tell you.'

Rose began to cry. 'You could be right, but I'm awfully afraid it's much more serious than that. I mean, you're right about it being connected with the invasion, but not that it's about village limits. Jack Robbs, who used to be head gardener – his nephew married an Imber girl and went to live there. The War Office own Imber as well, and last Monday *they* all had to assemble at the village school for a meeting.'

'And?'

'The Yanks are taking it over lock, stock and barrel, for training their troops for the invasion. Street fighting. They all have to be out by December the seventeenth.'

Eve was suddenly conscious of being icy cold. 'What do you mean, out?'

'What I say. Out! The entire village is to be evacuated.'

*

They had come early, Eve, Rose and Ernest, to make sure of
front-row seats. When the school doors had been unlocked
at nine o'clock, they were already waiting outside.

Eve had arrived in Staple Abbots the night before after
battling with her supervisor for two days' leave. She had been
saving what was left of her quota to take at Christmas, in case
one or other of the children came home, but her telephone
conversation with Rose had made all such considerations
irrelevant. If Rose were correct in her assumptions about the
reason for this meeting, then there would be no room at the
flat for anyone else apart from herself and her parents. For if
Rose and Ernest had to leave Abbey Court, where could her
father and mother live except with her? The prospect filled
Eve with dismay and foreboding.

Standard Five classroom had been denuded of its desks,
which had been piled up in other classrooms, and furnished
instead with rows of chairs lent for the occasion by the
Methodist chapel. Those villagers who arrived late and could
not find a seat stood at the back and sides of the room or
clustered in the aisles. Others, who could not even get inside
– and there were many – packed the corridor or spilled out
into the playground, relying on information relayed by word
of mouth to keep them abreast of the proceedings. Everyone
was in a high state of tension, the fate of Imber by now being
common knowledge.

Eve stared around her, trying to calm her nerves. There
was the same old cupboard in the corner, where the
stationery used to be kept and probably still was: pencils,
pens, blotting-paper and ruled or squared exercise books.
The front panels were defaced by scratches, cuts and the
carved initials of the most daring children, who had been
willing to risk a caning for one fleeting moment of
immortality. Did today's pupils, she wondered, continue the
tradition? Frank's initials were there somewhere. 'F.M.' He
had told her proudly that he hadn't been able to sit down for

a week after Miss Jillard had whacked him. The smell, too
– of chalk and ink powder and sweaty clothes – was exactly
as she remembered it, and brought back memories not only
of this school but of William Penn Road Juniors as well. The
walls looked as though no one had touched them since she
had left all those years earlier: the same dark brown dado,
blotched and peeling, with dirty beige paint above. And to
the wooden rail which divided the top half from the bottom
were pinned crayoned drawings, compositions entitled 'My
Holiday' or 'What I Want To Be When I Grow Up', sheets
of sums, and all with one thing in common – all marked ten
out of ten. How often had her own work hung there, to the
envy and annoyance of many of the other children? 'Teacher's
pet' they had called her: she had never really belonged. And
she had had Papa to thank for that; Papa with his liberal
notions of class equality which had failed so dismally when
put to the test.

Eve knew that she had never felt the same about her father
since Aunt Hetty had let slip the truth concerning Frank,
and her heart rebelled at the thought of sharing her tiny
basement flat with him and her mother. Her life would cease
to be her own the moment they stepped across the threshold.
Helena would grumble incessantly at the cramped and
unedifying quarters, particularly after the spaciousness of
Abbey Court; Marcus would be crabby because there was no
room to store his precious books. Eve crossed her fingers
tightly and prayed that it wouldn't come to that.

But she knew from the first second when the Land Agent
walked through the classroom door and took his place behind
the teacher's desk, that there was to be no reprieve; that Staple
Abbots's fate was to be the same as that of Imber. The man had
the uncomfortable air of the bearer of bad tidings, and refused
to look anyone in the eye. The message was identical. The
Americans wanted somewhere to train their troops in street
fighting and hand-to-hand combat; their snipers needed to
learn how to take advantage of the cover afforded by houses and
shops. The War Office had such provision at their disposal and

were anxious to oblige their powerful allies. Staple Abbots, like Imber, must pay the price.

His monotonous voice rumbled on in the stunned and incredulous silence. 'The Army will, of course, pay all removal costs and any reasonable storage charges for furniture until you can find alternative accommodation, or until you can return to your homes, whichever is the sooner. You have until December the twentieth to make alternative arrangements, which gives you just over a month.'

'But ... But what about the farms? The animals?' a voice from the back wanted to know, and there was a dazed murmur of support. 'We can't just abandon them, surely?'

'I'm afraid' — the Land Agent looked down at his hands, twiddled a pen on the teacher's desk — 'that the animals will have to be slaughtered. There is,' he went on smoothly, ignoring the general cry of outrage, 'no other option. As you so rightly point out, sir, you can't just leave them behind. The Americans,' he added, trying unsuccessfully to raise a smile, 'won't have time for milking cows or feeding hens.'

'What about damage?' Eve asked abruptly. 'Damage to property and land? It's going to be considerable, isn't it? Who pays?'

'Claims for compensation will be allowed after the end of the war.' Once again the answer was a little too pat, a shade too smooth to inspire much confidence. But the War Office, their landlord, had spoken and there was nothing that anyone could do. In twos and threes, the villagers emerged into the murkiness of the November day, moving like sleepwalkers.

'For God's sake, pinch me,' a man's voice said behind Eve. 'Tell me it's all a nightmare and I'm going to wake up.'

Turning her head she recognized Jeb Marston, Ellen's husband, now run to fat and beginning to lose his hair, his face grey with disbelief. She put out a hand and squeezed his arm, and he nodded without realizing who she was, his mind focused on how to break the news to Ellen when he got home.

'We'd better get back,' Rose whispered, her face drawn and pale above the collar of her old tweed coat, framed by the pixie hood she had knitted from oddments of wool unpicked and rewound from other garments. 'We have an awful lot to think about. And we have to tell Aunt Helena and Uncle Marcus.' As they left the school playground and began walking down Upper Lane towards the village High Street, she turned to Eve. 'They're your problem now, dear, I'm afraid. Wherever Ernest and I go, we can't take them with us.'

'Of course not.' Eve tried desperately to sound as if she didn't mind. 'They must come to me at the flat.' Truth took over. 'They'll hate it. It has one spare bedroom which I can use, and they can have the double bed I sleep on. Oh, dear! The place is really only big enough for one.'

Rose and Ernest barely heard her; they were too wrapped up in their own problems. A month was so little time in which to make all the arrangements which would be necessary. They would have to decide where they were going to live and then set about finding accommodation. Ernest pressed Rose's hand and murmured consolingly, 'It'll only be temporary. We'll be back before you know it.'

Rose nodded bravely. 'You're right, love. The war can't go on for ever. It won't be for long.'

As they walked along the High Street in the winter dusk, Eve felt her heart welling over with misery and indignation. Staple Abbots was her home, the place where she had been born and grown up; where she had first fallen in love. Maybe she hadn't lived there for many years, but it was still a vital part of her. They passed the general store and the Ring O' Bells, St Peter's Church and the turning to Lower Abbots. In that cottage over there, Miss Ellice had lived and carried on her dressmaking business. And opposite was the bakery, now run by Mrs Jenks's daughter and her husband. How was it possible that anyone could take it all away from them? Without so much as a by-your-leave, or a do-you-mind? Come to that, without so much as a thank you. Someone, sitting up in London in his Whitehall office, had looked at a map, at a small black dot on the edge of Salisbury Plain, and thought: 'Ah, yes! We own that. Turn out the inhabitants and we can let the Americans use it.' What was it to him, after all? Just a pinprick and a few statistics.

Her parents were on the watch for their return. Eve saw the drawing-room curtains twitch as they approached the house, and before Rose had time to dip into her coat pocket for her keys the front door was opened.

'Well?' her father demanded anxiously.

Ernest shook his head. 'Bad, I'm afraid, Uncle Marcus. The entire village has to be evacuated by the twentieth of December.'

'But that's impossible! They can't do that!' Helena's voice was sharp, didactic. 'Obviously there's been a mistake. We must all write letters to our MP. Who is he, Marcus?'

Rose slammed the front door behind her. 'There's been no mistake, Aunt Helena, and writing to anyone would be a complete waste of time and effort. Staple Abbots is War Office property and they can do as they like with it, except for the church and the chapel. But what good are those without a congregation? Oh no, there's no appealing.' She dragged off her pixie hood and flung it on the old gate-legged hall table. 'I'm going to make a cup of tea. Anyone else want one?'

They followed her into the kitchen and stood around, not saying much, while she filled the kettle. Helena was sulking. She was not used to being spoken to like that. Rose was usually so polite and deferential, knowing what was due to her elders. She demanded imperiously, 'Marcus! Who do we know at the War Office?'

'No one. Don't be so ridiculous, woman!' His wife's mouth fell open in astonishment, but he ignored it. 'And it wouldn't make any bloody difference if we did. Can't you understand that this is a decision made at the very highest level? By Churchill himself, probably. Find somewhere for the Yanks immediately, he's told all those brass hats in

Whitehall. And they've done it.' He turned his fierce gaze on his daughter. 'This is your fault, Eve! It's you we have to thank for being turned out of our home when we're old and feeble.'

It took Eve a second or two to assimilate exactly what her father was saying. When it finally sank in, her first thought was that he had become senile suddenly, without any warning. 'What on earth do you mean, Papa?' she asked. She noted that Ernest and her mother were also looking puzzled. Rose, busy with her own worries, was taking down cups and saucers from the old Welsh dresser and setting them on the table.

'I mean that if you hadn't played fast and loose with Donald all those years ago, if you'd married him as the rest of us wanted you to do, then we wouldn't be in this predicament today. He'd have stayed here, where he belongs. He'd never have gone to Australia and he wouldn't have sold out to the War Office. Staple Abbots wouldn't *be* theirs to commandeer.'

Eve stared at him, unable for the moment to say a word. The furious anger welling up inside her had literally robbed her of her voice. She had read of people being rendered speechless, but never realized until now that it could be a physical fact. Meanwhile, Ernest had taken up the cudgels on her behalf.

'Oh, come on, Uncle Marcus! That's a bit thick! Nobody could possibly have foreseen what would happen; not Donald selling to the War Office, nor this. You can't blame Eve.'

'No, I do think you're going a bit far, Marcus,' Helena protested. 'You can't *make* people fall in love.'

'No, but you can damn well prevent them getting married when they have!' Eve had finally found her voice, and her tone was vitriolic. She was trembling violently, and it was as much as she could do not to grab hold of her father and shake him until the teeth rattled in his head. 'I'm talking about Frank, Papa, and the way you and Uncle Arthur set about making sure that we'd never get married. And don't try to look innocent! I'm perfectly well aware that it was Uncle Arthur who paid Jenny Slade to seduce him, but you and Mama asked Uncle to take a hand. I don't blame Mama. She never made any secret of the fact that she didn't want Frank as a son-in-law. But you! Full of all those liberal, egalitarian ideals! I should have expected you to warn me what my uncle was up to, not condone his nasty little plans.'

Marcus had gone extremely pale, except for a high flush of colour along each cheek-bone. 'How did you find out?' he asked at length.

'Aunt Hetty told me. Oh, she didn't mean to. It just slipped out one evening when she and Mama were staying at Holly Lodge, after Lawrence's funeral. Mama had gone to bed. Aunt Hetty was tired and a bit befuddled because I'd given her some whisky to drink. And afterwards she was very hot in your defence, Papa. Very loyal. But then, she didn't see you through my eyes, did she? As a thorough-going hypocrite!'

'Eve! How dare you speak to your father like that!' Helena's sympathy had somersaulted in her husband's favour. Ernest looked disapproving, while Rose slammed the teapot down on the table, causing the tea to spill out through the spout.

'For goodness' sake!' she exclaimed. 'Haven't we enough present worries, without resurrecting old quarrels and disagreements?'

Eve said coldly, 'This was my *life* that was meddled with, Rose.'

Rose began pouring the tea with a trembling hand. 'Don't be sententious, Eve. I think you and your father owe one another an apology. You've both said things that you'll regret later. And the fact is that no one could have forced Frank to seduce Jenny Slade if he hadn't wanted to, any more than you breaking your engagement to Donald forced him to emigrate or capitalize on his inheritance by selling to the War Office.'

Ernest nodded. 'She's talking sense, Eve, Uncle Marcus.

Frank Mailer, Donald – they're the ones responsible. Nobody else.'

Eve hesitated, relishing her anger for a few seconds longer. Then, still a little reluctant, she went over to her father and kissed his cheek. It felt icy to the touch.

'I'm sorry, Papa. I shouldn't have said what I did.'

He nodded, groping for her hand, holding on to it with such desperate force that she felt her knuckles crack. It was then she realized that he was having difficulty in trying to speak. As he keeled over, Eve caught him. Seconds later, he died in her arms.

Chapter Twenty-eight

It was mid-January, 1945, just as Soviet troops were entering Warsaw, that Eve was told she could move back to Holly Lodge as it was no longer of use to any government department. The Americans had long gone, and for a while after their departure it had stood empty, only to be taken over again by the Ministry of Aircraft Production. But by the previous Christmas it was once more deserted, and on January 17th Eve received the notification she had been hoping for.

Over breakfast, she said to her mother, 'We can move into Holly Lodge whenever we like. I had a letter this morning.'

Helena sniffed. 'Thank God for that. This place gives me the creeps; it always has done. Living underground is bad for my catarrh. And then, of course, there are the inauspicious circumstances under which I came here.'

Eve spread a piece of toast with the mixture of margarine and butter which she blended from their rations. 'Mama, don't bring that up again, please. We've been over and over this ground so often. You know how bad I feel, even after eighteen months, about Papa's death. Let's leave it, shall we?'

Helena shrugged, knowing that she was being unreason-able and, worse, unkind by persisting with that line of conversation. But she had had a bad night, waking on two or three occasions with pains in her hip and shoulder joints. She faced, too, another lonely day while Eve was at work; and although she had made friends with several women of her own age in the neighbourhood, she couldn't play bridge and drink coffee for more than a few hours at a time, which left long, empty stretches when she had no one but herself for company. As a result, she felt hard done by and added peevishly, 'It's not even as if I can visit your father's grave, buried as he is in St Peter's churchyard.'

Eve sighed. 'Mama, that will soon be a thing of the past. The war's nearly over. I shouldn't think it could last much more than a couple of months. This time next year, you and Rose and Ernest will be back in Staple Abbots. I mean, the Americans must have left before D-Day, and as soon as peace is declared the War Office will start putting everything to rights. In the meantime, we've the move to Holly Lodge to keep us busy. I expect there will be quite a bit which needs doing there to make it habitable.'

'I'm seventy-three,' her mother protested. 'I shan't be much help, I'm afraid.' Nevertheless, her face brightened at the prospect.

In the event, however, Eve was pleasantly surprised by the state of the house: there was comparatively little damage, nothing remotely like that suffered in her imagination. Everything looked very shabby, of course; the paintwork was filthy, and so was the wallpaper which was lifting in several places. But this was only to be expected, and there was no structural damage. Indeed, all traces of that created by the bomb had been expertly repaired, and a new length of cheap linoleum laid along the landing. Her furniture, when it came out of store, looked equally shabby, but again not as bad as she had anticipated. By devoting almost all of her free time to cleaning and polishing, washing and ironing, stitching and repairing, she had the house looking reasonably present- able inside two months; and she and her mother were comfortably installed well before May 8th, VE-Day, which signalled the end of the war in Europe. There was still Japan to be dealt with, and no one could hazard a guess as to how long that might take, but for the time being it was impossible to think that far ahead.

Eve was woken in the middle of the night by the sound of church bells ringing and fireworks being let off some- where in a neighbouring street. She got up and looked out of the window, to see people streaming across the Downs. There had been rumours all day that Germany was about to surrender, and the news had at last been made official. She went into her mother's room, sitting on the edge of the bed and gently shaking her awake.

'It's over, Mama – the war in Europe. It's finished.' Helena struggled to shake off the web of sleep, then sat up and the two women hugged one another. 'And do you know the best thing of all?' Eve continued. 'Olivia and Ginny and Arnold have come through it all unscathed.'

But even as she spoke, she thought of Justine, and wondered if anything had happened to Jules before or since the fall of France. Perhaps soon she would get a letter. Please God, let it be good news! She thought, too, of Jeff, but hurriedly shied away from the recollection. The American losses on Omaha Beach on D-Day, and during the subsequent fighting as they moved up through France, had been so enormous that it was probable – indeed more than probable – that he had not survived. And what, anyway, was it to her if he hadn't? She would never see him again.

'Let's go out,' said Helena with a sudden burst of energy. 'Let's get dressed and go into town to join in the fun.' She pushed back the bedclothes. 'Do you have any petrol in that car of yours?'

Eve laughed excitedly. 'Yes, a drop or two. Come on, then. We will.'

They drove at a snail's pace down Blackboy Hill and along Whiteladies Road, in a queue of traffic which seemed to stretch for miles. Lights blazed from every house and shop window as their owners ripped down the blackout curtains. The pavements were thronged with civilians and service personnel, arms entwined, all singing 'Roll Out the Barrel' and other wartime favourites at the tops of their voices. But there were people too who stood silently, tears coursing down their faces; people for whom the war had been a robber and a destroyer, and whose lives would never be the same again. For the most part, however, everyone tried to forget his or her troubles, including whatever slaughter might still lie ahead in the Far East, and be happy that at least the killing in Europe had stopped. For once the English overcame their inhibitions and natural reserve, hugging and kissing complete strangers in the street, joining Conga lines that snaked across the road with a reckless disregard for traffic. Fireworks which had survived six years of storage in cupboards and sheds were let off, with more danger to domestic life and limb than almost anything else since the blitz.

Near the devastated heart of the city, Eve was forced to park the car in a side road, and she and her mother got out and walked. The Tramways Centre was packed with people standing shoulder to shoulder, bringing any sort of progress to a halt. Lights sparkled on the waters of the River Avon, in itself something of a phenomenon after all these years. And Eve astonished both Helena and herself by saying, 'Do you know what I'd like to do? I'd like to go to church.'

So they walked back to College Green and the Cathedral, once the heart of the great medieval Augustinian Abbey, which along with St Mary Redcliffe had survived the bombing, and sat quietly in one of the pews. The peace of the place washed over them, and the noise outside sounded like the breaking of waves on a distant shore. Refreshed, and with the realization that it was two in the morning, they made their way back to Gaunts Lane where Eve had left the car.

The return journey was easier and quicker than the outward one, as the majority of traffic was still heading in the opposite direction. A lot of people, especially the younger ones Eve guessed, would be reluctant to call it a night until dawn, and maybe not even then, but she could see that her mother had had enough. As she unlocked the front door of Holly Lodge the phone was ringing, and when she answered it was Arnold, extremely happy and slightly drunk, hoping that she'd heard the news and wishing her 'a happy peace'.

'Livvy's here with me,' he said. 'She wants a word.'

There were sounds of merriment in the background; a gramophone blaring 'The White Cliffs of Dover', the chink of glasses, much laughter. The RAF station was obviously throwing a gigantic party to celebrate the end of the European war.

'Mother? Isn't this exciting? Have you been out at all? Oh, good! We're having a whale of a time here, as I expect you can hear.'

Eve laughed. 'I certainly can. How's Andrew? Do you know when he'll be coming home?'

'Who? Oh, Andy! No, not a clue.'

Eve said with a touch of malice, 'I suppose you and Arnie and Virginia will all be demobbed fairly soon. You've been in right from the beginning, so you ought to get early release.'

Except for the 'noises off', there was a sudden silence at the other end of the line. Then: 'Yes,' Olivia answered stiffly. 'I haven't really thought about it, but I guess you're right. Well!' She gave a forced laugh. 'That's something to look forward to. Look, I've got to go. The party's hotting up and Arnie's pestering me for a dance. Take care of yourself. Love to Helena. See you soon perhaps.' She had almost replaced the receiver when she added, 'If you hear anything from Justine, be sure to let me know,' before finally hanging up.

Eve slowly mounted the stairs to her cold bed, with all its clothes tossed back just as she had left it when she got up. When she had undressed she looked in on her mother, ready to offer a hot-water bottle or a cup of warm milk; but Helena, who always swore that she could never get a wink of sleep if once she were disturbed, was already snoring. Eve returned to her own room, but was unable to settle. There was still a lot of noise outside, but it was not that which made her wakeful. As on many previous occasions, she found herself wondering anxiously what the future would bring for Arnold and Olivia and, above all, Virginia. She did so want Frank's daughter to be happy, and was so afraid she might not be. It was half-past three before common sense took over and told her there was nothing she could do, so she might as well stop worrying.

At last she began to doze, but it was a fitful rest and one dogged by dreams. Lawrence and Calanthe were on the landing, inspecting the hole made by the bomb, and from the hall her father was shouting, 'He'll never marry you, you know!' Another time she was in the churchyard at Staple Abbots, looking down at a grave. The inscription on the headstone was blurred, and she didn't know whose it was, but she was quite sure it wasn't Marcus's. She said to Aunt Josephine, who had suddenly appeared at her side, 'His is in America, you know. He was killed in the D-Day landings.' Somewhere nearby a bell began to ring; not a tolling from St Peter's belfry but a shrill blast of sound like someone pressing the front-doorbell, and keeping a finger on the button . . .

Eve sat up abruptly. Someone really was ringing the front-door bell. She glanced at her bedside clock, which showed seven-thirty. Dear heaven, it was time to get up – she had to be at work by nine – but who could possibly want to see her at this hour? It wasn't the day for paying the milkman, and in any case he always came to the back door. Ginny, of course, home on leave. How stupid not to have thought of her immediately! Eve climbed out of bed, pushed her feet into her slippers, ran a comb through her hair, dragged on her ancient blue silk kimono and went downstairs. The bell had stopped ringing some moments before, but as she crossed the hall it began again.

'OK! OK!' she called. 'I'm coming. Just be patient, Ginny, will you?'

She withdrew the bolts and pulled the door open. Jeff Hamilton was standing on the doorstep.

*

Eve telephoned the office at nine o'clock to say she wouldn't be in. Her supervisor didn't even ask her for a reason.

'We shan't be needed for very much longer. They're going to disband us as soon as possible, I believe, so don't trouble your head about it.'

By this time, Eve had dressed and taken her mother breakfast in bed. She wanted to keep Helena out of the way for as long as possible, and fortunately the older woman was still too tired after the night's excitement to enquire why her daughter wasn't at work. Eve and Jeff sat in the kitchen, drinking tea and eating all her week's ration of bacon with tinned tomatoes and fried bread.

When, in the past, Eve had imagined such a meeting, without ever seriously supposing that it would happen, she had pictured Jeff and herself falling into one another's arms in an orgy of tearful reconciliation. But in fact their behaviour was very restrained. 'Hello, Jeff,' she had said, as though she had seen him yesterday. 'Hi, Evie,' he had replied with equal aplomb, only the rapid blinking of his eyelids indicating that he was labouring under any stress. She had invited him in, and as he stepped over the threshold, dropping his kit-bag just inside the door, he had glanced curiously about him, obviously trying to remember the house as he had known it.

'You've done wonders,' he said, following her into the kitchen.

'There wasn't a lot wrong with the place,' she conceded. 'I only hope your lot have done as little damage at Staple Abbots as they did here, but I suspect that's too much to ask.'

'I beg your pardon? I'm not with you. Say that again.'

So while she made breakfast and brewed a pot of tea, Eve explained about the village. Jeff expressed his regrets, but said he knew these things went on and that a similar evacuation had happened down in Devon. When Eve had taken her mother her tray, they ate and exchanged news – for all the world, Eve thought, as though they were just two friends who had never meant anything special to one another. Jeff had survived the D-Day landings, the trek through France and the crossing of the Rhine without a scratch, but had seen many of his friends fall in action. Walt Morello had been ripped to pieces in a hail of snipers' bullets in the Ardennes.

Eve pushed aside her plate, no longer hungry. Outside, a bird sang joyfully in the lilac tree beyond the kitchen window. She thought of Lawrence and her father who, in a way, had both been victims of the war; of Justine and Jules whose fate, as far as she was concerned, still hung in the balance. But she had much to be thankful for. Realizing that she had spoken her last thought aloud, she added, 'I'm alive. I have my house back; Mother and I have found we can live together without resorting to murder; Ginny, Livvy and Arnold are safe. And now...' she dragged her gaze away from the window and the purple glory of the lilac tree, forcing herself to look directly at Jeff on the other side of the table '... I know that you're all right, too. What does the Psalm say? "My cup runneth over".' She laughed shakily.

Suddenly they were both on their feet and in each other's arms, hugging and kissing, alternately laughing and crying. They seemed to stay like that for a very long time, drawing comfort from their closeness; but at last they drew apart. Jeff lit a Lucky Strike and Eve made a fresh pot of tea.

'The great British panacea,' she said, with a laugh that broke in the middle. She asked abruptly, bitterly, 'Why did you never get in touch after you went away? You must have known that there was a good reason for my absence that evening.'

Jeff tapped ash into the white china ashtray in the middle of the kitchen table. 'I guess so. But I was confused. It was a confusing time. I suppose I thought that I was the most important person in your life, and that no one and nothing else should be allowed to take precedence over me. Christ! How selfish and self-centred can you get? But's that how I felt. Later on, when I'd come to my senses, I was going to write and say I was sorry.' He drew heavily on his cigarette again. 'But by then, I had a pretty fair idea of what lay ahead of us. I never believed, like some, that the Germans would just cave in. They're fighters, and fighters to the death. I knew it would be a long, hard, bloody struggle. I didn't know whether or not I would survive it. I came to the conclusion that it would be fairer to you if I stayed out of your life and let you forget me ... The trouble was, I couldn't forget you. So, when I was told that I was being flown home to await demobilization in the States, and when I discovered there was a thirty-six-hour stopover at Plymouth for refuelling, I caught the next train to Bristol. And here I am.'

Eve set the freshly filled teapot down on its stand and resumed her place at the table. 'So?' she asked, as she poured two cups. 'Where do we go from here? You're still married ... still a father.'

'Yeah. You're right. Nothing's altered.' Viciously, he stubbed out his half-smoked cigarette in the ashtray. 'Linda still writes to me every week; sends me photographs of herself and the boys. They're real fine kids that any Pop could be proud of. They write me, too. How they've done in class, baseball, looking forward to me getting home. That kind of stuff.' Jeff's face looked suddenly drawn and full of pain. 'What are we going to do, Evie?'

She sipped the hot tea and took strength from its warmth. 'We aren't going to do anything. But you know that, without me telling you. I can see by your eyes that you've already come to the same conclusion. You're going back to Plymouth, and from there to the States where Linda and the boys are waiting for you. And you're going to make a go of things.' She tried to smile, but only succeeded in grimacing. 'As I told you a long time ago, once you get home everything will be different. Oh, I don't suppose it'll happen overnight, but in six months' time, maybe even less, Europe and the war and ... and I will all seem like a distant dream.'

He reached over and gripped her free hand. 'Never!' he exclaimed. 'Never!'

Eve put down her cup and laid her other hand on top of his. 'I'm right,' she insisted gently, and knew with a terrible sinking of the heart that she probably was. 'If I'm not, and if things don't work out with Linda, you can always come and get me.' But she spoke lightly, jokingly, because she was quite sure that it would never happen. This was hello and goodbye, hail and farewell, a dream reawakened only to be lost again before it was more than half-formed.

'What will you do?' he asked miserably.

Eve gave her head a little shake. 'I haven't really given it much thought. I suppose the war isn't really over yet. There's still Japan; it depends how long they can continue alone, without their former allies. In any case, it won't affect the civilian population over here very much, except for those who have men in Burma. Censorship will be disbanded. For now, however, there's my mother to look after, and the children to visit once they're demobbed and settled.' She couldn't bear the thought of how bleak and unexciting and middle-aged it all sounded. But then, she was middle-aged and so was Jeff; she was forty-five and he was forty-seven. Too old for this welter of emotion which was tearing them both apart. Or perhaps one was never too old: Eve didn't know. She didn't know anything any more; she just felt desperately tired and wished to heaven that Jeff had never come to see her. Why hadn't he just gone back to America and left her alone?

But she wouldn't have wanted that, either. Something wet fell on her hand, making her jump, she realized that she was crying. Jeff got up, picked her up bodily as though she weighed no more than a feather and sat down in her chair, cradling her on his lap. He didn't say anything because, after all, what was there to say? They both knew that he had to go home, that he owed it to his wife and sons, that no amount of self-delusion could change that fact. But he rocked her gently to and fro, murmuring endearments against her hair, putting off the moment of parting.

Eve heard the rattle of crockery as Helena carefully

descended the stairs carrying her breakfast tray, which she insisted on doing despite all Eve's efforts to dissuade her. 'I can't be too much of a nuisance,' she would say plaintively. And this morning was to be no exception. Eve slid off Jeff's lap and went quickly across to the sink, so that her back was to the door when her mother opened it. Surreptitiously, she wiped her eyes.

'Mama!' She took a deep breath and turned, forcing herself to smile. 'You're up early. I thought you'd want to lie in after being out so late this morning.'

'I heard voices.' Helena permitted Jeff to relieve her of the tray. 'Who's this? You didn't say anyone had called.' She took in the uniform. 'An American!' she accused bitterly. 'One of those people responsible for taking our village away from us! I hope you've told him all about it.'

'Mama, don't start, please! It's nothing to do with Major Hamilton.' She performed the necessary introduction, adding, 'Jeff is on his way back to the States, to his wife and children. He just dropped in on his way home to tell me.' She didn't mention that he had 'dropped in' from Plymouth; there was no point in complicating the issue. Her mother's face had relaxed at the talk of a family, and her manner became noticeably less abrasive. She even managed a smile. 'Where do you come from, Major?'

'Philadelphia, ma'am.' And in response to Helena's request, he produced the now tattered snapshots of Linda and Drew and Jeff junior for her inspection. Eve could hear them chatting amicably as she washed up the breakfast dishes, but paid no attention to what they were actually saying.

Jeff was going. She glanced at the clock on the kitchen wall and saw that it was almost ten-thirty. In another hour, less, he would have vanished from her life for ever. 'I must get dressed,' she said. 'I feel terrible, slopping around in my dressing-gown at this hour of the morning. Will you stay to lunch, Jeff?'

'No. No, thank you.' He was suddenly on his feet,

gathering up the scattered photographs, cutting Helena off in mid-sentence. 'I . . . I ought to get along, if you'll excuse me. There . . . Well, there isn't any point in hanging about.' He turned to Helena and held out his hand. 'Ma'am, it's been a great pleasure meeting you, but I'm afraid I have to say goodbye.'

Helena shook hands graciously. 'Goodbye, Major. Of course I understand. Now I too must go up and get dressed.' She paused in the doorway, a frown creasing her forehead. 'Why aren't you at work today, Eve?'

'I'll tell you later, Mama – as soon as I've seen Jeff on his way. I'll be up in a minute.'

Helena glanced sharply from her daughter to the American, nodded briefly and disappeared upstairs. Eve and Jeff were left facing one another across the table. 'Well,' Eve said, after a moment, 'this is it, then. Goodbye.'

'Yeah. I guess it is.' He buttoned his tunic. 'Don't come to the door with me, Evie. I'll see myself out.' He spoke with difficulty, as if he could barely form the words. 'I don't want you waving me farewell from the doorstep.' He moved towards the kitchen door, then suddenly spun round, came back and took her in his arms, kissing her as though he would never let her go. But finally: 'I love you, Eve,' he said, then tore himself free. Eve made no attempt to follow him. Thirty seconds later, she heard the front door close.

Galvanized into action, she ran into the drawing-room and wrenched back the curtain, staring into the street. But he had already disappeared around the corner, to try to hitch a lift to the station. Eve sank into an armchair, covering her face with her hands. Why had he come? Why hadn't he left her alone, believing that he no longer cared anything about her? After a long time, she slowly got up and made her way into the hall. She really must get dressed. Now she was at home, she would have to cook lunch for her mother. And it would be an opportunity to wash those net curtains in the dining-room that had got so dirty. Deliberately, she let the ever-present domestic worries occupy her mind. It was as good a way as any to stop herself thinking.

As she crossed the hall, she noticed the little pile of letters which her mother must have picked up and placed on the table, and without interest she glanced at the top one. It bore a French stamp and there was something familiar about the handwriting ... With trembling fingers, she tore the envelope open.

Moments later, she was running up the stairs two at a time, shouting: 'Mama! Mama! There's a letter from Justine! She's all right! She and Jules and their family are all OK!'

Part four
1950

Chapter Twenty-nine

Justine threw her arms around her stepmother's neck and kissed her.

'You've come at last,' she said. 'Welcome to Marseilles. Is this all your luggage? Right. Stay here a minute while I find a taxi.' And she headed off towards a rank of waiting cars.

Ten minutes later, they had left the station behind and were speeding in the direction of the Hotel Châtain. Glancing out of the taxi windows, Eve was dismayed by the general ugliness of the city and by the decrepit, slightly sinister air of many of its old nineteenth-century buildings. As this was not the first time she had seen Justine since the end of the war – her stepdaughter, together with her husband and children, had visited Bristol on several occasions during the past five years – Eve was aware that Marseilles had been badly damaged by bombs before the fall of France. Nevertheless, she was disappointed that such an ancient city, which had been both a Greek and a Roman settlement, a great crusading port and the birthplace of the French national anthem, not to mention its links with the Foreign Legion, should prove to be such an unromantic place.

Correctly divining her thoughts, Justine pressed her stepmother's hand.

'When you get to know it better, Mama, you'll love it. Marseilles has an ambience all its own, and the surrounding countryside is beautiful. Now, tell me the news. First of all, you. How's the new job going? Do you get on with the headmistress? That's so important. And are you still living alone? Holly Lodge is a big house for just one person. Jules and I worry about you being there on your own.'

Eve smiled – a little irritated, as she always was, by oversolicitude, but grateful all the same for Justine's concern.

'Darling, I'm perfectly capable of taking care of myself. Heaven knows, I ought to be, at fifty! Moreover, I haven't had that much time to decide what I want to do. Six months isn't very long. The one thing I'm certain of is that I don't need to move. Not yet, anyway. As for the job, it was strange to start with, teaching again after all those years in Censorship and then looking after Mother until she died. But it's rather like riding a bicycle, you never really forget how to do it. But in any case, a private girls' school like Longhurst isn't exactly William Penn Road Junior Mixed!'

Justine laughed. 'I imagine not. It was always terribly sedate and ladylike when Livvy and I were there. And talking of Livvy, how is she? How's the marriage working out? You had some reservations about it the last time we mentioned the subject.'

Eve grinned and squeezed her stepdaughter's hand, delighted to be the bearer of good news.

'Well, I was saving this tit-bit until later, but now you've asked I can't keep it to myself any longer. Livvy telephoned from Plymouth two nights ago to say that she's expecting a baby in March of next year.' Justine gasped with excitement and the two women beamed at one another as Eve continued, 'She sounded happier than she's been in ages. Andrew's got a shore posting for the next twelve months at least. He spoke to me as well, and was as pleased as Livvy.' She heaved a satisfied sigh. 'I do believe she's got over Arnie at long, long last. She may have married Andrew for all the wrong reasons, but I feel in my bones that everything's going to work out fine.'

The taxi, whose pace had been reduced to a crawl for the past ten minutes in the press of traffic, began to pick up speed again.

'And Arnold and Ginny?' Justine enquired. 'What about them?'

Eve hesitated before replying. 'Ginny adores him, of course. And there's Rebecca: she'll be three this autumn, and is the apple of her father's eye. The only fly in the ointment as far as I can see is Arnie's ambition. He's quite happy at the moment, living in London and doing his old job at Wentworth School, but what he really wants is to go into politics, and that takes money. Ginny doesn't have any, except what I shall leave her one day. I sometimes get the impression that Arnold wishes he'd known about the Robartes fortune before he asked Ginny to marry him, but I hope and pray I'm wrong. There was a time, towards the end of the war, when I was afraid he might be willing to jeopardize both his marriage and Livvy's for the sake of it. But,' Eve added more cheerfully, 'that isn't likely to happen now. He's genuinely fond of Virginia and, as I said, he dotes on Rebecca. And with Livvy starting a family of her own, I think we have every right to be optimistic about the future. Now, how are things with you, my darling?'

Justine tucked a hand in her stepmother's arm and gently pressed it.

'Jules's parents have made us both full partners in the hotel. Isn't that marvellous?'

'Marvellous,' Eve agreed. 'Mind, you have put a great deal of your father's money into improving the business.'

'I'd have done that anyway, partly because there's nothing I wouldn't do for Pierre and Eloise, and partly because it's an investment for my children. Jules is the eldest son, and one day the hotel will belong to Étien, in his turn.'

'You're the most contented person I've ever known,' Eve said, kissing Justine's cheek. 'It's a real pleasure to be with you, and I'm looking forward very much to meeting your in-laws after all these years. You've talked and written about them so much, I feel I know them already. How are Jules's brothers and his sister?'

'Blooming, and their families too. Eloise is planning a big get-together next Sunday so that you can meet them all. At last! We're here. The Hotel Châtain! I'll pay the driver. No, I insist! He'll only overcharge if you try to do it.'

Eve did as she was bid, staring curiously out of the window. The hotel was in a side street off the Canebière, Marseilles's

most famous thoroughfare where, it was said, if you sat long
enough at one of the pavement tables you were bound to see
someone you knew pass by. The Hotel Châtain itself, and the
picturesque alleyway in which it stood, had survived a wartime
purge, in the name of hygiene, of most of the streets around the
old port; and as Justine had said on more than one occasion,
'We're so lucky still to be there.' It's early Victorian-style
façade was not imposing and it looked what it was, a
comfortable family hotel. Eve wondered idly what Aunt
Josephine had liked so much about it that she had been willing
to invest money in it rather than allow it to fall on hard times.
Perhaps she would find out when she went inside.

But indoors it was rather dark and old-fashioned, with lots
of red plush and heavy mahogany furniture. It seemed popular,
however, judging by the number of guests, and the smells
wafting through from the kitchen were delicious. The girl
behind the reception desk, who was busy with a visitor, waved
a hand and called out something in French.

'She says she'll tell the porter to bring up the cases later,'
Justine explained. 'Leave them there, Mama, and we'll go and
find Eloise and Jules.'

The family living quarters were at the back of the hotel, on
the top two floors. Jules was in the parlour, waiting for them
with his mother, an attractive, still dark-haired woman in her
late fifties who appeared, Eve thought, surprisingly nervous as
she greeted her guest. Why that should be, Eve had no idea;
Eloise Denon must have spent a large part of her life greeting
strangers and putting them at their ease. When she spoke, her
English, though accented, was almost as good as her son's.

'I am so pleased to meet you at last, Mrs Prescott. I've 'eard
so much about you from Jules and Justine. And of course, I was
acquainted with Miss Gilchrist. I can see a faint resemblance,
but you 'ave auburn hair.'

Eve laughed self-consciously. 'A lot of grey in it now, I'm
afraid. But please, you must call me Eve. I feel I'm practically
family.'

'Of course you are!' Jules exclaimed. 'And do you know, I've never thought of it before, but it's most appropriate that you should be here, at the Hotel Auburn.'

Eve blinked. 'Auburn? Is that what châtain means? What a coincidence! How very odd.'

Justine nodded. 'Isn't it? Although it's never struck me before. Mama, sit down and I'll ring for some tea and cakes. As a family we eat rather late, after the guests have finished dining, and you'll be famished by then. Where's Papa? He promised he'd be here to greet you.'

There was silence for a moment, then Eloise Denon said hurriedly, 'There – er – there's been some mix-up about the fish. He . . . he's gone to the market to sort things out.'

Justine pulled the bell-rope. 'Oh, well,' she shrugged, 'it can't be helped. Mama can meet him later. I don't suppose he'll be very long, and Étien and Marie will be home soon. They'll keep her occupied.'

Pierre Denon, however, remained elusive throughout the rest of the afternoon and evening, busy around the hotel and failing to put in an appearance at the family dinner long after his grandchildren had gone to bed. By the time he did finally come upstairs, Eve was feeling more than a little the worse for wear. The long cross-Channel and train journey of the past thirty-six hours, even though she had had a *wagon-lit* on the overnight express from Calais, had exhausted her. And although, like the majority of French children, ten-year-old Étien and seven-year-old Marie were well-behaved, they still demanded attention, particularly from Eve whom they had not seen for some six months and were delighted to meet again. On top of all this, she had drunk too much unaccustomed wine with the meal and her head was beginning to swim.

Eloise Denon was just pouring coffee when the dining-room door opened with a gentle click. Eve had her back to it and did not immediately turn her head, being far more fascinated by her hostess, who gave a start, spilling a trickle of dark brown liquid across the snowy linen tablecloth. The dark eyes widened in momentary alarm before being swiftly veiled by their curving lids. The coffee pot was replaced on its stand by a hand that shook slightly.

Jules exclaimed in English, 'Ah! Papa! Here you are at last! Never mind, better late than never. Let me introduce you to my mother-in-law. *Belle mère*, this is my father, Pierre Denon. Papa, this is Madame Prescott: Eve.'

Eve rose from her seat and turned, holding out her hand.

Pierre Denon was still standing in the open doorway. The bright light from the landing behind him cast him into shadow, but Eve could see that he was small and thin, with grizzled hair that had probably once been dark. For a moment longer he remained motionless and then, as though propelled by some unseen hand, came slowly forward, stopping within a foot or two of Eve and raising his eyes to hers with a look which both compelled and implored. One sinewy hand closed over hers.

'I'm very pleased to meet you, Eve,' said Frank Mailer.

*

Eve had no idea, afterwards, what she answered – or if indeed she said anything at all. The room spun suddenly about her ears, and she felt as though someone had placed a great stone on her chest. A thick yellow fog was gathering at the back of her eyes and she remembered thinking that she was going to faint. Her knees buckled and she sat down heavily in her chair, gasping for breath.

'She's ill!' Justine's frightened voice sounded somewhere above her head. 'Jules! Fetch some brandy, quickly!'

There was a flurry of movement, then a man's voice – Frank's voice! – said quietly, 'Let me.' An arm slid around Eve's shoulders, supporting her. 'Here, my dear, drink this.'

The fiery liquid slid down Eve's throat, making her cough and splutter but restoring her senses, or as many of them as she felt she could trust. Cautiously, she reached out a hand and held the edge of the table, tracing the shape and solidity of the oak beneath the cloth. It was real enough: this wasn't, after all, a dream. She stared across at Jules, his pleasant face a mask of anxiety and concern, then twisted her neck to glance up at Justine who was hovering worriedly beside her chair. Her gaze swivelled to Eloise Denon, who sat as though turned to marble, only her eyes alive and beseeching Eve's silence. And finally, she forced herself to look at her host. At Pierre Denon ... at Frank Mailer.

She put up a trembling hand and pushed a tendril of hair, dank with sweat, back from her forehead. Her chattering teeth closed once more on the rim of the glass and she took another sip of brandy.

'So – so foolish of me,' she stammered. 'I ... I must be more tired than I realized.' Justine murmured something about calling the doctor, and Eve flung up a forbidding hand. 'No, darling, no!' She recognized the shrill, almost hysterical note in her voice and made a determined effort to speak more calmly. 'I'm perfectly all right. Just a passing weakness caused by exhaustion and a lot more alcohol than I'm used to at one sitting.' She tried to laugh, but it was unconvincing and tailed off into a croak. 'I'm sorry, I've spoiled your evening.' She leaned against the back of her chair and closed her eyes.

Eloise Denon, her expressive features registering unutterable gratitude and relief, said warmly, 'Please, please don't apologize. We understand. Is ... Is there anything I can get you? You 'ave only to say.'

Eve shook her head and, after a few moments, rose unsteadily to her feet, shaking off Frank's encircling arm.

'I ... I think I'd like to go to bed, if ... if no one minds.'

Justine endorsed this decision. 'Quite right,' she said firmly. 'What you need is a good night's sleep.'

This, Eve thought, was the last thing she was likely to get, but all she wanted at present was to be alone. She allowed Justine to escort her to her room, but once there discouraged her stepdaughter's inclination to linger and help her undress.

'I really am fine now, darling, thank you. You run along. I'm sure there are a million and one jobs you have to do before you can get to bed yourself.'

Justine hesitated. 'We-ell, yes,' she admitted reluctantly. 'But only if you're sure . . .'

'Quite sure. I'll see you in the morning. Now, off you go.'

Justine looked for a moment as though she might argue the point, but Eve's improved colour and general demeanour convinced her that there was, thankfully, nothing seriously wrong, and so she gave in, kissing her stepmother good-night and enveloping her in an affectionate hug. She shut the door behind her and the silence of the room, broken only by the muted roar of the traffic as it prowled the length of the Canebière, closed around Eve. She sat where Justine had left her, on the edge of the bed, arms stiffly extended and fingers gripping the pink satin quilt.

He was alive! Frank Mailer was alive! She hadn't dreamed it. She hadn't imagined it. He was there, on the floor below her, a living, breathing man . . . flesh and blood and bone. If she got up and walked out of this door, down one flight of stairs and into the dining-room, she would be able to touch him, to hear his voice just as she had done all those long, lost years ago. How the transformation to Pierre Denon had come about, she did not yet know, but it was obvious that no one except Eloise had any idea of his true identity. Jules thought Frank to be his real father, as he was undoubtedly the father of his brothers and sister, although given Jules's age Eve knew that was impossible. The deceit, however, had been absolute.

Eve raised her hands and covered her face, pressing the fingers into her temples as though she would crush the bones to pulp. All these years! *All these years!* The words kept going round and around inside her head. He had left his parents to mourn him in their lonely old age, his daughter to be raised by other people, his wife to make her own way in the world. And herself? What had Frank bequeathed to her? That most insidiously inhibiting of all legacies, the 'if only' and the 'might have been' of the unfinished dream.

Slowly, Eve lifted her head and stared in front of her, not seeing the heavy mahogany dressing-table and chest of drawers, nor the thick-piled carpet in dusty pink, nor yet the solid brass lamp beside the four-poster bed. She was oblivious to everything except a growing sense of anger which threatened to consume her, like a fire burning suddenly out of control. She wanted to speak to Frank now, tonight! But she couldn't, not without rousing the suspicions of Jules and Justine. Yet, why shouldn't they be told? Why shouldn't Frank be exposed to them for the fraud that he was?

Without any recollection of having moved Eve found herself outside her bedroom door, standing at the head of the staircase. She could hear people talking and walking about, the chink of crockery as, presumably, her stepdaughter and Eloise cleared the table of the dirty supper dishes. Someone laughed, a deep-throated, contented laugh. Justine.

Eve shivered and drew back. However angry she felt with Frank, however bitter, she couldn't destroy her stepdaughter's happiness. Nor, she realized, was she willing to expose Frank without at least listening to his side of the story. And there were other people, too, whose lives would be ruined by a single, vengeful word from her. All Frank's other children. Lawrence's grandchildren, Étien and Marie. She went back to the bedroom and made herself undress, wash, clean her teeth and brush her hair. At last, still in a daze, she climbed wearily into bed.

She switched out the light and closed her eyes, but her mind was in too much of a ferment to sleep, ranging back and forth across the intervening years. Frank and Eloise must have realized from the very beginning who Justine's stepmother was; that one day they would have to meet her and risk their whole life being destroyed. No wonder they hadn't wanted Jules to marry Justine. Even less wonder that they hadn't been at the wedding. The unsettled climate of 1939 must have seemed like the perfect excuse; and afterwards the war, and the difficult period which followed it, had postponed the evil day for another eleven long years. Until tonight. For a moment or two, Eve could almost feel sorry for Frank. It must have been like living with the sword of Damocles hanging above his head.

Why hadn't he tried to warn her in advance? Sent her a letter? But what could he have said or written that would have lessened the shock? Perhaps, once she had at last accepted Justine's oft-repeated invitation to spend the summer vacation with them, he had decided that this was the best way, the only way, to let her find out the truth. Perhaps he had hoped that her visit would be delayed yet again, as had happened – for one reason and another – over the past five years. Perhaps he had prayed that by some miracle, they would never have to meet . . .

The tears welled up, forcing themselves between Eve's closed lids and trickling down her cheeks. A sense of betrayal, of having loved an illusion, someone who had never really existed, made her want to scream aloud in frustration. How much had that lost dream of Frank Mailer affected her feelings for Lawrence? For Jeff Hamilton? She realized now that she had never been able to give all of herself to either man; that there had always been a little corner of her heart which they could not reach. Had they both felt it, too? Was that why Lawrence had clung to his mother? Why Jeff had gone back to the States, determined to make his marriage work?

Eve sat up abruptly, switching on the bedside lamp and staring desperately around the unfamiliar room. She would never sleep at this rate. She reached for her book and opened it at the marker, but the words made no sense, so she closed it again and lay back against the pillows. Her whole body ached with fatigue, but her whirling thoughts refused to let her rest. She dozed and woke, dozed and woke until about four o'clock, just as it was getting light, she fell into an unrefreshing slumber from which she was eventually aroused, just after eight, by her stepdaughter bringing her a cup of tea.

Justine sat on the edge of the bed, her face puckered with anxiety.

'How are you feeling this morning?' she asked gently. 'I had hoped you'd be better after a good night's sleep, but you're still looking extremely tired.'

'Oh, I'm all right,' Eve lied gallantly, sipping her tea and trying to sound brighter than she felt. 'It always takes time for me to settle into a strange bed.'

'Well,' Justine smiled, patting her stepmother's hand, 'perhaps it's all for the best that my plans for today have been altered. It was my intention to take you on a sightseeing tour of the city, but Jules's parents have decided to monopolize your company, for this morning at least. They say they want to get to know you better, but that means Jules and I have to look after the hotel.' She grimaced. 'I must admit that I was a bit put out when Eloise told me of their intentions just now, but having seen you, as I said, it's probably no bad thing. You'll be quieter with them. I should only rush you around, trying to show you everything at once. Now!' She rose from her seat and stretched her arms above her head. 'I must go and see that all's OK in the kitchens. First, breakfast's at half-past-eight. Eloise says you're not to hurry. Come down only when you're ready. She and Papa will be waiting for you in the little breakfast alcove, at the far end of the dining-room.' She glanced at her wristwatch and let our a shriek. 'Heavens! I'm late.' She kissed Eve's cheek. 'I may see you at lunch-time – it depends when Jules and I are free – but Pierre and Eloise will look after you. 'Bye!' The door closed behind her.

Eve finished drinking her tea, then slowly got out of bed, gathering up her towel and sponge-bag before making her way to the bathroom. Half an hour later, she was staring at her reflection in the pier-glass which hung on one wall of the room. Her mirrored self, in the pale green linen dress and leather sandals, looked back at her, a little pale but seemingly calm and composed, giving no indication of the turmoil her mind was in. Then she took a deep breath, picked up her handbag and went down one flight of stairs to the family's living quarters on the floor below.

The dining-room door stood ajar and, as she paused, she could hear the low murmur of voices from within. Summoning up her courage, she pushed it open and, as she did so, Frank got up from his seat in the alcove and came to meet her, holding out both his hands.

Chapter Thirty

Eve ignored him and walked straight past to the small table set in the alcove, where Eloise was pouring coffee. The smell of hot, freshly baked croissants filled the air, and at any other time would have made Eve hungry, but now she felt as though her appetite had deserted her, never to return.

Eloise replaced the coffee-pot on its stand and said hurriedly, 'I have things to do. I'll leave you alone with Pierre. That is ... I mean, Frank.' The colour stained her cheeks and she looked flustered. 'You ... must 'ave a thousand questions to ask 'im.' She didn't even bother to enquire if Eve had slept well; the niceties of polite behaviour were so obviously irrelevant at such a moment. She added something in rapid French, and Frank nodded.

When Eloise had gone, Frank came slowly towards the table and sat down opposite Eve, who had her back to the window. He blinked, as though the strong sunlight pouring in through the dusty panes hurt his eyes. He stirred his coffee in silence for a few moments before asking abruptly, 'Do you hate me, Auburn?'

'Don't call me that!' she snapped, her voice ragged and charged with tears. She put up a hand which trembled slightly to touch her hair. 'Besides, it isn't auburn any more. It's going grey.'

Frank shook his head. 'It still looks auburn to me. And you haven't answered my question.'

Eve steadied herself with a sip of coffee while she tried to bring her emotions under control; tried to sound calm and detached.

'Why should I hate you?' she asked at length. 'You don't mean that much to me. But if you were to ask do I despise

398

you? – then the answer would have to be yes! A coward, a cheat and a liar! How else would you expect me to feel?'

Frank sucked in his breath. 'Strong words,' he said after a while, 'but I suppose I deserve them.'

'Yes. I think you do.' Eve's tone was icy, but with a flicker of rage burning underneath. 'Let's face the facts. For the past thirty-two years you have been officially dead, yet here you are, alive and well with a "wife" and family. I assume that the other three children are yours, but Jules can't possibly be, even though Eloise is his real mother. Just as you,' she continued with venom, 'are Virginia's real father. Haven't you ever wanted to know what happened to your child by Jenny Slade, Frank?'

He looked shamefaced, but replied defensively, 'I know all about her. I've seen snapshots of her. Justine unwittingly keeps me up to date. But, Auburn' – he stretched out his hand beseechingly across the table – 'I couldn't do anything about her without giving myself away. You must see that. And it isn't just *my* life which would have been wrecked by confession. There are so many others. Please! Just let me tell you my story before you judge me too harshly, before you decide what you ought to do. And thank you for not divulging the truth last night.' He gave a shaky laugh. 'Do you know that I was hoping against hope that you wouldn't recognize me? That you would fail to know me after all these years? Stupid! I would have known you anywhere, however big the crowd.'

Eve took another sip of coffee, but she no longer needed it as a prop and stay. Her mind was suddenly clear, the welter of emotions stilled. The detachment she had striven for was hers, and all at once she felt nothing but a great sense of fatigue. But it was a pleasant tiredness, as though she were drifting on the edges of a dream. All she wanted was to go back to bed and sleep, but she owed it, not to Frank but to Ginny and herself, to hear what he had to say.

'All right,' she said. 'I'm listening. Tell me the story.'

Yet again, a little colour stole into his lean cheeks at the note of contempt in her voice, but he merely inclined his head.

'Thank you. I'll make it as brief as I can.'

*

At the beginning of August 1918, the British forces were stationed in and around the ruined Belgian town of Ypres; 'Wipers' to the British Tommy. On the 15th July, the Germans had attacked along the River Marne, but within three days the French had repulsed them and they were in retreat. It was, with hindsight, the turning point in a war which had become a nightmare, leading to the Armistice three months later. But it was impossible to know that at the time. After four years of carnage, fighting back and forth across a few miles of blood-soaked ground, many infantrymen believed the Germans would never be defeated. Morale was low; fear and desperation the two emotions uppermost in the minds of men who had seen millions of their fellow countrymen slaughtered.

Frank had come late to the war, but his horror at the situation in which he found himself was as great as, if not greater than, that of men who had been in France much longer. It was aggravated by his parting from Eve, his growing hatred of Jenny and the stark contrast between the peaceful rural existence which he had voluntarily renounced and the devastation all around him. At first, his one ambition was to get himself killed as quickly as possible, but his love of life proved too strong and he started casting about for a means of escape.

He had met Eloise Denon when he and some pals had visited Le Coq d'Or, a village inn just beyond Ypres, on the French side of the Franco-Belgian border. It was owned by her father, Georges Truffe, a big, truculent man who originally hailed from Marseilles, and who had led a life of petty crime before he finally married and settled down to run the inn which his late father-in-law had left him. If there was one set of men he hated above all others, it was the French police, whom he regarded as his natural enemies, far more than he did the Germans. Indeed, he disliked the representatives of law and order whatever their nationality, and it was rumoured amongst the British troops that Georges had aided a number of deserters.

Eloise had spent most of the war in Marseilles, living out of harm's way with her aunt, her father's only sibling. However, in the summer of 1918 she had travelled north to see her husband, Pierre Denon, who had just been invalided out of the French Army suffering badly from shell-shock – a condition which, incidentally, the British Army authorities refused to recognize – and had left her four-year-old son, Jules, in his great-aunt's care. She served behind the bar of Le Coq d'Or while waiting for Pierre to recover sufficient strength to take him back to Marseilles, and she and Frank had been immediately attracted to one another.

'We seemed to hit it off right from the start,' he said. 'It wasn't love, but we liked each other. We liked the same things. We had the same sense of humour. And I got on well with her old man. In those days I was more than a bit Bolshie, and I sympathized with his contempt for authority.'

'You and Eloise slept together?' Eve asked, but she could guess the answer.

'A couple of times. But then my leave was up and I had to get back to the lines.'

Orders came that the British were to go into action on the 8th of August, to distract attention from the Canadian and Australian troops who were trying to free the railway lines north-east of Amiens. On the morning of the 6th a dawn patrol of three men and a sergeant, one of the men being Frank, was despatched to reconnoitre the path of the proposed advance.

'As usual,' he commented bitterly, 'intelligence was faulty and we wandered into the path of a German patrol. I can't remember exactly what happened after all this time, but I recollect a lot of firing, and a hand-grenade was thrown. My three companions were killed outright, but by some God-given miracle I wasn't even hit, so I lay perfectly still until the Hun disappeared, convinced that they'd done for the lot of us. Then I crawled over to see if there was anything to be done for the others, but they were all as dead as mutton. Jimmy Miles had copped it the worst. There were little bits of him strewn all over the place and his face had been blown clean away.'

The vague idea of deserting, which Frank had been toying with off and on for months, suddenly flowered into a practical possibility as he reflected that he and Private Miles had been much the same height and build. So, when he finally stopped being sick, he forced himself to overcome his squeamishness and planted his papers on the dead man's body, or as much of it as he could find.

'It was like a slaughterhouse, and it took me ages to find the necessary bits of poor old Miles. What remained of his own tags and papers, I buried. It was getting properly light by then, and I was terrified that someone who'd know who I was might see me. But my luck held. I managed to get to a deserted barn on the outskirts of Ypres, and holed up there for the rest of the day. That night, I made my way to Le Coq d'Or and threw myself on Georges's mercy.'

Frank's trust, it seemed, had not been misplaced. The landlord was only too willing to help and hid him in the cellar where he had, in the past, concealed a number of other deserters, both British and French. Some of Georges's criminal contacts were smugglers who, for a few free drinks, were willing to ferry a deserting Tommy across the Channel. But Frank could not return to England. He was 'dead'; he would have to remain in France. Georges shrugged and promised to see what he could do about obtaining forged papers for him.

And that was the way matters stood when Pierre Denon died suddenly in his sleep of an unexpected heart attack.

*

'And you took his place,' Eve said. 'All these years you've been impersonating a dead man.' She took a croissant and bit into it, suddenly hungry.

'Yes.' Frank swirled his coffee round the sides of his cup. He had drunk and eaten nothing. 'Although at times now, I find it extremely difficult to distinguish between Pierre Denon and Frank Mailer. Mostly it's the old life, in England, that seems unreal. After all, I've been Pierre far longer than I was Frank. As you reminded me earlier, it's been thirty-two years.'

'And Jules?' she asked. 'I take it he doesn't know you're not his true father?'

Frank nodded. 'He couldn't remember Pierre, you see. His father had been away at war since he was less than two. When I arrived here with his mother, in the late August of 1918, he accepted me without hesitation.'

'And what happened to the real Pierre?'

Frank spread his hands in a very Gallic gesture. 'I don't know. Georges undertook to arrange everything and it suited me not to ask for details. Eloise and I left almost at once for Marseilles, with me travelling as Pierre Denon, her husband. All the papers were genuine, of course, except for the photographs. There was less risk than you'd think. I was always small and dark and "foreign-looking", and the shell-shock served as an excuse for my inability to say very much until I'd managed to get to grips with the language. And Marseilles is the perfect place for anonymity. No one asks unnecessary questions, probably because so many of its citizens have something to hide. You know its reputation.'

'And people here accepted you?'

'No one in Marseilles knew Pierre. He came from the north.'

'And Aunt Josie? How does she fit into the picture?'

'She stayed here once, quite by chance, and recognized me right away. Oh, she was as shocked as you are to begin with, but she always had a great tolerance for people's weaknesses, and she realized it would do no one any good if she exposed me. Once she'd come to terms with the discovery, she accepted me and what I'd done without reservation. Eloise and I had just bought this place and were having great difficulty making a go of things. Our second son, Albert, was only a few months old and everything was getting on top of us. As well as offering a lot of sound advice about putting the business on a proper company footing, Miss Gilchrist arranged to lend us money which we later converted into shares for her. I like to think that, in the end, she got a good return for her money.'

'Oh, she did. Enough,' Eve added drily, 'to support your son-in-law through university. Isn't that ironic?'

There was a long silence before Frank said quietly, 'You blame me for not having done right by Virginia. But I couldn't foresee that Jenny would desert her.'

'That's hardly the point, is it?' Eve responded hotly, anger spurting up again. 'You abandoned your wife and child.'

'Look,' Frank argued desperately, 'I never knew her. Virginia, I mean. But I did know Jenny and what she'd done to me. And I hated her for it! That morning, stuck out there in No Man's Land, I didn't have time to stop and think. Maybe if I had, I'd have done differently. But at that moment, I just recognized a god-given opportunity and took it. I felt then that I never wanted to go back to England. I liked France, what I'd seen of it, and I didn't mind staying here. If everyone over there thought I was dead, what did it matter? I reckoned Jenny would probably be delighted to be shot of me.'

'She's quite likely married again, you realize that? A bigamous marriage. Not that I've any sympathy to waste on her! She deserted Ginny without a single regret, and she was in league with Uncle Arthur. Oh yes, I discovered that eventually. All the same, thanks to you she's unwittingly living a lie. Your parents endured a lonely, childless old age and died mourning the son they thought had bravely laid down his life for his country, but who was really living happily and prosperously in France. Your elder daughter doesn't even know you exist, and neither does your grand-daughter.' The bitterness and anger swelled and overflowed. 'And what about *me*, Frank? Didn't you give me even a passing thought? Wasn't *I* worth going back for?'

He answered savagely, 'Of course I thought about you! I don't think a day's ever passed but you've been somewhere in my head. Why do you think I called this place the Hotel Châtain?' He leaned across the table and gripped both her hands in his before she could divine his intention and withdraw them into her lap. His clasp was so urgent that she could hear the bones of her fingers cracking, though she refused to cry out. 'But there was no future for us, Auburn! Not after I'd married Jenny. Divorce for people like us was out of the question. And you *had* a future, a career, ahead of you. Your uncle was right. We could never have made a go of it. We were from different worlds!'

Eve laughed mirthlessly. 'Oh yes, my career! My brilliant career! And what, pray, has that been? Teaching in a second-rate, back-street school, looking after an invalid husband, your daughter, his two stepdaughters and, for the past few years, my mother. And then there was Arnold Bailey, who more or less adopted me. Always other people and other people's children. Never a child of my own!' She choked on the tears.

The pressure on her fingers eased as Frank lifted a hand and stroked her cheek.

'They're all your children,' he said gently. 'You've helped shape their characters, one way or another. What they are today, they owe to you. I never feel for a moment that Jules isn't my son because I'm not his real father. He may not have my blood in his veins, but there's a lot of the rest of me in him; in the way he thinks and acts. We may bear no physical resemblance to one another, but we're so alike in other respects that it would never occur to him to question his parentage.'

Eve released her hands, lay back in her chair and closed her eyes, letting the warmth of the sun slanting in across her shoulder caress her face. Her anger had evaporated once again.

'Why did you send him to Bristol to learn the English side of the hotel business?' she asked, curiosity overcoming self-pity. 'Wasn't that tempting fate?'

Frank smiled. 'I suppose in a way it was. A bit of bravado. But the Dorset had a good reputation in the trade, and it was a family hotel like our own.' His mouth twisted wryly. 'And how could I possibly have foreseen that, in a city the size of Bristol, the one person Jules would fall in love with would be your stepdaughter? Even had I known that you had a stepdaughter. Who could have imagined such a coincidence?'

Eve sighed and re-opened her eyes. 'If I believed in predestination and all that nonsense, I'd hazard a guess that fate was determined to keep our lives intertwined. But as I don't, I can't really offer an explanation.' She took a deep breath, struggling to shake off the lingering sense of unreality. 'Are you happy, Frank?'

It wasn't what she'd meant to ask, and a little while ago she would have said she did not care. But suddenly, the question seemed important. She needed to know.

'Far more than I deserve to be,' he answered gravely. 'I've grown to love Eloise. Not in the way I loved you, but perhaps it's more satisfying. You were always the dream, Auburn, not the substance. I can accept that now. We adore the children and our grandchildren. But what about you? Hasn't there been anyone else since your husband died?'

'An American,' she replied briefly. 'But when the war was over, he went back to his wife and two sons in the States.'

'Ah!' Frank raised his eyes and regarded her steadily across the table. 'What do you intend to do, Eve? About me, I mean?'

She smiled ironically. 'I didn't imagine for a second, Frank, that you were interested enough to ask about my personal plans.' When he would have protested, she flung up a hand. 'It's all right! I don't mind. The truth is, I suppose, that I really don't care.' She looked him full in the eyes. 'The answer is nothing. I'm not going to do anything at all. What good would it do if I decided to blow the whistle? I should harm Justine and Jules and possibly Virginia as well, so my only option is to leave matters as they are. I don't pretend to condone what you did, but I can accept that it was a decision made in extraordinary circumstances, and that once taken there was no reversing it, even if you'd wanted to. That was a truly terrible war; maybe worse than the one we've just lived through. What it did to the men who fought in the trenches doesn't bear thinking about. Perhaps the blame lies with the politicians who got us into it, and with the generals who so mismanaged it. Anyway, not being able to claim Ginny as your daughter is your loss far more than hers. And I'll go on looking after her for you, as I've done for all these years. No, you and Eloise have nothing to fear from me.'

Frank grinned crookedly.

'I never really thought I had, you know, but I had no right to be certain. I've treated you shabbily all my life, but if there's any justice in the world, you'll meet a man some day who's really deserving of you.' He reached out and raised one of her hands to his lips. 'Thank you, Auburn. You'll always be there, you know, in a corner of my heart.'

*

Eve opened the front door of Holly Lodge and the taxi driver brought her cases in after her. She paid and tipped him, then started opening windows. The place smelled stuffy after being shut up for four weeks.

Home! She didn't believe the word had ever meant so much to her as it did today. The house was like an old and trusted friend – solid, dependable, real. In stark contrast, the past month had an almost nightmarish quality. Constantly having to be on her guard lest she let slip even a hint of the truth had worn her down. She had wanted desperately to cut the holiday short, but dared not because she could offer no valid excuse to Jules and Justine.

She would not be returning to Marseilles. It might prove difficult thinking up reasons to refuse her stepdaughter's pressing invitations – 'Now you've been once, Mama, there's no getting out of coming again!' – but it would have to be done. Anything was preferable to enduring Frank's company, and he must indeed feel the same. Eve had a sudden, vivid, poignant reminder of him, here in Holly Lodge, when they were children, staying with Aunt Josie. Then the memory faded, leaving an aching void behind. Frank Mailer, so long a part of her, had vanished for good. In his place was a stranger, Pierre Denon, who meant nothing to her whatsoever.

She picked up the pile of letters lying on the mat and went into the kitchen, where she made a cup of tea before settling down to read them. There was one from Ginny, sounding contented and happy, and another from Olivia to say that Andrew was taking her on a celebratory holiday to Spain. (And Eve mustn't worry, she was feeling absolutely fine. Pregnancy? There was nothing to it.)

A franked, buff envelope marked the latest stage in Eve's running battle with the War Office, and she tore it open without hope, which was just as well in the circumstances. Nothing had changed since they last wrote to her. In polite official language, her informant was instructed to say that, as yet, His Majesty's Forces, Southern Command, were not in a position to allow the former tenants to take up residence again in the village of Staple Abbots. The village still played a vital part in the Army's training programme.

Eve sighed. Why did she bother? It wasn't as though she wanted to go back and live there herself. But it infuriated her that the War Office had reneged on its promise, and instead of allowing the villagers to return after the Americans had left, had taken it over for the Army as a combat zone. Moreover her father was buried there, and it had deeply distressed her mother, towards the end of her life, that she would not be able to lie beside him in Saint Peter's churchyard. So, joining forces with Rose and Ernest in Salisbury, and some of the other Staple Abbots exiles, Eve had waged a relentless campaign against authority, constantly bombarding the War Office with letters. But so far to no avail. Soon there would have to be a council of war, and other, more active methods considered to get their message across. But Eve wished she had someone to share the fight with her; someone to give her backbone when her courage failed.

The phone rang. Pushing aside her correspondence, Eve got up and went into the hall to answer it.

'Hello? Eve Prescott speaking.'

The operator's detached, uninterested voice informed her that there was a caller from the United States on the line. Would she please hold on a moment, while she was connected?

The United States? Who on earth...? Surely not! It couldn't possibly be, not after all this time! Eve tried to stay calm, but her heart was pounding and the hand holding the receiver shook.

'Evie?' He sounded loud and clear, just as though he were in the next room. 'It's Jeff! Jeff Hamilton. Evie, where've you been? I've been trying to contact you for the past three weeks!'

'I've been in the south of France,' she answered faintly. 'Jeff, is that really you? How ... How are you?'

'Oh, I'm great. Never better. On top of the world.' He sounded suddenly, desperately anxious as he added, 'Evie ... You've not ... not gone and got married again, have you? Or anything goddamm stupid like that?'

'No,' she said breathlessly. 'No, nothing so idiotic. Why? Why do you want to know?'

He let out a whoop that nearly deafened her, and which must surely have injured the ear-drums of any operator who was listening in.

'Because I'm a free man once more! Linda and I finally got divorced. The decree absolute came through just under a month ago, and I've been trying to get in touch with you ever since.'

'Divorced? You're divorced?' Eve repeated wonderingly.

'As ever was. The marriage has been going downhill for years, in fact ever since I came home after the war. We found it hard to pick up the threads of our old life together. We stuck it out for the sake of the boys; but they're pretty much grown up now, and old enough to understand. Linda's getting hitched again, and the boys like Clint a lot. So I'm footloose and fancy-free – but not, I hope, for long! Evie, Evie, Evie! Please, *please* say you'll marry me! Or, at least, promise you'll think about it seriously.'

'I don't have to think about it,' she told him. 'I'm standing here, grinning like the Cheshire cat from ear to ear. Of course I'll marry you, whenever you like.'

She heard him give a great gasp of relief, then he began to laugh, a trifle wildly.

'Our children may think we're too old for romance, but, honey, we know better. Don't move! Don't leave the house! My bags are packed and I've quit my job. I'm coming over. I'm catching the very next plane!'